Aaron looked grim. "Imagine for a moment that tiny, trusting elemental being bound in the same way you just were, *against* its will. It has no words of release from its prison, no hope of escape, no thought of rescue, no breath, no air, no heat, no hope of movement ever again and you'll know what that elemental feels when its lured from its own world of Briah and locked into this one by the pure gold of Assiah, a true prisoner. Complete innocence and trust forever bound by greed and avarice or the expectations of power, never knowing or understanding why or how it has been bound."

Brandon looked at him in horror.

"So now you know," Aaron gave him a humorless smile.

Yes, now Brandon knew and he wished to hell he didn't.

"Ready for that drink now?" Aaron asked.

Destiny Given - Dedicated...

To Alex, first son of my first daughter -

Go for the dream when you're able....
RTFM when you're not...

I'll probably be long gone before you read this, but...
Know I'll always love you -

...heart, mind, soul.

Leslie

Table of Contents

Prologue - The Story of Phineas Tristan

Phineas Tristan was a young boy who dreamed of a world of water.

He sailed in a boat that was just the right size. Dolphins swam beside him, leaping and calling to each other with cheerful chatter he could almost understand.

On clear and sunny days, Phineas would drop the anchor of his small sailing craft, and dive into the cool water to swim playfully with his dolphin friends.

Some days he even swam with a mermaid or two.

On one such occasion he sailed to a special island and found an underwater cave that boasted a small sandy beach within. The ceiling of the cave was high and sparkled with light.

There was long forgotten treasure on the little beach inside his cave. Pirate chests filled with golden coins and goblets. Swords with jeweled grips. Diamonds and rubies as large as his thumb were scattered on the sand. Leather bound books also lay on the small beach with handwritten words in an odd language he couldn't understand.

There were natural treasures inside his secret cave as well. Shells that were polished to rainbow colors, conch shells he could blow into that made music like trumpets. Pearls the size of marbles made from oysters who had long since died of age.

It was a child's private sanctuary away from the real and dangerous world outside.

As he became older, Phineas visited his secret cave less and less as the adult world called more insistently for his attention.

The day finally came when he wasn't a boy any longer. It was time to put away his childish dreams, return to the harsh world of Assiah permanently. He swam to his secret cave with his dolphin friends one final time and took one silver-blue pearl to always remember the childhood world he would he would forever leave behind.

The year was 1812.

Chapter 1 - Whilom

The fifth world of Whilom et Nebulae had been created from the innocent and lonely heart of a child. Lush and green, pure as the soul of that child, it thrived. The water of the lakes and rivers were clear and clean, the soil rich and fertile. The flowers in her garden were bright, abundant and could be found in no other world. Night fell only when she slept, the breeze blew only when she felt too warm, the rain fell only when she cried.

Celandine pushed her long dark hair behind her ears and shoved the rest of the heavy mass over her shoulders. Walking toward the sparkling blue lake in bare feet, she frowned at the rich green color of her clothing then leaned down and checked the texture of the grass.

Something was wrong. The color of the grass should be the same shade and softness as her short dress, but it wasn't.

She looked around her critically. In some places the grass looked faded, almost brown. Too many warm and sunny days, it was obvious she had been remiss in her duties. The blades were thirsting for moisture, a touch of rain would be necessary. A dark thought, a melancholy mood and the sky would cloud with her tears, the rains would come.

Today she had no sad memories, no reason to cry.

From the condition of the grass, she hadn't cried for a very long time.

Other, more direct means would be necessary.

Pulling her thoughts and energy together, Celandine sat down on the grassy bank of the lake, putting her bare feet into the water up to her ankles and thought of a light rain, feeling the moisture of the air build, condense, then create a light drizzle. "Softly, gently," she directed the fall of clean water. "*Geburah hod, Netzach, Ain Binah. Socair.* Softly, gently." She lifted her face to the now light sprinkle, urging the gentle rainfall to nurture - never harm.

From the vantage point of her position, she noticed a disturbance near the bank of the lake and rose to investigate. Smiling with compassion, she gently lifted the salamander away from the edge of the water. "Having a unpleasant adventure, little one?" she asked the tiny creature as she lifted it in the palm of her hand and kneeled down, protecting it from the rain with her body. "Shh, thou art safe." She stroked the elemental lightly to remove all the water from its skin and was rewarded when its orange and yellow flames danced sweetly once again. She smiled with the sheer joy of its natural animation. "Aren't thee the lively one!"

The salamander shivered with sparks of joy at the sound of her voice, blazing even brighter.

Celandine smiled. "Oh, 'tis true, thy flames are beautiful, but thou art too young and fragile to be here. The wet is not for thy kind. Quickly home now. *Ki Akal, Atziluth.* Go in peace, my tiny friend." The salamander vanished, returning to his home world.

She returned to the edge of the lake, again concentrating on the light rain she had summoned.

("Celandine!")

Celandine turned with mild surprise toward the voice. It was rare for anyone to visit her garden without forewarning or invitation. "Tansy? Why art thou here?"

(Tansy came to warn thee. Speak not loudly, it might hear thee!")

She reached out a hand toward the voice, lightly touching the presence next to her. "Why art thou invisible?" She grinned at the pixie. "Hiding will not keep off the wet."

("So the ghost does not see Tansy again! By the gate, Celandine, 'tis by the gate into Briah by thy garden. Look, no, do not look! Do not let it know Tansy has alerted thee!")

"A ghost?" Concerned by the unnatural fear in the pixie's voice, Celandine turned her head toward the gate. "There is no ghost, perhaps a play of light and shadow, less than thought."

("But, if only thought, a play of light and shadow,") the pixie complained, ("how can Tansy see it?")

"Well, I don't really know," Celandine smiled with amusement, "maybe thou art simply noticing thy own shadow for once. Art thee flying with thy eyes open today Tansy? Where be the adventure in that?"

("Tansy does not look for adventure!") A small splash of water flared where Tansy had obviously stamped her small foot.

Celandine laughed at the show of temper. "Thou art behaving like a flit!"

There was another angry stamp of a tiny foot. ("'Tis serious! Tansy is not a flit! It might be only shadow-mist now, but it was a shadow-taint! Tansy saw it clearly, at the meadow 'twixt Assiah and Briah! It saw Tansy, too!)

"Perhaps 'tis but a child dreamer from Assiah?" Celandine suggested.

("Tansy does not care where it is from! Make it go away! 'Tis no child! It looks nearly form true, Celandine, like it could touch Tansy if Tansy gets too close.")

"Form true?" Celandine turned again toward the gate into Briah.

She started to feel a small amount of concern.

(Please, Celandine. It scares Tansy. Tansy doesn't want to see it, nor want it seeing Tansy! 'tis a shadow-taint! If Celandine will not help Tansy, Orchis will help Tansy!")

"Orchis?"

Tansy again stamped her foot. ("'Tis is no child dreamer of Assiah Tansy sees, but a shadow taint! Thou does't not believe me. Orchis is my lord and Tansy will tell him!")

"Tansy, wait!"

The pixie didn't answer, she had left as silently and invisibly as she had come, leaving behind both a mystery and a stronger feeling of worry. Any ghost from Assiah was her concern, not that of Orchis. It was her world, her responsibility.

Celandine thought about Tansy's description. A shadow taint that was nearly form true? "Oh, five hells," she stood, moving quickly to catch up to Tansy and avert disaster.

Dealing with the arrogance and ambitions of Orchis was always a pain in the ass and it was going to make this a very long day.

Chapter 2 - The Magician

A month had passed since Paul Hunter, Aaron Zale and Pricilla Pierce had rescued Susan Warrender from Emma Coleman and The Order of True Life. For Paul, the entire experience had been a journey into a realm of both fantasy and horror. The real world he thought he knew was now skewed from a wholly different perspective. How much of it had been real, how much his own imagination, he still wasn't sure.

One thing was certain, life was more interesting and mysterious now than he had ever dreamed it could be.

He grimaced at the too routine corporate liability contract in front of him.

No mysterious or exciting fantasy here.

His intercom buzzed. "Mr. Zale has arrived, Mr. Hunter," his paralegal told him.

Paul looked up from the pages he hadn't actually been reading, put them back in their folder and his inbox, then tried to slow his heart rate, knowing this would be a difficult meeting. "Send him in." He stood, taking a deep breath. He lifted his charcoal gray suit jacket from his chair and put it on, straightened the sleeves then walked around to the front of his desk, automatically donning his professional lawyer expression.

The door opened all too soon, Aaron Zale walked into the room and shook his hand. "Paul," the famous Magician was looking at him curiously.

"Aaron, glad you could come on such short notice." Aaron Zale was a large man, well over six feet, broad shouldered, a modern day Viking down to the silver blond hair and his piercing blue eyes. Unlike Paul, he was dressed casually in jeans and sport shirt, yet somehow he never appeared casual. He had too much vital presence. Paul's office was large, but its spacious proportions seemed to shrink when Aaron Zale was in the room.

Daphne still stood at the door. "Would you like coffee, Mr. Zale? Mr. Hunter?"

Paul looked at Aaron hopefully.

"I'm fine."

Paul turned back to Daphne. "We're good, Daphne, Thank you. Hold any calls unless they're from The District Attorney, Mary or Susan."

"Yes, Sir," Daphne backed out of the room, closing the huge double doors behind her softly.

The quiet of the office was heavy, Aaron looked at Paul expectantly. "You sounded a little rattled on the phone, Paul. Problems with the casino contract?"

"No, nothing like that," he assured him, gestured to one of the two leather chairs in front of his desk and waited until Aaron was seated before resuming his own chair. Keeping his court face intact, he tried to decide how to start the conversation. Despite their very real friendship, Paul always felt slightly intimidated by the man. The over-large desk between the two offered a surprising comfort, which was a stupid thought, any threat from Aaron Zale would not be physical, he had other more effective methods of dealing with his anger. The news he was about to impart would not be well received. "I'm sorry if I interrupted your work."

"No problem, we were pretty much done for the day," Aaron replied, watching him curiously. "Nothing that can't wait."

"I, ah. Good. How's Pricilla? I haven't seen much of her."

"She's fine. Things have been a little hectic, but nothing major, just the normal difficulties of settling in." (And a few other problems he wasn't willing to share.)

"House working out?" At his suggestion, Aaron had purchased an exclusive estate well north of San Diego in Fairbanks Ranch, an area both secluded and secure. Reaching Aaron Zale was virtually impossible without invitation.

"The house has everything we need."

"The helipad?" Paul continued to stall.

"Finished last week," Aaron answered. "What's up, Paul? You sounded concerned when you called."

"You want a drink?" Paul asked next, glancing over at the office bar hoping Aaron would say 'yes' so he could join him.

"No," Aaron answered, recognizing a stall when he heard one. "I want to know what you're dancing around, couldn't tell me over the phone, and why you wanted to make sure Pricilla wasn't with me when I came here."

So much for leading up to the subject gradually. Paul took a deep breath and cut to the chase. "Curt's out on bail. He was released three days ago," he looked apologetic, and continued hastily, "I would have found out sooner, but it was done off-calendar. I'm not sure if you wanted to Pricilla to know. The last time she saw him..." he left that thought unfinished. The last time Pricilla had been near Curt, he had tried to drug and rape her. Pricilla had handled it alone, but at a heavy emotional price to both herself and Aaron.

The air in the room was suddenly as thick and oppressive as a thunderstorm charged with unspent lightening. If anyone other than Aaron Zale had been in the room with him, Paul would have shrugged it off as imagination, but with Aaron, it might actually be possible for lightning bolts to strike from the ceiling.

"How?" Aaron's, eyes blazed, but his voice was calm. "That little asshole confessed to at least a dozen violent rapes. They charged him with felony burglary and sexual assault."

"And by definition it meets the standard," Paul assured him.

"Then why the hell did they give him bail?" Killing the messenger would not only be bad form, but it would deprive him of additional information. Aaron also considered Paul a friend, one of a very few he trusted.

The room was still heavy with energy, Paul felt pressure in his lungs. "Criminal Law isn't my specialty, Aaron, but I'm guessing they had to. I did talk to one of the detectives on the case. Except for his breaking into Pricilla's hotel room, they can't prove anything substantial. The rapes he confessed to were never reported, the women they contacted said it was 'consensual sex', part of Church doctrine, or they simply claim they don't remember it ever happening. The attorney The Order of True Life hired for Curt had him plead 'not guilty' at the prelim. The judge tried to hold him by setting a large bail, but the Church posted it in cash without blinking an eye."

"So they just let him out?" Aaron asked incredulously.

"Pretty much," Paul answered, wishing Aaron would simply shout or rage and take the feeling of impending doom out of the room. "Additionally, the kid's remorse is very believable. He keeps sobbing when he's questioned and apologizes profusely for any and every wrong he may have committed toward Pricilla. His attorney is working on throwing out his confession, citing emotional distress. Hell, I wouldn't be surprised if he tried to turn the tables and accuse her of physiological abuse."

"Damn!" Aaron had an overwhelming urge to put his fist through a wall, but contented himself with a hard rap against the arm of the chair. "I don't want Cilla facing that bastard again, even in a courtroom. She already feels sorry for the little shit, God knows why."

The minor physical punch Aaron had given the chair had released some of the energy in the room, Paul relaxed somewhat. "What do you want to do? Do we tell her?"

Aaron was quiet for several seconds. "Hell, I don't know. I should have killed the son of a bitch when I had the opportunity. Its not like anyone would have missed the little shit."

"I would have helped you bury the body," Paul assured him,

brightening up at the idea.

"I appreciate that, but there wouldn't have been enough left of him to bury."

"Even better, simpler to argue reasonable doubt," Paul gave a twisted smile, imagining an even stronger easing of the room. "The guy's a sadistic menace, but the law is handicapped, Aaron. Even with Pricilla testifying against him, he'll probably only get probation."

Aaron nodded, considering private alternatives. "I hate this."

"I know. He'll commit again, animals like that don't change. I'm worried he'll look for both Pricilla and Susan. He was pretty much obsessed with both of them," Paul put in. "He called the Warrender house from the jail. Mary took the call. He told her to 'take care of Susan, to 'keep her safe', to make sure she ate properly. Mary said it was 'creepy', he acted like Susan was his girlfriend, not his victim. I think he actually believes it, he's completely delusional. I had Mary change the number, but I don't think it will stop him and Susan doesn't want to move in with me."

Aaron looked concerned. "Why not?"

Paul shook his head. "That whole 'butterfly - guide' thing, is taking its toll. Mary has been calling old friends, trying to help Susan find a new 'guide', learn to ground herself so she won't be as vulnerable to people like Miss Emma and Curt in the future." He gave a weak smile. "Mary, of all people, talking responsibility, wanting to teach Susan to ground herself. Talk about irony."

"Mary is stronger than you think, Paul."

"Maybe, but not physically strong enough to take on Curt if he shows up. The guy is insane, Aaron. He should be in an institution, at the very least. I've asked Aunt Mary to take Susan out of the country for awhile."

Aaron nodded. "Not a bad idea."

There was a slight shimmer in the air.

"A-Ron, I have a problem, I need your advice," a gentle hand rested on Aaron's shoulder while Pricilla made her announcement.

"Holy shit!" Paul stood abruptly, pushing his chair into the wall behind him, his heart started pounding too rapidly. Pricilla had materialized out of thin air, her beautiful self was standing next to Aaron where before there had been nothing. She was wearing what looked to be a chemise and silk shorts, they were white, very sheer and left little to the imagination. "How did you, where did you…?"

Chapter 3 - Oops

Aaron closed his eyes in annoyance and let out a quiet groan. "And now we have another problem," he decided with a heavy sigh.

"Pricilla?" Paul stared at her. Her hair was an impossible combination of blond on top, dark brown underneath. He'd asked her once if she was a natural blond or brunette, she had cryptically told him she was born blond, turned brunette after an illness and was gradually turning back to blond. Sometime later, he'd found out the real reason. He still had nightmares about it.

Pricilla looked at her surroundings, recognizing Paul's well-appointed office. *(Well. Damn! This is embarrassing! What the hell are you doing here?)* she asked Aaron mentally.

(Right back at you), Aaron answered in the same mental voice. *(What do you mean, you have a problem?)*

(Later.) "Hey, Paul!" she walked around the desk and kissed him on the cheek. "Sorry for the intrusion, I won't stay long. You look great, love the tie, did Susan pick it out?" She straightened the blue silk deftly, patting it into place and stepping back to admire her valet handiwork. "So! How's Mary? I called her yesterday, she must have been in her garden, there wasn't an answer, the phone just kept ringing, not even the recorder picked up."

"You, you just, you're not..." He looked down on her slight form, her legs were bare, as were her feet. Pricilla could look spectacular in a gunnysack, but dressed as she was, she could stop a man's heart. Damn, she had great legs, not to mention... "Whoa," he took off his suit jacket, putting it around her shoulders. "Here, you ah," he pulled it tightly around her. "You must be cold."

"Thanks," Pricilla smiled at him. "Ooh, Nice," she stroked the jacket with appreciation, "You need to give Aaron the name of your tailor, he just buys off the big and tall racks. He has absolutely no sense of style."

(You're taking pot shots at my clothes, while showing up out of the blue, wearing what you're wearing?) Aaron complained.

(The poor man's freaking out, work with me here, will you?) Pricilla suggested.

"How did you, uh," Paul took a deep breath unaware of the private conversation going on around him. "You're here. You weren't here before."

"Yup, nope," Pricilla smiled. "I'm here, I wasn't here before. Weird,

14

huh?" She looked imploringly at Aaron. *(Now what?)*

(I'm thinking, keep stalling.)

(Think faster. I'm running out of inanities here) Pricilla told him.

(You? Never.) Aaron returned.

Pricilla glared at him.

"Ah wha... How did..." Paul shook his head, he looked at the closed door to his office. "You didn't come through the door. You... Out of thin air. You just... not here... and you're wearing," he waved his hand at her near lack of clothing, "thin air, right?"

"No, Victoria Secret," Pricilla nodded with encouragement. She looked over at Aaron. "You see what a gentleman he is? Even completely thrown for a loop he still offers me his jacket. Did you even consider covering me up?" She slid her arms into the coat. At five three, the hem reached almost to her knees.

Aaron sat back in his chair and looked at her curiously. "Why would I do that? I think you look great in that almost outfit."

"Thanks. Lucky for you, I don't sleep in the nude," Pricilla countered.

Aaron smiled. "If you did, I think even Paul might have hesitated to offer his jacket when you showed up," he prophesized. He looked at his watch. *("Five hours, Cilla. I didn't expect you back for at least three more.")*

("And you were supposed to be at home or at the theatre. I'm early, get over it. Plans change, situations arise. In any event, I can't stay long,") she answered.

Aaron looked at her suspiciously. *("What do you mean, situations arise, you can't stay long? What situations? What's going on?")*

("Just a little problem in Whilom that I need to talk to you about. Okay, maybe a potentially large problem, but I need to talk to you. What are you doing here? You didn't tell me you were meeting with Paul today.")

("A legal issue,") Aaron waved it away. *("What kind of problem on the other side?")*

(It's complicated.)

"Uh," Paul was still sputtering, still unaware of the silent conversation going on without him, "what, uh, how did you..."

Pricilla looked at him with concern. "Sit down, Paul. You look a little shaken." She took his arm and helped him return to his seat. "I'm really sorry for popping in like that. You're not going nuts, I promise. There's a logical explanation," *(as soon as we think of one)*. "Take slow, easy breaths. There you go." She gave him an encouraging smile. "Can I get you anything? Water? Coffee? I know, Food! I'll bet you haven't eaten today." She looked at Aaron for help. *(Think of anything yet?).*

(Nope.) "You going to offer to go down to the local deli in that outfit?" Aaron asked curiously. "If so, I'd like a corned beef on rye. Mustard, no mayo. If you get arrested for indecent exposure, call for bail, it's apparently very easy to get."

Pricilla glared at him. *("You're not help-ing.")*

("Neither are you showing up in your pajamas,") Aaron countered.

("Which would not be an issue if you were where you were supposed to be,") Pricilla argued silently.

"Jeans and t-shirt in my briefcase," Aaron gave her a superior look.

"Really?" Pricilla walked back around the desk, reached down, retrieved his briefcase and opened it, pulling out the articles of clothing. "No bra, no shoes?"

"Don't push your luck, Cilla," Aaron suggested. "You're lucky I brought that much. You're driving me nuts with this thing as it is."

Pricilla sat in the chair next to Aaron, pulled on the jeans, then stood to shimmy the tight denim over her silky shorts, zipping the jeans with difficulty. Both men watched the reverse striptease with obvious fascination. "I'm driving you nuts? You should try it from my end of the spectrum," she took off Paul's coat, handed it to Aaron who handed it to Paul, scowled at the plain red t-shirt and put it on over the silk camisole of her pajamas. She rummaged through the case, then shook her head, closing it and turned to Paul. "Do you have a rubber band?"

"Uh. Yes. I think so," Paul rummaged in his desk drawer and handed one to her.

"Thanks," Pricilla pulled her hair into a quick ponytail and grinned at him. "That's better." She looked back at Aaron. "You really forgot shoes?"

"Oh, for the love of…" Aaron sighed heavily, pulled his cell phone and punched a few numbers. "Jacob? Check around the limo and see if Pricilla left any shoes under the seat. If she didn't, buy a pair of running shoes at Target or payless, six medium and bring them up to Paul's office. …yes, she's here, …yes, she's fine… Hell, Jake, I don't know why, bad sense of timing? Because she's trying to give me a heart attack? … keep laughing, Jacob, and I'll let Cassie put a salamander in your bed." he flipped the phone closed. "Now that you've entertained us with your wardrobe issues, maybe you'd like to explain why you're here?" he looked at his wife suspiciously.

"*Target* for shoes?" Pricilla looked horrified.

"Don't start," Aaron suggested.

Pricilla sat in the chair next to him and looked over at Paul. "Feeling better?" she asked him. "I really am sorry, Paul. It wasn't intentional. I wouldn't have spooked you for the world."

"Right. No problem," Paul lied, trying to slow his heart with little effect. "Not to be too nosy, but how the hell did you get in here?"

"Actually, it's Aaron's fault. Blame him. He's not where he's supposed to be," Pricilla answered, looking daggers at Aaron. *(Well?)*

Paul looked curiously at the magician. "Aaron?"

Aaron shook his head. "Not important," he told him. "A little illusion Pricilla and I been having trouble with."

Pricilla brightened and looked at Paul hopefully. "You like comfortable explanations, want to go with that one? It's an illusion Aaron and I were working on for his charity show and it went awry. I like it. Good answer. Simple."

"You popped in here, like a genie out of a bottle," Paul narrowed his eyes, "and Aaron was not expecting you. I don't think so. Simple isn't in the cards."

"Genie out of a bottle? Do all men think alike?" Pricilla asked with annoyance. "Aaron said that the first time too. I really hate that analogy, the whole master/slave thing is more than a little creepy. I am not a genie. I do not grant wishes."

"You appeared out of thin air, you were wearing…"

"Pajamas," Pricilla answered helpfully. "They came with a robe and slippers. Pretty, huh?"

"Very," Paul answered truthfully, then winked at her. "Worth an entire jar of crunchy peanut butter."

Pricilla dimpled. "Really?"

"Excuse me?" Aaron sat up. "What does that mean?"

"Inside joke," Pricilla told him, "get over it."

"You two have far too many 'inside' jokes," Aaron frowned.

Pricilla grinned, it lit up her face. "Oh, come on. I adore Paul! He's like the brother I never had. Or," she wiggled her eyebrows, "the lover I should have had. We were engaged once, if you recall. He even gave me a ring. I still have it. Aquamarine. Very pretty."

"That was a bogus engagement," Aaron reminded her.

"But we played it so credibly."

"Very funny." Aaron narrowed his eyes. "How credibly?"

"Jealous?" Pricilla asked hopefully.

"Yes. Happy?"

Pricilla looked at him critically, then slumped slightly. "No, you're not," she decided with a sigh.

Aaron took her hand, turned it over and kissed her wrist. "Yes, love, I am."

Pricilla melted almost instantly. "Thank you. Now you want to tell

17

me why you're not where you're supposed to be and how I ended up here?"

"I'd like the answer to that one myself," Paul put in.

"Side issue, Cilla, not important," Aaron answered at the same time.

She looked curiously back and forth between the two men. "You both look guilty of something."

"Just a small legal issue Paul and I need to discuss. Not important."

Pricilla looked at him for a few long seconds. "Okay, that's a lie and not even a good one. What aren't you telling me?" she countered.

"We'll talk about it later." After he took care of their current problem, Aaron promised himself.

Pricilla frowned, looked at Paul's guilty expression, then back at Aaron. "Ah ha! You heard that Curt's been released on bail, didn't you? You two are planning strategy on what to do about it without me." She shook her head. "Protecting the little woman, are we? What century is this again?"

Aaron turned in his chair and looked at her with angry suspicion. "How did you know he was out on bail?"

Pricilla gave him a superior smile. "The District Attorney called me last week before he was released. He also wanted to assure me that they would have Curt linked to an ankle bracelet and he's limited to travel between his place of business, specifically the Order of True Life, and home. Wasn't that sweet of him?"

"And you didn't mention any of this to me because..." Aaron looked furious, then suspicious. "Has that bastard tried to contact you?"

"Curt? No, of course he hasn't, there's a restraining order in effect. Besides, how would he even know where I am? You purchased a house that's a damned fortress in the middle of ten acres of nowhere."

"Knowing you and how much you pity the little schmuck, you probably told him."

"Please. I pity the child he was, not the psychotic monster he's become. How stupid do you really think I am?"

"Oh, I don't know. Stupid enough to think you can handle him by yourself, stupid enough not to warn me he was out on bail?" Aaron glared at her.

Pricilla gave an exaggerated sigh. "I didn't tell you because I knew you'd over-react, which, I point out, you're apparently doing."

"You haven't seen me over-react, yet," Aaron promised.

"Hello?" Paul put in loudly. "Personally, I've lost all interest in Curt and the Judge letting him out on bail," he assured them. "Can we get back to how you popped in here wearing only your pajamas?"

Pricilla turned her attention to back him. "Oh, that."

"Yes, that," Paul mimicked her.

"Hmm, well," Pricilla frowned. "You're really not satisfied with the 'problematic illusion' answer? It really is a great answer."

"Not even remotely," Paul assured her. "I may be an attorney, but some bullshit even I can't co-sign."

"Didn't think so," Pricilla confessed with a heavy sigh and looked at Aaron speculatively. *(I say we just tell him the truth. Destiny Given, there are no accidents, the Fool's journey is for a lifetime.)*

Aaron shook his head at her. "Paul doesn't want to get involved in any of this again, Cilla."

"Yes, I do," Paul assured him instantly, more than a little intrigued. "Someone tell me, I'm dying here. What's going on? How did she do that? What does she mean that it's your fault she ended up here?" Granted, Aaron Zale was a master magician, with a huge reputation for stunning his audiences, but this was beyond anything he'd seen on the stage and he was privy to a few of the very real magical talents Aaron possessed. "How did you do that?"

There was a soft knock on the outside door, it opened and Paul's Paralegal walked partly into the room, holding a pair of red sandals by the straps and looking confused. "Mr. Hunter, I don't know why, but Mr. Zales's driver brought these," she stopped suddenly and looked at Pricilla. "Oh! Miss Pierce!" she blurted out in surprise. "I didn't see you come in."

"Hi, Daphne! You looked busy, I just sneaked past to tell Aaron something," Pricilla told her, getting up and taking the shoes from her. "I was waiting in the limo and didn't even think about shoes until I got in here. Thanks." She looked appreciatively at the pearl gray suit the young woman was wearing. "Wow, that outfit is great! Where did you get it?"

"Here we go," Aaron muttered under his breath to Paul.

"One of the Outlet stores by Barona," Daphne told her, looking pleased. "It's a bit out of town, but everything's at least forty percent off."

"Forty percent? Really? Oh, we have got to go shopping together. I don't know any of the good places around here yet," Pricilla decided. "I'll give you a call later this week and we'll set it up, okay?"

"Sure," Daphne nodded. She looked at Paul. "Sorry for the disturbance, Mr. Hunter. Uh, I'd better get back to work."

Paul waited until Pricilla had returned to her chair and put on her shoes, then raised an eyebrow. "You do that very well."

"Do what?"

"Divert attention from the subject. She doesn't even remember bringing in the shoes, or wonder how you might have slipped past her barefoot."

"That had nothing to do with it," Pricilla looked at him disgustedly. "I like Daphne. Do you even notice her? She's smart, very pretty, has a terrific personality and thinks you walk on water. She also has great taste. Isn't she the one who decorated your condo? Are you still planning on selling it? The view is spectacular."

"True and its closer to the office, but in this economy selling it is," Paul thought about it, then turned his attention back to the conversation at hand. "Cute. Now you're doing it to me."

"Doing what?"

"Re-direction, sleight of hand, *diverting*. Trying to get my mind off the subject of how you 'popped' in here when even Aaron wasn't expecting you." He looked at her sternly. "'splain, Lucy."

"Men have such tunnel vision," Pricilla complained and sighed. She looked toward Aaron, he looked back at her blankly. "You're not going to help at all, are you?"

"Me? And be accused of trying to protect the little woman, or diverting the fool from his 'Destiny Given' journey of knowledge?"

"Okay, fine." Pricilla looked back a Paul, then tried to think how to begin.

"Take your time, I've got all day," Paul settled back in his chair.

"Ah. Well. You remember the Apocrypha of Seth-A-Ron? The key to the fifth world, etc., etc., etc. blah, blah?"

Paul sat up straight, his attention fully engaged. "Vividly. This has to do with that?"

"More than you can imagine," Pricilla nodded.

"What about it?"

"Uh," she frowned. "Do you remember the description of the fifth world?" she asked.

Paul nodded seriously. "'Misty green trees and deep green grass, the stillness of a dark and quiet forest, a calm, cold and dark blue lake,'" he quoted. "I was convinced it was Whilom, because it was the same description you gave me of your fantasy place. You said all places needed a name, or you couldn't find them again. Then Aunt Mary confirmed that Whilom was the name of the fifth world."

"Right," Pricilla nodded with encouragement. "What else do you remember? Who lives there?"

Paul frowned. "The elementals."

"Which ones?"

"All of them. Air, water, fire."

"The elemental of Earth also spends half her time in the fifth world." She reminded him.

"Oh, right," Paul answered, "I forgot."

"There you have it."

"There I have what?"

"That would be me."

"What would be you?"

"The elemental of Earth. Sort of."

"Uh," Paul stared at her. "Huh?"

"That's the problem."

"Uh, not getting this," Paul admitted, looking at Aaron for clarification.

"Trust me," Aaron suggested, "the way she's telling it, no one would."

"It's all so simple," Pricilla sighed with frustration.

"No, Love," Aaron argued, again kissing her wrist, "it isn't. I still haven't grasped the total situation myself."

Pricilla shook her head at Paul. "I understand Aaron missing all the repercussions of the apocrypha of Seth-a-Ron, but you're an attorney, you're supposed to read the fine print. Remember the Star of Solomon?"

"Vividly. Susan pulled it out of thin air when she became Cyrestis, the third daughter of the firmament. Believe me, that memory is etched in my brain." Even if it wasn't in Susan's memory, he added to himself. Another mystery he didn't quite understand, but he suspected Aaron had something to do with Susan's apparent memory loss.

"She didn't exactly pull it out of thin air," Pricilla argued, "Cyrestis pulled it out of Whilom, but that's a side issue. Sort of."

"Sort of what?"

"Side issue," Pricilla waved it off. "Do you remember what the star does?"

"Uh," Paul tried to concentrate. "Not completely. Aunt Mary said it was either a lock or key. If it was a key, it gave the user unlimited access to the fifth world. If it was a lock, then the fifth world would be locked away forever to all but the elementals who abide there."

"Exactly."

"Then Emma tried to use the star and she locked the world away," Paul remembered, "and everything inside it."

"No, not everything, you're still missing it. The world is locked away to all *but* the elementals who abide there. 'But', being the operative word, the fine print, as it were. The elemental of Earth also spends half her time in the fifth world."

"And you're the elemental of Earth," Paul finished, frowning.

"Got it. Well, not completely. Half in any event."

"Come again?"

"In short, without the unlimited access the key would have offered,

I'm required to flip back and forth between Whilom and Assiah like some kind of a demented yo-yo. Half my time here, half there. The fine print, as it were. If I spend more than half my time here, I just sort of "pop out."

Paul thought about it for a second, then looked at her in utter confusion. "Pop out of what?"

"This world and into Whilom," Pricilla answered calmly.

"You mean physically? Your body, not just your mind?"

Pricilla nodded. "Yup. If I exceed my time limit here, it grabs me back."

"That's, uh,"

"Cool, huh?"

"I was going to say impossible," Paul admitted, "but knowing you, I don't think so." he digested it for a moment. "That's one hell of a codicil," he understated. "When did this start?"

"Shortly after Cyrestis pulled the star from Whilom. The first time I disappeared was at the airport when we were on our way back from Vegas."

"You disappeared in public?" he looked horrified.

Pricilla shuddered and nodded. "Oh, yeah. Totally unexpected. Then Aaron panicked and summoned me back, turning it into a real debacle. Free magic act performed by the Amazing Zale right next to ticket counter. Very spectacular. Not to mention embarrassing as hell. I was wearing this little green outfit that..." then shook her head. "Never mind. Suffice it to say I felt like a standard magician's stage prop in the usual skimpy costume. He got all kinds of applause and gave autographs to rest of the passengers in the lounge area while I stood there, looking like a fool, not sure where the hell I was, even who the hell I was. Then he sent me back and I'm guessing he got a standing ovation."

"I'll bet he did," Paul looked at Aaron, who was sitting back in his chair, looking bored. He looked back at Pricilla, still feeling confused.

"Unfortunately, summoning me caused even more problems, he kept me a little too long, which screwed up the timing, so I was gone for nearly eighteen hours before I could get back on my own." She looked at Paul's bemused face. "It's complicated."

"Sweetheart, you're got me confused and I was there," Aaron put in. "Have you ever told a story straight out?"

"Hey. I'm doing the best I can. You want to try explaining this?" Pricilla countered, glaring at him.

"Not especially," Aaron admitted.

"What do you mean Aaron kept you too long?" Paul asked at the same time. "For that matter, what do you mean he 'summoned' you?"

"Ah. Remember the sylph?" Pricilla held out her hand, thought the words, a translucent silver-blue ball rested on her palm.

Paul stared at it, entranced as he always was. "I wish you'd teach me to do that." He held out his hand, silently asking to hold it.

Pricilla complied, handing it over gently.

"I love these things," Paul smiled at the spectral orb. It glowed from the energy of the tiny sylph inside it, tingling in his hand like a tiny electrical spark, throwing light on his desk. "It feels so real," he said softly. "I know it's only imagination, but it feels so real."

"Yeah... well, actually... no."

"No, what?"

"Not your imagination. I just 'summoned' it. While its here, it is real, a living, thriving, entity," Pricilla gave him several moments, then leaned over the table, "sort of. But it's not a thing, it's an elemental. It comes because it wants to, it considers us a friend, so it feels safe. It will stay because it doesn't know enough to leave us, or because it's having fun in a different place and wants to explore longer. They'll stay indefinitely, if you let them. That's why it's necessary to send them back," she reminded him. "*Ki Akal Briah*," she blew gently on the orb, pinching the top. "Go in peace, my friend." The orb disappeared. Pricilla sat up, leaning comfortably back against her chair. "Every elemental has to be returned to their natural world, or it will fade and die in this one," she reminded him. "Its not where it belongs. Like a fish out of water. Or, the mouse in Lenny's pocket."

Paul nodded, feeling suddenly sad at the loss of magic in his hands. It was always too brief. "You told me that before."

"It bears repeating," Pricilla told him. "The same rules hold true for all the elementals," she told him. "We can summon them for only a short time, then have to send them home where they belong, where they can thrive. Sylphs go back to Briah, Undines go back to Yetzirah, salamanders go back to Atziluth..." she left it hanging and looked at Paul hopefully.

Paul frowned.

Aaron broke the silence. "And Earth elementals go back to Earth, Assiah. Unless, of course, that particular Earth Elemental also resides in the fifth world. If she's summoned from there, she has to be sent back there."

"What?" Paul looked shocked. "You mean you can summon Pricilla like she does the sylph?"

"Pretty much."

"Well, he doesn't use an orb," Pricilla put in helpfully. "Genie without the bottle and without the ability to grant wishes," she added firmly.

"Wait a minute," Paul stared at Aaron. "If you don't send her back after just a few minutes, she dies?"

"Possibly," Aaron looked a little skeptical. "We're not sure. That's the standard theory, assuming the same rules hold true for Pricilla as they do the other elementals. We haven't tested it completely," he answered, thinking about it. "Personally, I'm guessing not. She belongs to both worlds, Assiah and Whilom, but she does fade a bit after about ten minutes when she's summoned." He considered it. "I'm pretty sure she'll go back on her own," he modified, "probably, but I give her a push, just to be on the safe side."

Paul sat up sharply. "Wait a minute! Probably? You think?" He looked at Pricilla with instant concern. "Ten minutes? You've been here for longer than that! Are you alright?" he looked at Aaron angrily. "Send her back!"

"Protecting the little woman, are we?" Aaron leaned back in his chair looking amused.

"No, no, you're still not getting it," Pricilla reached over and patted Paul's hand. "I'm fine. Aaron didn't summon me."

Paul looked confused. "Then how did you get here?"

"I came on my own. If I come back to Assiah on my own without being summoned, everything is normal. Well, almost normal. Since Aaron is my closest connection to Assiah, he's my anchor, that's why I showed up here. I always return to wherever he happens to be, wearing whatever I happened to be wearing when I disappeared." She frowned, considering it. "Which might be just a wee bit awkward if he happens to be somewhere even more public, like a men's room, or if I disappear out of the shower, naked. I could really cause a nice reaction if Aaron happens to be doing his act and I show up on stage, au natural. That's the reason I need to know where he is. He's supposed to have a predictable schedule so I know where I'm going."

"Oh. Uh," Paul frowned at her, then looked hopefully at Aaron. "Anchor?"

"Confusing, isn't she?" Aaron grinned. "I swear, she can make a duck daft. Too much information, love," he told Pricilla. "You're getting off point. Assuming, of course, that you have one?"

Pricilla gave him an annoyed frown, then turned her attention back to Paul. "So basically, to make a long story short, that's why I popped into your office wearing only my pajamas. Aaron's here and I was wearing pajamas when I left this morning. Of course," she glared at Aaron, "he's not supposed to be here, he's supposed to be at the theatre, rehearsing, or at home, where I wouldn't freak out my friends and cause any sensation."

"Sweetheart, you always cause a sensation, no matter what you're wearing," Aaron told her magnanimously.

"That's so sweet," Pricilla smiled at him.

"I'm lost again," Paul looked at Aaron for help.

"In a nutshell, she belongs to two worlds equally. Half there, half here, disappears without conscious control if she overstays here. When she comes back on her own, she re-appears to wherever I happen to be in whatever she was wearing when she left, unless I dabble and summon or send her back like any other elemental," Aaron summed up.

"Got it," Paul told him.

"You *got* that?" Pricilla looked incredulous.

"Not even remotely," Paul admitted. "I'm still imagining you popping on stage naked when Aaron is doing his act," he smiled at her. "It was a polite response. The lawyer way of diverting." He returned his attention to Aaron. "So, you and Pricilla are having 'normal' complications?"

Aaron looked at him blandly. "Yup. Same old, same old."

"Wow," Paul sat back in his chair.

Aaron shrugged. "Welcome to my world. Never a dull moment." He looked at Pricilla sternly. "So. All that aside, why are you here and not in the magical mystical world of Whilom where you're supposed to be?" he again looked at his watch, "for another three to five hours?"

"It's a long story."

"Sum up," Aaron suggested.

"It's not that easy," Pricilla frowned, "I keep losing some of it."

"Give it your best shot," Aaron raised an eyebrow.

Pricilla sighed heavily, threw up her hands, then stood, pacing back and forth in front of the door.

"Pricilla," Aaron looked at her seriously. "Don't think about it, love, the longer you're here, you'll lose more of it, spit it out."

She stopped pacing. "Okay, summing up. It's like this. Tansy saw a ghost from Assiah, so she went invisible, because she's never seen it before and she thinks its holding form true... I mean true form. It scared her shitless, because it showed up near her garden. Now she refuses to become corporeal unless she's further away from the gate so the shadow taint can't see her. I tried to explain to her that it's probably harmless, but she always was high-strung."

Aaron raised his eyebrows. "Tansy?"

Pricilla waved the question away. "Actually, Tansy is not really important. What is important, is that because she's still spooked, she told Orchis. Orchis is more than a little interested that any contaminate from

Assiah can be seen from outside the Briah gate and has become suddenly secretive. Secrecy and Orchis is not a good combo, believe me."

"Contaminate? Orchis?"

"Who's Orchis?" Paul put in.

"Just another troublesome issue I'll have to resolve, sooner or later," Pricilla answered. "What I am concerned about is that star missing from Whilom is the cause of the shadow-taint, and that Orchis might take advantage of it, creating more problems."

"What?" Aaron nearly shouted, looking at her in horror.

"You want me to repeat that?"

"No, I want you to explain that. Orchis who? Might take advantage of what?"

"The vulnerability of a shadow-taint. Orchis is..." Pricilla gave him a look of annoyance, then looked around the office concern, "Something's wrong. I shouldn't be here," her hand flew to her mouth in alarm.

Aaron sat up sharply. "What's wrong?"

"I," Pricilla frowned. "Oh, Damnit to five hells, I left the water running. Too much rain and I'll get a bog. I've got to go before I drown my garden. I'll be late coming home," She smiled at Paul, gave him a breezy, "later, Paul," hurried over to Aaron, kissed him quickly, then simply disappeared.

"Whoa!" Paul reacted first, still staring at where Pricilla had been standing. "Okay, that I will never get used to," he admitted. He turned his attention to Aaron. "That is so outside of normal, I'm not sure it even happened."

"Normal for whom?" Aaron asked him with a heavy sigh.

"Point taken," Paul conceded. He stared at the place Pricilla had just been and shook his head. "And I thought Susan turning into the Third Daughter was strange."

"You're the one who said you wanted to get involved again," Aaron reminded him. "We can go back to all this being an illusion. Want me to erase the memory of it for you?" he offered.

Paul answered quickly. "Hell, no! This stuff is weird, but a damned sight more interesting than my real life," he told him with a smile. "Okay. Assuming Pricilla really was here and I'm not suffering from a ruptured brain tumor, what was she talking about? Did you understand any of that? What problem? She left the water running? And the Star is causing it?"

"No, she got it to rain, then..." Aaron shook his head. "Actually, I have no idea," he admitted, again settling back in his chair. "That was off the chart bizarre, even for Pricilla." He frowned.

"Oh, good. I hate being the last man to get the punch line," Paul confessed. "Want a drink?"

"Scotch, neat," Aaron answered gratefully.

Paul walked over to the bar and fixed two drinks, then handed one to Aaron. "If all this flipping back and forth is caused by the Star of Solomon, or rather the lack of it, I'm thinking that you giving it to Emma, the wicked witch of evil, wasn't one of your better moves," he mentioned carefully.

"Ya think?" Aaron rubbed a threatening headache between his eyes with the cold glass of his drink.

"This has been going on since you got back from Vegas?"

"Sadly true."

"Will getting the star back fix it?"

"I have no idea," Aaron took a large sip of his drink. "For all I know, it could make it worse. Every time I mess with this crap I get kicked in the balls. It's been nothing but trouble since the day I was born into this stupid philosophy. It breeds idiots and I'm one of them. Cilla's right, I should have read the small print."

"You had other problems at the time. Pricilla was in a coma, Susan was in thrall, Mary was... well, Mary." Paul reminded him. "Back to now. What 'shadow' ghost or taint was Pricilla talking about? The one that Tansy saw in her garden? For that matter, what's a 'shadow ghost', who's Tansy? And who's Orchis?"

"Not a clue," Aaron shook his head. "Ghosts, taints, Tansy and Orchis. We have now entered the Twilight Zone." He frowned.

"So what now?"

Aaron drained his drink and looked curiously at the glass. Paul walked over with the bottle and poured another couple of inches into it. "Thanks," he saluted Paul with the glass and took another sip. "The name Orchis sounds vaguely familiar. Where have I heard that name before?"

Paul frowned as he put the bottle back on the bar, thinking about it. "I think it's the name of a flower. Actually, I think both Tansy and Orchis are names of flowers," he offered with a wrinkled brow. "I could check with Mary. Why? Is it important?"

"Maybe," Aaron tapped his fingers on his glass. "Damn! I know I've heard the name Orchis before, it's like the edge of memory."

"Hold on," Paul suggested, rolled his chair around to his computer and started typing. "Twenty-first Century to the rescue."

"I seriously doubt it's on the internet, Paul."

"Everything's on the internet, its magic for the masses." Several moments passed while he typed. "Yup, here it is. 'O-r-c-h-i-s, noun, from the Greek; Orchis, named for a testicle, from the shape of the roots. One:

A genus of hardy perennials, with tuberous fleshy roots; type of the Orchidacæ with small purplish or white flowers growing in loose spikes. Two: An orchid; specifically a variety with small purplish or white flowers growing in loose spikes'." He looked up from the screen. "Told you it was a flower."

"She used both as names," Aaron stated firmly. "We're looking for people, not plants."

Paul scrolled down the page. "Okay, I'll try a different spelling. How about this? 'O-r-c-u-s. Noun, Latin. In Roman mythology, (a) the lower world; Hades; (b) Pluto, Dis.'" He sighed. "Not especially helpful."

"Maybe it is," Aaron frowned. "Purple is a royal color. A plant or flower named for a testicle from the shape of the roots means male. The lower world is a hidden world."

"So," Paul encouraged, "That means what?"

"Not a clue," Aaron kept tapping his glass. "A hidden world," he put his drink down, stood up abruptly and started pacing. "Root in the form of a testicle... man-root, fertility."

"O-kay," Paul put all that together, "so... if we're still talking people, we now have a royal male, or at least some guy who wears purple, who's fertile, living in a hidden world," he smiled. "Confusing, but simple."

"Oh, shit."

"By your tone, I'm guessing this isn't a good thing?" Paul surmised.

Aaron turned and considered him sharply. "Hardly."

"You want to clue me in?"

"You sure you want to be clued in?" Aaron asked. "It's going to get complicated. And really, really strange."

"I prefer strange," Paul assured him, "reality is overrated. Besides, you're always telling me that all of this stuff doesn't really exist, right?"

"Keep that in mind," Aaron suggested.

("Beth Ce-Cill et Celandine akal Whilom et Nebulae et Assiah. Now!") Aaron mentally shouted.

The air shimmered. An incredibly beautiful woman materialized quietly into the room. Her hair was dark brunette reaching halfway down her back, her eyes a startling blue. She was wearing a tunic of silky green over one shoulder, Greek style, it barely reached the middle of her thighs, one side of the dress was slightly longer than the other. Her feet were bare. She looked like a sexy dream of fantasy.

"Jesus, Aaron! Would you warn a person?" Paul asked in a

horrified voice, jumping out of his chair.

The woman looked at him, startled, then smiled sweetly. "Oh, 'tis thee! Hello."

"Pricilla?" Paul choked out.

She tilted her head to one side, considering the question. "Thee called this one by that name once before. 'tis been a long time, yet one remembers. We became friends along thy journey through my garden of Whilom. Thou were seeking someone in Briah, were thee not? Did'st thou find her?"

It was Pricilla, yet not Pricilla, Paul took in her startling blue eyes and dark hair, his heart pounding. He remembered those eyes, the dark hair, even her clothing. He had met her once before, in what he thought was a semi-erotic dream, one that took place in Whilom. A fantasy world that existed on a level he still didn't quite understand. He had difficulty breathing, but managed to answer. "Uh, yes, thank you. I found her."

"One is so pleased for thee. A troubled heart can so easily crush a soul."

"That's very true," Paul answered, confused.

"Ce-Cill."

She turned toward Aaron. "One greets thee, Magus of power by eternal lemniscate."

"You're speaking in parables and with unnecessary formality, Cilla. Knock it off. It makes you sound remote from us, aloof." He looked her patiently. "Who am I? By what informal name am I called?"

She looked at him with concern. "Thou art A-Ron," she answered. "Dost thou not know thy name?"

"Just making certain you do." He told her, hiding his initial concern and pointed at Paul. "Paul is your friend in Assiah, isn't he?"

Pricilla looked back to Paul, frowned, then nodded. "Yes. Paul is a friend in Assiah. One remembers." She blinked, thought for a long moment and smiled. "I greet thee, Paul. How's Susan?"

The change in voice and manner was startling, it was more like the Pricilla he knew, her eyes had softened to more of a blue/grey, even her posture was more natural, less ethereal. "She's doing well."

"And Mary? There was something.... I couldn't get through to her by... phone. The... " Pricilla frowned while she searched for the word, "the... recorder didn't pick up."

"She's also fine," Paul confirmed. Okay, he could handle this. Go with the flow. Think of her as Pricilla in costume. A sexy, terrific costume that barely covered the necessary parts and little else. "Sorry you couldn't reach her. She changed the number. Crank phone calls. I'll give you the new number."

"I thank thee... you."

"You're welcome. Um, Pricilla, Just for the record, why are you wet?" he pointed to the floor, the tunic she was wearing was lightly dripping on the carpet.

Pricilla looked down at her clothing. "Oh. Please forgive one's dishevelment. The world desired moisture, One offered it the joy of rain, but this one... *I* was not attentive during the offering," she explained with mild embarrassment.

"Ah," Paul smiled, still confused. "Sure. Okay." He looked hopefully at Aaron.

"Ce-Cill? Are you saying you called the rain to water the plants?" Aaron asked, bringing her attention back to him.

"One was unable to cry, it was necessary for the health of the garden."

"So you controlled the weather and made it rain." He decided not to ask about the crying part.

"Such an act would be an impertinence, showing little respect. One does not control the weather, one asks assistance of the elements when there is need."

"But you made it rain."

"One must be ever vigilant, else the roots of fragile life will wither and die."

Aaron barely kept from rolling his eyes. "You're speaking like an damned oracle again," he told her.

"One does," Pricilla gave him a small smile. "Because it annoys the hell out of you."

Paul laughed. "Good one," he put in.

Pricilla grinned at him. "I do try, friend Paul."

"Damnit, Cilla! We don't have time for games," Aaron sighed.

Pricilla looked at him critically. "Then why did you call if not to play master Magician and his assistant? I'm *busy*."

"You didn't tell me Orchis ruled your world, Ce-Cill."

"Orchis?" Pricilla looked surprised at the comment. "His rule is within but a part of Briah," she answered, "none rule Whilom."

"Who is Tansy?"

"One known since childhood, perhaps conceived at that time."

"Yes, but what is she?"

Pricilla shrugged indifferently. "She is pixie, but believes herself to be a wayside fairy."

Aaron frowned. "What's the difference?"

"In appearance, little, but fairies trespass less. Tansy finds a difficulty recognizing boundaries. She often flits into Whilom from Briah without invitation, a true fae would not do so. Thus she becomes wayside by her very demeanor."

"And in her travels she saw a ghost?"

"A shadow-taint from Assiah," she corrected him, "and it saw her, or so she believes."

"You don't believe her?"

"It matters not. Tansy is easily frightened and in her worry, she expressed her fear to Orchis who she believes to be her King. His interest in a shadow taint of Assiah might be a concern, Orchis is overly ambitious, always searching for power and control."

"Does Orchis travel through other worlds?"

Pricilla considered it for several long moments. "None know the boundaries of Orchis' essence within the world of Briah."

"Can he travel into Whilom?"

"Orchis is of Briah. He would not trespass."

"But can he?"

"Whilom is not within Briah," Pricilla answered, unconcerned.

"I see," Aaron lied. "Why do you want the star?"

Pricilla looked confused. "One can not pull a star from the heavens above Nebulae. Should one wish to do so, t'would be a foolhardy dream with no substance."

"Focus on me, Ce-Cill, on Assiah," Aaron ordered. "I'm talking about the Star of Solomon."

"Solomon?" Pricilla rubbed the center of her forehead. "The spark of star pulled from Whilom by the Third Daughter of the Firmament?" she guessed.

"Yes. That star," Aaron said patiently. "If someone like Orchis obtained it, what power would it give him?"

Pricilla looked surprised. "There is no value to the star. It but opens doors from Whilom into the dreams and realms of children. It has no power to give."

Aaron tried again. "Do you think Orchis wants the star of... the star pulled from Whilom?"

Pricilla seemed baffled by the question. "There is no value to the star," she repeated. "Only one truth is certain, this One... *I* have merely been reminded of this one's... *my* obligations by Tansy's concerns of a shadow-taint. The spark... the Star... you speak of is of the fifth world, it belongs in the fifth world where this one... where *I* am bound, not to an unknown creature of Assiah who is not. It should have been returned. The sylph returned to Whilom, frightened from the... Star by one who should not have attempted to use it. Because of such disuse, it was not returned as was ordained. Its absence is clearly felt."

"Its return to Whilom was not in the apocrypha of Seth-A-Ron."

"There are texts and there are texts, A-Ron. Not all are written by the sons of Assiah," Pricilla answered.

"Meaning?"

"Thou art... *you* are the Magus of power by eternal lemniscate. Thy... *your* choice was made, it cannot be unmade. She looked pained. "Thou... *you* perceived the sephiroth of thy... *your* own Seth by thy own judgment."

"Meaning?" Aaron repeated.

"One not fully of Assiah travels the passageways of a different sephiroth or Seth," Pricilla said cryptically. "One cannot understand knowledge that is still hidden or not yet ordained. Not all paths venture through Assiah."

"Which means what?"

Pricilla shrugged. "The realms one travels is of its... *his* own sephiroth."

"Which means what?" Aaron asked again, trying not to show his irritation.

Pricilla paused, obviously having trouble with her answer. "Thou...*You*..." she tried again, letting out a frustrated breath. "Thou art the Magus of power by eternal lemniscate, bound to Assiah, yet not. Thou art mortal, yet not. Thou art essence of shadow, yet not." She gestured toward Paul, looking even more frustrated. "Paul art Mortal, bound to Assiah, yet not. It... *he* is essence of shadow, yet not. Its... *his* life-power manifests on a precipice of Assiah while on a journey of knowledge, yet not."

"Oh, for God's sake," Aaron frowned at her answers, it was another oracle statement, questions within answers within more questions. "Sum up, Pricilla," he suggested. "Make it simple for us mortals of Assiah, 'yet not'."

Pricilla looked stressed, almost in pain as she considered her answer, finally saying, "as with all being, the limits of worlds are confined to the bounds and anchors of Destiny Given, not taken. All are far more or less than what thou might perceive. Thou *are*, but thou are *not*."

Paul had been listening, growing more confused, but watched worriedly as Pricilla started becoming almost translucent like some kind of ghostly apparition. Her eyes were brilliant blue again, not gray. "Um, Aaron?"

"I know," Aaron nodded with obvious concern, walking up to Pricilla and cupping her face. "What is your Destiny Given, Ce-Cill?" he asked quietly.

"This One... *I* have no destiny. This One... *I* am elemental. It has been thus since my becoming," she answered, still struggling with words, her eyes moist with unshed tears.

"No, Ce-Cill, that's not true," he told her. "I am your Destiny Given, Love," Aaron assured her gently. "Mind, heart, soul. Always."

"Yes," She said gratefully and touched his face with relief. "Thou art my Destiny Given, A-Ron. Oft dreamed, but never forgotten. Mind, heart, soul. Always."

"Yes. Always." Aaron kissed her quickly, but possessively. *(Ki Ce-Cill et Celandine akal Whilom et Nebulae, go in peace with my heart),* he said the words mentally.

Pricilla disappeared fully, Aaron sat back down.

"Okay, that's it," Paul decided, walking over to the bar. "Logic has escaped the building. Insanity reigns. Next time warn a person, before you zap them out of the ozone, okay?" He held up his empty glass. "Refill?"

"Double," Aaron nodded, holding out his own empty glass.

Paul took it from him, walking over to the bar. "I'm guessing that was a 'summoning', right? The same way Pricilla calls the sylph. You called her?"

"Pretty much."

Paul quietly refilled the drinks, handed Aaron his, then leaned against his desk rather than returning to his seat.

"Thanks." Aaron took a long pull of his Scotch.

"Towards the end, she was fading. I could almost see through her."

"She wasn't exactly here."

"Is that what she meant by mortal, yet not, essence, yet not?"

"An annoying play on words." Aaron answered.

"Yet not," Paul gave him a weak smile.

"At this point it's just esoteric bullshit," Aaron answered. "While she's in her 'elemental, yet not' state, it probably makes perfect sense to her. Evidently, elementals have their own playbook and their own language."

"Strange."

"You claimed to prefer strange," Aaron reminded him.

"I'm re-thinking that claim. Is she going to keep popping in and out of here?" Paul asked.

"No. Not unless she does it on her own. The Amazing Zale is done with his illusions for the day," he smiled at him, "you can relax."

"Illusions. Right. Not that I'm complaining, mind you. But that was some outfit she almost wasn't wearing. Is that what she looked like when she showed up at the airport?"

"Oh, yeah. At least then it wasn't molded to her body from rain, or I would have had a riot on my hands."

Paul imagined it for a moment and smiled. "No argument there. What happened to the clothes and shoes she put on before?"

"Nothing. She'll be wearing them when she comes home. Apparently what's made in Assiah, stays in Assiah."

"And that's the outfit she wears in Whilom, so it stays in Whilom, like the dark hair and blue eyes." Paul frowned. "Weird."

"Trust me, it doesn't get any less so with daily acquaintance to it."

"Did she really forget who I was, or was she putting me on?"

Aaron shook his head. "No, she wasn't putting you on. She has to be brought out of her other persona and fight to retain it when she does. It takes a few moments for her to acclimate the two worlds together in her mind. Even after she does, she has to be reminded. Grounded. Unfortunately, after only a few minutes, she starts reverting back. Apparently, it's difficult for her to maintain colloquial speech for very long after she's summoned. She's not really here, not really there. It's like waking up in a middle of a dream. She gets disoriented, frightened, and the longer she's here, the worse it gets and the more fragile she becomes."

Paul looked at the area where Pricilla had been standing, then walked over and touched the carpet. There was no water, nothing to show she had ever been there. "Here, yet not," he said in an almost whisper. "Essence, yet not."

"Oh, God. Now you're beginning to sound like an oracle," Aaron groaned.

"Sorry," Paul returned to his feet, looking a bit sheepish. "So! Now that I'm over my looming heart failure, what was that about? Why did you summon her back?"

"I summoned her back for a few answers."

"Got that, yet not," Paul couldn't resist.

Aaron glared at him. "Finished beating that dead horse yet?"

"I may have one or two left," Paul smiled. "Or not. Who is Orchis?"

Aaron took a long sip of his drink and looked annoyed. "Evidently a fae king of some kind. I don't really know. As Pricilla mentioned, there are texts and there are texts."

"Fae?" Paul repeated. "You mean like fairies, elves, gnomes, leprechauns, hobbits?"

"And more, according to Pict legend. The mischief-makers, the fantasy sparkles in the sky you see as a child, all of it. I've never read anything especially virtuous about any fae, except maybe for the Brownies."

"What do they do?"

Aaron shrugged. "Apparently, if they like you, they'll clean your home and milk your cows, taking half the milk, unfortunately, but still. As for the rest of the group, they trick, seduce and basically create havoc for mortals. They never exactly lie, per se, just twist the truth to get what they want. Not good or evil, they simply play for their own enjoyment and if someone gets hurt or dies, they don't particularly give a damn. We're nothing but essence of shadow. You no more exist to them than they do to you, no harm, no foul if you happen to get hit by a car while they're amusing themselves. There are very few records and those were made from oral legends, which changed in the telling over the centuries."

"So is Orchis a bad guy, or a good guy?"

"Hell if I know," Aaron admitted. "I only skimmed through a few of the texts outside my own path. God knows I had enough crap to study on that level. Besides, fairies were the 'sissy' stuff, beneath my notice. Susan and Mary could probably tell you more about them than I can."

"You're right, that's right up their alley," Paul nodded, "I'm surprised Susan hasn't already added them to her books. Strange though, I always thought Whilom was empty, except for the elementals."

"True, but it's her world. Pricilla was just a child when she created Whilom. Naturally she would add a bunch of magical and fantasy creatures to populate it. What kid wants to stay in a fantasyland alone? She probably has a few unicorns running around Whilom as well. What little girl wouldn't? Both her mother and father were True Science scholars, encouraging fantasy and imagination in children is part and parcel of the doctrine. Those would be just the kind of fairy tales they would have told her."

"Ah, huh," Paul poured more scotch into his glass. "Basically, then, everything in Whilom is imaginary, including the people. Figments of Pricilla's childhood imagination."

"Exactly. Well, probably. Maybe." Assuming Pricilla actually created Whilom and wasn't pulled into it by unknown Seth, he added to himself.

"Ah huh," Paul generously cosigned that bullshit, it was the least he could do for a friend. "So! Out of curiosity, does any of this old legend describe what Orchis, who doesn't or probably doesn't really exist, looks like?"

Aaron looked annoyed. "I don't know. Probably a 'Shining One', like all the fae. More beautiful than mortals can bear to look upon, the absolute epitome of perfection in male form, wings and size optional. He would be extremely vain, selfish and possessive. A master seducer of women." He grimaced. "Worse, according to Pricilla, he's ambitious as

35

well."

Paul raised an eyebrow. "There's the news every human male wants to hear."

"Oh, yeah. Especially when he knows his own very beautiful woman is in obvious contact with said seducer."

Paul let out a breath of heavy air. "So. Do you really think he wants the star if it has no value?"

"Again, I don't know," Aaron drained his scotch. "And I'm not convinced it has no value. Maybe it can be used to trap Pricilla in his world permanently. Maybe to stir his golden cup of ambrosia, for all I know. One thing is certain, if he does want it, I definitely don't want him to have it."

"Even though you say that Orchis, the 'absolute epitome of male perfection' doesn't or probably doesn't really exist."

Aaron glared at him. "That sounded suspiciously like another version of 'or not'."

Paul smiled. "So. Are you going after the star?"

Aaron tapped his empty glass in frustration. "Probably, fool that I am. The question is, how?"

Paul walked over, took the empty glass from Aaron's hand, then carried it back to the bar to refill it. "Not a problem," he decided, adding a bit of soda to the remaining scotch in his own glass to dilute the effects of his last two drinks. "You know where it is. Use your powers of illusion, break into Emma's house, whap the old bitch over the head and steal it from her. If you happen to run across Curt while there and he gets in your way, kill him." He leaned against his desk, looking hopeful.

"An admirable plan, Counselor," Aaron cracked a smile, "and my first preference as well," he admitted, "but, to stay within the rules of the Apocrypha of Seth-A-Ron and the dictates of the very beautiful and very sexy Cyrestis..."

"Careful," Paul cut in at the mention of Susan.

"You can ogle my woman, I can ogle yours," Aaron smiled and continued, "the star has to be used, destroyed, or 'freely given'. We know Emma can't use it, she tried, she failed. I doubt she'd destroy it..."

"And since the last time Miss Emma saw you she ran screaming into the night, I don't think freely giving it to you is going to be a viable option," Paul finished for him. "She has good reason to fear and hate you. Extremely problematic doesn't begin to cover it."

"No good deed goes unpunished," Aaron gave a humorless smile. "When I burn bridges, I don't screw around, do I? I'll probably have to simply buy the damned thing from her through an intermediary and pay only ten times what its worth." He told him. "I've had people watching the pawn shops and antique jewelry sales since she obtained it, so far, no luck."

Paul looked confused. "Doesn't it defeat the purpose of 'freely given' if she sells it?"

Aaron waved that away. "Semantics. 'I freely give you this one of a kind artifact of an ancient embodiment for whatever the buyer is willing to pay'." He sighed heavily. "It depends on who wants it and why."

Chapter 4 - Freely Given

The weather was cold, still early spring, made even colder by the lack of humidity. Considering the season, there should have been at least a little moisture in the air, but it was bone dry, no hint of rain in the immediate future.

Brandon Grayson stood on a dirt rise above the dying vineyard and studied it critically. On a small gravel pad next to him, someone, years before, had put a park bench overlooking the land below, presumably to admire the flourishing grapes during better times.

No one would be enjoying the scenery from that bench now, and there was no way Brandon was going to sit on it. The old weathered thing looked ready to collapse.

As for the view of the vineyard, it didn't look too bad from this distance, but up close, it was pretty much in the same shape as the rickety bench. The field was old and tired, needing extensive cultivation - or a good fire to put it out of its misery. The once thriving plants below were all dead. Even the few scattered weeds looked dry and sickly. Stakes stood in the cracked mounds of dirt looking like forgotten grave markers bound together with rusting wire. Some stakes were still shrouded with decades old bird netting.

There was an irresistible challenge in that, a fierce need in his soul to bring back life and purpose to the soil.

Brandon turned at a small sound behind him and watched Amme, alias Emma Coleman, walking up the dirt path toward him. She was a vile old woman, banished from the Crescent for scandals unknown. Currently, she was calling herself 'High Priestess' of some kind of cult church named 'The Order of True Life'.

She was complete nut job as far as Brandon was able to determine.

Unfortunately, if she had obtained the Star of Solomon as she claimed, she had become vital to his purpose. For sixteen years he had investigated, searched out the small clues in ancient texts, carefully not violating the rules of The Apocrypha or his clan's sephiroth.

However personally distasteful he found Emma Coleman, one had to deal with the tools they were given.

There were no accidents.

Emma stopped several feet from him and let him look his fill. She had used the last of her stored energy to create a false glamour of beauty and youth, believing she could, if necessary, seduce Brandon Grayson for the information she needed without offering him payment. She would enjoy the encounter, it peaked her sense of justice. He was young, no more than thirty-five, if that. A tall and handsome man, virile and fertile, with dark hair, a firm jaw and brown bedroom eyes. His snug jeans, leather jacket and matching boots made him look like a bad boy.

She liked bad boys.

Still, it was more than his good looks and masculine strength that drew her. His great grandfather had been handsome as well, she had tried unsuccessfully to teach him into the joys of his sexuality before he was a teenager. Unfortunately, the Grandfather was too unenlightened to understand the gifts she was offering him. He had turned on her, complained to his guide, forcing her rejection from the Crescent. It was only right that his great grandson pay for that insult with some of his own vitality. "I have what you need," she told him in a softly sensual voice.

Brandon managed not to crack a smile at her ridiculous attempt at seduction. He'd done his research thoroughly as he always did when dealing with unknown adversaries. And, he knew without a doubt she was definitely an adversary. She might be wearing a flirty blond wig and the clothing of a twenty-year-old street hustler, but he was more than aware that the disguise covered the well-used body of a woman nearing ninety who had the heart and perversions of a vampire. One word and he could dispel the false veneer she was clinging to so desperately, but he didn't bother. "Do you?"

Emma stilled in confusion. It was as though he could see right through her carefully applied glamour. She frowned at his lack of interest, reached into her purse and held out a padded envelope. "The Star?"

"You have the Star of Solomon," he said skeptically.

"Yes," her voice was still husky with sexual promise.

"I see," Brandon did not reach for the envelope. He looked at her curiously. "I merely requested confidential information about the star and where it might be found, not the star itself. Was it an oversight on your part that you didn't advise anyone you had a lead, or was it that you had intentions of keeping the star for yourself?"

"No," Emma lied. "But the opportunity to obtain the star was put in my path and I was certain you would want me to make the effort for you," she purred.

Brandon was losing patience. "You were wrong," his voice was flat.

"I did get the star and have brought it to you," she held out the envelope again. "Check for yourself," she suggested.

Brandon was not impressed by her words. If the star was genuine, chances were she had stolen it, in which case he could not take it. "Did you steal it?" he asked bluntly.

"No! I swear on my soul!"

That would be assuming she had had a soul. Brandon continued to frown. If she truly did have the star, there were a number of pitfalls he could fall into just by accepting it, even if she had obtained it legitimately.

"Where did you purchase it?"

"I didn't. It was given to me freely."

"Who offered it to you 'freely'?"

Emma lowered the packet and looked at him suspiciously. What was wrong with this man? Maybe he was gay. That would explain it. He certainly wasn't interested in her as a woman. "The Magician."

Brandon raised one eyebrow. "What Magician?"

"The true Magus of Power by eternal lemniscate! He was not playing the part," Emma swallowed the bile in her throat at the memory. "He was the true Magus!"

Brandon froze. Outwardly he kept from showing the horror he felt. The participation of anyone of the Major Arcana forced him to fully recognize the very deep and dangerous waters he was now drowning in. If he went through with this mad quest, there was no turning back.

Then again, the chances always were that he would probably have had to deal with the Magus at some point.

He'd just rather wait a decade or three.

"I didn't know that the destiny of a Major Arcana was given!" Amme continued.

"Not my problem," Brandon answered callously.

"I put myself in harm's way! I lied to an ancient embodiment! I faced the true Magus of power! You owe me!"

"I owe you nothing," he started to turn away. "I offered a commission for information about the location of the Star or the Third Daughter of the firmament, not in anyone's participation in a ritual well beyond their sephiroth."

"But you still want the star," Emma suggested desperately. "It was given to me freely. By the dictates of the Apocrypha of Seth-A-Ron, it must be offered in the same way."

Brandon turned back, his expression cold. He needed the star but he didn't want any dealings with this woman or the Magus. He considered his options, then inwardly sighed with resignation. "This transaction ends here. I offer one payment, freely given, agreed on by both. You either freely relinquish the star, or try and find another buyer. What's your price?" He was willing to go to fifty thousand for the damned thing, but expected to pay far less.

This time Emma licked her lips not as a sexual enticement, but because they had gone dry with fear. "You are third generation True Science, Minor Arcana."

Brandon looked at her sharply. "Your point?"

"My payment is knowledge."

"Knowledge." Brandon frowned.

"Freely given," Emma said.

"No," Brandon answered instantly. "Not freely given. I will break no rules of The Apocrypha in any knowledge I give you," he told her. "I agree to two questions, but only within those bounds."

"Three."

Brandon hesitated, then nodded. "Within those bounds and after I verify that the star is true," he told her. "Three questions."

"Agreed," Emma handed him the packet containing the star.

Brandon opened the envelope and slid the delicate necklace into his hand. It was centuries old and as light as air, exactly as described. But he knew it was more than simply beautiful. In the right hands, it could be an artifact of unlimited power, the key to unlock all four elemental worlds; but he was interested in only unlocking one.

Emma waited impatiently. "It is the true Star. I swear it."

He had known it was the true star when he touched it, but it was damaged. It should have felt alive in his hands, this was nothing but dead metal. He studied it more closely. The elemental that was supposed to adorn the center was missing. According to what little he had learned about the Seth of A-Ron, the key was no longer usable.

In short, the star was undoubtedly real, but ultimately useless. He should have expected it, but the hollow, twisted feeling in his gut was close to overwhelming. As far as he knew, enticing any elemental to give power back to the Star was impossible, but that was a problem for another time. For now he wanted information and was loath to ask anything of this woman. He needed to question without her knowing why he wanted the answer.

"You claim it is the true star." He looked at her with feigned doubt as to her credibility. "Tell me its providence. Who was the third Daughter of the Firmament?"

"I don't remember her name."

Probably not a lie, if Amme really had faced the true Magus of power, he would have wiped it from her memory. "What do you remember about her?"

Emma paused, her brow wrinkled in concentration. "She was connected to Solomon in some way. Still first generation, unprotected."

Brandon nodded, that dictate was well documented in his own studies. "What is the true name of the star? From which world was it pulled?"

"Its name?" Emma looked surprised at the question. She shook her head. "No other name or world designation was mentioned."

Brandon contained a sigh of disappointment. Again, probably true. She would never have been trusted with the information. This was going nowhere, fast. "Who called forth the Third Daughter and by what name was she summoned?"

"I don't remember," Emma frowned with annoyance, her memory hazy.

Brandon started to hand back the package as though it contained nothing. "Then I do not verify the Star."

"Wait, wait!" Emma concentrated, stepping back from his outstretched hand. "A woman. An older woman. I think I knew her once. She was the guide of a butterfly unprotected. That's all I remember."

"By what name did she call the Third daughter?" Brandon tried for another clue.

Emma shook her head. "I don't remember!"

"You spoke to an ancient embodiment and don't remember the name?" he asked incredulously.

"I... no."

Again, Brandon held out the package. "Then I do not verify the Star," he told her.

Emma held up both her hands. "I swear it is the star!"

"Then *remember*. Describe the summoning. Use whatever abilities you have," Brandon directed in a different voice, using his own true science talent to clarify the woman's memory.

"I... I can't remember," Emma again shook her head.

Damn. How deep was the block the Magus put on her? "*Boaz, Amme. Yod Atziluth et Kether et Nun*, you will remember," he told her.

Emma stood perfectly still, her eyes slightly glazed as though in a trance.

"Who is the Magus? What is his name?"

"I... I don't know."

Brandon frowned with frustration. "Remember what you can of the ceremony," he tried another tact.

"The guide told us to sit down. She..." Emma stopped.

"What was the guide's name?"

"I don't remember."

Another dead end. "Then tell me the guide's exact words," Brandon demanded in a quiet voice, losing patience. "Release the memory of what you heard during the ceremony. *Jachin, Amme. Kether et Nun. Jachin.*"

Emma answered almost instantly, picturing the moment, hearing the words. "We sat down. The guide spoke...'I, *Terias*, guide of the unprotected, release the power to unbind the memory. As I cannot in body, thus must I in Spirit. Awake, *Cyrestis*. The third daughter of the firmament must now arise. *Jachin, Cyrestis,* thy slumber ends, thy time is now, *Jachin et Assiah, et Hod et Kether, Jachin.*'"

Brandon memorized the key words as she spoke them. *Terias, Cyrestis, Assiah, Kether.* The two ancient names of the guide and Third Daughter, one unnamed and hidden world on Assiah. "What question did the Third Daughter first ask you?"

"She asked if I was the woman that all men dream of," Emma answered.

Brandon almost laughed out loud. "And how did you answer?"

Emma's voice took on a superior air, re-playing her part as the High Priestess of the Major Arcana. "Yes, Third Daughter, I am the High Priestess of the Major Arcana," she said, her head gave a pompous bow as though she were meeting the Third Daughter again.

High Priestess? Right. And he was the King of Siam, Brandon shook his head in disgust. "Did you introduce yourself in that way in front of the Magus?" How insane was this woman?

Emma's posture lost its arrogance. "Yes." She looked annoyed. "The bastard smiled."

Brandon wouldn't have been surprised if the Magus had fallen on the floor laughing. How this woman thought she might even have a chance of pretending to be Major Arcana was amazing. "Did the Third Daughter use any words to cause the Star to manifest?"

Emma's voice was still hesitant, even in her trance. "No. Only gestures."

"What gestures? Picture them. Describe them."

Emma closed her eyes, visualizing Susan Warrender's hand movements. "I don't remember all of it, my attention was diverted."

"Tell me what you do remember," Brandon's tolerance was wearing thin.

Emma closed her eyes, then crossed her arms against her chest. "Old magic styling. Keys crossed," she unfolded her arms, bringing them down, then up over her head, "circle the earth," she crossed her right hand over her left, "silver over gold. " Emma frowned. "There was more, the room darkened, somehow she brought shadow from light, then light from shadow, but I don't know how."

Words thought, but not spoken, Brandon nodded, vaguely familiar with the doctrine. He'd have to do more research on it. Keys crossed. Silver over gold, air and earth, shadow of an unnamed world. "Describe the Star when you first saw it."

"The Star and chain were within a white light, hanging a few feet off the table, it cast no shadow. The center of the star was lit from within by a small light."

Brandon paused for a moment, then asked, "was the light silver with blue or white with flashes of blue?"

"I just saw the blue."

Meaning that the elemental needed to activate the star was either a Sylph or an undine. Silver or white to attract it from the shadows, the gold of the star to bind the elemental to Assiah. A sylph he might be able to summon and bind, an Undine was more problematic. Brandon let out a light puff of annoyance. "What was the next question of the Third Daughter?"

"If I would use the star, give the star to the Magus of power by Eternal lemniscate, or destroy the star."

Brandon thought about it for several long moments, Emma standing still as stone. Then he came to the obvious conclusion and almost groaned with the senselessness of it. "And you said 'you would use the star to make the world manifest', despite the fact that to the High Priestess of the Major Arcana, all is manifest," he determined. The woman was even more ignorant than he had imagined.

"Yes."

"And how did the Magus answer the Third Daughter?"

"He said he would keep the world eternal, manifest to none but the elementals of life. Then she gave him the star."

"Then what happened?"

"He said, 'fear not, Cyrestis, the... world will remain eternal, I shall not make it manifest', then he handed the star to me, and said, 'my burden now falls to thee, High Priestess', " Emma told him, frowning.

Brandon stiffened. "What burden?"

"Three choices. To use the star, give the star away freely, or destroy the star."

"And you tried to use the star," Brandon concluded.

"Yes. But it doesn't work!"

All for nothing. "*Boaz, Amme. Yod Atziluth et Kether et Nun*, You will return to the ignorance the Magus decreed. *Jachin.*"

Emma blinked at her release from the hypnotic spell, remembering nothing that was said from when she had first entered the trance. "I swear to you I have given you all the information I remember!"

Brandon hesitated for several long moments. "Should I verify the Star, you must relinquish all claim, freely given, before any payment of knowledge is made."

"I relinquish all claim," Emma told him without hesitation, "freely given."

"Then I verify the star." Brandon could feel the statement settling on his shoulders like a heavy lead coat, sealing the transaction.

It was not a comfortable feeling.

Emma nearly sagged with relief when Brandon put the star back into the envelope and placed it into the pocket of his leather jacket. "It was very strange," she told him. "Nothing made sense! The Third Daughter chose the Magician. The Star was his, she gave it to him! It was the key to the fifth world! Why would the Magus have given it to me?" she asked curiously.

"Because there is no fifth world," Brandon stated contemptuously. "You were seduced by religious nonsense, a ridiculous myth that has no validity."

"But there is! The Seth A-Ron, the Seth A-Netzach..."

"Neither are in your Sephiroth and can be only understood by those following those paths. As for why the Magus gave the Star to you, once the terms were given, it was predictable. His actions were dictated by the Seth-A-Ron," Brandon told her. "He had the same three choices as the ancient embodiment. Use it, destroy it, or give it to you. Even if such a fantasy world existed, as Major Arcana, the Magus was required to keep it eternal, manifest to none. You stated you would manifest it."

"I don't understand," Emma frowned.

Brandon sighed at her continued ignorance. "You pretended to be second key of the Major Arcana, did you not?"

"Yes, but..."

"He gave it to you so you would try and use it, knowing you had to fail and would lock the world away, making it eternal, manifest to none."

"That's insane! He could have used it himself!"

"Not and remain faithful to his Destiny Given," Brandon answered firmly. "The Magus would never violate any elemental world, he certainly wouldn't destroy it. He took the only safe option. 'Manifest to none' includes himself. By giving it to you, he kept his word to the Third Daughter and it remained protected. You have two questions left."

"No! I was curious, not asking a question," Emma looked horrified.

Brandon shrugged. "It was knowledge you apparently did not have, therefore it was a valid question. I freely gave you a specific answer, within our agreement. You have two more questions."

Angry but resigned, Emma took several moments, carefully deciding on her next question. "Can the Magus be defeated?"

Brandon looked interested. "The simple answer is no," he told her. "The Magus is forth generation True Science by birth and Destiny Given, which means his lineage starts with Phaedrus. He is the only known Key of the Major Arcana legitimately given. Within the bounds of True Science, he cannot be defeated unless he intentionally defiles The Apocrypha. The chances of any true born generation committing such an act, voluntarily or otherwise, is virtually non-existent. We are taught the dictates from birth. The Magus is, however, mortal and can lose that mortality on this plane of existence as can any mortal man."

"How?"

"The Magician can die of old age or be killed, like any man, but his Destiny Given does not change, nor do his dictates. He is always the eternal lemniscate, dead or alive. Where his Sephiroth takes him after death, depends on his own personal shin. True death is irrelevant to a Key of the Major Arcana."

Brandon held up a hand before Emma could ask her final question, his curiosity was now seriously engaged. "You mentioned that your interaction with the Magus of Power cost you a great deal. You're wasting your time and mine. Perhaps if you explain the problem you are so obviously skirting around, your last question might elicit a more useful answer."

"The Magician placed a shin upon my soul," Emma said in a rush. "I need to know how to remove it."

Brandon looked confused. "The Magus would only make such a momentous judgment if you violated The Apocrypha is such a foul way that you could never be redeemed. Participating in the choosing of the star might create a serious bend, it was certainly foolish to attempt, but would not justify such an irreversible action." He looked at her with true horror as the thought hit him. "Did you harm the Third Daughter with your knowledge of the Apocrypha?"

"No! I never would do such a thing! I knew better than to touch her. From the moment I met her, I used no True Science in my dealings with her. There was always a buffer between us. I swear it!"

Brandon let out a breath of relief. Had she personally harmed the Third Daughter, her actions would have become his the moment he had accepted the star. "If that is true, for what action did he place the shin upon your soul?"

"It was another issue that had nothing to do with the Third Daughter," Emma waved it away.

"Be more specific," Brandon demanded.

"I punished one of my congregation, a boy named Curt. A cruel young man. Evil. Very evil. He is in jail now for rape and other atrocities against women."

Brandon frowned. "Then I don't see the crime," he looked at her suspiciously. "In what way did you punish this 'Curt'?"

"I took away his ability to call the salamander. He deserved punishment."

"He could call a salamander?" Brandon's eyes widened, he took a step away from her. "He was true child of fire?"

"He was evil!"

"But he could still call and befriend an elemental of Atziluth?" Brandon persisted, his voice hollow.

"No!" Emma shook her head. "Its heat, only, not its physical presence. It was a minor talent only, he was untrained, clueless. He was not a true child of fire. His parents never heard of True Science before they died and left him to me."

"What was his family name?"

"Hollis," Emma answered. "A family not known to the arcana. I taught him control from the time he was six years old, they would have been incapable."

"Six? This boy was untrained and unprotected, an *accidental* butterfly when he came to you?" Brandon's eyes became hard.

Emma shrugged. "Perhaps," she admitted, then added quickly, "but he was out of control! He knew nothing, started fires accidentally, always getting into trouble. Without my help he would have become a menace to society!"

"Your help," Brandon repeated, his gut twisting. "You never became a qualified guide."

Emma nodded eagerly. "Exactly! And therefore any mistakes I might have made in his training of the basics of True Science cannot be used against me," she added, anxious to make her point. "I was kicked out of the crescent. I am no longer even numbered arcana. The Magus has no jurisdiction over me!"

"You…" Brandon's eyes flashed in anger. "If you had simply killed the boy with a gun, you would be right. That would be a temporal matter, only of interest to local authorities. But to take away the natural abilities of a child of fire, accidental or not, you would have had to use your knowledge of True Science, as well as whatever you taught him. If the boy had the power to call an elemental in *any* aspect, he could not have been completely corrupted, not if he could still reach into Atziluth. That's basic knowledge of a simple acolyte and you were well beyond that when you were rejected from the crescent."

"But…"

"No," Brandon frowned at her. "You willfully, knowingly, harmed an untrained, accidental butterfly, took away his last vestige of innocence and used your knowledge of True Science to do it."

"I am no longer arcana!" Emma's voice was a near scream, as

though volume alone could prove her point.

"Untrue. By using True Science, you once more firmly placed yourself under the jurisdiction of the Magus of Power, arcana or not. He is First Key. If you use knowledge of True Science in any form, you must abide by the laws of True Science and His dictates."

"It was a simple mistake!" Emma persisted with a near wail.

"One that can never be rectified," Brandon answered in a hard voice.

"How do I escape the shin?"

Brandon waited several long moments before giving the final answer that his bargain required. This horrible woman was the very antithesis of everything he had been taught to believe in. No one harmed a butterfly, they were protected completely until they were placed under the jurisdiction of a qualified guide and released. "You don't. Don't pretend to be naïve, Amme. You know the rules. You play the game, you pay the price," he told her harshly.

"That's not fair!"

"Fair? I repeat. The Magus is Destiny Given. By your actions, you gave him no choice. By ripping off the wings of a butterfly, born or accidental, you defiled The Apocrypha knowingly, without remorse. The Magus was required by The Apocrypha of the Major Arcana to place the shin upon your soul, making you ill-dignified and useless. You condemned yourself beyond redemption."

"But what can I do?" Emma wailed.

"Nothing." Brandon stated emphatically, then turned his back on her. "Your final question has been answered. Don't contact me again, Amme," he walked away quickly.

Emma sat abruptly on the shaky wooden bench by the path, her posture defeated.

A life without purpose

Brandon continued down the path to his car, feeling emotionally dirty after his contact with 'Miss Emma'. He walked the long way around at a fast and heavy pace, feeling the need to vent some of his anger. Had he known of the shin the Magus had placed upon her and the atrocity she had committed, he would never have spoken to her. She had placed his own soul and reputation in danger.

His gut twisted as he thought about it. An accidental butterfly. For an untrained child to retain enough innocence that he could still imagine an elemental or fantasy world was more than a little rare. Emma Coleman must be one hell of a con-woman to coerce his parents into leaving their child in her care.

At his black Lexus twenty minutes later, Brandon opened the door and sat in the driver's seat, leaving his long legs on the outside, considering his next step.

Did he even have a next step?

His cell phone started chirping, he didn't have to look at caller ID. "Hey, Dad."

"Well?"

Brandon dredged up an enthusiastic voice from somewhere in his tired psyche. His father was a true believer, if he had any inkling of what he was trying to accomplish, he would try to stop him. "Well what?

"The grapes? The reason you went down there?"

"Oh," Brandon managed to focus his thoughts back to the real world. "It's all good. The vineyard has sandy soil, no clay, dry but not played out. It should take cuttings easily with a little work. The only real expense is additional irrigation. Natural moisture is a bit uncertain down here. It's small, only about sixty usable acres, but it will be profitable when we add our name. Anton Larousse has agreed to oversee the operation."

"I thought there was an active well on the property. Is it dry?"

"No, it's still active and produces sufficient amounts, but the water is uncertain for the grapes, too much calcium for our label. It should be okay for general landscaping. We might be able to filter out the extra minerals if the vineyard gets too expensive to stay profitable, but I don't want to count on it."

"Your call. The estate itself?"

"More than a hundred years old, forty odd rooms, updated utilities. They'd been using it as a showplace for tourists, then tried to turn it into a bed and breakfast, but closed it down almost two years ago when they went bankrupt. The contractor and structural engineer checked it out, both say the basic structure is sound. A professional scrubbing, a few nails, new carpets, and it will be more than livable."

"Nice benefit. How long for the cleanup?"

"Anton estimates six months after escrow closes, unless something unexpected crops up."

"Then you're ready to bid?"

"Absolutely. They're talking almost twenty million right now, but in this economy, we'll lowball. I'm guessing we can bring that down almost a quarter. Maybe a third. They haven't had any serious offers for more than a year. They want a quick sale with a short escrow."

"They're desperate."

"That's the way I read it," Brandon agreed. "I'll let Renaldo broker the deal. It will be ours in less than ninety days."

"Good. Not a wasted trip like you predicted," his father answered.

"No," Brandon laughed without humor. "It was not a wasted trip at all."

There was a long pause. "Now tell me what's really going on, Bran."

There were times when the strong mental connection he had with is father was more than annoying. There was no way he would tell his father about actually conversing with a former arcana member who had been condemned as ill-dignified and useless. Brandon felt he was already too close to the abyss and he had no intention of dragging his father down with him.

"Brandon?"

Brandon shook off the need to tell his father about the shin on Amme's soul and the accidental butterfly she had defiled. "What do you know about the Magus?" he asked instead.

"The *Magus*?" his father repeated, obviously surprised by both the question and the change of subject. "All I really know is to stay the hell away from him. Everything else is unconfirmed rumor."

"I'll take what I can get. Tell me the rumors."

"Why the interest?" came the suspicious question.

"Just humor me, Dad."

There was a slight hesitation. "Well, supposedly, his lineage can be traced directly back to Pyrrho of Elis. He was Destiny Given in Kanpur when he turned thirteen, but it was only a formality. It was known he would be Magus the day he was born. His sephiroth and Seth were preordained. He was never a true butterfly."

"Jeez," Brandon grimaced. "That must have been one hell of a lousy childhood."

"Yup. The poor kid never stood a chance," Augustus agreed. "I doubt he had time to play rugby in his off hours."

"Anything else?"

"Not much and nothing good."

"Tell me."

"As I said, nothing good. I heard through the grapevine that Emil Hamish was his guide, then some hellacious rift happened between them twenty or thirty years ago. Nobody knows exactly what occurred, but whatever it was, it was very, very, ugly."

"How ugly?"

"Ugly. Hamish screwed up, somehow. There was a serious bend, almost a full breach. One of the most ancient Apocryphas of the Major Arcana had to be invoked by the Magus himself to correct whatever happened."

"Damn!"

"Tell me about it," Augustus agreed. "In any event, the Magus managed to divert the disaster, but I heard it cost him part of his soul. Hamish permanently gave up his status of Guide because of it. The most current rumor is that The Magus is on semi-speaking terms with Hamish again, but their relationship is still a little shaky. 'Stitched with the slightest thread of spider web' was the expression I heard."

"Emil Hamish is still alive? He must be ninety years older than dirt."

"Not only that, but still with Vanessa. Somewhere in Colorado, according to my sources."

"Don't know her," Brandon told him.

"Nice lady, she was your great, great Grandfather's guide. Or maybe his father's, I'm not sure. She must be close to ninety herself."

"Have you ever met him?"

"No, but my godfather did. Emil's arcana name is Hasimah, if that helps. The guy's a legend in the circle."

"No, I meant the Magus," Aaron explained patiently.

"The Magus? Hell no, 'knock wood'. I don't know who he is, or what name he uses publically and I really don't want to know. He prefers his anonymity."

Brandon took the star out of his pocket and studied it. "I may have a way to get around that."

"Don't follow it," Augustus suggested in a harsh voice. "The Magus is extremely powerful. First Key. Stay in the Minors. Playing in the Majors is serious shit, Bran."

"I know. Hopefully I can avoid it. I'll find out more in Bourgogne."

The silence on the other end of the phone was deafening. "Dad?"

"Sorry. Just thinking of major illnesses I could fake to con you into coming home so I can lock you in your room and weld the door shut."

Brandon laughed. "Thanks, Dad, I needed that."

"I wasn't joking, the thought has merit. I don't suppose I could talk you into letting this go?"

"Grandpére is dying, Dad. They're predicting six months at most. I'm the next in line."

"I know," Augustus answered, resigned. "It's all your mother's fault. If she wasn't so damned gorgeous, witty, intelligent and good in the sack, she never would have suckered me into marriage. Cunning, that woman."

Brandon grinned. If any two people had been born for each other, it was his parents. "Yup. Mom definitely pulled the wool over your eyes."

His father let out a heavy sigh. "If you have to take on your grandfather's quest, Brandon, remember to 'keep your sword pointed upward'."

"'Through the cypress and storm clouds'," Brandon finished the favorite quote of his father's with a smile.

"Expect more clouds than cypress, Son. Give Grandpa Rose my best regards," Augustus said heavily.

"I will."

"I love you, Bran. Try and give me a few grandkids before you get yourself killed, will you?"

"I'm not as easy to trap, Dad, but I'll do my best. Go hug that sneaky woman you married."

They disconnected the call.

Brandon looked at the Star in his hand critically. Had he known of the shin placed on Emma Coleman's soul, he would never have taken it, but now he was under its three pronged edict. Use it, destroy it, or give it away freely.

That was the bottom line. Use it, destroy it, or give it away. Should he use it? Could he use it? Without an elemental to lend it power, the star was virtually useless.

But he still might be able to use it. Workable or not, it still had value.

As a bargaining chip to find out where the Magus was hiding, if nothing else.

Chapter 5 - Page of Wands

Three months without a word, without knowing if Susan was alive or dead. Curt had called the chapter house trying to find her, but she wasn't there. She'd left the Order since the last time he'd seen her. He'd said cruel things during their last discussion, he did remember that. He needed to find her, she was his responsibility, she belonged to him. She would not be able to survive without him.

Finally, he had called her Aunt Mary in La Jolla. With relief, he learned that Susan was there, she was unhurt.

But she wouldn't to talk to him. Without his guidance, she had returned to her old family, her old life.

He knew then that she didn't really belong to him anymore. Despite the hurt of that knowledge, his worry for her lifted. Susan, his Ayin, might no longer be his, but she was safe, that was the most important thing.

Ayin was safe.

Maybe it was for the best. In his own way, he loved Susan, but he had treated her badly. Even Emma had told him that he treated her badly. And Emma should know. Manipulation and treating people badly was Emma's stock in trade, not a character trait he ever should have adopted.

("In you, I can see a beautiful little boy who had loving parents, who were coerced into giving custody of you to Amme before they died. Over the years, this little boy was sexually and emotionally molested and manipulated until he learned to believe that the only love open to him was an old, profoundly barren woman who knew a few magical tricks to keep him interested.")

Pricilla had told him that and he knew it was true. He could have been someone else, someone good, but Emma had turned him into a monster.

The Order of True Life finally hunted him down while he was in jail. They hadn't heard from Emma for more than three months and the Order was in chaos without her leadership. He was second in command they had decided, the one most closely connected to her. Without her guidance, they needed him. Within twenty-four hours after they found him, his bail had been posted and he was out. The church members used their own personal money for the exorbitant bail.

There was an irony to the justice system. There was a reason the world was so fucked up. He didn't deserve to be out, he was a monster.

He told the police that, he told his attorney that, he even told the Judge that, but no one seemed to care about the facts, he was bailed out anyway.

So, he went to the only place he knew. Curt looked around the empty Victorian house he had lived in with Miss Emma for the last few years. She wasn't there, or he would have killed her immediately, putting himself back in jail under new charges, ones that wouldn't allow him out on bail.

Monsters should be in jail, not on the outside where they could hurt innocent people.

He knew Emma wasn't gone for good, he'd still have that chance of redemption. In the cupboard next to her favorite chair, he found the wooden box holding her cherished tarot cards. She'd never leave her cards for more than three days at a time. They ruled her life.

Just as she had ruled his.

He looked around the house critically. Home. This wasn't his home. Without Emma's false illusions of attractive comfort, it was simply an old, dusty, rundown house. She enjoyed playing with people's minds, getting them to see what she wanted them to see.

It had never been a real home, it was just another prison, one made by Emma herself. He knew that now. Pricilla had told him the truth, she was the only one who had ever told him the honest truth.

("It's a simple scenario, Curt. Emma needs your youth, your innocence, the magic elixir of your gender and she's drinking every drop of it, every chance she gets. You weren't born a jerk, Curt, any evil you now possess has been carefully planted by Emma. You do not carry that aura around you naturally.")

He had broken into her hotel room to drug her, enjoy her fear, rape her, make her like what he did to her, make her his. Emma had told him she belonged to him, that he could have her.

Somehow, Pricilla had stopped him from violating her, made him listen to her, told him the truth.

(Given a normal upbringing, I can see also that you would have been a strong, powerful, intelligent and very kind man of great importance and depth.")

God, how he wished he had become the man she had described. He could have been loved and respected for himself, not be the monster that Emma had created.

Pricilla was forth generation True Science, she knew things he could only imagine. She had showed him so much. She had called the salamander without words. She had simply held out her hand and it had come to her. It had blazed and flickered in her palm, a living, breathing elemental of fire. She had let Curt touch it. It had been beautiful. So very beautiful. He would never forget it.

("Yes, he is beautiful. The very first elemental. Older than man. Older than the Earth herself. Without him, life would not exist. You've only used his heat. You've never actually seen a real one in this world, have you?")

He never had. Emma had taught him how to call the salamander's fire, he had used it for frivolous needs, heating her fucking tea, starting a fucking fire in her fireplace, but he had never known how glorious a creature it truly was.

And then Pricilla had sent the salamander back to it's own world and the beautiful creature was gone.

("Ki Akal, Atziluth, go in peace my little friend.")

And that's when he knew exactly what he had become, worse, what he could have become. *(My little friend).* Pricilla had treated the salamander like a cherished friend, not a pet, not a slave. She had spoken to it with love and respect. She even told him why, something Emma had never revealed to him.

(It thrives on love and trust. Why do you think he let you touch him just now? Why do you think he came to you all those years? You saw it, Curt, he was dancing for you! Do you think he would have done that for someone like Emma? The elemental of fire trusted you, Curt. He liked you. That's the only reason he would ever let you touch him or use his heat.")

He had learned so much, now it was too late. Emma had lied to him. She had told him never to make a friend of the Salamander, that it was his servant, nothing more, to call it his friend was religious nonsense. Finally, after years of treating the elemental the way she had trained him, the salamander, the heat he had used so indifferently to warm a teapot or heat a bath, wouldn't come to him any longer.

He hadn't known. It had wanted to be his friend, but he had treated it like a slave. It didn't take a psychiatrist to tell him the score. He had abused the salamander and every other friend he might have had, the same way Emma had abused him. The same way he had treated Ayin. No. Not Ayin, that was the name he had given her, not her real name.

Susan.

(Given a normal upbringing, I can see also that you would have been very kind man of great importance and depth.)

A man who would have been kind, maybe even a man Susan could have truly loved with no tricks, no drugs, no coercion.

Yes, he knew the truth now, but it couldn't change anything. He had become as evil and cruel as Emma. The salamander would never return to him, neither would Susan.

Emma would pay for that. She would most surely pay for that. He would make certain she would never harm another person, another innocent. First he'd take her power, then her life. Then he would go back to jail where monsters belonged so everyone else would be safe.

First take her power...

Curt eyed Emma's cherished box of tarot cards. Seventy-eight cards that helped her plan her schemes, map out her manipulations. Force innocent people to her will.

He sat in her chair and opened the box, checking its contents. With surprise, he noticed that the box contained more than just her cherished cards. On the top there was also a small velvet drawstring bag. He opened it curiously, spilling the contents in his hand. He now held a gold brooch with two blue stones and a silver bracelet with a green stone. At the bottom of the box, under the Tarot cards, lay a golden knife with a blood red stone.

He put the jewelry back into the velvet bag and slipped it into his pocket. He'd find a safe place for them later. He touched the blade of the jeweled knife thoughtfully, then set it aside on the circular table next to him.

And then, one by one, he lit every foul card with one match each, letting their ashes drop into the chest as they burned. He may no longer be able to summon the salamander, but he still loved fire. Fire would cleanse everything.

Perhaps it could even cleanse a little of his evil and permanently tainted soul.

***

Two days later when Emma came back to the house, Curt made sure she saw the ashes of her precious cards before he killed her. He knew it would make her suffer more than the golden knife he thrust into her black heart.

Curt called the police himself, making certain the monster he had become would be locked away forever.

While waiting for the police to arrive, he set fire to the house.

He watched it burn with Miss Emma's body smoldering inside, rejoicing in the living flames as though they were the salamanders he could no longer call. The grass of the lawn was brown and dry from lack of water, the sparks from the house jumped into it, grateful for the food, flickering and dancing to the sounds of the oncoming sirens.

It was beautiful, so incredibly beautiful. He danced and laughed in a circle around the brilliant flames that so reminded him of his beloved salamander, his heart full of pure joy.

He would always love fire.

Chapter 6 - Troubles and Sorrows

Pricilla opened the front door wearing white shorts and a red sleeveless top, her mostly blond hair in a ponytail. "Hey, Paul," she greeted her visitor. He was dressed professionally in a dark suit and blue silk tie, carrying a slim briefcase. "Cassie said you were coming over and that you sounded a bit rattled on the phone. What's wrong?"

Paul looked around worriedly as he walked through the door. "Cassie is the new housekeeper, right?"

"Not exactly, more of a long term guest. She's studying to be a chef, just playing the part of housekeeper during her summer vacation. Cassie is Jacobs niece, her folks are in Greece."

"How old is she?"

"Just turned eighteen." She thought about it. "No, nineteen."

Paul lowered his voice. "Is she in on all the woo-woo stuff like Jacob?"

Pricilla grinned. "'Woo-woo stuff'?"

"You popping in and out, calling sylphs, that stuff?"

"Oh, *that* stuff. Like Jacob, Cassie's second generation and can pretty much handle the 'woo-woo' stuff. Up to a point anyway. A Page of Wands, she's more into salamanders, than sylphs. Out in the world of real she has to hide her talents. Here, she's like a kid with a new toy, enjoys conning the salamanders into lighting the Barbeque and candles without matches. Aaron is not amused, he's trying to break her of the habit, even if the salamanders do get a kick out of it." She smiled. "In any event, you may speak openly without fear of being considered a nutcase, everyone who works or stays here is crazy as a loon."

"Good," Paul sighed in relief, "then I'll fit right in. Is Aaron here?"

"No he's been held up at the theatre, something about the stage lights. He'll be back soon. Come on out to the patio, I just mixed up a pitcher of lemonade." She walked him through the living room and out the French doors. "Unless you want something stronger?" she gestured toward the circular bar near the center of the patio. "Aaron keeps it well stocked. I think I'm driving him to drink."

"Still no handle on the popping back and forth?"

"We're working on it." She walked over to the table near a huge pool that looked like it was spilling off into the canyon behind it. "Sit, relax. I've been meaning to thank you for finding this spectacular house. Fabulous view at night." She sat down at the table, filled two glasses with ice and poured the lemonade. She waited until Paul had taken a sip, then asked, "So. Why did Cassie say you were rattled when you called?"

Paul took another sip, then set the glass down on the table with an audible click. "Have you heard from the District Attorney?"

"The D.A.? No," she frowned. "Why?" She held up a hand. "Don't tell me, let me guess. The hearing on Curt has been postponed again, or he chewed off his ankle bracelet and hitched a ride to Mexico."

"Nothing that mundane," Paul answered with a grim smile.

Pricilla looked concerned. "Oh, five hells. What did he do?"

Paul paused. "Let's see." He thought about how to say it.

"Paul?"

"Okay. Summing up - Curt killed Emma with some kind of ritual knife; burned the house down with her in it; called the police to turn himself in, waived his rights to an attorney, then spent six hours in interrogation, cheerfully explaining his actions. The police, in a fit of rare sanity, thought it might be a good idea to have him checked out through County Mental Health. He'll be locked up with them for at least seventy-two hours before being charged and arraigned. My guess is he'll be institutionalized for life."

Pricilla just stared at him, eyes wide.

Paul took a sip of his lemonade to ease his dry throat, then continued. "Emma's body is still in the morgue, looking a bit like what the cops call a 'crispy critter', so they won't be completely sure of the cause of death until the autopsy, but the preliminary report suggests it's the big knife sticking out of her chest and not smoke inhalation or a heart attack." He paused and took another long drink of his lemonade.

Pricilla opened her mouth to say something, anything, and ended up with, "Uh... More lemonade?" she lifted the pitcher hopefully.

"Thank you, yes."

She filled his glass to the brim, her hand surprisingly steady. "So, uh... " She bit her lip. "Emma's dead?"

"Deader than a doornail. Officially, her identification is still pending, waiting for verification of her dental records, but that's merely a formality. It was definitely Emma Coleman."

"Umm... I'm not exactly sure what to say," Pricilla understated.

"Oh, that's just my lead-in. It gets even more complicated," Paul assured her, lifting his briefcase. "I received a package today, before I heard the news. It was postmarked two days ago."

"From who? Whom?" Pricilla asked with concern, as he opened the briefcase and pulled out a large padded envelope.

"From Curt, the knife wielding fire bug himself," Paul answered. "Inside was a note for me, asking me to give this to you." He handed her a small wrapped box with her name on the outside. He lifted his glass and saluted her with it. "Happy days." He drained the newly filled glass. He then took the pitcher and filled it again, drinking half.

Pricilla looked at the small box in her hand with horror, fighting the urge to shove it back to him. "Shouldn't I... um... I don't know, give this to the District Attorney or something?"

Paul shrugged. "Its not like it contains the murder weapon, they already have it. It doesn't fall under the rules of evidence any more than if he sent you a gift last Christmas. Of course, being from Curt, you might want to have the bomb squad check it out before you open it." He looked at her seriously. "Or Aaron."

Pricilla looked annoyed. "Why does everyone assume Aaron can handle everything and I can't?"

"Because we men are bigger, stronger, smarter?" Paul suggested, puffing out his chest with a smile.

"Right. Sell that to Susan, I'd like to be there and listen to her answer," Pricilla bit her lower lip, then unwrapped the box. Her hand was less than steady as she lifted the lid. There was a folded note on top of a small velvet bag. She unfolded the note, it read, "'Thank you, Pricilla, for telling me the truth. I think these would be safer with you. Your friend in peace, Curt'." She handed the note to Paul so he could read it.

"Your friend in peace?" Paul looked up from the paper with unveiled sarcasm. "That kid really does need to be in County Mental Health."

("You told the salamander to go in peace, you called it your friend."... "He trusted me? He liked me? Is that why he quit coming to me? Because I hurt him?")

At the time he had seemed like such a lost little boy and it had crushed her heart. Pricilla shook off the words and the pain they caused her, then opened the drawstring bag, spilling the two pieces of jewelry into the palm of her hand. "Oh, that's nasty," she looked with horror at what she held.

"Those look old," Paul said as he looked at the antique gold and jewels, "And they're probably stolen, but what's nasty?"

"This," Pricilla put the bracelet down on the table and gently touched what looked to be a brooch. "Someone apparently thought it was humorous to trap an undine," she answered, still staring at it. "It can't be Emma's work, she doesn't have the skill and it's a hell of a lot older than she is. Was." She corrected, then looked more closely at the brooch. "Damn. And a sylph."

"What?"

"See where it's separated by the gold? One side is an undine, the other a sylph. Both living, both trapped."

"Trapped? Why would anyone want to do that?" Paul asked, looking at the brooch curiously where she pointed out the separation. He saw the flicker of light on the silver side and felt a wave of melancholy. A tiny sparkle of light just like the one he had held only a few days before. "Why?" he asked again.

"It probably gives the owner some kind of bullshit power I don't know about," Pricilla looked angry, then balanced the brooch carefully as she blew on it softly. "Ki Akal Yetzirah. Ki Akal Briah." She blew on her palm a second time. "Go in peace my gentle friends."

The stones flickered with life, then abruptly flashed, surrounding Pricilla in a huge bubble of blue water that pushed Paul off his chair, knocking over the table, pitcher and glasses in the process. Thankfully, the table, pitcher and glasses were acrylic and didn't shatter.

"Holy shit!" Paul pulled himself up off the cement deck, his pants were soaked in lemonade. He stared incredulously at the round blue globe now surrounding Pricilla.

"Well," Pricilla frowned from within the bubble, "this is awkward." Her words echoed back to her.

"What?" Paul saw her lips moving, but couldn't hear a sound. He stepped closer to the bubble, touching it lightly, then slapped it. "What *is* this thing?" He could see ripples move like water within the walls of the sphere, but it felt solid. "Are you alright? Can you breathe in there?"

"This is seriously annoying," Pricilla slumped against the wall of the bubble from the inside.

"What?" Paul asked. He hit the wall of water more forcefully. "I can't hear you! Can you get out? What can I do?"

Pricilla touched her right ear and shook her head, showing she couldn't hear him either, then shrugged. "Call Aaron?" she mouthed the suggestion.

Paul pulled his cell phone from his jacket, flipped it open, nothing happened. The damned thing was soaked with sugar and lemon, its crystal face broken from his fall. He looked at Pricilla. "Its dead," he showed her the phone. "I'll call from the house," he told her, then pantomimed what he planned to do. He positioned his thumb and little finger to his ear and used the universal circular dial with his finger and suddenly wondered why people mimed a rotary dial when no one even had rotary phones in this century. Did kids today even know what a rotary phone was? Even he hadn't seen one in years.

Pricilla waited patiently while Paul pondered the issue, then shook her head and pointed toward the bar. "Over there."

Paul looked where she pointed, there was a wireless phone hanging on the wall next to the bar. "Right." He walked quickly over to the bar and picked up the phone, staring at it stupidly for a moment, then hit the contact list. Aaron's number was on top, he punched the button.

"What's up, Cilla? Wait a second," Aaron said before he continued. "Jacob, I don't think we need to put a blue transparency on that spotlight, it's washing out half the stage."

"Aaron. It's Paul."

"Paul?" Aaron repeated. "Why are you calling from my home phone?"

"I'm at your house. On the patio."

"Did we have a meeting?" Aaron asked curiously.

"No. I came over to tell Pricilla about Curt and,"

"What about Curt?" Aaron interrupted him angrily. "Has that little bastard been trying to contact her? Do we need another restraining order, or should we just cut through all the red tape and kill the little creep?"

"Not necessary. He's back in jail."

"Damn," Aaron answered. "For what, another rape?"

"No. He killed Emma, torched her house, called the police and turned himself in."

"Ah." There was a very long pause. "Where's Pricilla?"

"She's here, but..."

"What's wrong?" Aaron asked with concern. "Is she alright?"

"Uh..." Paul looked at the bubble surrounding Pricilla. "Well... yes and no. We're having a bit of a problem at the moment."

Aaron sighed. "Don't tell me, let me guess. She wants to go down to the jail to commiserate with the little schmuck and you've taken her car keys like the true friend you are, right?"

"No. Nothing like that. Curt's a side issue at the moment. She's..." He looked again at Pricilla who was now sitting cross-legged on the bottom of the bubble, her right palm resting on her chin, her elbow on her knee, watching him on the phone. "Um... It's a little hard to explain."

"It always is with Cilla. Put her on the line."

"That isn't possible at the moment." Paul cleared his throat.

"Why?" Aaron asked in a calm voice.

Paul's voice quavered with unexpected amusement at the whole insane situation. "Because she can't reach it?"

"And she can't reach the phone because..." Aaron persisted patiently.

"She's... Um... She's stuck in a bubble?"

There was a long pause. "She's taking a bubble bath on the patio?" Aaron asked, confused.

"No, she's trapped inside a bubble." Paul knew he was going to lose the battle in a moment and burst out laughing.

"Ah. Huh." A short pause. "O-kay. Could you describe this bubble?" Aaron asked curiously.

There was comfort in the fact that he could call Aaron with such an outrageous bit of lunacy and have it treated so casually. Paul bit his bottom lip, hard. "It's a," he controlled his voice with difficulty. "It's... Well, it's blue," he started, trying to keep his voice somewhat level. "And its big, I'd estimate about six feet in diameter."

There was another long pause. "Well. That's new."

"It certainly is for me," Paul admitted, finally letting go with a choked laugh.

"Leave it to Pricilla to figure out a way to trap herself in a bubble," Aaron sighed. "I'm guessing she's in no immediate danger, or you'd sound a little more concerned."

Paul looked at Pricilla, she was watching him with obvious frustration, her elbows braced on her knees, both palms now holding up her chin. "She looks okay for now. Any suggestions as to what I should do? I'm a little out of my element here."

"Well," Aaron considered the problem, "it's just a bubble," he pointed out reasonably. "Can't you simply pop it and let her out?"

"Pop it? Uh, wait a second." Paul rummaged through the barbeque tools and found a long skewer, then walked back over to Pricilla and poked at the bubble with it. "I don't think so," he reported into the phone. "When I prick it, it ripples, but it seems pretty firm." He looked at Pricilla again. "And Aaron? She looks a little pissed off."

"Well, that's to be expected," Aaron answered, "no one likes it when you try to pop their bubble."

Paul barely controlled a laugh by coughing. "True," he grinned.

"What's she saying?"

"I have no idea. Thankfully, the bubble seems to be soundproof."

"Interesting," Aaron sighed heavily. "Well. So much for getting any more work done today. I'm on my way. I'm taking the helicopter, so I should be there in about fifteen. Stay around for dinner. I'm grilling salmon this evening."

"Okay. Are you going to let Cassie light the barbeque? Can I watch?"

"No and no. Doesn't anyone want a normal life anymore?" Aaron asked.

"Where's the fun in that?" Paul asked.

Aaron hung up, apparently deciding not to dignify the question with an answer.

A teenage girl bounced out onto the patio, her short curly brown hair was colored with bright red streaks and bobbed with youthful animation. She was wearing cutoff jeans and t-shirt that exclaimed, "Cry me a river. No really, please! The rivers we have are drying up, or haven't you noticed?" She skidded to a stop. "Pricilla? Did you and your friend want some nachos?" She looked at the bubble and blinked. "Whoa. That is so cool!" She looked over at Paul. "Hi. I'm Cassie. Do you want me to call Mr. Zale?"

"I've already called him," Paul told her, wondering how he was going to explain a six foot wide bubble on the patio with Pricilla sitting inside.

"Okay. Do you want to have some nachos with your bubble?" Cassie asked, grinning.

"Sure," Paul answered, then walked over to the bar. Pricilla was right.

They were all crazy and he fit right in.

Chapter 7 - Bubbles and Beer

"Well," Aaron decided as he walked around the bubble with Pricilla still inside. "At least it's an attractive bubble."

Paul had taken off his coat and tie, sat in his now dry, but still lemonade ruined trousers, and was sitting casually on a comfortable barstool behind the bar, drinking his second beer. There were three taps, he had chosen a rather tasty blend from Ireland that had a definite kick. He looked at Pricilla's bubble critically. "Yes, yes it is. Very pretty as far as bubbles go," he agreed, sipping his beer. A definite kick, the Irish undeniably knew their beer. The effect was rather relaxing. "Am I slurring?" he asked Aaron with mild curiosity.

"Not yet." Aaron had tried unsuccessfully to communicate with Pricilla both verbally and mentally with no luck. "Draw me one too, will you?" he walked back to the bar and sat down, looking over at the bubble, with mild interest.

"No problem." Paul took another pilsner glass from the cupboard and looked at the names on the tap handles. "Guinness, Smithwick or good old bud, Sir?" It was a nice break playing bartender. Practicing law was boring. Maybe he should consider a career change. He smiled to himself. From Torts to taps. What a swell idea!

"Bud's good," Aaron decided. "The Guinness is a little too strong."

"That explains my fuzzy head," Paul nodded, filling the glass, rather satisfied with himself when he was able to keep the foam to a minimum. He put it on the opposite side of the bar as Aaron sat down. "Have you ever thought of changing careers?" he asked conversationally.

"Hourly." He kept his eye on Pricilla and her bubble.

"When I was a kid I wanted to be a professional baseball player. I was great in Little League, not so bad in High School, either." He looked at Aaron curiously. "What did you want to be when you grew up?"

"I wanted to be a kid," Aaron answered, still looking at Pricilla and the bubble, "being a grownup is a pain in the ass."

"They didn't have a baseball team in Law School, but my dad was determined I go, he didn't give a damn about baseball. Why don't parents ever ask you what you really want to do?"

Cassie spoke up as she walked toward the bar with a plate of nachos, "because adults never listen. They think they know what's best for you, even when they don't," she told them. "I had an idea while I was making these," she announced, as she put the plate on the bar. "What say we roll the bubble into the pool? Maybe it will dissolve. If not..." she grinned, "well, there's no point in wasting a perfectly good bubble. We could play dodge-ball or something. Pricilla might even enjoy it."

Paul laughed.

Aaron groaned. "Go in the house and play a video game or something, Cassie."

"A video game?" Cassie gave him a look of horror. "What am I, twelve?"

"Whatever. Twitter a friend. Bake a cake. Anything."

"Bake a cake?" Cassie brightened. "Can I..."

"No," Aaron answered before she could finish the question.

Cassie gave him a frustrated look. "Fourth generation get to play with bubbles, I get cartoon Wii games, is that fair?" she asked Paul.

"Not fair at all," Paul agreed wholeheartedly.

"Cassie," Aaron glared at her.

"I'm going, I'm going." She stomped back into the house. "Scream if you want more nachos," she called over her shoulder, "I'm attaching my video game to the surround sound while I twitter with my little friends and bake a cake with environmentally suspect electricity."

Aaron groaned. "You find me a house with ten thousand square feet and it's still too small with a teenager in it."

"Kids liven up a house," Paul disagreed.

"I could do without lively for a year or two," Aaron decided with an exasperated exhale. "Explain to me again how exactly how this newest disaster happened?" He picked up his beer and took a long drink.

Paul munched on a nacho and thought about it. "Well, Pricilla opened the box that Curt sent her, said something about the brooch inside being nasty, that it contained both a sylph and an undine. Then she said something else in the crazy language you people sometimes use, the bubble just whooped up out of thin air," he threw his hands up in the air to demonstrate, "and it pushed over me and the table. Crash! When I got up, she was inside the bubble, looking out." He took another nacho. "These are pretty good," he decided.

"Kids always make good nachos," Aaron took one and also munched, "I think they live on them. Where's the brooch now?"

"I think it's in the bubble with her. I couldn't find it," Paul told him. "Oh! He looked around the bar then spied his objective right in front of him. He brushed his pants to take the salt off his hands. "This came from Curt too," he picked up the velvet bag, opened it and handed the bracelet with the green stone to Aaron. "What do you think this one does?"

Aaron looked at the bracelet with interest. "Not a clue." He studied the stone. "No trapped elemental in any event." He put it down on the bar top, dismissing it.

Paul looked slightly disappointed. "Oh. So it's not a counter-spell to the bubble or something?"

"If it is, I have no idea how to work it," Aaron shook his head, glancing again at the bracelet. "Do you remember what it looked like?"

"Huh?" Paul grabbed another nacho. "What what looked like?"

"The brooch, Paul."

"Oh. I only saw it for a moment," Paul thought about it, trying for a visual memory. "A little garish for my taste." He considered it. "My great-great grandmother might have liked it. Mother always said her taste was all in her mouth, that she gravitated toward tacky jewelry when she was alive."

"Was it broken in any way?"

"The brooch?" Paul frowned, trying to remember. "Didn't appear to be. But I didn't see the clasp on the back. It might have been broken, clasps tend to break easily. I had tie tack with a lousy clasp, once. Must have had it fixed weekly," he rambled on. "Finally I just quit wearing tie tacks altogether. My mother keeps giving them for my birthdays, I don't think she's noticed yet. The last one was the scales of justice. Do you believe that? Like every lawyer in the country doesn't have one. I think they give them away as party favors at graduation. Mother has no original thoughts. That reminds me. Mother's birthday is next month. I wonder if it's on my desk calendar, I forgot it last year. Mothers get so touchy about things like that," he shook his head. "First they act like its no big deal, then remind you about it for months."

"The brooch, Paul. What did it look like? Etchings? Design?" Aaron asked patiently, trying to get him back on topic.

Paul paused for a moment. "Right. The brooch. Well, it was gold, had a yin yang type of decoration, I think. It had blue stones inset on the top. One was lighter blue than the other."

"Ah. Earth, wind, water."

Paul blinked. "Okay!" He looked at Aaron expectantly. "And that means what?"

"No idea," Aaron sipped his drink calmly, keeping his back to the bubble with Pricilla in it. "Is she starting to look even more pissed off to you?"

Paul peeked over Aaron's shoulder and at the bubble. Pricilla was back in her Aladdin position, glaring at them. "Yup. Probably annoyed that we're sitting here drinking beer and eating nachos. She's been in there almost an hour."

"Serves her right for fooling around with things she doesn't understand," Aaron decided, swallowing another sip of beer. "Earth, wind, water," he started tapping his glass, thinking.

"You said that before," Paul noted. "I didn't understand the first time. What does it mean?"

Aaron frowned. "Well, assuming the gold is relatively pure, it's an element of Earth. Sylphs are wind and air elementals, Undines are water elementals." He looked at Paul curiously. "Was there a strip of gold between the yin and yang?"

"I think so."

"Ah. Got it. The undine and the sylph are kept separate by the earth elemental."

"And that means what?"

"It means we're dealing with something pretty nasty."

"That's what Pricilla said."

"So, using her heart, not her brain, she tried to release them and got trapped inside herself," Aaron concluded, then shook his head. "Double trapped, gold on the back, gold on the front to keep the elementals separated," he took a nacho and munched thoughtfully.

"Clear as mud," Paul decided. "Ready for another beer?" he asked hopefully. He'd need to practice drawing one if he decided to become a professional bartender. Maybe he should invest in an old fashioned English style Pub, one near his office. He could be a part-time bartender and learn the trade before he quit law altogether. He'd have to look into the liquor laws. Torts to Taps. He really liked that. Good name for a pub.

"Oh! Simple," Aaron broke into his thoughts.

Paul frowned. "What's simple?"

Aaron took a long sip of his beer to wash down the nacho. "She's trapping them, they're not trapping her. As an Earth elemental herself, she simply took the place of the gold and bound them to herself."

"Oh. Right." Paul nodded. "That makes..." he shook his head, "...absolutely no sense to me." He decided. "Am I slurring?"

"Not yet," Aaron got off his barstool, walked over to the bubble and got Pricilla's attention by slapping on it. "Go. To. Whilom," he told her, making sure his mouth moved with clear exaggeration."

Pricilla looked at him with astonished surprise and promptly disappeared, the bubble disappearing as she did.

Aaron gave a satisfied sigh, reached down to the ground and picked up the brooch that remained behind. He frowned at it. "Back where they were, trapped inside. End of second problem, back to the first." He walked over to the bar, put the brooch carefully on it, touching it gently. "Poor little things." He picked up his beer looking angry.

Pricilla materialized next to him, took his beer and sipped it, then gave it back to him, adding a gentle kiss in the process. "Thanks. I can't believe I didn't think of that."

"Who can think clearly inside a bubble?" Paul asked supportively. "Ale, lager or beer?" he held up a new glass.

"Lager." She looked at the brooch on the bar and ran a finger over it. "Sorry, little friends. We'll think of another way to get you out of there." She shook her head. "Just babies, all they really want to do is go home." She picked through the nachos and took one that was more cheese than chip.

Aaron raised an eyebrow. "You talked to them?"

"Not really. They talked more to each other than to me. They've never been together before. In the same space, in any event. If your next question is who trapped them, I don't know. All I really know is that it wasn't their choice." She took the glass from Paul. "Now what do we do?" she asked Aaron.

"For now, eat, get drunk and sleep on it until I do some research."

Paul raised his glass. "Way ahead of you," he announced. "I'm working on the drunk."

"So you are," Pricilla smiled at his alcoholic slur. "Thanks for sticking around, Paul, you're a good friend."

"Not sure about that," Paul answered more soberly. "First Susan's problem, now this. I never seem to bring rainbows into your lives."

"You don't create problems, Paul, just bring them to our attention," Aaron argued. "Someone else committed this atrocity," he nodded toward the brooch. "We don't know who, we don't know why and we don't know when," he frowned. "And, at the moment, I have absolutely no idea how to undo it."

Pricilla frowned. "Maybe you're not the one who's supposed to."

Chapter 8 - *Knight of Swords by Destiny Given*

Aaron watched Brandon Grayson walk out onto the patio. The superficial research he'd managed to obtain about him had been favorable. CEO of his family's centuries old wine business, successful, somewhat ruthless in negotiations, well respected. He was dressed casually for this meeting in khaki cotton pants, light blue Polo shirt, loafers, no socks. He was thirty-seven, but had no gray in his dark hair to show that he had experienced any real stress in his life. Third Generation True Science. Cool customer, very sure of himself.

And for some reason, though they were near each other in age, Brandon Grayson made Aaron feel just plain old.

Aaron came out from behind the bar, ready to face what promised to be his next problem. "You must be Brandon. Hamish told me to expect you." He held out a hand. "I'm Aaron Zale."

"Mr. Zale," Brandon shook his hand firmly. "Thank you for seeing me." He had been quietly investigating everything he could find on Aaron Zale ever since he had learned the name. All he had been able to discover were details of his public persona, information readily available to the world at large. Fifteen years before he had exploded onto the stage with his magician's act, performing almost exclusively for charities. He was known mostly for his altruism and debunking bunko artists.

Unfortunately, Brandon had been unable to find anything useful about Aaron Zale's exalted position in the hierarchy of True Science, not even his birth name or date. Physically he was a large man, white blond hair, eyes that seemed friendly and filled with humor.

Somehow, with the title of Magus, First Key of the Major Arcana, Brandon thought he'd be more intimidating.

"Just Aaron," he gestured to the circular bar.

"Aaron, then," Brandon smiled and sat on one of the bar stools. The patio was huge and well-proportioned, several canvas fans circled silently above, not especially cooling, just moving the hot summer air with an artificial breeze. The pool beyond the patio looked cool and inviting. If he lived in this part of the state he'd probably never get out of that pool.

Aaron walked back around to the serving side of the bar. "What can I get you? Ice water, beer, ale, Scotch? We even have a very nice Riesling from one of your own vineyards."

"Ice water, thanks. It's a warm day."

Aaron pulled a bottle of water from the refrigerator under the bar and handed it to him. "Its worse in Vegas, anything under a hundred feels like spring." He tapped a beer for himself then discreetly flipped a switch under the counter. A light mist added itself to the breeze of the fans, cooling the atmosphere considerably.

Brandon looked casually toward the doors to the house. "I understand you were recently married," he said conversationally. "Congratulations."

Aaron smiled. In point of fact, he and Pricilla had been formally bound since the moment she had been born, but the more traditional civil ceremony was less than a year old. "Thank you." He hadn't missed Brandon's concern when glancing toward the house. "My wife is forth generation, Brandon, she's more than a little familiar with the problems True Science generates. She's also elsewhere at the moment. We're quite private." He assured him. "Anything you want to talk to me about is confidential."

"This about the Star of Solomon."

"I see." Aaron had stiffened as he took a sip of his ale, but managed a look of mild interest rather than shock. "I wasn't aware that the Star was within the sephiroth of a Page of Swords."

"Not directly, no."

Aaron nodded. "What is your interest in the star?"

"You gave the Star to Amme, alias Emma Coleman."

Aaron raised an eyebrow. "You're well informed."

Brandon reached into his breast pocket and placed a velvet box containing the star on the counter between them. He opened it. Even without direct sunlight, the metal shimmered like liquid gold. "Amme gave it to me."

("And so returns the proverbial bad penny,") Aaron said to himself. He put down his ale and looked with loathing at the star. Months he'd been searching, now he didn't want to touch the damned thing. He closed the top, looked directly into the eyes of Brandon Grayson and pushed the box back to him. "Quite a gift. It should fetch a good price. You should have it appraised before you put it on eBay." He took a sip of his beer. "If Amme was a friend of yours, I'm sorry for your loss."

The friendly look in Aaron's expression was no longer evident. Brandon recognized the fact that this conversation was going downhill rapidly. "She was not a friend of mine. She gave me the star for information on how to remove the shin you placed making her ill-dignified and useless."

Aaron raised an eyebrow. "And what did you tell her?"

"I told her it wasn't possible. When I understood the damage she had done to an unprotected butterfly, worse, an accidental butterfly, I removed myself from her filth as quickly as possible."

"Then we'll start on a clean slate," Aaron decided, accepting the answer as truth. "Why did you seek me out?" Why Hamish had given his direction was now obvious, the Star of Solomon would have been more than a little motivating as a bargaining chip.

Brandon regretted he hadn't taken the more potent drink he'd been offered. "Because I need your help."

"As Magus."

"Very much so."

"One can run but cannot hide," Aaron offered a grim smile, but the humor was back in his eyes. "Okay, hit me. What kind of help do you need from the Major Arcana?"

"Can the Star of Solomon still be used?"

"Not without an elemental to give it power," Aaron answered.

"If it contained an elemental?"

"Possible. Do you know how to bind an elemental against its will?" Aaron countered.

"No," Brandon answered. "Can it even be done?"

Aaron thought regretfully of the brooch Pricilla had received from Curt. "Unfortunately, there is a darker side of True Science some people have explored successfully in the past. Long past, I hope. I've seen the results. Heartless and utterly cruel, doesn't even begin describe the consequences."

Brandon looked with concern at the necklace. "Is the Star of Solomon one of those consequences?"

"No," Aaron assured him. "The elemental that temporarily attached itself to the star did so of its own free will, it was not coerced in any way and left of its own free will." He nodded at the necklace between them. "It was never bound. That may look like Assiah gold, but its from... well, not here."

"The fifth world," Brandon guessed, sipping his water. The air on the patio was somehow cooler now.

Aaron raised an eyebrow. "Not all legends are based on fact."

"But some are," Brandon answered.

"So some ancient Seths claim," Aaron answered noncommittally. "Why is the mythological fifth world of interest to you, Brandon?"

"Have you ever heard the legend of Phineas Tristan?"

Aaron sat on the chair on his side of the bar. "Enlighten me," he suggested, showing polite interest and sipping his beer.

Brandon had thought exposing his family's dirty laundry would be difficult, but surprisingly Aaron's posture and casual question put him more at ease. "In short, when Phineas Tristan was a boy, he took something from Yetzirah. A direct violation of the Apocrypha."

"An artifact of power?"

"No," Brandon shook his head quickly, "just a small talisman, a piece of Yetzirah that would remind him of his secret world."

Aaron looked interested. "When did this happen?"

"Eighteen Twelve. Right after the war started."

"How old was he?"

"Not quite thirteen. He believed the talisman would keep him safe when he joined the Navy."

"A good luck charm?"

"More or less," Brandon answered. "Not that it was necessary, he never saw action. He had hopes of being a cabin boy on one of the ships, but ended up as a cook's helper in some Politician's mansion, far from the action in the Atlantic."

"There are no accidents. Maybe that was the luck he needed. Was he relative of yours?"

Brandon nodded. "A distant relative, yes."

Aaron quickly did the math. "Was he second generation or third?" Each generation was a hundred and forty four years long, bringing something back from an elemental world would be quite a feat for someone with such little training in the doctrine of True Science.

"Second, on the cusp of third," Brandon was curious about the question, but went on without asking the reason for it. "It's my family's obligation to obtain redemption for Phineas by returning the talisman."

"Redemption?" Aaron furrowed his brow. "If young Phineas did or even could transport something from Yetzirah to Assiah, it was a minor transgression only. Regardless of the beliefs of the times, he was boy, not a man, probably not old enough to shave. I'd guess his voice hadn't even changed yet. The actions of a child are always forgiven. Redemption is unnecessary."

"By the values of his descendants, they are the actions of a man, not a child," Brandon told him. "The keys had been crossed to him that year. There was also a little matter of a sixteen dollar sign up bonus, a hundred and sixty acres and three months pay promised upon discharge from the military after thirteen months of service. Almost a fortune in those days. He collected those acres, the bonus, the three months pay and eventually became a very wealthy man with that stake. In short, whether he thought it was a good luck charm at the time or not, his knowledge of True Science was used for personal gain. A direct violation of the Apocrypha. As have all Phineas' male descendants before me, I took the burden of his abuse of the doctrine and vowed the return of the article he took."

"And offered to take on the responsibilities of his self-imposed sephiroth and its dangers," Aaron finished for him. He shook his head, picking up his glass again. "I don't suppose you considered making that vow a really bad decision?" he asked, taking a sip of his drink.

Brandon managed a laugh. "So my father has mentioned once or twice."

"Wise man," Aaron told him.

"He is," Brandon agreed. "But his side of the family isn't directly affected by Phineas' actions. It's a matter of family honor on my mother's side. I still have to try."

Aaron put down his beer. "No, you don't," he argued. "True Science is not a religion, Brandon, the sins of the father do not trickle down to his heirs. As Magus, I can release you and your mother's family from any promises made, past to present. No harm, no foul. No shin upon your soul, or that of your mother's family. It will cost you nothing."

"Thank you for the offer, Aaron, but I gave my word of honor to my Grandfather before he died. I have to at least try to return the article Phineas stole from Yetzirah."

Aaron grimaced. "Very noble, but again, not wise. If you commit an adult vow to a child's innocent indiscretion, you, and your family, are obligated to far more than you might want to give."

"So I've been told. Can you help me, Magus?"

"Damn." Aaron let out an audible breath. "If you don't allow me to release you from your vow, as Magus I have to formally accept said vow. At that point, you will create another chapter, another Seth, call it the 'Seth-A-Tristan et Yetzirah' and it will follow your family around like a plague until resolved. Worse, as Major Arcana, I'll have to write the damned thing in some cryptic nonsense that even I won't fully understand when I'm done. Is that what you really want?" It would also be added to his own ever increasing sephiroth as Magus, but he didn't mention that little caveat, it was part of his mantle as First Key.

Brandon didn't hesitate. "Yes. Without a formal Seth, my mother's family has tried for generations and failed. With a formal Seth, we stand a chance of succeeding."

"Do you speak for the entire family of Phineas Tristan? Past, present and future?"

"With or without a formal Seth made by the Major Arcana, this obligation will follow my family." Brandon hesitated, then revealed the last of his secrets. Names had power, it required total trust before being given. "My full name is Brandon Tristan Grayson. Every male descendant of Phineas Tristan is given and will be given the first or middle name of Tristan so that we are always reminded and connected to his 'indiscretion'. We have been and always will be committed."

Aaron's eyes widened. "Your ancestors added this obligation to your familial apocrypha," he realized.

"Yes. Phineas Tristan himself decreed it before his death."

"He placed a shin upon the entire family," Aaron determined.

"Yes. His remorse and guilt were very genuine."

Aaron let out a heavy sigh and nodded, accepting the inevitable. He made a casual wave toward the house, sealing it from the outside from all possible interference, physical or visual. Cassie was at the beach with friends, but he'd learned in the short time she'd been with them that teenagers never followed a reliable schedule. They were always early or late. He then took a long sip of his beer, put it down on the bar and looked at Brandon with a serious expression.

"Are you ready to make that vow here and now, accept a formal Seth, or would you like to give yourself some time think about it for awhile?" The tone of his voice suggested the latter.

"I am more than ready now, Magus. A formal Seth is necessary, I'm convinced of it."

"As you will it." Aaron nodded, then he started the ritual, knowing that once started, it had to be completed without pause, knowing the consequences to Brandon could be fatal. He sincerely hoped the favorable information he had on Brandon Grayson, and his own instincts about the man were accurate. "Then I ask you formally, Brandon Tristan Grayson. By your own free will do you take on this obligation, adding a formal Seth to your familial apocrypha?"

"By my own free will," Brandon answered firmly, feeling a small electrical charge up his spine. The fact that his full name was used for the question bothered him.

Aaron nodded, his eyes focused on Brandon's. "I ask you twice. Brandon Tristan Grayson, by your own free will do you take on this obligation adding a formal Seth to your familial apocrypha?"

"By my own free will." Brandon answered. The top of his head now tingled with that small electrical charge. It felt similar to the same uncanny feeling he had at thirteen when he had taken on his formal sephiroth.

Aaron looked him forcefully in the eyes with a mesmerizing effect. He used a voice with a slight accent Brandon didn't recognize. It sounded old, archaic, a voice from a century long past. "Then I ask thee thrice, as Magus of Power by Eternal Lemniscate," his voice changed more prominently foreign when he used the title, it was deeper, powerful, echoing within an invisible chamber that suddenly encircled them both. "'Will you, Brandon Tristan Grayson, *by thy own free will,* be formally bound to the 'Seth A Tristan et Yetzirah' and the obligations of chivalry'?"

Brandon froze. Everything seemed to just stop. Aaron Zale might have seemed like a regular man before, a mere stage magician, but now he was the true Magus of Power, first key of the Major Arcana. His eyes had gone from friendly blue to merciless slate cobalt. The air around Brandon had become stifling, circling him with pressure from all sides, making it hard to breathe. There was no outside world, only this invisible, impenetrable chamber. At that point, he felt completely out of his element. This was no simple sephiroth given to a boy when he reached his maturity. This was a formal Seth. A situation far outside his knowledge or understanding. It could only be given by someone of the Major Arcana or by prior Apocrypha dictates at birth.

Brandon suddenly remembered his father's warning. ("The Magus is extremely powerful. First Key. Playing in the Majors is serious shit, Bran.")

The intimidation Brandon hadn't felt from Aaron Zale before, now hit him forcefully. The question was very real and formally stated. This was deadly serious, possibly fatal. There was absolute power here, pulled in from the very Earth by just a few spoken words. A new Seth was being formed, it encased him, weighed him down with an uncomfortable geas he could literally feel.

Aaron was watching him intently now, patiently waiting for his answer, acting as if he had all the time in the world.

But there wasn't time. Brandon could barely breathe. He couldn't swallow. He couldn't move his head, his arms, his body. His eyes were paralyzed open, he couldn't blink, he couldn't move his focus away from the Magus.

Brandon knew with absolute certainty that he had to say the words or his throat would freeze, his vocal cords would no longer function. He would stay solid as stone, a living statue.

Living death.

("Playing in the Majors is serious shit, Bran.") He had heard his father's warning, but not really taken it seriously.

Aaron Zale, the Magus of Power by Eternal Lemniscate, first key of the Major Arcana, was still watching, still waiting. His eyes were still a cold slate of merciless cobalt blue, almost black with intensity.

Seconds passed, each one feeling like an hour. If possible, the air became even more stifling. Brandon was literally bound in ribbons of invisible wire made of impenetrable air. Formally bound. Not figuratively bound, but physically, literally, mentally bound. There was only one way to pull himself out of the trap he had willing put himself into. He could either accept the formal obligation, or ask to be released from it. He knew if he did, he would not have a second chance. He doubted the Magus ever gave second chances. "I will formally be so bound," he finally said the words. He didn't recognize his own voice. Somehow it had also sounded ancient, archaic.

"'Do you, Brandon Tristan Grayson, renounce the status of Page and take on the quest of a Knight of the Sword bound by the 'Seth-A-Tristan et Yetzirah'?"

Breathing was almost impossible now, his lungs felt like they were going to collapse if he couldn't take a breath. Brandon had to respond or he would be held in this vacuum forever. He'd never be able to move again. Breathe again. Everything was quiet. So horribly quiet, a tomb of silence sealed from without. He knew there would be no sound again unless he spoke. He looked with near panic at Aaron whose eyes were as unforgiving as stone. "I do," he answered. Instantly, the pressure of the ropes of air eased but still held him tightly in their grasp.

"So it will then be written," The Magus announced, his voice still heavy with power. "The mantle and burden of Knight of the sword falls upon thee, bound by the Arcana and the obligations of chivalry. All minor arcana within the sign of the sword are henceforth under thy protection and jurisdiction. Thou art bound from this day forth to the Seth A Tristan et Yetzirah, as are thy descendants. 'May you keep your sword upraised to the highest ideals of your mantle.'"

('May you keep your sword upraised'.) His father often used that phrase as a simple, almost meaningless, expression telling him to keep his guard up, but from Aaron Zale's voice of absolute power, it was very different. It had true meaning, almost a command. "Through the cypress and storm clouds," Brandon gave the prescribed answer automatically.

Finally, Brandon could breathe freely. He took a deep lungful of air, then consciously blinked, just because he could.

Aaron looked at him knowingly, hiding his relief that Brandon had actually survived the ritual. "Well. Wasn't that fun?" he said in his normal voice and smiled, lifting his ale and saluting with it. "Welcome to the wonderful world of Destiny Given. Trust me, it sucks and there's no way out once you're been given the mantle. God knows I've tried."

"Uh..."

Aaron smiled. "Not what you expected?"

"Four Hells, no," Brandon answered honestly, still taking in deep breaths. He'd never take the simple act of breathing for granted again. "I knew you were Major Arcana, I knew your title carried more responsibility and dictates than are stated, but... My family have been followers of True Science for almost five centuries, but still..."

"Still, in your heart of hearts it was all just a load of bullshit,"

Aaron finished the thought. "An archaic philosophy based on wishful thinking and pseudo religious fantasy."

"Pretty much," Brandon admitted with a weak smile.

"Some of it is," Aaron told him. "Most of it, unfortunately, is based on real True Science, hence the name."

"So I just found out."

"Only minimally," Aaron looked seriously at Brandon. "That was only a minor binding," he told him, "agreed on, willingly, by both. Your free will, thrice given, my acceptance thrice received."

"*Minor* binding?" Brandon asked incredulously.

"Minor," Aaron assured him. "And even that I don't do often and seriously try to avoid," he told him. "You asked me earlier if it was possible to bind an elemental against its will."

"Yes," Brandon frowned, not sure where this was going.

"As third generation, you have summoned an elemental, a sylph of air, then released it within a few moments as you were trained to do so by your guide. Is that correct?"

"Yes." It had been a long time, but Brandon still remembered the doctrine, the sylph, and the wonder of it.

"That sylph comes to you, willingly, out of friendship, trust and joy."

Brandon nodded.

Aaron looked grim. "Imagine for a moment that tiny, trusting elemental being bound in the same way you just were, *against* its will. It has no words of release from its prison, no hope of escape, no thought of rescue, no breath, no air, no heat, no hope of movement ever again and you'll know what that elemental feels when its lured from its own world of Briah and locked into this one by the pure gold of Assiah, a true prisoner. Complete innocence and trust forever bound by greed and avarice or the expectations of power, never knowing or understanding why or how it has been bound."

Brandon looked at him in horror.

"So now you know," Aaron gave him a humorless smile.

Yes, now Brandon knew and he wished to hell he didn't.

"Ready for that drink now?" Aaron asked.

Brandon looked at the empty bottle of water that he didn't remember drinking. He had a suspicion he had sweated out every drop after the 'minor' illustration of the power of Major Arcana. "Scotch, neat," he nodded.

Aaron pulled a glass, poured a healthy portion of a very expensive scotch and handed it to Brandon. "So! Aside from ruining your day and permanently destroying your life and perception of reality and the Major

Arcana power of True Science, is there anything else I can do for you?"

Brandon took a large swallow of his Scotch. "I'm not sure any more. Hell, I don't even know where to go at this point. Any clues as to how to get in to Yetzirah without the Star of Solomon?"

Aaron laughed. "Great, now he asks the hard questions," he looked up for inspiration, then back at him. "Not personally, no." He took a deep breath and frowned. "There is one who might have the knowledge you need, but I make no promises."

"Another Key of the Major Arcana?" Brandon asked.

"Not exactly."

"Who then?"

"No one you'll be likely to meet on your own," Aaron answered. "But, the nature of the Seth you just bound yourself to necessitates knowledge outside both Major and minor Arcana."

Outside the Arcana? Brandon looked intrigued. "Can you introduce me?"

"With strong reservations," Aaron answered. "First, I suggest you put the star back in your pocket, keep it well hidden."

Brandon pocketed the box containing the Star of Solomon and looked at him curiously. "Why?"

"You wanted an introduction to someone who might help, you're about to get one," Aaron told him. He walked around the bar and stood in a more open area of the patio. He looked again toward the house and silently called a second seal for added privacy *(Boaz et Assiah ki Briah. Yod Assiah et Kether et Nun)*.

Until released, the house was now as impenetrable as stone. Nothing could enter or leave.

"Now?" Brandon had turned in his chair, watching Aaron with confusion.

Aaron nodded. "No time like the present. Keep your questions short and to the point. You will only have a very finite amount of time."

"Alright," Brandon agreed, wondering what new horror he was about to experience.

("Beth Celandine ki teth Whilom et Nebulae. By Seth-a-Ron and my Destiny Given, I formally request your presence.") Aaron said mentally, wondering if he was making a colossal mistake.

The air shimmered. Pricilla quietly materialized a few feet in front of Aaron. As was her usual attire when being summoned, she was wearing the lush green, off-shoulder dress, her feet were bare. "One greets thee, Magus of Power by eternal lemniscate," she said formally to Aaron with a slight nod of her head.

"And I you," Aaron answered in an equally polite voice. His heart jumped painfully. This was one of the very few times he had called her formally by the Seth-A-Ron and his mantle, with no reminders of her earthly bond to Assiah or him. He hated it. It always unnerved him.

At the moment, she was fully Celandine, not Pricilla, someone he didn't completely know. Aaron studied her from Brandon's perceptive, almost seeing her for the first time. Mortal, yet not, essence, yet not. Was this what others felt when he wore the guise of Magus? Did his posture and voice change into someone he never saw in the mirror? What did Celandine see when she came to him in this form while ungrounded? The real him, her husband, lover and eternal mate, or merely the Magus, a stranger, a man she didn't know?

"I would have you meet Brandon Grayson." he gestured to Brandon.

Brandon had risen to his feet in shock, barely keeping his jaw from dropping and holding back a wholly inappropriate quantity of swear words. He looked incredulously at the beautiful woman who had appeared out of thin air. She was slim, with dark hair falling in soft waves down her back. Her hair was adorned with a small white light at her temple. The tiny light was an unprotected sylph, he realized with shock. Who *was* this person? Was she even real? How was it possible for a sylph to be in Assiah without protection?

The woman looked at Brandon curiously, then nodded her head in acknowledgement. "One greets thee, Brandon Grayson."

Her eyes were a startling blue, adorned by a face that was almost ethereal. Brandon swallowed, not sure exactly what to say. "Hello," was all he was able to manage.

"Brandon is the heir of Phineas Tristan," Aaron added to the introduction.

Pricilla cocked her head to one side, considering Brandon. "The missing pearl of Yetzirah," she nodded, never taking her eyes from him. "The undines remember thy ancestor fondly and with great sorrow at his passing, twelfth son of Tristan."

Brandon was openly shocked by her words. How did she know about the pearl?

"Was the pearl an artifact of power, Celandine?" Aaron asked with concern.

"Nay, merely noted by its absence," Celandine told him. "A token only, taken by an innocent child of Assiah with both fear and despair in his heart."

Fear and despair. Brandon's stomach twisted. Who was this woman who could wear sylphs in her hair, communicate with undines, who

80

apparently knew what his ancestor had felt when he took the pearl?

As though he had asked the question out loud, the Magus answered him.

"Brandon," Aaron's voice was hollow. "This is Celandine." He added the rest almost reluctantly. "Elemental of the fifth world."

Chapter 9 - Celandine

Brandon was struck dumb, his heart beat erratically.

Elemental of the Fifth world.

Impossible. This woman was an elemental of a world that only existed in myth and legend. Good Lord. What the hell kind of Seth was he getting into?

"Brandon," Aaron said sharply. "Her time is finite, remember? You have a question for Celandine. Ask."

Brandon couldn't take his eyes off her. Questions? Where to start? He had nearly a million. What was the fifth world, where was the fifth world? Hell, why was the fifth world? What kind of elemental was she? Earth, wind, fire, water, or something completely unknown?

"Brandon," Aaron said again, speaking more forcefully. "Yetzirah? Your quest?"

Celandine looked at him curiously. "Thou art on a quest, Brandon Grayson?"

At her voice he snapped out of his stunned paralysis. Oh, lord, what was her name again? He could barely concentrate. "Yes... Celandine," his muddled mind finally remembered. "I am on a quest. The pearl of Yetzirah, though merely a token to my ancestor, must be returned from where it was taken."

"It is to be returned by thee?"

"Yes. I am honor bound."

"Thy quest is in vain," Celandine said firmly. "Thou art a Page of sword. A gate into Yetzirah is closed to thy kind." She frowned and turned to Aaron. "Magus of Power by Eternal Lemniscate. Why does one sense upon Brandon Grayson the essence of a world that belongs to him not?"

Brandon touched the pocket containing the star, then noticed Aaron giving a stiff negative motion of his head. He quickly dropped his hand.

"Brandon's quest to right the wrong of his ancestor consumes him, Celandine. He has newly become a Knight of the Sword. Perhaps that is what you sense," Aaron suggested.

"Perhaps," she looked doubtful.

"He follows the Seth-A-Tristan et Yetzirah."

She frowned. "One knows not of this Seth."

"The Seth-A-Tristan et Yetzirah is newly written," Aaron explained.

Celandine paused for a moment, then nodded her head in

acceptance "By thy sephiroth and thy Seth, Magus of Power by Eternal Lemniscate, so it will be noted by all worlds."

Noted by all worlds, Brandon repeated in his mind. Which worlds? Who *was* this being?

"Ask what you need to know to help you on your quest," Aaron suggested to Brandon using a 'hurry-up' gesture with his hand. "Celandine's time is finite."

Brandon didn't need to hear the words 'change the subject.' He nodded his understanding. "Is there any gate I can enter from Briah into Yetzirah?"

Celandine looked at him with suspicion.

"Celandine," Aaron broke in. "As Magus of Power by eternal lemniscate, I formally beseech your assistance for a Knight of the Sword on a quest to defend his family's honor."

Celandine turned her attention to him sharply. "A *formal* request, *willingly* given, Magus of power by eternal lemniscate?"

"A willing request to be placed within both the sephiroth and Seth of my Destiny Given," Aaron answered. "Twice formally given."

"So it will be noted by all worlds," Celandine looked reluctant, but nodded. She paused and tilted her head as though she could hear something no one else could. She caught Brandon's eyes with a meaningful look. "A Page on the cusp of both worlds might serve a Knight of the Sword on a quest of honor who is bound to a Seth newly written and noted by all worlds." She turned her attention to Aaron and added, "one quest begets the other. Two of Earth, two of air, one of water. So it must be written."

"Thank you, Celandine," Aaron answered. "We will intrude on your time no longer. *("Ki Celandine...")* He paused for a split second before he released her, desperately needing to reaffirm their relationship, remind her of who she was in Assiah. *("Carry with you my heart, my mind, my soul, Ce-Cill.)*

Celandine looked at him curiously for a moment, then smiled gently. *(Always, A-Ron. Heart, mind, soul, oft dreamed, never forgotten.)*

(Ki Akal Whilom et Nebulae), Aaron released her, holding on to her parting words tightly. More and more it felt like she was pulling further and further away from him.

Before he could blink, Brandon watched the elemental of the fifth world shimmer out of sight. "Holy shit!" he blurted out the words he had wanted to say during the entire experience.

"Tell me about it," Aaron responded and went back behind the bar, drawing another beer.

Brandon also walked over to the bar. His hand shook as he took the bottle of Scotch from Aaron and freshened his drink as well. "How the hell did you do that?"

Aaron looked grim. "The guise of Magus has both its perks and its problems," he told him. "You just witnessed a serious combination of both."

Brandon looked concerned. Nothing was free, and he knew the cost wouldn't be to him. Aaron Zale had willingly made a formal request of the elemental on his behalf. Twice given. An unbreakable vow. "How much did that cost you?"

Aaron recovered his more mild expression, sidestepping the question. "Just a well deserved reminder of ignorance that everyone needs now and again. There are texts within texts, I don't think we've even scratched the surface of True Science knowledge. We'll never know everything." He shrugged. "Nothing in life remains stagnant."

"'Every step in a sephiroth lengthens the path, every answer you find gives you more questions, more responsibilities'," Brandon quoted from his childhood studies.

"I always hated that truism," Aaron laughed. "On the plus side, you did get the first answer you needed."

Brandon thought about it and nodded. "I need to find a Page. One on the cusp between Briah and Yetzirah."

"Which begs the next question," Aaron nodded with amusement.

Brandon laughed lightly. "Where do I find this Page?"

Aaron nodded. "And when you do find your Page that question will be answered; then you'll get the next question."

"What the hell do I do with him when I find him? And so on and so forth," Brandon nodded thoughtfully, then asked, "Was Celandine real?"

"As real as any other elemental," Aaron answered. "Not to worry. Celandine is part of my sephiroth, not yours. In an hour's time, you won't remember ever meeting her, or that there even is a Fifth World. It will return safely to myth. At most it will be a fleeting dream, nothing more, a memory you think is there, but can't quite touch," he told him. "Unless she wills it otherwise," he added.

"I rather hopes she doesn't," Brandon answered truthfully. He pulled the box holding the Star from his pocket. "Celandine sensed this, didn't she?"

"Yes. It belongs in her world."

"And you didn't want me to give it to her."

"It's complicated."

"Not for me." Brandon snapped the box shut and handed it to him. "Your complication, Magus. Freely given."

Aaron sighed heavily as he opened the jewelry box, lifted the star from within and looked at it with resignation. "Nothing's free," he assured him. He looked at the doors to the house. *(Jachin et Assiah Ki Briah. Yod Assiah et Kether et Nun)*, he silently released the blocks he had placed to keep this meeting private. "Go and find your Page, Knight of Swords. By then, the full Seth-A-Tristan et Yetzirah will be formally written. Study it well when you receive it. You can trust that your own unpleasant complications will soon follow, as well as more questions and more difficult answers."

Chapter 10 - Page of Cups/Swords

Roberta Bethany Griffin had sometimes watched Brandon Grayson when they were both children. She was only seven when she first saw him. He was almost eleven, but they never actually met. Generally she peeked from around a large tree in the park-like grounds of the French chateau his family called home.

Roberta was not a pretty girl in those days and she knew it. Oh, her parents told her she was beautiful, of course, but she looked at all the popular magazines, she knew the score. She was gangly and skinny, had kinky red hair and hazel green eyes. Her nose was too small and she had too many freckles. She had huge dimples that looked like holes in her cheeks. She had been so terribly shy, so embarrassed by her self perceived ugliness. She always hung back, watching, but never speaking to the other children.

She was very lonely.

But in her own secret world she had beauty. She had friends who though she was wonderful. She was never alone there. On one side were dolphins and otters and seals. There was one burly sea lion who made her giggle with his loud barking voice. On the other side were bluebirds and butterflies, sparrows and doves. A parrot with bright wings that flared with brilliant colors through the trees. At night there were Lunar moths, nightingales, owls, night heron, mocking birds and a few whippoorwills.

And then there was Brandon Grayson. She barely noticed other children who came near the gates of her secret dream world, but Brandon had always seemed special. Him, she noticed. He was real, not fantasy. When he was in Briah, he became a hawk or owl, maybe a golden eagle, but sometimes... Oh, *sometimes* he took on the shape and form of a magnificent Griffin. The body and heart of a lion, the wings and the head of an eagle.

She loved him then. He became the symbol of her very own name, her favorite creature of mythology.

Her Griffin. It gave them a connection, a bond between them that she would keep as her own special secret. But even there, just as in the real world, she only watched him from behind a large tree.

She was nothing more than a shadow to Brandon, he never saw her.

As all children do, Roberta grew up, leaving her childhood dreams behind. At thirteen she entered high school and realized she was not so very different from other children after all. They were all a little clumsy and gangly. Quite a few were as lonely and shy as she was. Some had braces, some had noses that were too big or too small. She made real friends who supported each other through puberty, pimples and boys. They laughed together, cried together, fought with each other and were no longer lonely.

Eventually, Roberta became a woman. Her body filled out proportionally to compliment her average height, her clumsiness turned into graceful movements (with the help of five years of ballet). Her shyness turned the corner into confidence. Her kinky red hair turned into a less curly auburn.

(But she still had too many damned freckles.)

Best of all, Roberta's fantasy world as a child had given her a true passion as an adult. She studied ornithology and lepidopterology (although she never mounted a butterfly in her life.). When her passion shifted to marine biology, it became her purpose and career. She swam with dolphins and killer whales. She found sharks and other predators of her water world glorious. They all had a purpose, they were all beautiful to her. Her professional colleagues called her 'Bobby the Mermaid', she spent more time in the water than on land.

And there was another side to Roberta Bethany Griffin, one she kept very private, because it embarrassed the hell out of her.

She was born to True Science, third generation. It was part of her childhood training, but she never took it very seriously. She was a cusp child born between Aquarius and Pisces, Briah and Yetzirah, never quite fitting into the aspects of either side. According to her father, she was a Page of cups with mostly green eyes, according to her mother, she was a Page of swords with mostly brown eyes. Silly stuff really, but she loved them both unconditionally and left them to their True Science superstitions while she traveled through a more normal world that was based on reality.

She was in Australia trying unsuccessfully to braid her long hair into some kind of order that might look good on a lunch date with her new diving buddy, when her mother called. Almost before she flipped open the phone and put it to her ear, her mother exclaimed, "Bobby, sweetie!"

"Mom!" Roberta tried to put the same enthusiasm in her voice, still scowling at her hair in the mirror. She looked like hell. No make-up and her nose was peeling. She leaned closer to the mirror and carefully, painfully, pulled off the largest bits of skin that looked like dead fish scales. "Ow." She grabbed a tissue and blotted off the blood that wept from one abrasion.

"Sweetheart? Are you okay?"

"Fine, Mom. Just dinged my nose."

"You're picking at your skin, aren't you? Wear more sun-block, Bobby, you're going to look like an old lady before you turn thirty."

"Mom, I'm thirty-three."

"Okay. Before you turn forty, then. What time is it there?"

"A little before noon."

"Saturday, right?"

Roberta grinned. "Right."

"And Friday here," Geneva decided with a smile in her voice. "I really love that. It's like I'm talking into the future somehow. What are you doing?"

"Getting ready for a lunch date."

"Really? Is he good looking?"

"He is and he's a friend."

"In other words, you're not sleeping with him." Geneva Griffin gave out a disappointed sigh.

"Did you have conversations with your mother that were this personal?" Roberta asked curiously. "Somehow I don't think it's customary. Aren't you supposed to assume I'm a virgin until I'm married or something?"

"No, dear, that's your father's role. And then they only pretend until you're about twenty-five. Even men aren't quite that naïve. So! Are you going to sleep with him?"

"Mom. I refuse to discuss my sex life with you. It's..."

"It's what?"

"Mostly non-existent," Roberta confessed. And had been since her second almost serious relationship during her last year in college. A 'free love' child of the sixties she wasn't.

"Ouch. Sorry, baby. We all have our slow seasons. Did I ever tell you that your dad and I went without sex for almost a month? It was only the one time, but it was simply awful. We were miserable."

"Thanks for sharing, Mom, but I really don't want to know about it," Roberta assured her.

"It was right after my appendectomy. I was too whacked out on drugs to pay attention," Geneva's voice smiled again. "But when I was better, whoa! did we make up the time!"

"Mom," Roberta said quickly. "Really. Seriously. I really, really don't want to know the details of your sex life with Dad." Certainly she saw her parents hug and kiss, often, but to imagine them in bed together doing more than sleeping? Not too weird.

"Always so stuffy," Geneva decided. "I didn't call about that in any event."

"I'm so relieved. What's up?"

"Do you remember Brandon Grayson?"

"Ah... sounds vaguely familiar, but... no. Refresh my memory," Roberta suggested, struggling with a lock of hair that refused to be braided. Length took out most of the curl, but there were always a few rogue hairs that refused to be tamed. Sideburn curly queues hadn't been in fashion since...

Nope, they never really were in fashion.

"You met him in France, a Bastille party at his grandfather's chateau. They served a lovely Chignon Blanc from their own winery as I recall. You were seven."

"I was seven?" Roberta repeated. "Mom, that was thirty years ago!"

"Twenty eight. You just reminded me that you're only thirty-three. Honestly, Bobby! When was your last MRI?"

"Okay, let me think. Grayson... Bastille Day, France," Roberta's head was swimming. "Chinon blanc... Alsace?" Then she had a flicker of memory. "My Griffin?" Just as suddenly as the flash of memory surfaced, it disappeared.

"No, dear, Grayson. He's not one of our Griffin relatives and it was Loire, not Alsace. Alsace is known for its Riesling, not Chinon Blanc.

Roberta's heart sank. "Tell me this isn't a True Shi... Science thing, Mom."

"This isn't a True Shi... Science thing," Geneva answered promptly.

"Thank God."

"Sweetie, get with the program, of course it's a 'True Science thing'." She gave a loud huff of annoyance. "Seriously, Bobby, sometimes I think my lightening fast wit is completely wasted on you."

Roberta rolled her eyes, then noticed another fleck of skin peeling off her nose. Question to self. Pull it off, or smooth it down with lotion?

"Lotion, Sweetie, or you'll bleed again."

Roberta jumped back from the mirror. "Stop that!"

"I will when you quit pretending it's all fantasy."

"Fine," Roberta gave a heavy sigh. "Tell me about your True Science thing. My date gets here in," she looked at her watch, "twenty seven minutes and I still have to put on my makeup."

"Just lotion, Bobby, that powder crap you use will just make the peeling worse. Anyway, you're done there, your contract was up two weeks ago and you're needed here, ASAP."

Roberta frowned. "For what?"

"Brandon Grayson needs a Page."

"Tell him to buy a book," Roberta suggested, "they have lots and lots of pages in them."

"There you go! You do have your mother's wit! You've made me proud, darling. I'm wiping a happy tear from my eye as we speak," she assured her. "A.S.A.P., Bobby," she said in a no-nonsense voice. "I've booked a flight from there to Montreal, it leaves at two tomorrow, your time. It's prepaid, First Class, so you can catch a catnap. Only twenty hours! You'll still be home before you leave!"

"But..."

"Roberta Bethany Griffin! You're third generation. Brandon Grayson is a Knight of Swords. He is also third generation and needs a Page."

"But..." Oh, damn, her mother used her full name, she was going to lose this one if she didn't think of some credible excuse, hopefully with a True Shit excuse her mother would buy. "Whoa. Back up! He's a Knight?"

"Boosted up this year by the Magus himself, according to my sources."

"Holy sh... Mom, I'm on the cusp, remember? Nobody, nothing! No solid footing on one side or another. No formal sephiroth! By True Shit... uh... I mean, by True Science perception, I'm flaky and unreliable. Clumsy, trip over my own feet. What kind of Knight made by the Magus wants a clumsy Page who's liable to drop his proverbial sword while she's tripping over her own uncoordinated feet? Is he insane?"

"Sweetie, you grew out of 'clumsy' years, well, months... okay, days ago."

"Cute. Thanks, Mom, I feel so much better now. You're always such an ego booster."

Geneva laughed. "Trust me, you're perfect for this Seth."

"Wait a minute. A *Seth*? You expect me to follow a *Seth*? But..."

"Honey, You weren't going to sleep with the guy, anyway. It's only lunch, not a candlelight dinner and he's too young for you. Even more telling, you're wearing something out of some cheap sales catalog, you're not wearing the Victoria Secret underwear I sent you, or your FM shoes."

"That's CFM, Mom.

"Really? Well, hell. I get used to one colloquialism and they come up with another one. What's the 'C' stand for?"

"Never mind," Roberta looked down at her flat sandals (definitely not CFM shoes) and had to concede that she was wearing catalog clothing and plain white cotton underwear. And, her diving buddy was five years younger than her, which was definitely a turn off. "But..."

"See you tomorrow at PET airport. Love you, Bye." The line disconnected.

Roberta looked in the mirror and sighed. "Swell. Unruly red hair, cotton nappies and a trip home to Mother." She scowled at her reflection. "Wimp. You. Are. A. Wimp."

Oh and God help her, she was supposed to follow an unknown True Science Seth? When she didn't even have a formal Sephiroth? Could her life get any more screwed up?

Bracelet of Assiah

The text Aaron was trying to decipher was a combination of ancient Greek, peppered with runic life symbols. He looked again at the bracelet that had arrived with the brooch and frowned. The same cryptic symbols were on the band as in the text, but in an odd order. The most he'd been able to determine so far was, "to hold to the true world, the green hills of our creator."

Not terribly illuminating. What he did know was that the bracelet felt fraudulent somehow. It was an unusual antique, to be sure, but it did not feel like a true artifact of power.

Something was definitely off about it. It felt too... ordinary. Yet he knew it wasn't.

Aaron turned to texts from the Roman Empire, then Christian biblical texts. A subtle hint there led him to more ancient apocryphas, more dry script that had, for one reason or another, been banned by whatever Catholic pope was in power when they were hidden. Some of the material on his desk had been stolen centuries before from the dusty vaults of the Vatican, some had been found and hidden away by True Science scholars.

Now they were all hidden away here. In truth, this library was the major reason for a house that was big enough for an army. After renovation the library was nearly two thousand square feet and two stories high. If the entire house burned down, this one room would remain standing. Fireproof, waterproof, earthquake proof, humidified, sealed from outsiders, containing books and scrolls most people didn't know existed.

Books he often wished he didn't know existed.

They all contained secrets and lies, truths and deceptions, they were all cryptic. The huge library was stacked to the ceiling with manuscripts and ancient scrolls, crumbling texts, all of them held truths and lies, dust and decay. Hundreds of them would need to be copied before they fell into ashes.

He looked up at the clock on the wall. Pricilla had been gone this time for more than fifteen hours. It was an experiment of a sort. If she spent more time there, perhaps she could also spend more time here. She called it her "overtime plan." She slept with him throughout the night, but it seemed shorter each time.

What the hell did she do in Whilom that could pull her back so

Whilom Magic - Destiny Given

completely? He had an urge to summon her as an elemental, just to see her, but the thought of going through the ritual formality, her short bursts of clarity, then again back to the formality was more than he could bear. Each time it took longer for her to talk naturally; when she did it was for shorter periods of time.

When she did return as herself, if he asked her to tell him about Whilom, she would start, then lose the memory. Did the same thing happen to her in Whilom? Did she quickly lose the memory of Assiah, of him, of their life together?

The very thought tore him apart.

Oft dreamed, never forgotten. Celandine said those words every time he summoned her now.

Oft dreamed. Was he becoming only a dream to her in Whilom?

Aaron forced himself to look away from the clock, unroll another scroll, pretend he wasn't worried and actually gave a damn about the bracelet in front of him.

It took several minutes to realize he'd found the information he needed. As was everything else, when you quit looking for it or lost interest, you found it.

According to the text, the bracelet wasn't just old, it was ancient. It was a royal Albanian armband, not a mere bracelet, and while it might not feel like it, it was definitely an artifact of power. "To clasp to the world, those who are lost to the other. To take away the madness, to hold to the reality of this world and no other." Underneath the description was an intricate drawing that matched the design of the armband in detail. More cryptic words claimed that once the armband was attached it could not be removed by any natural or supernatural power until the death of the wearer.

Hold to the reality of this world and no other.

It took a moment to sink in, then Aaron froze in disbelief. Take away the madness. He stared at the bracelet in both horror and fascination. In those ancient times, fantasy and belief in any religion other than what was currently in fashion was considered blasphemy or madness. Demons and other entities were beaten or burned out of anyone who believed differently.

Take away the madness.

He let out a slow breath. Belief in other worlds would definitely be considered 'madness'. To take away those alien ideas or beliefs without physical punishment would actually be considered an act of kindness, a cure for insanity. No beatings, no burnings, no hangings. Except for the very wealthy. With enough money or favors, the wealthy could always escape punishment. The very value of the almost pure gold and jewels that adorned the bracelet showed that it would only be used on persons of significant wealth or political importance.

Until death. Only then it could be removed so the person could go to the world of the accepted religious hereafter.

Hold to the reality of this world and no other.

Not the reality of Briah, not Yetzirah, not Atziluth. More to the point...

Not the reality of Whilom.

Aaron couldn't take his eyes off the armband.

A gold shackle to take away the madness, hold to the reality of this world and no other.

Pricilla's elemental world had been Aaron's nemesis for as long as he could remember. It had been her sanctuary, a safe place to go when the real world was too devastating, too difficult. A fantasy haven for a six-year old little girl who had lost both her parents. A child who had thought they had died because she had made an innocent wish to be able to stay with him, not travel with them to yet another archeological dig. A wish twice given, heart, mind, soul, because even then, she loved him and never wanted to be without him. He'd pulled her out of her six-year coma by using the full power of his Magus abilities in True Science, damn near killing himself in the process, and losing a part of his soul.

To bring her back, he had to erase the innocent love she had for both her parents, and for him, so she could survive without self-hatred. His own love for her had to be buried, hidden. He had to stay away from her to keep her from regaining those memories on her own.

It had taken more than two decades before he could cross the keys back to her, bring back her memories. Bring back the love between them that meant everything to them both.

And always would.

'To hold to the reality of this world and no other'.

Aaron found himself increasing attracted to that promise of normalcy.

(Do you know how to bind an elemental against its will?)

Celandine was an elemental. He looked again at the armband with the green stone of Assiah and an unbreakable lock of pure gold. If Pricilla put it on, there would be no world other than Assiah for her. It was an increasingly tempting thought that couldn't be ignored.

He could hold her here, with him, she would never be able to return to Whilom unconsciously or physically.

Aaron got up from the desk, taking the artifact with him, then walked to the bedroom and put it in the wall safe. Sooner or later, he would have to make the decision. Permanently taking away Pricilla's world from her was an ugly thought, but with his abilities as Magus it was possible.

Maybe even necessary.

If it took a shackle to keep her with him, he would. They couldn't lose each other again.

It would destroy them both.

Chapter 11 - Knight meets Page

Roberta looked toward the huge open-air pavilion tent where the wine exhibit was taking place and sighed. This 'wine picnic' was held annually by the Grayson family to woo their wealthy cliental into yet another snob fest. This time it wasn't in France (which might have at least been interesting), but in Temecula, California. She'd never even heard of the place before, now she knew why.

According to her digging on the internet, wine and wineries were about the only thing of interest in Temecula. Bicycle rides through wineries, balloon trip over wineries, wine tasting in wineries... If you wanted to join the country club set, there were a number of golf courses and tennis clubs. Lakes? Sure. All manmade with stocked fish. The ocean? Thirty plus miles away on twisting roads.

Yep. Fake water, domesticated fish. The perfect place for a marine biologist.

Roberta let out a huge sigh of annoyance. Her mother was going to owe her big time for this one.

Okay, where to start? Finding Brandon Grayson in this madhouse wouldn't be easy, everyone here looked suspiciously alike. The women wore sundresses of modest (expensive) style and color with large hats to keep off the sun. It felt like she had a stepped back in time into the world of The Great Gatsby.

Roberta was dressed in a similar light blue linen dress, her hair in a careful chignon, but she had forgotten the hat that was supposed to be part of the very expensive outfit her mother had talked her into (one of many such outfits her mother had talked her into before going on this stupid True Science mission.). The men were just as vain as the women in their clothing, they wore equally casual (yet elegant) outfits; twill pants, sports jackets, no ties, the first button or two open.

How very trendy. Yawn.

Roberta was a cut-off jeans and t-shirt type person. Always had been, always would be. She detested shopping for clothes she'd never wear more than once. She seriously disliked snobby formal gatherings, although she had to attend them more often than she liked for ecology fundraisers. She had one little black dress that she wore every time to those fundraisers. It was a great dress. Polyester. No hand washing, no drycleaning, it could be thrown into the washer and dryer with nary a wrinkle.

("No, darling," her mother grimaced at, admittedly, her catalog clothing, especially the wash and wear little black dress. "And what's with these awful shoes?" She'd held them up by the straps, not quite holding her nose. "Did you find them at a yard sale? You've been raised in the best of families, gone to the best schools. Do you want people to think you're some kind of a country bumpkin going to a county fair?")

Damnit, she liked county fairs. They certainly suited her more than this pretentious wine tasting reception. She was not impressed by people who sniffed and swirled their glass of wine before taking their first sip then clicked their tongue while tasting it and declaring, "it's a little too dry or too wet, its too acidic, too fruity..." Roberta always had the urge to roll her eyes and declare, "Get over it people! Its not dry, it's liquid, therefore it's wet, it's acidic because, hello! It's alcohol. It's made of grapes, which is a fruit, therefore it's fruity. Duh?"

Since she had promised her mother she would attend this wonderful hoop-la, she would have to stay awhile to meet Brandon Grayson before she could escape.

Sadly, no one was wearing a nametag, she'd have to ask around pretending that she didn't think wine was simply overpriced grape juice with a vague alcoholic kick and try to mingle. She walked over to the long table, making it through the group of pre-drunk snobs surrounding it and was greeted by the pseudo bartender with dark unkempt hair who was a little less formally dressed.

Generally, the folks serving the drinks had the most useful information.

"Hello," she tried her most winning pseudo smile.

"Well, hello there," the bartender returned, giving her a broad wink. "What are you drinking, Sweetheart?"

"What do you recommend?"

"Ah." He pulled the cork from a new bottle. "Fils Gris Riesling is today's debut," he told her, holding the bottle across his forearm to show her. "'A modest little wine with questionable breeding, but I think you'll be amused by its presumption'."

Roberta laughed. "Thurber?"

He grinned. "Mangled and misquoted," he admitted, "but apt in this case."

"I'll take your word for it. To be honest, all white wines taste pretty much the same to me."

"Shh," he smiled, handing her a crystal glass of wine. "Me, too, but since my Uncle owns the label," he nodded over his shoulder, "you didn't hear me say that."

"Me three," said an attractive brunette walking up to them. Like Roberta she had forgone the fancy hat. More telling, she had her hair in a cheerfully casual ponytail. "Pour me some of the same, Don. I'd ask you to spritz it, but Uncle Auggie would have me flogged."

"Sure thing, Sis."

"Uncle?" Roberta looked from one to another, trying to hide her surprise. "You're both Graysons?"

"Only on our maternal side. Mom was happily married out of it," the woman answered, "we're from the more liberal side of the family," she smiled, holding out a hand and leaned closer, "we occasionally imbibe a pint or two of domestic beer," she admitted. "I'm Vicky Lawson," she nodded toward the bartender. "This is my reprobate twin brother, Donald."

"Don," he corrected.

"Roberta Griffin," she answered, shaking Vicky's hand with a smile, "friends call me Bobby."

"Bobby it is then," Vicky answered.

"Nice to meet you too, Don."

"Always nice to be noticed by a beautiful woman," he smiled and tilted his head. "Do I detect an Australian accent?"

"More of an affectation I picked up the last few years," Roberta admitted with mild embarrassment. Her mother had noticed the same thing and chided her about it. "I was born in Canada, but I don't spend much time there."

"Then Australia here I come," he gave her another wink and a grin.

"Don't waste time on him," Vicky linked arms with Roberta. "Married, two teenage kids, shameless flirt, but no follow through," she assured her. "Come on, Bobby. Let's look for some fresh, less domesticated and more original meat. I'll introduce you around."

Okay, maybe they weren't all so snobby.

"Who's that pretty young woman in the blue dress with Vicky?" Charlotte Grayson asked her son innocently, nodding to the far side of the lawn.

Brandon glanced over at his cousin and her companion who had several men talking to them animatedly. Flirting probably, if he knew Vicky. "No idea," he made his voice firm, his mother had a habit of trying to fix him up at these affairs. His cousin Vicky wasn't a great deal better. She thought any unmarried male was fair game. He looked away from, admittedly, a very attractive woman and kept searching for the man he was expecting. "Did your friend tell you when this Robert Griffin was going to arrive?"

"Not precisely. Do quit obsessing," Charlotte suggested, dodging the question. She let out a light laugh. "Oh, look! How fun is that?

Madeline Hennessy is wearing one of her Liza Doolittle creations again," she noted. "I swear most folks come to these things just to see her newest design."

Brandon dutifully checked out the hat. It was incredibly huge, reminding him of a beach umbrella with feathers. "It should make her very popular," he answered, "it casts more shade than the main pavilion." He again looked at his watch.

"You have no sense of whimsy," his mother retorted. "I think she looks wonderful. Such a lovely girl, I can't imagine why she's still single, can you?"

"Hmm," Brandon didn't rise to the bait. He could easily understand why Madeline Hennessy was still single, she had the IQ of a flea and wore insane head gear. He took a sip of wine to keep from saying so out loud. His mother had been pushing Maddie at him for years.

"Ah!" Charlotte smiled in enthusiastic anticipation. "I believe Vicky is coming over here to introduce us to her new friend. Be gracious, dear."

Brandon turned to his father. "Reign in your wife, Dad, she's scheming again."

"And sleep on the sofa for a week? Not a chance in hell. Fight your own battles, Son." Augustus looked curiously at the pair coming toward them. "At least this one's not wearing a flying saucer on her head," he noted, as he took a sip of his own wine, then put on a smile as his niece walked up and kissed him on the cheek.

"Uncle Auggie, Aunt Charlotte, Brandon," Vicky smiled at them then blinked at Brandon with the same not so innocent expression on her face as his mother's. "Look who I found! This is Dr. Roberta Griffin."

Roberta shook hands with both the older Graysons. "It's very nice to meet you."

Augustus gave her a warm and brisk squeeze of her hand. Charlotte enthusiastically took both her hands and patted them gently. "Bobby, dear! Your mother and I are old friends. I'm so glad she could talk you into coming. And all the way from Australia! How are things 'down under'? Where are you staying?"

"The Weston," Roberta answered, feeling an odd friction in the air, her polite smile faded when she looked at the ill-disguised annoyance on Brandon Grayson's face. Her expression cleared. "Well! I see our mothers have a great deal in common." She forced the smile back on her face. "Not to worry Mr. Grayson. I have a round-trip ticket and would be happy to use it."

Chapter 12 - Kether et Nebulae

They were sitting in Brandon's massive office at the winery. To Roberta, the atmosphere and furnishings felt as pompous and arrogant as Brandon Grayson himself. Deep, thick, burgundy (or would that be Merlot?) colored carpet. Polished oak panels, floor to ceiling bookshelves (beveled glass doors, naturally), and a large oak desk, ruthlessly polished to within an inch of its life (no doubt a priceless antique worth a small fortune) that thankfully separated them.

Trying to ignore her surroundings, Roberta looked curiously at the sheet of paper Brandon had given her, then looked up at him with confusion. "The True Science parable of the beginning of life?" she asked. "This is your Seth?"

"No," Brandon answered, still trying to decide how to undo the damage caused by his first reaction to Roberta Griffin. He had flubbed it badly. Finding out that his Page was a woman was one thing, recognizing his instant sexual attraction to that same Page was another. Showing his initial shock was his third error. A very bad first meeting all around. She was now cool and distant, the dimples he had first seen when she had met his father and mother hadn't been evident since. Obviously the attraction was not mutual. "The Magus sent it along with the Seth, and strenuously suggested we read it."

"Okay," Roberta looked skeptical, but silently re-read the story she had learned as a child.

~

And So Started the Life of Kether et Nebulae

The star burned and it flared, discarding parts of its essence away from its core.

*

One spark burned and it melded, its heart liquid stone.
It clung close the star with despair, all alone.
But the star never saw it. The star didn't care.
It had thrown away refuse, nothing more, nothing rare.
The spark went unnoticed, forgotten, ignored.

*

The spark circled the star in the space of rejection.
It had movement without purpose, an empty life of its own.

It called itself Atziluth.

*

The surface of Atziluth cooled, but its core...
...it burned hot with rejection, forgotten, ignored.
The surface soon melted, it steamed and it rose.
Again and again, it steamed and it rose.
The newly formed air would not be ignored.
It was not simple refuse. Atziluth would not throw it away.
It would exist with fresh hope, it would live without fear.
It would not go astray, it would always be near.

It would call itself Briah.
*

Briah froze and it steamed and it cooled and it grew.
It rose far above and it fell down anew.
It created glaciers and lakes that became rivers and seas.
It played on the surface and did as it pleased.
The newly formed water would not be ignored.
It was not simple refuse. Atziluth would not throw it away.
It would live with fresh hope, it would live without fear.
It would not go astray, it would always be near.

It would call itself Yetzirah.
*

Yetzirah flowed and it stormed, it warmed and it cooled.
It created mountains and valleys that rose when it pooled.
The newly formed land would not be ignored.
It was not simple refuse. Atziluth would not throw it away.
It would live strong and firm, it would live without fear.
It would not be rejected, it would always be near.

It would call itself Assiah.
*

Assiah had warmth, it had air, it had mountains and seas.
It had butterflies, birds, it had and fishes and trees.
It had movement and purpose, a true life of its own.
It did not go unnoticed...

....It was seen by the star.
*

"Damn." Roberta grabbed a tissue from her purse and dabbed at her eyes. "This stupid thing has always made me cry," she explained her less than adult reaction. "I never figured it out. Is the star finally sorry it rejected the spark, or is it now planning to destroy it out of jealousy for what the spark has become?"

"Not a clue," Brandon told her. "I don't think parables are supposed to give the ending away, just make macho boys think and sissy girls weep."

"Very nice." Roberta smiled.

The quick flash of dark green eyes and prominent dimples was a gift. Brandon returned her smile carefully, hoping not to repeat his previous mistakes.

He had a beautiful and very sexy smile, warm and compelling clear brown eyes. Roberta put on her business game face so he wouldn't realize her attraction to him. This was business. She knew his type, he would want to keep it strictly business. "So, explain to me why we're re-reading this? It was the first story we were taught when coming out of crystalis. A pretty tale, but old news."

"Evidently the Magus thought we needed a refresher," Brandon answered. "You're saying True Science is merely a 'pretty tale?'"

"No, I'm saying I honestly don't care if it is or not," Roberta responded truthfully. "I study fish and water mammals. I go to them in their own natural habitats. Real life is more comfortable."

"Do you plan on raising your children in the belief?"

"If I ever have children, yes. I like the philosophy. It keeps kids safe. They need that initial cocoon. True Science gives them the first six years growing up with total safety, complete innocence, unconditional love. When they come out of crystalis their guide teaches respect for all life, all elements, ecology in its purest form. It's a healthy upbringing." She shrugged, dismissing the topic. "So! You met the Magus. How far off the beaten path is he?"

Brandon thought about Aaron Zale. "Formidable. He seems normal enough at first. Personable, likeable, a good sense of humor. As First Key he is extremely powerful. As fourth generation, he's learned to summon elementals from all the worlds, undine, sylph, salamanders. He's not arrogant with his Destiny Given, or his abilities, it's more like he's resigned to the responsibility. Never deviates from his sephiroth, prone to extreme retribution when anyone else does."

Roberta frowned. "What kind of retribution?"

Brandon considered the fate of Emma Coleman, alias Amme. "For a major offence against the Apocrypha he is fully capable of putting a shin upon a soul, making it ill-dignified and useless."

Roberta looked dubious. "He can really do that?"

"Not only can, he *has* done that," Brandon assured her.

Roberta's eyes opened wide. "What kind of a major offense could be that horrific?"

Brandon looked grim. "The intentional harm to an unprotected butterfly with no remorse, no justification."

"Who in the four hells would be stupid or cruel enough to intentionally harm a butterfly?" Roberta asked with horror.

"In the one case I know about, a woman who was banned from the guide circle for some pretty nasty activities. After she was banished, she used the little True Science she did know and removed a butterfly's natural ability to call an elemental. A salamander."

Roberta's face lost all color. "She did *what*?" Outside of True Science, no one really understood what that meant, but Roberta was raised in the doctrine, she definitely did. Such an action would literally rape away the very heart and soul of an innocent child. She felt the bile rise in her throat and swallowed rapidly to keep from tossing up her lunch.

Brandon looked concerned. "Are you alright?"

Roberta swallowed several times more, but the nausea became more intense. She gave a quick shake of her head, then stood hastily, almost running to the bathroom she had noticed earlier. She just made it to the door, shutting and locking it before she started dry heaving into the toilet. There was no relief, nothing came up, but her stomach cramped with the unexpected violence of her body.

Splashing cold water on her face didn't help. She wet a washcloth then lowered the lid of the toilet and sat down on it, shaking, holding the cloth against the back of her neck. Her heart was pounding, her mind was in turmoil.

Oh, God. What kind of villains would she be dealing with? What had she gotten herself into?

No, what had her mother gotten her into? Had she known what she would be facing?

Roberta threw the washcloth into the sink, putting her head in her hands. What kind horrible monster would be so cruel to a child? Why?

(I'm saying I honestly don't care if it is or not...)

She was such a damned liar. Roberta sat up slowly, holding open her hands at chest level. "*Ki Teth, Yetzirah*," she whispered softly, using the True Science words she had learned as a child that made everything in the insane belief worth learning.

A small sphere of water appeared in her hands, the tiny swimming undine inside magnified by the water around it. It was so delicate, so beautiful, so joyful in its water antics. It was performing just for her and let her know it.

All elementals came only out of pure love and innocent curiosity.

103

They always wanted to play, to show off. They were giving a personal, magical gift.

A very private gift. Roberta always summoned an undine secretly. As a child she called it often, as an adult she called it rarely and only on days when she needed to remember she had a special, magical friend she could always depend on, who would never let her down. It had been her lifeline, a fragile gift she had taken for granted. As a child on the cusp she could also summon a sylph of the air, but rarely did, the undine had always been her favorite.

All elementals had the same gentle souls. Her grandmother had been a Page of Wands, the salamander she had been able to call had glowed with joy, its tiny lizard-like body threw off sparks lighting up the room with its cheerful essence. Her grandmother had been so delighted with the thrill, her smile could light up the room on its own. As a little girl, she had badgered her grandmother often to summon the salamander, not really to see the elemental, although admittedly it was beautiful, but just to see her grandmother's amazing and wondrous smile when she held it in her hands.

(It had movement and purpose, a life of its own... It would live with fresh hope, it would live without fear. It would not go astray, it would always be near...)

Shit. She had needed a reminder of a childhood story, she had taken her perfect Yetzirah companion for granted for too damned long. "*Ki Akal Yetzirah*. Go in peace my beautiful, wonderful friend."

She looked at her now empty hands, still feeling the joy and mourning for the sadness of any child who could no longer summon the perfect gift, a joyful, compassionate friend in their moment of need.

Chapter 13 - The Pearl of Yetzirah

Brandon watched the door Roberta had exited worriedly. Obviously, if the information about Amme had effected her that harshly, she wasn't as far removed from True Science as she wanted others to believe. Good news and bad news. He opened the padded envelope that came a few days after the Seth-A-Tristan et Yetzirah, gingerly taking out the vile brooch Aaron Zale had sent him. The short note that had come in the small box gave very little information, none of it encouraging.

"Brandon," said the letter, "Unfortunately, here is the complication I warned you about. According to what little research was available, the horror I have sent you was created by five black 'magicians', (as they called them in those dark days). Evidently this artifact, (and, unfortunately, several others still outstanding), was the reason the Arcana of Guides was originally founded in the first place. Treat it with kindness, use it with compassion.

"This brooch is now part of the Seth-A-Tristan et Yetzirah and the formal sephiroth of both you and your Page."

Brandon looked at the brooch binding the sylph and undine with concern, bordering on horror, remembering the Magus' words on the day he had met him.

("You asked me earlier if it was possible to bind an elemental. Imagine for a moment being trapped in the same way against your will. No words of release, no knowledge of good and evil, no hope of escape, no thought of rescue and you'll know what an elemental feels when its lured from its own world and locked into this one by the pure gold of Assiah... now you know.")

Brandon frowned at the bathroom door. If merely hearing about the crime Amme had committed against a butterfly had affected Roberta physically, what would the knowledge of this "complication" do to her?

He should never have mentioned Amme's crimes.

So why had he? *("Now part of the Seth-A-Tristan of both you and your Page.")* Because, he answered his own question, not telling her about the brooch would be a breech of the trust he needed to establish between them. Any other action would be a black lie of omission.

("Welcome to the wonderful world of Destiny Given. Trust me, it sucks and there's no way out once you're been given the mantle. God knows I've tried...")

His new mantle of knight had gained about a thousand pounds with

105

the possession of the brooch. He looked at the door again and grimaced. Well, he had found his Page, alienated her at first meeting, made her cry with a childhood parable, then caused her to get sick in the bathroom. Not a promising start. Was there a snowball's chance in hell that she would willingly enter into this quest? He put the brooch back into the envelope, then into his desk drawer.

Yes, he'd tell her, but not just yet.

Brandon read the second page of the Magus' note, still frowning.

"As for the Seth itself. Saying 'It will so be written' doesn't necessarily mean that I fully understand the bloody thing, only that I write it down as per the dictates of my Sephiroth. It is written in English, rather than the customary Greek as a courtesy to all who follow The Seth-A-Tristan et Yetzirah per your family sephiroth. The obligatory twelve stanzas are for you and your Page to decipher, depending on whatever situation you might need to resolve.

"At this point, as a Knight of the Sword, you are on your own." - *Aaron*

For about the fifteenth time, Brandon opened the leather portfolio with the formal Seth bound inside. It was not computer generated, but written in archaic script with a fountain pen and black ink. There were no hesitation marks. He knew it had been written in one sitting without pause. Apparently "written by his hand" meant exactly that. He skipped to the end of the Seth. The salutation from the Magus still stunned him.

~ And thus it has been written unto The Apocrypha
  ~ In the Year Six Hundred Seventy Four
  ~ by the customary count and Shin of True Science
   ~ forever expanding the knowledge of Pyrrho of Elis
   ~ determined by his sephiroth and Seth
   ~ In the year Three Hundred Forty Seven (BCE)

~ by the hand of the Magus of Power by Eternal Lemniscate

Unbelievable, impressive, and more than a little intimidating. Pyrrho of Elis. An accolade of Pythagoras himself. Which meant it was not written into 'an' apocrypha, but 'The' Apocrypha. As Forth Generation, it also meant that Aaron Zale was definitely related to Pyrrho of Elis, as his father had once suggested.

Hell of a heritage.

As for the Seth... *(for you and your Page to decipher)*, in English or not, it was a complete and total riddle. He also knew from his studies that there was no particular sequence or line that could be reliably followed.

106

Roberta came out of the bathroom almost twenty minutes after she had gone in. Brandon noted that her freckles were more prominent. She was still a shade pale, but exceptionally calm. "Are you alright?"

"I'm fine," Roberta nodded, somewhat embarrassed, but still feeling cheered by the visit from the undine. "Sorry about that. Sometimes..." she gave a weak smile. "I've been through all the training, studied all the doctrines, kept up on the basics when my mother or father were around, but..."

"Still, in your heart of hearts it was all just a load of bullshit," Brandon finished the thought, using the same words Aaron had used on him. "An archaic philosophy based on wishful thinking and religious fantasy."

"No. Not really," she shook her head, surprising him a little. "I know it's real, just thought it was unnecessary. I've been on the periphery for a long time. By the age of thirteen, since I was given no formal sephiroth, normal life became more interesting, less introverted."

"Less complicated," Brandon added.

"That too," Roberta agreed. "So, assuming I take this on. What's the Seth you're bound to, what's the objective, who do we badger for the information, what kind of villains do we have to vanquish and what country do we invade to get them?"

Brandon smiled, oddly more confident. "Its not that easy."

"Nothing ever is," Roberta answered with resignation. "So. Aside from having me refresh my memory of the life of Kether et Nebulae, what do you need me for?"

Brandon took out a velvet bag from his inside coat pocket and offered it to her.

Roberta reached across the desk and took it, spilling the contents into her hand. "What's this?"

"You're a Doctor of marine biology, maybe you can identify it."

Roberta looked at it. "Phylum Mollusca gestation, calcium carbonate secretion," she smiled innocently.

"I have absolutely no idea what you just said," Brandon admitted.

"In short," Roberta gave him a genuine smile, her eyes sparkling, "its a pearl made by a parasite, a bit of sand, or something else that lodged itself inside some kind of mollusk."

He smiled back, it was impossible not to, her dimples almost demanded it. "Anything else you can tell me about it?"

She looked at the pearl again, rolling it around on her palm with her forefinger. "Well, all I can say for certain is that it's a natural sea pearl not cultured artificially, not fresh water." She pursed her mouth. "I'd say it was in its host for a long time. As pearls go, its larger than average. I

107

doubt it's from any known oyster."

Brandon looked interested. "I thought all pearls came from oysters."

"Oysters are only one kind of mollusk," Roberta assured him, "there are more than twenty different species that can produce a pearl." She shook her head as she studied it. "This one is more than a little odd, though, and it's not from any known oyster or sea snail. Melo Melo Pearls are large and round, that fits, but they range from tan to dark brown, occasionally orange. The blue rainbow luster makes it looks almost abalone, but doubtful. I've never seen one from an abalone this symmetrical before." She looked at it more closely. "The color... silver blue, with no flame, no greens, no gold, not even a hint of pink. That's strange, even for Abalone. Add the size and almost perfectly round shape, it makes it even more unlikely."

Roberta shook her head, grimaced slightly, then balanced the pearl on her palm. "Scratch Abalone," she decided. "It could be from a conch, but again, no flame and they're generally more teardrop in shape, so that doesn't fit either. Scallop, maybe, but the color... I don't think so." She frowned, annoyed that she couldn't identify it. "Not a deep water pearl, not the China sea, not the South seas, not North or South America, not the Mediterranean..." She looked at him sharply. "Not from Assiah at all," she studied his eyes, her own eyes wide with shock. "This is from Yetzirah."

"You're good."

"No," Roberta answered, "I'm seriously confused. How in the four hells did anyone manage to get a Yetzirah pearl from there to here?"

"Better question," Brandon countered, "how do I return it from where it was taken?"

"Return it?" Roberta looked shocked. "That's your Seth?"

"Pretty much."

"But," Roberta was incredulous. "Those were just dreams we had as children to find a safe place! Its not as though anyone can physically go there," she told him and added, "trust me. If I had ever left my bed or meditation to physically go to an elemental world, Mom or my guide would have definitely noticed I was missing."

"Mine as well," Brandon assured her. "But, someone obviously accomplished it, or they couldn't have brought that back with them," he nodded at the pearl.

Roberta looked again at the impossible pearl. "Do you know how to physically get into an elemental world?" she sounded shocked.

"No," Brandon admitted quickly. "Even if I did have that knowledge, I'm a sword. I'd end up in Briah, not Yetzirah. You, on the other hand, being on the cusp, have a foot in both worlds."

Roberta looked unconvinced.

He handed her the portfolio. "Here. It's the only copy I have. Do you have a eidetic memory?"

"Not photographic, but after two or three readings I have a memory that's fairly close to one. If it's in rhyme or song, I'm even better," she answered. "Some old tunes I wish I could forget." She took the portfolio, opening the beautifully tooled front cover carefully, looking at the impressive lettering with near awe. "Well, no song or rhyme here, it's not even easy to read," she sounded irritated as she squinted at the Seth he had given her. "Why the ancient script and spelling?"

"It has to be written by the dictates of the Magus' Sephiroth," Brandon explained. "Whether or not I succeed, it's a formal Seth. The original has already been added to The Apocrypha of the Major Arcana. Probably in ancient Greek. I doubt colloquial language or computer generated pages would fit the image. This translated copy will go into my family archives."

Roberta frowned, considering the ramifications. "In short, if you don't succeed, it will follow your children's children in perpetuity until it's resolved."

"If you willingly decide to take this on, it will become your sephiroth."

"My formal path." Not a strict obligation, more of a designation. It was also a bribe, but he didn't know her. As a child she had always wanted to be given a clear path, a sephiroth she was meant to follow. It was a 'right of passage' for most True Science kids when they hit puberty. As an adult, however, it was more problematic. She had created her own sephiroth outside of True Science. She had traveled the world searching for adventure, new sea creatures, new challenges.

More importantly, she loved what she did and was damned good at it. A True Shit sephiroth was no longer on her 'to do' list.

"Are you willing to take this on?" Brandon asked carefully.

Roberta avoided the question by scanning the Seth quickly, then again reading the first stanza. "'One quest begets the other. Two of Earth, two of Air, one of Water." She read out loud, regarding him suspiciously. "We're both of Earth, we're both of Air and I'm of water."

"Exactly. Between us we hit the Trifecta."

Which was why she was sitting in on this pseudo job interview. She wasn't wanted or needed for her hard earned skills as a Marine Biologist, she was wanted and needed because she just happened to be Third generation, born on the right day at the right time, in the right place.

Are you willing to take this on?" he asked again carefully.

She didn't miss the wording of his questions. Willing. Willingly.

That was the key issue. By True Science terms, that meant total commitment. No. She didn't need a sephiroth, or a 'ticket to the prom' any more to be accepted by her peers. She had movement and purpose, a true life of her own. Yup, the Kether-et-Nebulae really was a story worth remembering. If she ever found out who the Magus was, she'd send him a thank you note for the reminder.

Brandon was losing her and knew it. "When's the last time you had a real challenge, Bobby?" he tried, using her nickname intentionally.

"I swim with sharks almost daily, Mr. Grayson."

"Even hang-gliding becomes routine after awhile," he countered. "Fun, but no real challenge."

Well, hell, he'd found her weak spot. That was a true dangling carrot. Swimming with sharks had lost the adrenalin rush she used to get. Oh, the danger was still there, but with care and intelligent precautions even chasing and tagging sharks was merely an indulgence, one she wasn't able to do as often as she wanted. Lately, her job entailed more politics than adventure.

And Yetzirah! A water world of true fantasy, a world no one had really studied. Kids might play there in their dreams, but never really saw it through adult eyes and curiosity.

It was almost an irresistible lure. No fund raising, no board meetings, no lecture circuits explaining the dangers of pollution and climate change or the need for the preservation of valuable sea life. A chance to travel to an elemental world, see sylphs and undines in their own habitats...

Damn. Was it bait for a bored and jaded marine biologist, or the chance of a lifetime?

Brandon made a calculated decision. "If you'd like to take the Seth back to your hotel with you, read it, think about it, sleep on it, I'll understand." If nothing else, he'd have to see her again to get the Seth back and hopefully come up with a new strategy before she bolted.

"That might be best," She stood, gathering her purse, looked at the portfolio she had put back on the desk and picked it up.

Brandon also stood. "I'll see you tomorrow then." He gave her a confident smile that was wholly false. "Would you join me for breakfast?"

"Lunch," Roberta suggested. "I'm still a little messed up on my time zones."

"Lunch then," Brandon agreed. "I'll have a limo pick you up and bring you here. We can dine on the patio where it's private. Noon?"

"Noon," she agreed, walked to the door and closed it gently behind her, not looking back.

Nope. Not one of his better business meetings, Brandon decided heavily, sitting back down with a frown. When she saw the brooch and realized what else they were up against, he had a feeling he might never get her on board.

Chapter 14 - The Seth-A-Tristan et Yetzirah

Roberta Worked through the handwritten Seth with difficulty. The script itself was old-fashioned, more like calligraphy than regular writing. The words were formal and cryptic. She copied it down on the hotel stationary so she wouldn't have to re-decipher it when (if) she read it a second time.

<u>Seth-A-Tristan et Yetzirah</u>

One quest begets the other.
Two of Earth, two of air, one of water
*

Realize thy knowledge and convention of innocence
One may be coaxed yet not coerced.
One may be touched yet not imprisoned.
*

A life of despair has no purpose
A life of fear has no movement
A life without despair has no existence
A life without fear is foolish
*

A world without despair or fear is subject to jealousy and avarice.
*

Purpose has meaning to all being, or has no meaning
Movement explores the unknown, or remains stationary
Existence has no meaning or name unless it is fragile
*

To be blind to danger is imprudent
To see danger where none exists is cowardice.
*

An Elemental of Fire will not consume thee
An Elemental of Water will tempt thee
An Elemental of Air will seduce and deceive thee
An Elemental of Earth and Nebulae will contest for thee

*

Thy path is long.
One gate will open to thee, one other will not.
*

Travel worlds known to thee.
Reject that which has no purpose to thy quest.
*

Be not consumed, be not deceived, be not driven from thy path
Be not known by elements unknown to thee.
*

Reject thy certainty.
*

Diomedeidae may aid thee, if thou will it.
Diomedeidae will be lofty, denying thee thy purpose
One quest begets the other
Thy chivalry defines thy outcome.
*

Pure, unadulterated... Gobble de goop. Drum roll, eye roll.

Roberta shook her head as she read her copy of the Seth for the third time, then sat back in the hotel desk chair, unbraided her hair and combed it out with her fingers. She'd already put on an oversized t-shirt (that her mother would freak about if she saw it) to 'sleep on it', as Brandon had requested.

Right. As though, after reading the stupid Seth, she'd be able to sleep at all.

God, what a mess. Mom, why me?

Almost predictably, the phone rang. Roberta picked it up. "Hey, Mom."

"Handsome, isn't he?" were Geneva's first words.

Roberta considered her answer, remembering her initial reaction to Brandon Grayson. Tall, incredibly well-proportioned, fabulous eyes, gorgeous grin... "Very," she admitted. "But don't get your matchmaking hopes up, Mom. Your friend Charlotte, aka his mother, already tried that ploy, it didn't work for either of us. He's not interested and I'm too confused."

"Well, it was worth a shot," Geneva's voice smiled. "Did you even like him?" she pressed.

"Since what we exchanged was more or less in a business setting, I honestly don't have an opinion."

Geneva took on a more serious tone. "I know its against the Apocrypha to give me the details, but how bad is the Seth he needs you for? Is it dangerous?"

Define dangerous, Roberta thought to herself. "Its complicated," she answered instead.

There was a long pause. "Baby, are you scared?" Geneva sounded incredulous.

"I don't know what I am. Don't worry, Mom, I'll work it out."

There was a long pause. "Yes," Geneva told her, her voice taking on an almost dreamy tone, "you will."

Roberta stilled. "Anything else?" she asked the question carefully, recognizing the tone of her mother's voice. Part of her mother's sephiroth was full empathy, with a touch of knowing. Sometimes it really freaked her out, other times it had prevented her from making a disastrous decision.

Another long pause. "Until you decide this is truly your sephiroth, do not ask for more than you have already been given. What you currently know determines."

"Determines what?"

There was a pregnant pause. "I have no idea," Geneva laughed, her voice back to normal. "Occasionally this True Shit crap even creeps me out."

"You want me to do this," Roberta decided.

"No, I'm not saying that. What I want, all I've ever wanted, is for you to be as happy with who and what you are as I am with you. There's a big difference. Get some rest, Bobby. Know that I love you and so does your father."

Of that, Roberta never had any doubts.

(It would live with fresh hope, it would exist without fear. It would not go astray, it would always be near...)

Again, the parable of Kether-et Nebulae flashed in her memory. It was the very basis of how True Science children were raised. No anger, no telling a child to 'grow up' before his or her time, imagination encouraged, protected and applauded, never reigned in or ignored. It wasn't just a child's story, it was another priceless gift. She had needed the reminder of who and what she was.

"And I love both of you. Forever and always, Mom."

"Forever and always." Geneva repeated. "Sweet dreams, baby."

"Thanks, Mom, you too."

Roberta picked up the hotel stationary she had written her translation on, read it one last time, then shredded the paper into tiny bits, and tossed them into the trash.

Dreams

Roberta looked with awe at the ocean in front of her and smiled. She'd forgotten how beautiful it all was. In the waves far offshore the dolphins were surfing. Within the waves she could see their shadows easily. Her childhood friends, Nerida, Nixie and baby Jennifer leaped into the air and called out to her, their voices gleeful when they saw her. An undeniable invitation. They were in a playful mood and wanted her to join them. Grinning, she walked into the water, wearing the silver gray swimsuit she always wore when in the waters of Yetzirah. She eagerly swam out to join them in their games.

Adelie. This was hers, her place, her world, her sanctuary. It had been such a very long time.

She always knew her friends, her other family, would be waiting for her, welcoming her back.

Brandon abruptly woke from a troubled dream. More of a nightmare. Ever since he had been a teenager, he had been able to sense a wrongness, a foreboding of things to come. Grapes were fragile unless carefully tended. Every vineyard his family owned had been saved by his instant recognition of danger to the vines, from root to leaf. He could sense weather, dry summers, cold winters, mold, blight, phylloxera aphids destroying the rootstock. He always felt the dangers before they could take hold. His instincts made the difference between success and failure, death and disease.

This was different, more of an imperative. His instincts were screaming at him, telling him to take a stand and fight the rot. Somehow between meeting the Magus and finding his Page, his need to follow the Seth-A-Tristan et Yetzirah had become crucial. Waiting would be disastrous; there was no time to hesitate. It was no longer a Seth he could leisurely take his time fulfilling, not something he could pass on to his heirs.

A parasite, a wrong element, a rot had been invading, creeping slowly but relentlessly, destroying something precious. Unfortunately, he wasn't sure what that rot was destroying.

What he was sure of, was that he had an enemy. Somehow, he would have to combat it.

Soon.

"Pricilla?" Aaron woke up instantly and brushed her cheek until she woke. Her eyes were slightly glazed with sleep. "What is it, Ce-Cill? A nightmare?"

Pricilla gave a weak smile, her eyes cleared. "No, love," She kissed him gently. "Just a thought that came from nowhere."

In the past few weeks, Pricilla had been drifting more and more into dreams. At night it wasn't so worrying, but the daydreams she slipped into at odd hours were starting to frighten him. It was as if the two worlds of Whilom and Assiah were colliding. Soon he would have to make a decision about the armband. The shackle. "What thought, Ce-Cill?"

"An essence, yet not, shall be absorbed by the Seas of Yetzirah."

An essence, yet not. Damn. It wasn't fully Pricilla he was holding, only half. Celandine, her other half, was also in the bed with him. It was like loving two women at the same time, separate, but still one. Essence, yet not. He let out a careful breath, thinking the words, not saying them out loud. *("Ki Celandine, akal Whilom, Akal Nebulae. Keep with you my heart, my mind, my soul.")*

(Always, A-Ron Oft dreamed, never forgotten.) he heard the words in his mind.

But the words came from Celandine, not Pricilla.

Aaron held Pricilla closer. "Stay with me, Ce-Cill. I love you, don't leave me."

He looked across the bed to the framed landscape on the wall, the one covering his private safe. The one that contained the armband of Assiah.

Should he banish the world of Whilom for the world of Assiah, exile Celandine, send away half of the woman he loved?

Secrets and lies, problems and solutions...

Betrayal or loss...

"Stay with me Cilla," he repeated.

Time was running out.

Chapter 15 - Bound

"So. Tell me about Roberta Griffin," Brandon suggested, after they had finished lunch and lingered over iced tea. It was warmer than hades on the patio, but the fan was making a serious effort to at least keep the bugs away.

Southern California weather was not trying especially hard to entice him to live here permanently.

"Well," Roberta tried to ignore the whirling noise of the fan, it was driving her nuts. She didn't mind the heat, but the constant windstorm blowing across her sleeveless white silk shirt was giving her goose-bumps. Her mother was definitely more into fashion style than practicality. "Mostly I study sharks and Manta Rays, then give lectures on my findings."

"Why sharks and mantas specifically?" Brandon asked curiously.

"They are all endangered, some species are near extinction. Without sharks, the whole ecosystem of the ocean is in danger. The oceans cover more than two thirds of the planet. That ecosystem goes, everything follows."

Brandon looked interested. "I wasn't aware that sharks were endangered."

"Few people are, fewer people care. They are always ready to save the whales and dolphins, but not much else. Sharks and rays were here before the dinosaurs, they've survived everything but man. In the past twenty years, more than seventy percent of all sharks have been destroyed, hunted for sport and food. Some people kill them out of simple fear fueled by movies and the media. Accidents with nets and over-fishing take out tens of thousands more every year. They're slow to breed; saving what's left of the remaining population is pretty much impossible without intervention.

"As for the Manta Rays, they're related to sharks, so now they're on the menu as a cheap substitute for shark fin soup. Mantas breed even more slowly, a pup every two years or so, if they are lucky enough to find a mate. They're beautiful creatures, more graceful than you can imagine. Some have wing spans more than twenty feet wide," she told him almost wistfully. They are incredibly beautiful creatures.

"You love what you do," Brandon realized.

"Yes. And, I could go on for hours in lecture mode, but before your eyes start to glaze over, I'll stop." She pulled the leather binder holding the Seth out of her oversized purse and set it on the table. "This is what you really want to discuss."

Brandon nodded, sorry he hadn't met her under different circumstances. Her passion for her work fascinated him, almost a much as her freckles, dimples and beautiful face. "What's your take on it?"

"As Churchill once said, 'it's a riddle, wrapped in a mystery, inside an enigma; but perhaps there is a key'," she quoted.

Brandon barely smiled. "It is that. What else?"

"That, somehow, being born at the right time and place," (and for no more legitimate reasons), she added mentally, "I'm part of that key."

There was tired resignation in her voice. Brandon had been fully prepared to push her cooperation before she knew all the facts, now it felt immoral to even try. She had a life she wanted, he would be taking her away from that, perhaps for a long time. Maybe permanently, if his nightmare of danger was true. "I should tell you all the complications before you consider being bound to a new sephiroth," he told her. He pulled a padded envelope from his inside pocket, holding it out to her.

(Until you decide this is truly your sephiroth, do not ask for more than you have already been given. What you currently know determines.) Roberta glanced longingly at the envelope, then back at him, shaking her head, not taking the offering. "I don't need to know the complications. I will be your Page, Sir Knight of Swords." She gave him a weak smile. "What the hell. I'm between assignments at the moment."

Brandon hid his surprise, but put the envelope back in his pocket. "You Willingly agree to take on a formal sephiroth?"

"Yes." She tried not to wince at the word 'willingly'.

Brandon pushed his glass aside.

Roberta stiffened. He was prepared to do this right now, she realized, a little surprised. Why the haste? Usually, an acceptance of a formal sephiroth was made, then a date was set, the entire family was there, like some kind of religious baptism. Flowers, fancy clothes, a party to follow. A celebration of adulthood similar to a Jewish Bat Mitzvah or a Mexican Quinceanera. 'Today I am a Woman and/or man' was the theme. At the age of thirty-three, it was almost embarrassing. ('Today I am a woman'. Goody, goody, goody. Whoop-tee do! I'm all grown up now, Mommy and Daddy!)

"Willingly," she answered with only a minor hesitation, but still feeling stupid.

"Formally?"

"Formally," she answered, ready to get this whole damned farce over with.

Brandon nodded. "What's your full name?"

Names had power. Giving her full name freely to someone who knew how to use that power was always a risk. She hesitated only a moment. "Roberta Bethany Griffin."

Brandon put his hand on the cover of the leather bound Seth and tried to ignore the instant sting of the contact. "Put your hand on top of mine," he told her. "Don't break the connection, unless you change your mind." When she complied, he felt a more powerful connection as it extended from the Seth, through his hand, then shot up to hers. He took a deep breath. "Roberta Bethany Griffin. Do you willingly follow a sephiroth given to you by a Knight of Swords who is bound to the Seth-A-Tristan et Yetzirah?"

"I will willingly follow," Roberta answered, feeling a small line of electricity through her hand, down through Brandon's and further, maybe even into the Seth itself.

Okay, this was more than a little weird.

"I ask you twice. Roberta Bethany Griffin. Do you willingly follow a sephiroth given to you by a Knight of Swords who is bound to the Seth-A-Tristan et Yetzirah?"

"I answer twice. I will willingly follow." The surge of energy grew thicker, stronger. Roberta had to fight the urge to break the connection.

Maybe this wasn't such a good idea after all.

"Then I ask thee thrice. Roberta Bethany Griffin. Do you willingly follow a sephiroth given by a Knight of the Swords who is bound to the Seth-A-Tristan et Yetzirah?" His voice had changed, it was deeper, resonating with power.

"I answer thrice. I will willingly follow." Damn! The electrical charge through her hand split into three lines of power, one to the head, one to the heart, one to the groin.

"The path of your sephiroth has been given," Brandon announced.

Roberta quickly pulled her hand off of his. "Four Hells! What was that?" She briskly rubbed her palms together to ward off the sting.

Brandon looked concerned. "Are you alright?"

"Have you given a formal sephiroth before?" Roberta asked him.

"Twice. Since the Magus changed my Destiny Given, it comes automatically with the extension of my sephiroth," Brandon answered. "The last was my cousin's daughter and son on their thirteenth birthdays. She giggled all the way through it. He shrugged and went to play racquetball afterwards." He answered "Of course, at the time, I wasn't directly touching my Seth, nor was it mentioned, so this was probably a bit less humorous. Are you alright?" he asked again.

"Well, I don't feel like giggling, or playing racquetball," she assured him.

"Was it painful?"

"No." She laughed. "Actually, I feel like I need a post glow cigarette." (Yup, today she was a woman.)

Brandon looked at her in shock.

"Sorry," Roberta cleared her throat and took a sip of her cooling coffee. "I have an inappropriate sense of humor when I'm stressed."

Brandon grinned. "Good for you too, huh?"

Roberta cleared her throat. "Okay, then." She smiled and nodded toward his coat pocket. "Tell me about the complications in that envelope."

Brandon's humor instantly faded as he pulled the envelope back out of his pocket and handed it to her. "I wanted to show you this before, but you kind of jumped the gun on me. A little complication to the Seth."

Roberta opened it, looked at the brooch curiously, then read the note from the Magus. She put down the note and studied the brooch more closely. "Are those elementals?" she frowned.

"Yes. Sylph and Undine."

Roberta could see a miniscule flicker of light in one stone, tiny but sluggish movement in the other. "They should be dead, but they're not," she told him, staring at the brooch with an almost scientific curiosity. "How are they able to survive?"

Brandon felt a surge of annoyance that Roberta didn't seem as outwardly horrified by the brooch as he had been. "They're bound, unwillingly, by Assiah gold."

"Unwillingly." She touched the stones gently. "A whale sealed in a too small aquarium unable to swim. A living butterfly pinned under glass unable to fly." Her voice was soft, but her expression was one of pure, unadulterated sorrow, her lips tight with fury. "That's about as nasty as it gets. Still alive, but not living the life they are supposed to live." She looked up at him her eyes blazing. "What psychotic asshole did this? How and why was it done?"

Brandon handed her the note that came with the brooch. "Even the Magus doesn't know. It was done centuries before his time."

"They've been in there for centuries? How do we release them?" Roberta looked even more horrified.

"That's our problem to figure out."

She looked again at the letter from the Magus and grimaced. "'Treat it with kindness, use it with compassion'," she read out loud. "I've got the kindness and compassion covered, but use it how?"

"I'm not completely sure, but I think it's the rest of the key."

"The rest of the key," Roberta wanted to physically hit something, but kept her emotions in check. Screw the rest of the damned Seth, this was more important to her. She gently turned the brooch over, then turned it over again and studied the front with the two elementals trapped inside. "Five black magicians to create this. You and I to fix it." She looked up at him sharply. "The first part of the Seth. What do you want to bet that those five black magicians were made up of two of earth, two of air, one of water?" she asked.

Brandon stiffened, "I wouldn't take that bet," he told her. "What are you thinking?"

"As you said, together we hit the Trifecta. If it takes that combination to trap them, doesn't it follow that it would take the same combination to release them?"

"It fits," Brandon nodded.

"It's a working theory," Roberta answered. "You've been concentrating on the pearl, but the Magus gave you this. First stanza of the Seth, 'One quest begets the other, two of earth, two of air, one of water'." She frowned. "The question is, which quest comes first? The quest to fix this, or the quest to find a way to Yetzirah and return the pearl?"

"Figuring out that detail is my part of the key," Brandon decided, feeling the certainty the moment it occurred to him. (One quest begets the other.) "Three," he muttered almost to himself. He carefully took the brooch from Roberta and studied it. "Thrice to accept the Seth, Thrice to give the Sephiroth, five black magicians, two of us. Two from five is three." He kept his eyes on the brooch, frowning. "We keep using the word 'key'. You're part of the key, I'm part of the key, the brooch is part of the key. Three again. That can't be a coincidence."

"Lost me," Roberta admitted.

"Keys."

"'Keys'," Roberta repeated.

"Keys open doors," Brandon said slowly.

"O-kay," Roberta said, "what doors?"

Brandon stood, the need for urgency he had the night before was suddenly and forcefully pressing on him. "I need to check a few of the minor arcana apocryphas."

"You figured it out?" Roberta asked.

"Yes," he nodded absently. "I think I have. All but the fine tuning."

"Care to share?"

Brandon stood abruptly. "I'll have the car take you back to your hotel. Pack lightly as though you're going on backpacking trip." He looked at the dial on his watch. "Three days. Three keys. The three of us. We'll leave at eight fourteen day after tomorrow. I'll have the car pick you up at seven." He walked out of the room and back into the house, heading rapidly toward his library. She heard a door slam in the distance.

"The three of us? What three? What keys? Leave for where?" she asked the closed door where Brandon had disappeared.

Perfect. The arrogance she had felt when she first met him was in full force. The line had been drawn. He was the boss, she was the employee. Her newly given 'peasant Page' sephiroth to his 'noble Knight' Seth.

Swell. She should have followed her first instincts when she met him and used that return ticket to Australia. Unfortunately, by formally agreeing to the sephiroth she couldn't get away from it. Quitting her new job because she had a jerk for a boss was not an option. "Nice talking to you," she called out.

"Ma'am?" came a confused voice.

Roberta looked over at the entrance from the patio back into the house, the man who had driven her here was standing just inside. "Sorry, just talking to myself," she picked up her purse and followed the chauffeur who would drive her back to her hotel.

Chapter 16 - Farewells

For that day and half of the next, Roberta was forced into her least favorite activity.

Shopping.

Since all she had brought with her to California was well-tailored casual and snobby accessories she had to buy only days before, (as per her mother's instance), she went shopping for Brandon's cryptic 'backpacking trip'.

Pack lightly, he told her. Sighing heavily, she went to the first outdoor retail store she found, wearing a ridiculously expensive beige linen outfit that suggested she would be going to a posh country club later to have lunch with 'the girls'.

Embarrassing.

It didn't start well. The 'helpful' little blond employee at the sporting good store, ("Hi, I'm Kristin!") who was dressed like a movie version of an Outback crocodile hunter in shorts, seemed to have more questions than answers. "Will you be backpacking in the mountains?" the girl asked, smiling broadly.

"Um, not sure." Roberta answered.

Kristin's smile faded somewhat. "Will you be fishing?"

"Not sure."

The helpful employee's smile faded a bit more, but she gamely pressed on. "Do you know what kind of weather you'll be backpacking in?"

"Not a clue," Roberta answered.

"Predicting the weather is always difficult," Kristin nodded, still trying for a positive outlook. "Well, an all weather jacket will be a must," she decided.

"Okay."

Kristin showed her an enormous circular display of colorful jackets. "These are all forty percent off," she said proudly.

Roberta looked at one of the labels. The $300.00 price-tag had a red line through it, $180 replaced it. "Great bargain," she didn't quite groan, then grabbed the first one she found in the right size at the least price. It was dark green camouflage.

"How large is your backpack?" Roberta's helpful shopping guide asked her.

"Don't have one," Roberta admitted, then decided a lie would cut through the rest of her non-answers. "My boyfriend is really into nature and backpacking, he thought it might bring us closer together. I think this is a test to see if we're compatible or something." She added in a whisper, "I just want to give him the impression that I know what the hell I'm doing. All he did say was to pack lightly."

The sales girl nodded and grinned, her previous chipper attitude returned with a vengeance. "Gotcha! We'll get ya looking like you're a pro," she promised.

"Great," Roberta answered with as much enthusiasm as she could muster.

When done, it only cost her one thousand eight hundred and seventy-two dollars to duplicate the same items the preservation society had purchased for her last backpacking trip to the inland rivers and lakes in the real Australian outback.

Small wonder they were always running out of funds if they shopped for these types of 'bargains'.

Back in her hotel room, as she was ripping off price tags and viciously stuffing her new four hundred dollar backpack with over priced freeze dried foods, first aid kit, and camelback water carrier, she mentally practiced several blistering remarks to make to Brandon Grayson. ("By the way, *Boss*, before we go any further, shouldn't we discuss my pay grade, work hours, overtime, my medical benefits, days off, personal days, retirement plan? More importantly, do I have a damned expense account for this stupid sephiroth?")

Okay, childish as hell, but thinking up more comments made her feel better. Just to be more childish, she sent the receipts for her little shopping excursion to her mother.

A mother's guilt was a beautiful thing. She called her on her cell phone.

"Bobby?"

"Hey, Mom. Uh..." Suddenly, tweaking her mother about her expensive shopping trip didn't feel so important.

"Are you okay?" Geneva's voice was heavy with concern.

"Fine. I just wanted to call because..." Why had she really called? "Apparently, Brandon Grayson and I are going on a trip."

"You've agreed to a sephiroth," Geneva concluded, quietly.

"Yeah. I can't tell you where we're going, mostly because I don't know, nor can I tell you how long I might be gone, because I don't know that, either. I just wanted you to know that I may be out of touch for awhile. Or not. For all I know we're off to the backside of Timbuktu where they don't have phone service. I don't want you to worry if you can't get hold of me for awhile."

There was a long pause. "Or possibly never seeing you again," Geneva answered tonelessly, in her knowing voice.

Roberta felt a severe chill at her words. "I love you, Mom," she put all the emotion she could into the statement. "Is Daddy there?"

"I love you too, baby," came the response in a soft voice that sounded suspiciously close to tears. "Here's you father."

Roberta's conversation with her father was almost as short, and just as heart wrenching.

***

By the time Roberta was led into the library on the designated morning, she was wearing her new clothes and her professional Doctor Roberta Griffin face. She put the new (and far too expensive) backpack down next to her feet (newly adorned by stiff two hundred dollar camping boots that would take a month to break in), then put her ('bargain' priced) jacket on top of it.

Brandon, she noted, was wearing ordinary jeans, a well worn leather jacket and equally well worn, probably comfortable, black boots. His backpack was not new and seemed like it had seen some heavy use. That irritated her more than a little. "So, what's the plan?"

Brandon looked at her sharply. The soft clipped up hairstyle she had been wearing when he had seen her last was now in a long braid hanging halfway down her back. She might look more casual, but seemed more official and uptight in appearance. "Is something wrong?"

"No," Roberta lied. "You walked out of our discussion a little abruptly the other day, I'm just feeling a bit out of the loop."

"Oh," he grimaced. "Sorry. I've been wracking my brain over this Seth for weeks, barely slept trying to figure it out even in my sleep, then when we were talking and... you could say I had a sudden epiphany and I had to check it out."

"Been there, done that," Roberta told him truthfully, thinking of all the assistants she had rudely ignored when she thought she had a breakthrough in the lab. "No apology necessary."

"Yes, it is. I really am sorry."

"Forget it," Roberta suggested, letting her frustration go. She looked at the fortune of gear at her feet. Mostly. "So. What was your epiphany?"

Brandon gestured to one of the wing-back chairs. "Sit, relax, have a cup of coffee. We have about," he looked at his watch, "thirty minutes."

"Until what?" Roberta a sat in the chair indicated. There were two coffee cups, a silver carafe between them, a silver creamer and another silver dish containing sugar cubes. One cup still had a small amount of white coffee in it, she filled the other one, black, and took a sip. Excellent blend.

Brandon rubbed the back of his neck and started pacing. "In the wine industry, I can sense when to reap, when to sow," he told her, "even when to do the cuttings. Its part of the sephiroth I was born with and given formally when I turned thirteen." He looked slightly embarrassed.

"Which would explain why your family has the most famous and productive vineyards in the world," Roberta put in.

"Partly, yes," Brandon shook his head. "This is hard to explain."

Roberta shook her head. "Not really. My mother's sephiroth has what I call moments of 'knowing'. I've more than learned to listen to her advice when she enters that area of her personality. Everyone else in the family recognizes it as well." Even the night before when she had the horrific feeling of a final 'goodbye forever' when she talked to her parents.

"Then you understand," he looked relieved. "According to my 'knowing', the time to sow is this morning, at eight fourteen. The moment of the full moon."

Roberta looked out the window at the clear blue sky. She'd have to take his word for it that there was a full moon out there, somewhere. "Okay, so we leave at oh eight-fourteen. Where are we going?"

"It's more a matter of how we get there, then where we're going," Brandon answered cryptically.

"Brandon," Roberta said firmly, not allowing the evasion. "Where are we going?"

"Yetzirah and Briah."

"What?" Roberta stared at him. "That's impossible!"

"I don't think is."

"But," Roberta decided to humor him. "O-kay, let's say it is possible. How?"

Brandon took a deep breath and combed his fingers through his hair. "If I'm right, it's almost too simple. The Seth-A-Tristan stated, 'realize thy knowledge and convention of innocence. One may be coaxed yet not coerced'. When you summon a sylph, you're coaxing it, like a child coaxing a butterfly or hummingbird to land on his finger. You hold it for only a moment, then release it, sending it back to Briah."

"As per the dictates of The Apocrypha," Roberta nodded. "Coaxed yet not coerced. Ask, never demand an elemental's compliance."

"Exactly. We were looking only at the whale and butterfly imprisoned in the brooch, not considering the too small aquarium and glass trap you mentioned at lunch."

Roberta nodded with false encouragement, still not knowing where the hell he was going with this.

Brandon continued. "We're not just working with two elementals, we're dealing with three elements. Gold is an element of Assiah, the undine is an element of Yetzirah, the sylph an element of Briah. If we can coax an undine and sylph back to their worlds from here, wouldn't it follow that we can also coax the Gold back to Assiah from there?"

"And yet," Roberta put in, "still being confused, I ask again, how do we get there?

Brandon ran his fingers through his hair. "I'm probably saying it wrong," he answered. "To stay within the 'two of earth, two of air, one of water', we both touch the gold, two of earth, we both touch the Sylph, two of air, only you touch the Undine, one of water. We coax all of us, at the same time, to your cusp world that touches all three in the same way. Then we release the elements back to their own worlds. Gold to Assiah, undine to Yetzirah, sylph to Briah."

"Through my cusp world on the way back to their own," Roberta repeated.

"Exactly."

"I'm not sure if that's brilliant, or just insane," Roberta answered. (Or if I'm just too dimwitted to figure out what he's saying), she added to herself.

"That's the beauty of it," Brandon went on, fully aware of her inner doubts. "If it works, we're there. If it doesn't work, we're no worse off than we are now and we'll try to think of something else."

"But you have a *knowing*," Roberta determined, trying not to sound as skeptical as she felt.

"Yes. I have a 'knowing'. I know this will work, by realizing my innate 'knowledge and convention of innocence'." He gave her a confident smile. "Only one detail is missing and then we're set."

"What?" Roberta asked, not trusting his 'I'm a used car salesman, I have a great deal for you, trust me,' smile.

"The name of the world we coax them to," he looked at her directly. "Your world. I need the name of your world and a formal invitation to go there."

Roberta froze, her gut clutched. That 'trust me' smile wasn't even remotely amusing any longer. Children in True Science named their own secret places and that name stayed a secret. It needed a much stronger trust than she had given him before with her full name. To give the name of her secret world and an actual invitation to it, gave the other person power, an open entrance into a world that wasn't theirs.

Brandon waited.

Roberta took a deep breath and finally nodded. "It's called Adelie."

Brandon still waited.

She took another deep breath. "I formally give you an invitation to Adelie." It actually hurt to say it, as though she was giving part of herself away.

"I accept your invitation and I promise to keep the name of your world safe," Brandon answered, knowing what it cost her. "Adelie," he repeated. "Unusual."

"It's a type of penguin. Clumsy on land, graceful in the sea," she explained. "Pretty much the way I felt when I was six." Pretty much the way she was feeling at the moment, she added to herself.

Brandon had a flash of memory of a little read-headed girl hidden behind a tree, then the memory was gone as though he'd never had it. "Trust works both ways. Roberta. The name of my world is Faucon d'épée. I formally give you an invitation to Faucon d'épée."

She gave him her first real smile of the day. "I accept your invitation and promise to keep the name of your world safe."

"We're partners in this," Brandon said seriously. "Equal trust."

"Equal trust," Roberta agreed, feeling a little less insecure.

Brandon looked at his watch, then at the backpack at her feet. "You have everything you need?"

"Freeze dried food, water, personal necessities, a change of clothing. I've backpacked before," she assured him (a hell of a lot less expensively, and in much more comfortable boots).

Brandon looked at his watch, took his own loaded backpack from the chair in front of his desk and put it on. "Let's try this then," he took the envelope containing the brooch and opened it, throwing the empty envelope on the desk. The velvet bag containing the pearl he had already put in his jeans pocket, but patted the pocket again to make doubly sure.

The night before he had put his affairs in order, put the new vineyard in the capable hands of Anton Larousse. If this worked, there was a strong possibility that it would take more than a little time to finish the quest.

Assuming they could return at all. "It's almost time."

Roberta also slipped on her pack. "Do you really think this might work?" she sounded unconvinced.

"It feels right." He held out the brooch and took her left hand in his right, then kissed her hand lightly. "For luck," he told her. He put his left thumb under the brooch touching the gold, his forefinger gently over the sylph. Roberta, put her right thumb over both the sylph and undine touching the gold of Assiah by using the thin line between the two.

"Wait!" she said abruptly. "Assuming this works, how do we get back?"

"Again, simple. We release ourselves back to Assiah from your cusp world the same way we release the gold."

"Right," she answered, still more confused than enlightened.

"You ready?"

What the hell. She was dressed for adventure, she had to start somewhere. 'No guts, no glory'. She took a deep breath, holding his free hand tightly. "Ready."

"Think like a child. Trust yourself. Remember how you felt. 'Realize thy knowledge and convention of innocence'," he instructed, then also took a breath. "Together we coax the Gold, then we coax the sylph and you coax the undine. I've set the alarm on my watch. On the first chime we both coax the gold, Assiah et Adelie, second chime we both coax the sylph, Briah et Adelie, third time you alone coax the undine. Two of Earth, two of air, one of water."

The first chime sounded, "Two of Earth," Brandon said.

They said the words together. "Ki Akal Assiah et Adelie."

"Two of Air."

The second chime sounded,

Again, they spoke the words together. "Ki Akal Briah et Adelie."

"One of water," Brandon looked at her expectantly.

The third chime sounded, Roberta spoke alone, "Ki Akal Yetzirah et Adelie," then she added out of habit, "go in peace my beautiful, wonderful friend."

They both vanished from Brandon's office.

Pricilla was posed on the diving board at the pool in the middle of the last jump before she dove in when she felt the pull. She looked with concern at Aaron who was talking on the phone at the poolside table. "Aaron?"

He looked up, putting up a finger to show he heard her, but had to finish listening to the other side of the conversation.

Pricilla gave him an apologetic smile. "I have to go, love, sorry." She finished the dive, going toward the water.

Aaron was watching her, not sure what she was apologizing for as her hands hit the water. "Five hells!" he put the phone down abruptly and stood. There was no splash, no ripple in the water when Pricilla simply disappeared.

Crossroads - Adelie

"Well," Roberta was still holding Brandon's hand and let it go, using it to help cradle the water ball holding the undine. "That almost worked as advertised."

Brandon used his own hand to gently hold the sylph in his left hand. "Not exactly what I hoped for, but at least the gold of Assiah is gone," he pointed out.

"So is everything else we brought with us from Assiah," Roberta advised him. She looked down and laughed, mostly at herself. Instead of her overpriced camp clothing, she was wearing a blue gray shirt with a v-neck tie closure and dark green pants, also laced. On her feet were soft brown shoes. All that self-made angst about overpriced clothing and gear for nothing. "This is too weird," she continued to laugh. It was an adult version of the clothes she had worn when she visited Adelie as a child. Even the hair band that had been holding her braid was gone she realized, as her unraveling hair fell over her shoulder. "Apparently what's wholly of Assiah, stays in Assiah." She grinned. "You look very, uh, fashion trendy, yourself."

Brandon looked at his own attire, he was wearing a blousy white shirt, soft leather vest and pants, his shoes were also of soft leather. It was the same 'Robin Hood' outfit he remembered wearing in Briah as a kid. At least it wasn't too embarrassing. He'd never given in to wearing the 'merry men' tights and the pointy hat with a feather or carried a longbow and arrows. He looked around at their surroundings and grinned. "But we're here. We're actually here." To their right was a vast ocean that went on forever, to his left a deep forest. They were standing on a dirt track, separating the two.

Roberta noticed his curiosity, then looked around herself, studying with adult eyes a world she had only known as child. "Welcome to my world."

"Thank you for the invitation," Brandon stared down at the sylph in his hands. It was still in a bubble of air, still not completely free. "Let's finish this part of it. These little guys have been imprisoned long enough," he suggested.

"Agreed. The sylph you can release here, air travels easily where it will. But the undine," she smiled at the tiny creature swimming inside the bubble she was holding, "This little guy needs his own element before I

130

let it go." She started walking toward the ocean. "You take care of yours, I'll take care of mine."

Brandon looked down at the bubble of air and pinched the top, bursting it. "Ki Akal, Briah. Welcome home, my friend." He grinned as he watched the tiny flicker of light soar up and over into the trees. He felt good, as though he were a true hero, an honest Knight of Swords. God only knew how long the poor sylph had been trapped, now it was truly, completely free and he had been the one to unlock the prison door. He turned to see if Roberta felt the same satisfaction after releasing the undine.

His smile faded, his feeling of euphoria instantly died. She was out in the ocean, maybe a hundred yards away, swimming strongly. Three dolphins swam beside her, a smaller one raced on ahead. "Roberta! Where are you going? What are you doing?"

As he ran toward the water, a tidal wave of dark blue ocean rose up almost a hundred feet high in front of him, blocking his view. It stopped, just hanging there, waiting for him to try to pass. He stepped back a few feet, the water rushed back down and into the sea, not leaving as much as a ripple.

(One gate will open to thee, one other will not.)

Damn, damn, damnit! She was fully in Yetzirah, completely out of his jurisdiction. "Roberta!" Brandon tried again to reach the ocean, the wave again rose to block him. He pounded on the impossible wall of water, drenching his hands and clothes, but unable to get through. Again he backed up a few steps, again the wave went back into the sea. "Roberta!" She kept swimming further away.

She didn't hear him, she never even turned her head to look back at him.

Chapter 17 - Yetzirah

Brandon paced until he got tired, then plopped heavily on the sand about a yard from where the water would rise if he tried to get past the gate into Yetzirah. He watched the waves and let out an annoyed sigh. He'd been sitting there for close to an hour. He could barely make out the top of Roberta's head now. Still, he kept calling to her, whistling to her, willing her to look back.

He cupped his hands around his mouth one more time. "Roberta!!!" he yelled.

Terrific. Less than five minutes after they'd arrived and the quest had already gone to hell. "Damnit, Roberta!" Even going back to Assiah was no longer an option. He had to send her back, she needed to send him back according to the formula he had divined from the Seth-A-Tristan-et Yetzirah.

"Roberta! Damnit! Get your butt back here!" he yelled for the umpteenth time.

"Thy companion hears thee not, she is unknown to thee and will not heed thy call," a musical voice came from the left of him.

Brandon turned, startled, then his eyes widened, staring in astonishment, unbelieving. On a rock a few yards into the water sat an honest to God mermaid. Brilliant red hair flowed down her back, her large breasts were exposed, her tail was a shimmering blue and green with an added silver sheen.

Well, if he hadn't believed in a fantasy world before, this was a very vivid reminder that he wasn't in Assiah any more.

The mermaid gave him a coquettish smile. "Dost thou find my form lovely, Son of Assiah?" she posed, her face tilted toward the sun, thrusting out her breasts more prominently, nipples erect. She swished her tail in the water provocatively.

Brandon took a deep breath. Okay. A mermaid. A talking mermaid that positively oozed sensuality. He could almost see the pheromones drifting toward him. Well, he temporized, she oozed sensuality from the waist up, in any event.

Terrific. He didn't know anything about Yetzirah, except that he couldn't get through the damned water wall to reach it and now he had to deal with an over-sexed mermaid that was half turning him on.

She turned to him, her lips formed into a pout, annoyed that he didn't answer. "Dost thou *not* find me lovely, Son of Assiah?" she sounded incredulous at that possibility and flipped her tail angrily.

To imagine he could converse with or even imagine this creature was beyond him. Now what? Think, Brandon, think. What did he remember about mermaids? Very little, he answered his own question. All he remembered was that they sat on rocks and combed their hair, usually wore half seashells to cover their breasts (the cartoon mermaids evidently took liberties to get their G rating) and lured sailors to their deaths for sport.

A mermaid. Think. They were beautiful, selfish, vain, deadly and... vain. Also, he thought with a glimmer of an idea, she was on the other side of the gate, in Yetzirah. She was half fish and could swim like one. With a little persuasive charm he might be able to get her to swim after Roberta and drag her back. He got up from the sand and bowed. "You are very beautiful," Brandon assured her, going for the vanity. Her pout remained, so he added carefully, "you are so very, very, lovely you took my breath away and I was unable to speak or move for a moment."

She preened and smiled. "Thou art forgiven," she decided, with a sassy flip of her tail.

Score one for vanity. "I need my companion to return, beautiful lady, but she is too far away to hear me. Could you get her for me?"

She looked interested. "Perhaps," she looked toward Roberta and the dolphins, then back at him, her expression sly. "Dost thou request the siren's call, Son of Assiah?"

The Siren's call? Not his first choice, but, "Will she hear your call? Will it bring her back?"

"Perhaps." She shrugged, batting her eyelashes. "If she wishes it."

Drawn to her eyes, Brandon noticed they were a brilliant, spectacular, green. Every male cell in his body came to attention. Damn, she was gorgeous. Sensuous... and those incredibly beautiful eyes, a man could...

Whoa! Damn! Had he actually been considering sex with a fish? Shaking off lustful thoughts he was fairly (hopefully) certain were not his own, he decided to cut to the chase before he forgot his own name and drowned in the water wall before he could reach her and do whatever it was men did with an anatomically incorrect species.

The mermaid smiled with a 'come hither' expression.

Nothing was free, he reminded himself, ignoring his increasingly interested libido that apparently had a secret life of its own. "At what cost to me if she comes to your siren's call?" Brandon managed to ask, forcing himself back to a modicum of sanity.

She considered Roberta and the dolphins, while swaying a little on her rock throne. "Let us see..." she mused, then turned and smiled at him.

"Thy price could be... thy companion's passion for the sea!"

"No!" Brandon answered instantly, horrified at the thought. "Her passions are her own. They are not mine to give."

She gave a heavy sigh and thought for a long moment. She smiled, looking at him innocently, her tail swinging gently in the water. "Upon thyself is a bobble rare. Wouldst thou give it as adornment for my pretty hair?"

A bobble? Brandon padded his pants. felt the lump of the Yetzirah pearl and sighed in relief. He had completely forgotten it since arriving in Adelie. Between losing all his worldly possessions, releasing the sylph and Roberta's desertion, he was apparently going brain dead. Now a mermaid who wanted the pearl, the very basis of the Seth-A-Tristan et Yetzirah, their reason for being here.

The mermaid was still looking at him expectantly for an answer. Charm. He needed to use charm. Vanity, thy name is mermaid, he reminded himself. "The bobble is all wrong for you. Your beautiful hair needs no adornment, it's so lovely as it is. To add anything to your hair would take away from its perfection."

She gave a delighted tinkle of a laugh. "Thy words are pleasing to me. Wouldst thou offer thy friendship willingly?" she asked. "I would ask for a kiss to give me bliss, but the waters find your source remiss."

Willingly. There was a probable trap there. Brandon thought about it for several seconds not sure exactly what she meant or how to respond, again remembering those sailors who had been lured to their deaths. "If you will return that friendship," he answered carefully, "I will offer you my friendship willingly."

She sat up with a regal posture. "Then I will aid thee, voices three," she turned back toward the water and started singing.

"Bethesicyme, Bethesicyme, daughter of Amphitrite, near daughter of the oceans be,
"Come to me, sister, come to me! Thy sister Rhodes doth call to thee!"

Four hells! Her voice was uncanny, impossibly covering three octaves at the same time. Brandon had to cover his ears, but he could still hear her song, it was both enchanting and mesmerizing.

Again she sang the words with three voices, the music rising and falling with the rhythm of the ocean.

"Bethesicyme, Bethesicyme, daughter of Amphitrite, near daughter of the oceans be,

134

"Come to me, sister, come to me! Thy sister Rhodes twice calls to thee!"

He could feel the pull, even though it wasn't directed at him. If the myths of the sirens' song held any truth, he could more than understand why sailors steered their ships into the rocks.

"Bethesicyme, Bethesicyme, daughter of Amphitrite, near daughter of the oceans be,
"Come to me, sister, come to me! Thy sister Rhodes thrice calls to thee!"

His ears were ringing so loudly from the impossible sound of her singing, he almost missed Roberta's voice when she spoke.

"Darn it, Rhodes!" She was near the mermaid's rock in waist deep water. "Why do you use the siren's call?" she sounded annoyed. "You know I don't like that! It hurts my ears." She had some sea grass in her hands and gave it to Rhodes. "Will you fix my hair for me, please, sister? Please? I can never get the back of it straight, I forgot to tie it in a ribbon and it tumbles in my eyes. Please, Rhodes? Pretty please?"

"Sister," the mermaid answered, smiling as she leaned over and worked on Roberta's hair with deft fingers. "Thou hast been led astray." She looked over at Brandon. "Thy companion is handsome with a pleasing way. Wouldst thou leave him to mercies mine, or is this son of Assiah thine?"

Roberta stood still as Rhodes finished working her hair into a smooth braid with the sea grass twined within her hair like a ribbon. She looked at Brandon with confusion and frowned. "Son of Assiah? My companion?"

Brandon gave her an irritated half wave. "Hello, remember me? The person you came with?"

Roberta still looked confused, shook her head and frowned, looking back at Rhodes for more information.

"Tis to his shame, Bethesicyme, he doth not know thy name," Rhodes told her sadly.

"Why are you talking so silly?" Roberta asked the mermaid, tilting her head curiously.

"Your name is Bethesicyme?" Brandon asked Roberta at the same time.

Roberta's face cleared. "Oh! Hello, Mister!" She glanced toward the mermaid then back at him, with an expression of worry. "What did you give my sister for her siren's call?"

"Fear not, Bethesicyme," Rhodes answered before Brandon could speak. "He offered mere friendship, willingly."

"Willingly?" Roberta's eyes opened wide as she continued to look at Brandon. "Wha' for?"

"For her friendship in return," Brandon answered. "Is that going to be a problem?" There was a small splash, when he looked toward the sound, both the rock and the mermaid were gone.

"You never know with Rhodes," Roberta answered and walked out of the water, "she can be naughty and only talks in rhyme when she's after something she's not supposed to have. She can talk like a reg'lar person when she wants to." As she walked back into Adelie, the gray swimsuit she was wearing changed back into the blue gray shirt and deep green pants she had on when they first arrived.

Brandon looked at her with surprise. "How do you do that?"

"Do what?" Roberta asked curiously.

"One moment you're wearing... then you're wearing," he gestured at her clothes, then touched the beautifully designed braid now hanging over her shoulder curiously. "And your hair's dry."

Roberta shrugged. "I would never swim in my clothes! That would be silly!" her voice was that of a child. "And if my hair's wet, it just drips in my eyes and gets my shirt all wet. That would be silly, too!" she paused. "Does my hair look too grown up?" she sounded a little worried by the possibility.

"No, it looks very nice." *Grown up.* "Oh, shit!"

"Ooh... That's a bad word," Roberta told him, her eyes wide with shock. "You shouldn't say bad words, Mister. That's naughty."

Brandon took her arm, walked closer to the Briah side of Adelie and pulled her down to the ground, urging her to sit in front of him, knees touching. "We need some rules here," he told her.

"Rules?" Roberta glared at him. "No! This is my world! You can't make up any silly rules!" She started to get up.

"Roberta," Brandon said carefully, pushing her back down by her shoulders. She frowned at him, her eyes showing that she was willing to throw a temper tantrum. "Bobby," he added gently, lifting her chin into his hand. "Listen to yourself, sweetheart. You're sounding like a little girl. Your hair looks grown-up because you are all grown up now. This isn't the dream world you remember. We're here, physically, not in our imaginations."

"But..."

"You're not a child," Brandon reminded her and kissed her softly, carefully keeping the contact innocent as though she was really the young girl she acted. "*Jachin*, Roberta Bethany Griffin. You're a woman, not a child." He kissed her again, this time it was a little less than an innocent kiss and he detected a slight response. He touched her forehead with his. "That's it, Bobby, concentrate. *Jachin*. We're all adults here. Be the grown-up woman you are, not the child you once were. *Jachin*," he repeated for the third time.

Roberta touched her lips as she pulled her head back, searching his eyes. "Okay, that was strange," she said in her normal voice. Seeing his expression she grimaced. "Thank you. Excellent strategy."

Brandon smiled. "Curled your toes, did it?"

"If it did, I'd keep it to myself," Roberta returned the smile. "Very bad for a working relationship."

Brandon stood, then pulled her up by both hands. "Just another complication," he said cheerfully. He let go of her hands and looked around at their surroundings. "This world of yours seems a little... bleak."

"Well," Roberta studied the dirt track between the forest and ocean with adult eyes. "This part of it could use a decorator," she admitted. "But it's only my 'landing site' as it were. All of Yetzirah on one side of the gate, Briah on the other. I really didn't care how the path in between looked. Besides. Who plays in the road?"

"Good point, where does the road go?"

"Not a clue," Roberta admitted with a grin. "Like the curious chicken, I just crossed the road to get to the other side." She gestured to the right, "Briah there," she gestured to the left, "Yetzirah there."

Brandon nodded, "Well, I should at least be able get into the Briah side," he told her, then looked back toward the left, remembering the wave of water with annoyance. "But getting into Yetzirah is going to be a major problem for me. The entrance to that part of you world did a really good job of blocking me out."

"You're a sword, not a cup. It's natural that it's closed to you."

"I know. That's the problem."

"Because of the pearl? That's not an issue. I can take it into Yetzirah for you." She looked at the ocean, remembering her relapse into childhood when she'd entered the water. Maybe not. "Or, you could simply throw it into the water yourself. Since it's originally from Yetzirah, it should pass through the gate with no problem."

"I'm sure it would," Brandon agreed. "Unfortunately, it needs to be returned to the island cave it was taken from and I'm the person who has to take it."

"Either I missed that part of our discussion regarding 'complications' or you failed to mention that little stipulation," Roberta raised an eyebrow and looked out at the ocean. "So. We have two more complications."

"Two?"

Roberta nodded. "You can't get into Yetzirah and, even if you could, how are you going to find the cave you need to return the pearl to?" she asked shaking her head. "That's one big ocean, Brandon. Lots of islands, lots of caves," she assured him.

Brandon nodded. "Any suggestions?"

Roberta considered their options. "Well, I don't know how to get you into Yetzirah, but my sister might be able to help with the second part, she likes exploring caves, she probably knows them all. Of course it might take a year or two to get her back once she starts searching. She's easily distracted."

Brandon thought about the half naked Rhodes and turned to her. "About your 'sister', Rhodes."

Roberta's eyes twinkled. "Flirted with you, did she?"

"Mostly she just posed to show off her impressive... attributes," Brandon answered. "What concerns me is that she asked about the pearl. She wanted it for payment before she would help me. I didn't give it to her, but it was a close call."

"What?" Roberta looked toward the sea. "Why did she want it? More to the purpose, how did Rhodes even know about the pearl?"

"She says she sensed it."

Roberta shook her head. "I don't think so. She can't even sense me until I cross into the Yetzirah side," she told him. "That doesn't sound good."

"You didn't tell her about it?"

"The pearl? When? I didn't even notice she was here until after the siren's call." Roberta thought about it. "Who else knows about the pearl?"

"You, me, the Magus and..." He had a flash of memory that eluded him before he could grasp the significance.

"And?"

Brandon shook his head. "Something I can't seem to remember."

"Something?"

Brandon thought about the dream he'd had before they started, a wrongness. "No, not a wrongness, more like a..." He tried to find the right words. "An obstacle." That almost fit, but more of a... "Something is running interference." There. That was a perfect fit. Not a 'wrongness', an 'interference'.

"Something? What kind of 'thing'? Why would you think..."

"I have to get going," Brandon announced abruptly, interrupting her, and started quickly walking into the trees further into Briah. "There's a wrongness in Faucon d'épée."

"Hey!" Roberta had to run up to catch him, tripping over the uneven ground, finally grabbing him by the arm to get his attention. He kept walking, ignoring her. "Hello? Remember me? We were having a conversation?" She yanked more forcefully on his arm. "Hello? Brandon!" she said sharply, "stop!"

Brandon stopped, turned and looked at her curiously. "Je ne vous ai pas vu, Madame, pardonne s'il vous plaît ma violation. Est-ce que je vous connais?"

"Ah... Oh, damn," she answered, recognizing the young and innocent expression. "Time to grow up, Sir Knight." She stood on tiptoe, grabbed his face in her hands and kissed him, pulling back after a brief moment of contact. "Jachin, Brandon Grayson," she said. "Come on, snap out of it! Grown woman, grown man, remember? Wine, women, song?"

Brandon gave her a blank look, she tried the same words in French. "*Jachin*, Brandon Grayson. Rupture hors de elle. La femme développée, adulte, se rappellent? Vin, femmes, chanson?" Still nothing. She glared at him with frustration. "*Jachin*, Brandon Grayson. Please grow up. You are not a boy, you're a man. A very handsome, full grown, sexy man." He blinked. "*Jachin*, Brandon Grayson," she added a fourth time. "You are a handsome, sexy man. *Jachin*."

"Thank you," Brandon grinned. "About time you acknowledged that fact." He kissed her again, with a lot more passion, pulling her close. "I think this attraction complication has some nice side benefits going for it, don't you?"

"Jerk!" Roberta punched him in the shoulder. "You were faking it!"

"Only after the third 'Jachin'," he answered honestly, reluctantly letting her go, "Apparently three's the magic number around here, that's when you came out of it, too. Wow! that was strange! Not the kissing part," he assured her quickly, "before that. I honestly felt like I was ten years old again."

"Trust me, I know the feeling," Roberta assured him, concentrating. "'Realize thy knowledge and convention of innocence.'"

Brandon nodded. "Then, the second line in that stanza to the Seth. 'One may be coaxed but not coerced' There were two parts to the stanza. My guess is the first part was to get us here, using the innocence of a child, the second was how to snap us out of it so we wouldn't get lost in that childhood."

"Coaxing by kissing? Damned good thing we didn't become children at the same time," Roberta remarked.

"Luckily, I didn't start thinking like a kid until I'd been on the Briah side for several minutes, I had no problem when we were in your 'landing zone' closer to Yetzirah." He thought about it worriedly. "When you became a child and I didn't, I made the stupid assumption that I was immune." He shook his head. "We could fall into a lot of unexpected traps here. We need to keep reminding ourselves of the words of the Seth."

Roberta nodded in agreement. "I wish I'd taken more time to memorize it. I really hate riddles. They only make sense after the obvious consequence. Worse, I've never had a sephiroth, or followed someone with Seth before, I have no real knowledge of what in the four hells I'm doing."

"Your first sephiroth, my first Seth. A fantasy world that's no longer a fantasy. Blind leading the blind."

"Great confidence builder, Sir Knight. The good news for me, you're the Senior blind team member. You get to take all the blame when things get totally screwed up," she smiled. "Anyway, back to my original question before you went all French snobby on me. Don't do that again, by the way, your accent throws me. I only speak French-Canadian, with whole other colloquialisms," she told him. "Speaking of which, why were you speaking in French at all? My mother told me you were born in Napa."

"We moved to my Grandfather's chateau in France when I turned eight, I didn't return to the states and start speaking English again until I was eighteen. It took two years after we got back to the states before I was able to even think in English again and shed the accent."

"Got it. Damnit, I'm off track again," she noted. "Back to the original question. Where are we going?" She seemed to be asking that question a lot lately.

"Faucon d'épée," he told her. "I'm pretty sure it's this way, but I need a reference point." He started walking into the trees again.

"What kind of a reference point?" Roberta asked, catching up and taking his hand.

Brandon looked at their hands. "Are we going steady now?"

"Ha, ha. Just keeping adult contact so we don't revert back into our juvenile selves."

"We've already faced and conquered that portion of the Seth," Brandon assured her, but didn't let go of her hand. "Besides, if kissing doesn't work the next time, we can try some heavy petting," he grinned. "Then, if that doesn't work..."

"Men. They never want to actually work for the final payoff by dinner, dancing and even minimal courtship," Roberta complained. "Nope, they use any feeble excuse that comes to mind." She squeezed his hand gratefully. She didn't want to admit it, but this whole experience was beginning to feel damned scary.

Brandon gave equal pressure to her hand in return. "Scared, Bobby?"

"Yes. But you were supposed to pretend you didn't notice and just keep up the sexual banter so I wouldn't dwell on it," she told him. "Okay. We're going to your world in Briah because you need a reference point. Reference point to where or what?"

"The island in Yetzirah we need to find. It can be seen from the cliffs near Faucon d'épée."

"You have cliffs overlooking an ocean in your world? That's cool."

"Sorry to disappoint. They're in my Grandfather's world, not mine." Brandon answered. "I've never actually seen the cliffs," he admitted.

"Oh. And you can get into your Grandfather's world from your world?"

"Hopefully, yes. I've never actually been there, but I understand they're close to each other. The borders might even touch. He gave me a formal invitation and a verbal map to it on the day he died. It was part of my inheritance, the same as the pearl." He answered.

"You're going to explain that rather cryptic statement on our way, right?" Roberta asked. "What inheritance?"

So, for the second time in his life, he told a virtual stranger the story of Phineas Tristan and what the Magus had called a minor transgression that had become his formal Seth.

Diminishing Star

("Beth Celandine et Ce-Cill akal Whilom et Nebulae. Now!")

Aaron was pacing the living room floor when Pricilla finally materialized, wearing her usual green Whilom clothing.

"I greet thee, Magus of Power by Eternal lemniscate."

"Celandine... Ce-Cill," Aaron said gently. "What's my name?"

"Thou art named, A-Ronaday et Elis et Pyrrho et..."

Aaron held up a hand, stopping the litany of his full name. "My informal name, Ce-Cill."

"Thou art A-Ron," she answered curiously.

Aaron let out a sigh of relief. "I need you to come home now, Ce-Cill. I need you need to come back to Assiah, now." *(Ki Celandine akal Whilom,)* he added mentally, releasing her.

Moments later, Pricilla was next to him, wearing the bathing suit she had been wearing before she unexpectedly disappeared. "Hey!" she said cheerfully.

"Thank God," Aaron pulled her to him, holding her tightly.

"What's wrong?" Pricilla pulled back to see his face. "What was the urgency?"

"You were gone almost twenty hours," Aaron told her, "and you left before you'd been here for less than three hours."

Pricilla grinned. "So you decided to call me back from Whilom like a truant kid who was late for supper? And Celandine is some neighborhood mom who's going to send me home? Does that mean I don't get any dessert tonight?"

Aaron took her face in her hands. "This isn't even remotely funny, Love. You're starting to spend more time in Whilom than here. Its like you need that phone call to your Celandine self to remind you to come home. This is the third time this week."

"Oh. I'm sorry, Aaron. Sometimes I get caught up in some little details and I forget about..."

"About me?" Aaron asked her.

"No!" Pricilla answered him quickly. "Never about you. But Assiah seems so... I'm sorry, Aaron."

"Assiah seems so what?"

Pricilla bit her bottom lip. "Not real sometimes. More like a dream. A wonderful dream, but... a place I want to find, but its just a little past my... as though I have to be asleep to..." she couldn't think of how to explain it. "Assiah is a fantasy, a world of..."

"Fantasy. The way Whilom used to be to you," Aaron suggested. "'Real, but not. Essence but not'?" He quoted her own words, "Oft dreamed, never forgotten?"

"Yes," she admitted, looking a little frightened. "This isn't good, is it?"

Aaron closed his eyes and took a deep breath, then kissed her deeply. "We'll figure this out," he promised.

Hopefully before one day she wouldn't answer his call at all, believing both he and Assiah were only a dream she could never physically find.

Despite the incomplete information he knew about the Assiah armband, not knowing exactly the consequences, it was becoming more and more obvious he would have to use it.

Trap an elemental willingly or unwillingly.

Bind and shackle the love of his life.

Chapter 18 - Briah

"I need a break," Roberta announced. "We're going in circles."

They had been wandering around for several hours. "Maybe my internal compass stayed on Assiah," Brandon sounded discouraged. He leaned against a tree while Roberta flopped on the ground, her head cushioned on a pile of leaves, her forearm covering her eyes.

"Great. More good news," she muttered.

"It might have been wiser if we hadn't conquered my 'childhood innocence' part of the Seth so quickly," he continued, "I remember knowing exactly how to get to Faucon d'épée when I started walking into Briah as my child self, now I'm not sure where the hell we are."

"We're still in Briah," Roberta told him, "That's pretty much all I'm sure of."

"In short, we're lost," Brandon slid down the tree and sat.

"To be honest, at the moment, I seriously don't give a damn," Roberta yawned. "I'm just tired. Swimming is so much easier than walking."

Brandon relaxed against the trunk of the tree. "It will be dark soon, I suggest we camp out here tonight. Maybe after a few hours of rest, we'll think of something." He looked around. "There are enough leaves to make a better pillow with my vest." He smiled at her. "You going to make one with your shirt?"

Roberta lifted the collar of her Briah designed shirt and peered inside. "Nope. I'm nekkid under here, not even a bra. That's way too fast for a first date."

"Your count's off," Brandon started ticking off fingers. "We're on our third date," he advised her. "First date we had wine in my office; second date, lunch with a rather stimulating skin to skin connection, as I recall; third date... well, there was some pretty decent kissing going on there for a moment or two, but then you stated we're supposed to have dinner and dancing before I make a more aggressive move," he frowned. "That prerequisite is not only outrageous, by the way, but might be an insurmountable problem for me."

Roberta smiled. "First date you made me throw-up, second date you tied me to a sephiroth, which I'll grant had its interesting, electric, even encouraging moments, but then you walked out abruptly canceling even that thrill. As for the third date... Okay, I'll give you the pretty decent kissing," she admitted, "but I'm still not getting naked until after that dinner and dancing, maybe not even then. I need to be courted and wooed," she told him. "'I'm a good girl, I am'," she added in a bad cockney accent.

Brandon sighed. "Women always have a way of minimizing romantic encounters," he complained. He leaned more comfortably against the tree. "Damn. I am really hungry."

"Do you want apples, oranges, bananas, cherries, strawberries or pears for dinner?" she asked, lifting the arm from her eyes just enough to see him.

"If we're going to wish for food, I'd prefer a nice prime rib with au jus and horseradish, Yorkshire pudding and an excellent Fils Gris Bordeaux 1979, to go with it. Or, grilled Chicken with rice pilaf and a Fils Gris Chardonnay, 1994. Add sautéed vegetables on the side of either entree, no mushrooms. I'll forego the Chocolate soufflé for dessert and instead top if off with a good Cognac."

"I'll order that right up for you," Roberta answered. "If you don't mind, however, I think I'll have the Chocolate soufflé or a Drambuie for dessert."

"If we're going more casual," Brandon continued, "order a giant angus burger with fries and a Classic Coke, or even the damned freeze dried food from our backpacks, that we no longer have," he told her, then looked depressed. "Okay, that was a mistake. Now I'm really hungry. Whose lousy idea was it to talk about food?"

"Yours, but I don't think food was the original topic of discussion," she smiled. "You were just making up excuses for getting me nekkid."

Brandon grinned. "Very true and it's still a good plan, but now I'm more hungry than romantically inclined."

Roberta laughed. "Well, prime rib is out, but if you'd look up, you'd notice you're under an apple tree. At three o'clock, there's a banana tree, five o'clock, orange, pear and peach trees and somewhere in the brush are raspberries and strawberries. Maybe some carrots, as well, but I'm not sure. Those we'll have to search for." She covered her mouth and yawned again, then closed her eyes. "Wake me up when you get back to the romantic banter, but be warned, I still want the dancing before I'll even consider getting nekkid."

Brandon looked up. Impossibly, the tree he had been leaning against really was loaded down with apples. "Not to be critical, but apples aren't supposed to grow on cypress trees," he told her.

"My world, my rules. I never spent much time in Briah, I was more comfortable in Yetzirah, I liked it better there. Besides, what did I know about horticulture at age six? I wanted apples in my world, that's where they grew."

"You're kidding, right?"

"Nope. Its all part of the snack bar I added as a kid." She told him. "Eating sushi when it's still wiggling with life didn't appeal to me, so I put food on this side that didn't stare at me with wounded eyes. What did you snack on in your world, hot dogs and beans, a Big Mac with fries, or Chateaubriand and truffles?"

"Freshly killed squirrels and rabbits, mostly." Brandon started climbing the tree for the apples.

Roberta uncovered her eyes and asked, "out of curiosity, what kind of wine goes with squirrel and rabbit? White or red?"

"A domestic Zinfandel would be best, I think," Brandon said with a straight face. "But, since I was in the form of a hawk when I dined on such haut cuisine, I never found out."

"Not to mention you were underage."

Brandon rolled his eyes. "Please. My family owns wineries. I was wine tasting before I was eight." He hoisted himself onto a low hanging branch, plucked several apples and threw one down to her. "Heads up."

"Thanks," Roberta grabbed the apple that landed next to her and sat up with a groan. "I'm getting too old for camping." She bit into the apple. "Perfect. Always just crisp enough, never a bruise. I made great snack food when I was a kid."

Brandon sat comfortably on one of the large branches, also munching on an apple. "You also made a great climbing tree," he told her. "Sturdy but with just enough give."

"Doesn't give you splinters either," Roberta told him. "Another one of my kid rules." She looked at him curiously. "What are you wearing? You look almost invisible in that tree. Even your hair color blends in."

Brandon looked at his pants, they were exactly the mottled color of the branch he was sitting on. "Huh. Must have been something I did as a kid to stalk prey when I was in Faucon d'épée. You manufacture a swimsuit in Yetzirah, I'm suddenly clothed in ever changing camouflage when I'm in a tree in Briah. Weird," he dismissed it with a shrug. "So. What other kid rules does your world have? Always perfect weather?" Brandon speculated, devouring the apple.

"When I'm in Briah, yes, but on the Yetzirah side there are a lot of spectacular storms. Lightning, thunder, hail, waterspouts, you name it. I don't make any rules there."

"Why not?" Brandon threw the apple he had eaten down to the core into some bushes several yards away, then pulled another one.

"Nothing's stationary in the ocean except a few islands and I'm not so sure about those. You can't stake a claim and announce 'mine' in the middle of the sea." She thought about it. "Then again, there might be some underwater cities like Atlantis. That would be cool."

"You made underwater cities?"

Roberta mused. "I honestly don't remember." She shrugged. "Fantasy dreams, regular dreams, children's books, they all seem to merge together after awhile," she told him. "What nifty things do you have in your world?"

"Lots of trees to land on, a stream to drink from. The stream is about the width of the one we passed twenty minutes or so ago, but mine has big fat tasty fish to catch," he thought about it. "Maybe a cote or two when I wanted to take a rest. I don't remember half of what I created in Faucon d'épée."

"Sounds wonderful. I look forward to seeing it. I've never been invited into someone's world before."

"I've never invited anyone in before. It'll be nice to share it and explore my childhood fantasies." He smiled, thinking about it. "Damn, it was fun being a kid."

"I know. I miss it too. I was never scared, never worried about getting hurt. What's it like to fly?" Roberta asked wistfully.

"You've never flown?" Brandon looked surprised, "not even as a butterfly or a sparrow when you were in Briah?"

"Nope. I never changed shape in either world. It was my fantasy to fit in, just as I was." She stood and brushed off the back of her pants. "Apples are great, but about as filling as water. I'll go find some bananas." She started off into the trees.

"Don't wander too far, stay in sight," Brandon warned her. "And while you're shopping for food," he called at her retreating back, "see if you can find some of those hot dogs you mentioned. A man has to eat!"

"Men! Keep a nice house and he still bitches about his dinner. Complain, complain, complain. And my mother wonders why I never married," Roberta muttered loudly.

Brandon grinned as he watched her walk away. They may not have resolved the issue of finding Faucon d'épée, or figuring out where the cave in Yetzirah was, or even how to get there once they found the information, but he was actually having a great time. She was beautiful, smart, adventurous and held her own when he tried to get too bossy.

It was curious that he hadn't met her before. Third generation True Science families were not all that numerous. There were always parties to bring couples together. Formal sephiroths often merged together, some matches were automatic because of it. He'd even heard some children were bonded and virtually married at birth, preordained by some of the ancient apocryphas. His own parents had been twelve and fifteen when they were betrothed and had been joined at the hip from that day forward.

So why hadn't he met Roberta? Why had she never been given a formal sephiroth before now? They could be one of those perfect matches. He had a feeling or 'knowing' they were. They fit. He wanted to stay 'fitted'.

"Thou art a shadow man, yet thee hold form true," said a tiny voice.

He had been watching Roberta so avidly, he almost missed the small creature that landed on the branch next to him. After meeting a mermaid, it seemed almost commonplace to see what appeared to be a fairy, he didn't even jump in surprise. She was a pretty little thing with glossy brown hair and rainbow colored wings. Her miniscule dress also seemed to be rainbow hued. "Hello. Who are you?"

"This one is called Tansy," she answered in a sweet and friendly voice.

"It's very nice to meet you, Tansy."

"Where art thou going, shadow of Assiah?"

"Why do you call me a shadow?" Brandon asked curiously.

"Tansy hast seen thee before, through the Briah gate, near Tansy's garden," the fairy answered. "But thee was not in form true."

Brandon stilled. If she'd seen him, even as only a shadow, she knew where Faucon d'épée was located, it was the only fantasy world he knew, even in dreams. So. How to get directions without offering any more promises he might later regret? "Are you sure, Tansy? Where is your garden?"

The pixie pointed in the direction they had come from. "'Tis very far. Can'st thou fly? Tansy could lead thee," she offered.

"I would very much like to fly with you, Tansy, and to see your garden, but my companion cannot fly."

The little fairy looked sad, letting out a heavy sigh. "'Tis a very long journey using only thy feet. Perchance as long as a sun-day and moon-evening," she told him. "Still," she gave a tiny smile, "the sun-days are pure, the moon-eves are clear, 'twill be a lovely walk for thee and thy companion."

"Hello," Roberta stood below, looking up at them.

"Roberta, I'm sure you remember your friend, Tansy?"

Roberta paused, then smiled. "Tansy? 'tis a lovely name, but this one knows thee not. Art thou lost, pretty Tansy?" she asked.

"Tansy is never lost, her wings are most fine," Tansy answered, then looked at Roberta curiously. "Thou holds thy form true like the shadow man of Assiah."

"'tis my choice to do so," Roberta answered.

"Thy choice?" Tansy's eyes opened wide. "Is this *thy* garden then?"

"It is."

"Dost the shadow man trespass within thy garden?" Tansy asked with horror at the very idea.

"Nay, pretty Tansy, fear not for my garden. My companion was invited."

Tansy bit her bottom lip. "Dost Tansy intrude?" this time she looked concerned.

Roberta shrugged. "'tis as nothing, Tansy. Thou art forgiven thy trespass into this one's garden. A wayside fairy knows few borders on such pure days." She held up the bunch of bananas she had brought back. "Wouldst thou care to sup with such as ourselves?"

"Thou art very kind," Tansy gave a little sigh. "But the sun-day fades, Tansy must leave before the even-fall," she answered, and disappeared.

"Well, that was interesting," Brandon said, as he jumped down from the branch, sitting next to her. His clothes immediately changed back to the original non-camouflage colors. "And more than a little strange."

"'Curiouser and curiouser, said Alice'," Roberta agreed.

"So what was with all the 'thees, thys and thous' you were spouting?"

Roberta shrugged. "According to all the girlie books my mother made me read, fairies prefer formality. They use it to impress."

"She really wasn't one of your childhood friends?"

"Nope, never saw her before," Roberta gave him a stern look. "Hey, I may have tea parties with mermaids and Nereid, but I draw the line at playing with fairies. Big bugs with people faces. Blech."

"But you still offered her dinner," Brandon pointed out.

"I'll have you know, Sir Brandon, I was given lessons in the proper etiquette of a Lady," she told him pompously. "Offering dinner to a guest, even an uninvited one, is considered de'rigeur in all civilized cultures." She gave a heartfelt sigh. "Sadly, our table has been determined to be inadequate for fairy bugs." She sat on the ground, pulled a banana from the bushel and handed him the rest. "Such a pity," she added with a cheerful smile. "So! Do tell. Did you and Tansy have a delightful tête â tête while I was shopping for our dinner?

"Actually, Tansy seemed very helpful," Brandon told her, peeling the banana and taking a bite.

"In what way?"

"Apparently, she saw me as a shadow near her garden. I was at the Briah gate at the time. Assuming she did see me, I'd have to have been in Faucon d'épée at the time."

"Huh." Pricilla looked thoughtful.

"More importantly, she told me to go that way," he nodded toward the way they'd come, "so I'd be able to find it again. She even offered to lead the way if I'd like to fly with her."

"How suspiciously kind. During this seductive offer did she also bat her pretty little eyelashes like Rhodes and tell you how handsome you are?"

"Now, now," Brandon patted her hand consolingly. "No need to be jealous, milady. I told her I couldn't leave you behind. Since you don't have wings that are most fine, she told me it's about a two day walk; if I understood her measure of time correctly."

Before Roberta could respond, there was a sudden breeze, the wisps of hair not bound in her braid whipped around her face in a flurry of unruly curls. She pulled it back with annoyance and tucked it behind her ears. "Well! That was rude."

"What was?"

"I believe our little Tansy was eavesdropping. That was her, leaving the scene of the crime as it were. Sneaky little wayside fairy."

"Ah. 'An Elemental of air will deceive thee'," Brandon quoted. "The Magus nailed that one in the Seth. It wasn't even an oblique riddle. I had a suspicion the directions she gave me were bogus."

Roberta nodded in agreement. "I have a suspicion that's why they call them 'wayside' fairies."

Chapter 19 - Orchis

"We have been told thou hast news of import," Orchis sat negligently on a throne of beautifully carved wood, etched with leaves and flowers. He wore royal purple, his golden hair flowed down his back. His eyes were pure violet, a perfect compliment to his clothing. He wasn't wearing his full glamour, but still glowed with his own inner vanity.

The small pixie bowed in midair. "Tansy spoke with the shadow taint from Assiah and its companion, my Lord, they held form true!"

Orchis looked at her sharply. "Form true? Of what shape?"

"The shapes of a mortal man and woman of Assiah," Tansy told him.

"A mortal woman shape such as that of Celandine?" Orchis asked, more than interested. "Was she as beautiful as Celandine?"

"Celandine is Celandine!" Tansy giggled. "None look as Celandine!" she giggled again.

"Of course not," Orchis tried not to sigh with aggravation. To Tansy not even two daisies from the same bush were similar. Pixies were notoriously simple minded. Dealing with them was difficult, if not impossible, but if you managed to keep them focused, they made excellent spies. One just had to remember to talk in short sentences. He tried a different tact. "Tell us of this woman shape of Assiah," he said patiently.

Tansy flickered her wings, trying to recall. "It had sprinkles of fairy dust upon its skin."

Orchis was already bored with Tansy, but pushed on. "Anything else you can remember of her?"

Tansy concentrated. "It had hair of sunset newly gone. A ribbon of sea green adorned its tresses."

This time Orchis did sigh. This was going to take time and Tansy had the attention span of a flit. "And her color eyes?"

Tansy concentrated. "Eyes of sun-leaves turning from the early frost," she decided.

"Did the shadow man of Assiah call her a name?"

"It called her milady," Tansy remembered.

"Ah, a lady then, with courtly manners?"

"Yes, My Lord. "It seemed most gracious at first," Tansy added, then squinted her eyes, "but then it called this one a fairy bug when it could not see Tansy!"

Orchis hid his amusement. "That was most unkind of her," he told her.

"Tansy is not a bug!" she pouted.

"No. Tansy is Tansy, not a bug," Orchis' lips twitched.

Tansy gave him a shy smile. "Thank thee, my Lord."

"And what of the shadow man in form true? Did the lady call it a name?"

"The lady called it 'Sir Brandon'. It was dappled like the tree it sat upon," Tansy told him. "It spoke with kindness, but its words were remiss in their sounding."

"Remiss?"

"It spoke with no formal graciousness, not like the woman form."

Orchis decided to forego getting more information about the man, this entire conversation was tiring. He instead asked for the information he truly needed. "Now, Tansy. Didst thou stray the shadow man from his course as you were also bade?"

"I did my Lord!" Tansy boasted, "I did!"

"Very Good, Tansy," Orchis told her. "When they did not see Tansy, did they speak of a childhood world?"

"Yes, my Lord! The childhood world of the shadow man!" Tansy answered enthusiastically.

Orchis nodded with encouragement. "Did you hear the name of this childhood world?"

"Yes, my Lord."

"Did you hear the name of this childhood world twice?

"Yes, my Lord."

"Did you hear the name of this childhood world thrice?"

"Yes, my Lord!" Tansy's wings fluttered with excitement.

He looked at her sternly. "Did you listen true?"

"Tansy did, my Lord, as you bade her."

Orchis nodded. "By what name was the world of the Shadow man called?" he asked carefully. "Say it true," he admonished firmly.

"The name of the world is 'Faucon d'épée,'" she answered. When she said the name, it was in the exact tone and voice of Brandon Grayson.

The voice of a man coming out of Tansy's tiny mouth made his lips twitch again. "If thee listened true, then I hear thee true. Thou will tell me true the name of the world twice."

"The name of the world is 'Faucon d'épée, Faucon d'épée'. Tansy listened true, Tansy tells thee twice." Again, the name of the world was in Brandon's voice, each separate, with the slightly different pitch of someone speaking it two different times.

"Then I hear thee true, I hear thee twice. Thou will tell me true the name of the world thrice."

"The name of the world is 'Faucon d'épée, Faucon d'épée, Faucon d'épée.' Tansy listened true, Tansy tells thee thrice." Once again, the name of the world was spoken in the voice of Brandon Grayson, but with the slight differences that proved a distinct inflection each time and that she had heard it three times.

"Then I hear thee true, I hear thee thrice," Orchis nodded with approval. "Did thee also hear the name of the world of the mortal lady?"

Tansy shook her head. "Nay, my lord. No other world name was spoken."

A disappointment, but Orchis had other spies, he would soon learn the names of both worlds. "Now, Tansy, this is very important. Tell Celandine not of the shadow man or woman who hold forms true."

"But..." Tansy puffed out her lower lip, unhappy. "Celandine is Tansy's friend true, my Lord," tears formed in her eyes. "Should Tansy not speak true to Celandine?" her wings drooped down to her side.

This was going to be a problem. Orchis thought for a moment. "Thy friend Celandine was worried before when thee told her about the shadow taint, Tansy, dost thou remember?"

Tansy nodded sadly. "Yes, my Lord, Tansy made Celandine worry."

Orchis shook his head at her and tsked with obvious rebuke. "That was most unkind of you, Tansy. Most unkind. Dost thou want to make Celandine worry again?"

Tansy shook her head, her wings drooped even lower. "Nay, my Lord. Celandine is Tansy's friend true. Tansy is sorry for Celandine's worry."

Orchis leaned toward her and whispered. "Keeping this secret, would be a kindness to Celandine," he told her. "Then Tansy would not make her worry."

Tansy's wings lifted. "t'would be a kindness secret?"

"Yes, it would," Orchis agreed. "And a kindness secret is a very fine thing indeed," he assured her.

"Tansy has a kindness secret!" her wings flickered in excitement, swirling her around in dizzy circles. "Tansy has a kindness secret! Tansy has a kindness secret!"

Orchis groaned. He had every intention making Celandine his willing consort, killing her friend would probably hinder that ambition, so he resisted the urge to bash the little 'fairy bug' into the nearest tree. He smiled, liking that description, he'd keep it. "Hush, sweet Tansy. Hush now." He waited until Tansy settled down. "Even a kindness secret must be kept a secret."

Tansy looked confused, then her wings swept up to straight points. "Oh! Tansy understands!" she whispered in a low voice to Orchis. "Tansy must not tell she has a kindness secret, but keep that kindness secret a secret as well!" She opened her eyes in awe.

Orchis felt a little dizzy himself. "Yes. Thou art very wise, pretty Tansy," he assured her.

"Now Tansy has two secrets!" She started air dancing again, calling out so all could hear, "Tansy has two secrets! Tansy has two secrets!"

Four hells! He hated dealing with flits! Orchis had a vision of this going on forever, ordering Tansy to keep the secret that she needed to keep two secrets secret. "Tansy!"

Tansy was instantly in front of him, here eyes sparkling with pride. "Tansy has two secrets, my Lord!"

"Yes, I know. Tansy has two secrets," Orchis carefully kept from adding any more. "A very fine thing indeed. And because you do, you may sit at the small table and sup with the court. There is fresh honey and nectar, made just for you from scarlet Lambertia flowers. You can have all the nectar you can drink. Even more, if you like."

Tansy's eyes opened wide with delight at the unexpected treat. "Thank thee, my Lord!"

"You are most welcome, pretty Tansy," Orchis answered. Problem solved. A few days in court getting drunk on nectar wine made from potent Lambertia flowers and the 'fairy bug' would soon forget she ever had a secret of a secret. If not, maybe he could find a male pixie to keep her occupied for a time. A sterile male pixie, he decided. Briah definitely didn't need another 'fairy bug' flitting around his court.

More importantly, now that he had the name, he could enter Faucon d'epée without invitation. He could enter any world of Briah with a name thrice given and thrice received.

Faucon d'épée, he repeated to himself. A strange name for a dream child of Assiah to give a world, but it had a courtly sound, very fitting for a King of Fae.

Chapter 20 - Memories

They had finished their meal of fruit and the few carrots Brandon had found, then wandered off on opposite sides of a small stream to take care of their personal needs.

"Need a toothbrush?" Brandon asked Roberta as they met back again at the stream.

"Very funny. Since my toothbrush and toothpaste are in Assiah still in the backpack that didn't come with us, I will forego answering that very personal question." She looked at him with annoyance.

"You know fish," Brandon smiled, "I know plants. Green grape leaves for toilet paper and this," He walked across the stream using some flat rocks that bridged it and handed her a twig, "is a little trick in learned in Africa about fifteen years ago," he told her.

Roberta looked at the twig suspiciously, "and that trick would be?"

"Licorice root. You probably imagined them in your fantasy world because they have pretty flowers, but they do have other uses. I've already removed most of the outer bark, chew the end and Viola! you get a homemade toothbrush." He held up the one he was holding. "Looks like this when you're done, works great," he started working on his own teeth demonstrating the procedure, then pulled it out of his mouth. "Floss and brush, nifty and cheap," he smiled, "and actually better for your gums and teeth than those plastic nylon things you get at the corner drug store. Kills bacteria and bad breath. Chew off the other end in the morning and you get a new toothbrush."

"Huh." Roberta looked at the end of the twig. "Okay, that's useful," she decided, wetting it in the water, then followed his instructions. She brushed her teeth and gums, the flavor was sweeter than sugar. She rinsed her mouth with several hand cups of water to flush the taste. Admittedly, though, her mouth did taste extremely fresh.

They returned to the clearing they had claimed for the night and sat with their backs to the cypress/apple tree, tired but oddly content. "We need a campfire," Brandon decided.

"No marshmallows," Roberta answered. "Besides, I don't know if anyone can start a fire here. Kid rules and total protection, remember?"

"Probably a good thing," Brandon answered, "I may know how to make a toothbrush, but I never learned to make a fire by rubbing two clichés together."

"Ha." Roberta gave a soft laugh and looked to the other side of the clearing at the trees. They sparkled with tiny twinkles of light. "This place looks like wonderland at night."

"It does," Brandon agreed. "Sylph lights. I always wondered what sylphs did at night. Apparently they sleep in trees."

"I don't know," Roberta mused. "Maybe they're just here for us to enjoy tonight. Maybe the sylph you released this morning brought all his friends around to show us they're all free, they're all happy. They want to show us how much they like us," she gave a comfortable sigh. "I always feel that way when I summon an undine. It's like its giggling with glee inside its little bubble of water." She smiled wistfully. "They always cheer me up when I'm feeling a little less than appreciated."

"You still call undines?" Brandon turned his head and looked at her curiously.

"At least once a month, sometimes once a week," she answered, looking at him curiously. "What, you don't call sylphs when you're feeling blue?"

"Not for a long time," Brandon answered. "The sylph I touched this morning was the first I held in... I don't know how many years," he told her. "I'd forgotten how it makes me feel. Young, fearless, special, magical... Oddly real, as though I'm connected to something very important." He reached over and took her hand. "Come over here and snuggle," he suggested. "I promise to behave until after we've had that dance."

Roberta scooted next to him, he put his arm around her as she settled into his shoulder. "This is nice."

"It is," Brandon agreed. "I say we forget the Seth. We could live here and chuck it all, Swiss Family Robinson style. Build a tree house near the stream to run the waterwheel to pull up and lower supplies. I could make some pear wine. You could sell apple cider and homemade tooth brushes to the fairy bugs." He kissed the top of her head. "Our kids could dance with sylphs in the moonlight."

"Hmm. That would be good. No pollution, no over fishing, no rush hour with gas guzzling engines, no smog, no war, no global warming."

Brandon looked at the beauty of sparkling sylphs in the tree. "People have really screwed up our world, haven't they?"

"That we have," Roberta yawned. "I'm really getting tired of the ecology lecture circuit. The fanatics who show up, run out and picket cattle ranches or start illegal whale wars. Others use it as an excuse to blow up oil Derricks. The rest of the audience is there to prove they're politically correct. They write a check to join the WSPA or to save the rain forests, then fire up their SUV's, go home and use that contribution as a tax credit for the IRS. Everyone else has just quit listening and don't give a tinker's damn." She snuggled in closer. "I'm not sure why I even try anymore."

"Because you care." Brandon kissed the top of her head, again, then held her for a long time, feeling her drop quietly into sleep. "I'm falling in love with you, Bobby," he said softly, as he also fell into sleep.

"Hmm. Good," she answered, dreaming she heard Brandon say something wonderful. "Because I think I've been in love with you since I was seven years old." She fell more deeply into sleep.

Neither consciously heard the other.

Chapter 21 - The Star Returns

The nightmare was always the same. Painful. Horrible.

"I am not a child, A-ron," Pricilla looked at him confidently.

Aaron didn't answer, but took a deep breath. "Jachin, Hod Hasimah et A-Ron. Binah, Ce-Cill. Et Binah, Hasimah et A-Ron."

Pricilla's face turned blank. "Hod Kether Binah, yesod, A-Ron?" she looked confused.

"Yes, Ce-Cill, Hod Kether Binah yesod. Shin Tau, Netzach Chesed. I release the keys, Hasimah et A-Ronaday. A-Ron et Celandine..." he paused for a split second. "Celandine et Whilom."

Pricilla stilled for a moment, then looked at him and smiled beautifully. "I love you, A-Ron," she touched above her left breast. "Heart," she touched her forehead, "mind," she touched her center, "soul."

Aaron forced the remaining words, keeping his voice void of emotion. "Jachin akal, Ce-cill, Celandine. The memory awakens. The time is now. Jachin akal. Know the cost. Remember the cost. Know all the truth of your love for me. Heart, mind, soul."

Pricilla froze at his words, gave him a look of complete anguish, then went completely limp in his arms. "Oh, baby, I'm so sorry," Aaron held her for several long minutes.

Finally his, fully his... and once again so out of touch to him. A prisoner once more of Whilom. Damn the place to hell.

"Aaron?" Pricilla was shaking him gently, then with more force. "Wake up, A-Ron. please, wake up," she felt a moment of desperation.

Aaron's eyes flashed open. Seeing her safe, he pulled her to him. "This has to stop. I can't lose you again, Cilla. I won't survive it a second time."

"You won't lose me. You were just dreaming," Pricilla kissed him gently.

"No, Love, it's not just a dream," he took her face in his hands. "I'm losing you again. Everyday, you stay a few minutes longer in Whilom. Sometimes you leave without any warning, before you've been here for an hour. Everyday when you return, it takes you longer to orient yourself to me, to Assiah. Its like there's a small piece of you missing, if just for those few moments."

He'd have to use the armband, send Whilom back to harmless

158

dreams, or he would lose her to that world forever, he knew it. He couldn't lose her. Willingly, or unwillingly on her part, she would wear the Assiah shackle.

Pricilla touched his cheek gently, noticing his distress. "You're wrong, Aaron. It doesn't matter where I am, you're still with me, heart, mind, soul. I may have to orient myself to Assiah for awhile, but never to you." She kissed him again. "You are always there," she repeated firmly. "You're my anchor, my true reality. Heart, mind, soul. Always."

"I'm always there," Aaron repeated, then sat up sharply, letting go of her. *('A-Ron et Ce-Cill et Celandine. I release the keys.')* Her anchor. No. He shouldn't be her anchor. She should be her own anchor. "That's the answer!"

With Aaron's abrupt movement, Pricilla fell back on the mattress unexpectedly. "Hey!" she lifted up on her elbows. "The answer to what? What was the question?"

Aaron stared at her. "The keys were crossed. You're not a child," he announced.

Pricilla gave a heavy sigh. "Considering some of the things we did together less than," she looked at the bedside clock, "an hour ago, it's a damned good thing, isn't it?"

"Ce-Cill," Aaron glared at her. "Do not be a smartass when I'm having an epiphany."

Pricilla yawned, pushed up her pillow, then spied his pillow, pulled it from his side of the bed and added it to hers, making a more comfortable backrest as she leaned against it. "Okay, big bad Magus of power by eternal lemniscate. Hit me with this midnight epiphany."

He took a deep breath. "I haven't been completely honest with you," he admitted.

"Got a mistress on the side?" she asked. "If you do, call her, tell her to run fast, I'll probably kill her in the morning," Pricilla promised, covering up another yawn. "I'm too tired tonight."

"The armband with the green stone." He hesitated.

Pricilla looked as confused as she felt. "What about it?"

"It's an artifact from Assiah. I found its description in one of the original apocryphas of Natzach through Beburah et Assiah."

"Natzach through what to Assiah?"

"Beburah. Its a Seth written during the dark days of Pope Innocence the third."

"A little outside my sephiroth," Pricilla rolled her eyes, "I have no idea what that means. From the History Channel I do know that Pope Innocence was not all that innocent. What did this Natzach through whatever Seth tell you?"

"That the armband is fully of Assiah, it can never be removed from Assiah."

"O-kay," Pricilla gave him a confused smile. "That clears that up. Can we go back to sleep now?"

"Pricilla, the star belongs in Whilom. It should never have been removed from Whilom."

"Since it came from there, I'll agree with that." She hid another yawn. "Actually, I think I mentioned that to you a few months ago. Not that you ever listen to *my* brilliant epiphanies."

"Celandine also said it."

Pricilla shrugged. "Same difference." She a stifled another yawn.

"Cilla, I have the star."

"What?" Pricilla was suddenly wide awake. "Not as intriguing as a mistress on the side, granted, but it does beg the question. Since we've been going nuts trying to hunt it down, why in the five hells didn't you mention you finally found the damned thing?"

"Because..." Aaron rubbed his forehead viciously. "Pricilla, I've hated Whilom most of my life. It separated us for too damned many years."

"I know," she answered gently, "I'm sorry, Aaron. And now it's doing it again."

"I was wrong. I can't hate Whilom, it's part of you, of who you are. It always has been. You are not two people, you're both. I love all of you. Not just the parts I understand."

"Thank you," she frowned. "I think," she added. "Where is this going?"

Aaron tried to explain. "When I call you as First Key, not just as A-Ron and you come as Celandine, how do I appear to you?"

Pricilla looked at him thoughtfully. "For one, you're usually wearing clothes." She grinned. "Not that I'm complaining, mind you."

Aaron looked at her expectantly. "On a more serious level?"

"Well," she frowned, considering the question more seriously. "A little more pompous maybe." She shook her head. "No, that's not it. Intense. That whole 'Magus of Power by Eternal lemniscate' mantle you wear is a tad... more... I don't know... you?"

"Because The Magus is a mantle I can't shed completely even if I want to."

Pricilla shrugged. "You were born with it. Destiny Given. I don't fully understand it, you walk a different sephiroth than I do. You were trained to be magus since the day you were born. It's as much a part of you as that sweet little birthmark you have on your butt," she glared at him. "The one that only I, by the way, will ever see."

"Possessive, I like it," Aaron grinned.

"Good, you're stuck with it," she told him. "So, why are we discussing the obvious? What does this have to do with the Star?"

"Pricilla, the Star is your birthmark. *Your* mantle. You are Celandine, the elemental of Whilom. You created it when Whilom created you." He got out of the bed and walked over to the wall safe.

Pricilla watched him. "You know," she told him. "You really, really look good naked," she observed.

Aaron stopped punching in the numbers and turned toward her. "Pay attention."

Pricilla grinned. "Oh, believe me. I am. Wanna fool around?"

Aaron finished punching numbers. "Let me finish my epiphany first." He pulled out the box with the Star in it and the envelope with the armband of Assiah, "then, believe me, we'll get right on that rather intriguing offer."

"Honeymoon's over," Pricilla said sadly.

"Never," Aaron told her, coming back to the bed and kissing her quickly, "I will never let that happen."

Aaron held the envelope in one hand, the box with the star in the other. "We have two choices here. Assiah, or Whilom."

"What?"

"You can be permanently bound to Assiah by wearing the armband for life, once on it can never be removed, or you can continue to travel to Whilom."

Pricilla bit her lip and took a deep breath. "If it means staying with you, I choose Assiah."

"Wrong answer. Too bad, so sad." He put the envelope on the nightstand and handed her the box containing the star. "I choose Whilom, you don't get a vote. Put it on."

Pricilla opened the box and looked nervously at the Star. "Aaron, I'm not sure about this. It could send me back permanently."

"No, it won't," Aaron told her firmly. "Without it, you're crippled, without the total control you were meant to have. If you wear the armband, it will strip Whilom from you, take away what makes you, you." He noticed her eyes filling with tears. "That would be the wrong thing to do, love. It would strip you of who you really are. I can't, I won't, let that happen. Ever."

Pricilla looked at him, worry etching her face. "Aaron, I..."

"It's okay, Cilla," he assured her. "This is right. You have a different sephiroth than mine and I don't completely understand it any more than you do my mantle, but this feels right. It's not going to take you away, just add the little bit of Whilom that you're missing when you're here. The piece you have to keep going back to find because you're not complete without it. Put it on, love. Accept it willingly. It belongs to you. It always has."

Pricilla continued to look at the Star with trepidation. "You're sure?"

"Yes. I'm sure. I am Magus of Power by eternal Lemniscate. First Key. Trust me." He glared at her. "Obey me, woman."

"I think I'll go back to pompous," she decided. "Willingly, huh?"

"Yes. Willingly."

Pricilla took a deep breath, removed the Star from the box and quickly put it on, closed her eyes and waited for whatever was going to happen. "Am I still here?" she asked in a worried voice.

"Still here." Aaron laughed. "Take a look."

Pricilla looked at her chest where the star had been dangling just a moment before. It was gone, but somehow she still felt it. "Where is it?"

Aaron grinned, stroking her hair. It had almost turned totally blond over the past few months, now it was back to dark underneath, blond on top. "Where it belongs, love. Inside Whilom. Inside you. Its your Destiny Given." He held her close then looked over at the padded envelope on the nightstand and shuddered.

He'd have that destroyer of dreams and fantasies melted down into a paperweight in the morning, jewels and all. It would be a daily reminder that the temptation to use it could have turned him into the blackest of magicians, blacker than the five who had trapped the sylph and undine with the gold of Assiah.

Pricilla stroked his chest with feather touches and whispered, "Now that the drama's over, and since I'm still here..." she paused for effect. "...wanna fool around?"

Chapter 22 - The Eagle Flies

"Why do you think Tansy bothered to give you false directions yesterday?" Roberta asked Brandon curiously, as they got ready to travel. "We were already lost, what was the point?"

"Maybe because we're not really lost," Brandon answered. "When we were washing up in the stream, I had another knowing."

Roberta looked up at him with interest. "Okay. Are you going to put me in the loop this time?"

"The stream we washed up in. We follow it upstream. It will lead us directly to Faucon d'épée."

"Why does that sound familiar?" Roberta frowned, an old memory trying to surface.

"Familiar? What sounds familiar?"

"Following the stream. I think I used to follow that stream for some reason, but I don't remember exactly why. Something I did as a little girl. Looking for something, I think."

Brandon looked interested. "What kind of thing?"

Roberta let out a puff of air. "Not a clue. If it helps, I remember it was something nice." She smiled. "I think it was a tree. A big tree. A very special tree."

"How far did you go before you found this 'special' tree?"

"I don't know." Roberta shook her head. "It couldn't have been too far, I never spent more than a few hours in my world. Eight, tops, when I was sleeping through the night."

Brandon hoisted his vest, which he had turned into a makeshift backpack filled with apples and several of the twig toothbrushes. "Then let's find out where this stream goes," he decided. "The worst that can happen is that we'll find your tree and determine that it was 'special' because it had pink roses or something equally mundane."

"Hey," Pricilla argued, "I happen to like pink roses," she told him.

"Good, I now know what to get you for our anniversary," Brandon answered. "Are you ready to leave, or do you need another bathroom break?"

"I'm good for now. Lead on, fearless leader," she answered.

They walked for over an hour at a very fast clip when Roberta finally called out for a rest, seriously out of breath. "Hey," she choked out, bending over, her hands on her knees. She looked up at him. "Slow down. This isn't a race, is it?"

Brandon stopped and looked back at her. "We can't take another

163

break. We have to hurry." His voice was strained.

Pricilla heard it. "Why? What's the rush?"

"There's a blight in Faucon d'épée," he told her with concern. "I can feel it." He started moving again.

"A 'blight'?" Roberta answered, ran up to him, taking his arm to stop him. "Like a disease in one of your vineyards?"

"More of a... wrongness than a blight, but its getting bad. We have to hurry," he said again. "Seriously, Bobby, this is important. We have to go. We don't have time to slow down."

Roberta continued to hold him in place. "Wait. You said that before," she said with concern.

"When?"

"When you reverted into being a boy. You said you had to get to your world because there was a 'wrongness'." She studied his face. "Comment vous sentez-vous? Quel âge avez-vous ? Quel est mon nom?"

"Your name is Roberta," Brandon smiled, amused, "I feel fine. As for my age...." He kissed her, then pulled her closer and kissed her again. "Well past my puberty. Definitely not a boy," he assured her.

Roberta smiled. "Definitely not a boy," she agreed.

Brandon's expression again turned serious. "But, man or boy, we have to get to Faucon d'épée. Now. There is something very wrong there. We have to hurry."

"Okay," Roberta thought about it. "Then you need to fly."

Brandon looked at her as if she were insane. "What?"

"Fly," she repeated. "We're in Briah, Brandon, change shape. I can't, but you can. Scout ahead. Be a hawk, be an eagle. Use those eagle eyes, find your world, look for whatever is wrong. We can't fix the problem unless we know where to look for the problem."

Brandon looked thoughtful. "I'm not sure I remember how to fly."

"Of course you do," Roberta squeezed his arm. "We're in Briah. An elemental world. A magical world. You magically changed your clothes when you got here. You changed them again into camouflage without thinking when you climbed into the apple/cypress tree, then changed back again when you got down. Everything you did as a child, is still inside you. If you can change clothes without even thinking, you can fly. This is part of Briah, you can fly, you can change into a bird and fly."

Brandon looked up into the impossibly blue sky, then back at her. Was it possible? "I can't leave you."

"Do you feel a blight here?" she asked.

Brandon paused, feeling with all his senses. "No."

"Then you can leave me with no worries. Find out where that blight starts. I'm a big girl. I'm perfectly safe. I'll keep following the stream, so I

164

can't get lost," she told him. "Eventually, I'll catch up with you. If not, you can fly back and get me. The stream will lead you back. Consider the stream our 'water brick' road," she smiled. "All streams lead to back to me."

Brandon still looked unconvinced.

"Brandon. You have a *knowing*. You have to go and I can't keep up. You can do this."

"I'm not sure I..."

"Be sure. Look at that beautiful blue sky," Roberta continued, looking upward. "Think of the updrafts. Remember the joy, the feeling of the wind beneath your wings." She smiled at him, her eyes twinkling. "You know you want to show off your beautiful eagle wings. Be a golden eagle. I love golden eagles."

Brandon gave her a stern look. "You're coaxing."

"Coaxing, not coercing," she answered. "But I really do want to see you as a golden eagle. I really, really, want to see you fly and soar above the trees," she told him. "Run, fly, Brandon. Relive that fantasy, be a kid again. Fly," she repeated, then added quickly, "but don't forget that you are a grown-up," she warned. "I'm not quite sure I know how to kiss a juvenile eagle."

Brandon pulled her to him and kissed her. "Believe me, Sweetheart, I plan on staying a grown-up. You still owe me that dance and I plan to collect." He looked down on a face he found more beautiful with every moment they spent together. "You know I'm crazy about you, right?"

"I know you're crazy, in any event," Roberta kissed him back, throwing in more than a little passion.

Brandon held on to both her arms. "You'll just follow the stream, no detours. Promise me. I need to know you're safe."

"No detours," Roberta assured him.

"Don't you revert to childhood either," he told her firmly.

"Not going to happen," Roberta promised. "Now go. Fly for me, Brandon Grayson, be everything beautiful that you are, everything you always wanted to be. Just remember to come back for me."

He kissed her again, handed her his makeshift knapsack. "I'll always come back for you. I just wish that you could fly too," he told her, then ran toward the trees, his arms wide as he lifted and changed.

"And I wish you could love me, just as I am and not want me to change. Not a bird, not a mermaid, just the real me," Roberta whispered, too soft for him to hear.

A moment later, a golden eagle flew high above Roberta, letting out a hunting cry that sounded suspiciously like glee.

Roberta looked up at the sound. He was circling above. As an eagle, Brandon's wingspan was nearly eight feet across. He made a damned glorious bird, graceful, powerful. She waved at him and started walking upstream.

Brandon flew high in eagle form, watching from above, making sure Roberta followed the stream as she had promised. She had been right, there was no 'wrongness' in Adelie, but he still felt a concern. It didn't feel right not being with her. More, he wanted her to be with him. He wanted her to fly with him, feel the wind beneath her wings. The joy. They should be together, sharing it all. She was part of Briah, not just Yetzirah, why couldn't she fly?

(I never changed shape in either world. It was my fantasy to fit in, just I was)

It had been such a strange comment, but his eagle mind let it go. Catching the updrafts, he let the wind carry him aloft. There was absolute freedom here, no worries, nothing to stop him. He could fly for hours in this form.

Or, maybe not, he realized when he had to use his wings more forcefully to catch another updraft. He wasn't a young eagle any longer. Many of his brethren had been known to live up to forty years but they weakened with age, most no longer mated, didn't help care for their young because they'd all grown and left the aerie, built their own cotes.

Brandon felt those years now. His energy was low. He started circling, looking for small prey. But he would find nothing to sate his hunger in this world, he knew. He could sense it. He didn't feel like he could kill anything here.

But, he knew where he could. He had his own hunting ground. He knew his way to Faucon d'épée now. The stream twisted and turned, but he flew the most direct route. He needed fresh meat, he needed strength.

And he needed something more, something important, but his eagle brain didn't remember exactly what that something was.

Roberta watched Brandon go, took a brief bathroom break, then walked for nearly an hour by the stream before she stopped to rest. Damn, her feet hurt. She took off the soft leather boots she had designed as a child. At that age, the flimsy shoes seemed to be enough to protect her feet from pine needles on the ground, but not a great deal more. She put her bare feet into the stream and leaned back on her elbows, sighing with relief. Oh, that felt good. Damn, she must be getting old. She had cherished memories of running along this stream with so much energy, so much childhood glee. She had been free, lighthearted.

Young.

Roberta stilled as a doe and its tiny fawn walked up to drink daintily from the other side of stream and she smiled. They both looked up and saw her, studying her with mild curiosity, but they didn't startle, not even when she sat up quickly. No fear, just acceptance that she was a natural part of the scenery. She could probably ford the stream, walk overt to them and pet them, but she didn't. She watched them for a long time, then splashed her feet to get their attention. They looked up, showing that they knew she was there, then just leisurely drank their fill. A few minutes later they quietly walked back into the trees.

They were beautiful. Perfect.

She pulled an apple from Brandon's vest/backpack and looked at it critically. Still the perfect apple. Never a bruise, always perfectly ripe. She pulled one of the bananas. The banana was a perfect yellow, no brown spots, no imperfections, perfectly ripe. She put the banana back into the pack, then crunched the apple thoughtfully, looking around herself with adult eyes.

The stream burbled gently. If she cupped her hand and drank from it, it would be sweet and pure. If she bathed in, hell, if she peed in it, it would stay sweet and pure. It couldn't be polluted, it could never be tainted. Always clean, always safe.

Everything was perfect. Every burst of color, every bush, every tree. It was a fantastic botanical garden that needed no caretaker to rake or pull weeds. The grass… it was as manicured as a golf course. A golf course without sand-traps, without gopher holes.

And wasn't that just... perfect.

Perfection was nice, but it had its drawbacks. No campfires, no hot food. No meat. She could, probably, catch one of the fish in the stream, have a little sushi, but it felt wrong. This wasn't a fishing stream, just a place for the fish to swim, to mate, to make more little fishes.

Still hungry, Roberta pulled out the banana again and looked at it. She had a quick flashback of the peanut butter and banana sandwiches she had shared with her roommate in college. But, sadly, no peanut butter here. No butter of any kind. No bread. No grilled cheese sandwiches.

She missed peanut butter, she missed cheese.

Chocolate. Oh, God, she missed chocolate. Chocolate peanut butter cups. M&M's, chocolate sundaes with nuts and a ton of sinfully unhealthy whipped cream.

Enough of that, she decided. She took her feet out of the water to put her shoes back on, her feet dried instantly, ready to do just that.

No need for towels. Damn it, she missed towels! She liked towels. She wanted the feeling of friction when she got out of the shower and scrubbed her back with a towel just because it felt good.

But that was an adult luxury. Kids didn't need that scratchy rubdown. They didn't want to linger. They were too ready to jump out of the tub and go play, naked, if their parents didn't catch them in time.

Roberta gingerly felt the braid Rhodes had made in her hair and looked at the tip. Not a hair was mussed except for the stubborn curlicues that always fringed the sides of her face. She didn't have a mirror, but they probably curled perfectly too. No hairbrush needed.

Wasn't that just... perfect?

With a suddenly heavy heart, Roberta put on her shoes, got up and started walking slowly upstream.

The be-damned, beautiful, *perfect* stream.

Chapter 23 - The Blight

Three hours later, still following the stream, Roberta found the oak tree. At that moment, everything fell into place.

She knew this tree. She would hide behind it and watch Brandon Grayson fly as an eagle, a hawk... and something else. Something important, but it wouldn't come to her. She had watched him from behind that tree, wishing, dreaming she could go inside his world, watch him up close, cheer him on, thrill at his joy while he flew. Perhaps, she had dreamed, he would want her there, perhaps he could be her friend. All those lonely years as a child, all she wanted was a friend.

Now Roberta had a feeling, a *knowing*, that had she not been so shy and had come out from behind that tree and waved to him, he would have waved back, he would have become that friend. Perhaps, even then, he might have invited her into his secret world.

Even if she did have curly red hair and too many damned freckles.

Her heart had been heavy for three hours, now it lifted completely. She walked inside the World Brandon had invited her into, anxious to see what he had created. She looked up into the clear blue sky, searching for a golden eagle. He wasn't there now, but she knew he would find her soon. He had promised to come back for her and he would.

She walked further into Faucon d'épée. It was a beautiful world, Roberta was amazed by it. A lot of trees, but not quite a forest. A meadow, but not a finely manicured lawn. It was wilder than her part of Briah. No one mowed or raked this lawn. A few branches littered the ground, wild flowers grew where they would. Rocks and boulders were scattered randomly. It was more natural than her world and more perfect because of it. Rabbits darted, squirrels and chipmunks chattered in the trees. As a child she had wanted the comfort of friends, a cure for loneliness, a little silly fun swimming with Rhodes and her dolphin friends. It had been a perfect fit for a shy child with little confidence.

Brandon had created his world for adventure, freedom from family obligations and responsibility. His world reflected that need. (Oh, please. My family owns wineries. I was wine tasting before I was eight.)

Ironic, really. Now he enjoyed a quiet retreat, conversely, she liked and enjoyed adventure. It was as though they had changed roles as they aged. Her world was more what he needed, his world was more her style. The two worlds together would satisfy both their needs.

That really would be perfect.

Roberta went further into Faucon d'épée enjoying the slightly uneven terrain. She stopped abruptly within only a few hundred yards from the entrance. A short distance away was a beautiful white stag. He raised his head, looking at her curiously, then timidly started toward her. It had a very large rack of antlers polished as white as its coat, the animal probably outweighed her by a hundred pounds or more, not including those very sharp looking antlers.

Roberta stood perfectly still. This was not one of her tame deer in Adelie, she had no intention of going up to it and patting it on the top of the head like some well trained dog. Or horse, she corrected, reevaluating its size. That was one damned big stag.

The stag suddenly startled, then started running full tilt toward her.

Four hells! Was it attacking? Had she gotten too close to its family?

And then she heard the sound that had motivated the stag's sudden fear. High pitched, staccato, menacing. The stag was still running toward her, as though by reaching her it would be safe. It was on a zigzag course, but still trying to reach her.

Then she saw them. Hyenas. There were eight. No. Ten. The pack was only about twenty yards behind the stag and they were closing fast. Two moved to one side, two to the other, flanking the stag on both sides, two others staying behind it nipping at its heels so they could bring it down should it somehow reverse course. The other four were running full speed to get to the front of the stag, cutting off every exit.

The stag was part of Brandon's world. But those hyenas were definitely not his creatures and she knew it instinctively. These were ugly, scraggly, rabid. What were they doing here? How did they get here? Brandon had said he felt a "wrongness" in his world. Was this was part of what he had felt? They must be. Those damned hyenas didn't belong here. They tainted everything around them.

She hated them on sight.

She knew these bastards plan. They were going to take the Stag down, laugh at its pain, rejoice in its death. She couldn't let that happen. She'd never allow that kind of desecration in this world. It belonged to Brandon. By his invitation it also was her world to protect.

Roberta didn't actually think about it, just dropped her bundle of apples and bananas, picked up one of the larger branches on the ground and started running toward them, yelling at the top of her lungs, making as much noise as possible, determined to give the Stag a chance to get away.

Damned if she'd let those evil predators hurt that beautiful animal.

She kept running, finally getting herself between the white stag and the hyenas, then started swinging her branch in a wide circle, still yelling, screaming...

Hoping both she and the stag could escape, both find their way to safety without serious injury.

Faucon d'épée

It had taken the golden eagle less than an hour to find its way to Faucon d'épée. The food he needed for strength was plentiful. He fed on a fat jackrabbit, then rose again into the air. Searching, tracking. Not for food, for something else. Something was wrong here.

This was his usual hunting ground, yet somehow, it wasn't. At one point he saw a white stag, even that felt wrong, it was neither predator nor prey. He dismissed the stag and kept flying, looking for more obvious signs that his hunting grounds had been somehow invaded. For more than an hour he flew. Finally, exhausted, he rested in his primary cote for a time, then started his search again.

His world was contaminated. He could feel, almost smell it, but his eagle eyes couldn't see it. More hours passed. His hunting grounds were large, whatever was lurking, whatever was invading his world, would not be easy to locate.

Further and further he flew, to the very edge of his world, then further still, into another world he could enter. His Grandfather's world. "Emboîtement de corneilles". Crow's nest. His inheritance. It would be as large as his own, he knew, but he couldn't linger here. He saw the cliffs from a distance, but didn't venture further toward them.

There was something more important he had to do than explore another world, something vital. He had to turn back, go back into his world, find the contaminate, the poison.

When he crossed the border back into Faucon d'épée, again he felt the wrongness. It was stronger now, more menacing. Dangerous. His wings felt heavier, his eagle heart beat twice its normal speed. Not from weariness this time, but from a taste of fear. Even fear was a challenge for the bird, he was no coward, he would find the enemy and kill it as quickly as he would a snake or rabbit. He was the alpha predator here, none could take that position away from him. This was *his* hunting ground.

From high above, he noticed a sparkling stream and realized something else was wrong about his world. Something important was missing that should be here and wasn't. His heart thudded painfully.

His mate. That was what was missing. He shouldn't be here flying alone, he had a mate, they should be flying together. He had to find her.

The eagle let out a loud, "kyee-ee!" and dove. He dove low, staying mere feet above the stream, following the twists and turns searching for her. He called again, louder this time. There was no answer. A memory of auburn hair, green eyes and sun freckled skin flashed in his mind.

Had the enemy he'd felt somehow trapped her, or had she not yet entered his hunting ground? Was he merely feeling alone and abandoned, or was she in danger? They had made a nest together in a tree. No. They had made a nest on the ground.

That couldn't be right. They were eagles, they should be nesting high, not on the ground where their fragile offspring would be vulnerable to the elements.

("Don't forget that you are a grown-up,") he heard a voice in his mind. ("I'm not quite sure I know how to kiss a juvenile eagle."). It was a human voice, not one of his own species, but a voice he thought he should know.

(I will always come back for you.) He'd made a promise.

Then he remembered. Roberta, the name flashed in his mind. She wasn't an eagle, yet she was still his mate, he had to find her.

Why wasn't she flying with him? They would be safe now. Above the dangers he knew were below. Masters of the sky, hunting together, playing in the winds together, searching together for whatever was encroaching their world. Safe. He would damn well force her to learn to fly! It wasn't safe on the ground.

She wasn't safe alone. Maybe she had been hurt, their world was safe for children, maybe not for adults. Maybe she'd injured a wing... no, an arm.

("I've never changed shape in any world.")

In any world. Oh, Hell. She was born on the cusp. He remembered now. She had another world, one she told him she was more comfortable in. Maybe she had become lost or hurt and went to her world in Yetzirah for safety or help, not his world in Briah where there was an obvious taint, a poison that could hurt her. Obvious danger that might have frightened her away, where an unseen enemy treated her like prey.

He flew on, backtracking, his eagle eyes watching the stream, searching, going back to where they started.

Back to Adelie.

Chapter 24 - Rhodes

Flying to what Roberta called her 'landing zone' took less than three hours at his top speed. He turned back into human form as he landed. It was the easiest thing in the world. It was as natural as breathing. Oh, yeah. He was definitely going to teach Roberta how to fly and be damned if he'd allow them to be separated again. Not in Assiah, not in Briah, not in Adelie. They were a team. More, she was his mate, whether or not she was aware of that fact. He'd make damned sure she knew they were mates.

Yetzirah would always be an issue, he admitted to himself, she could escape him on that side of the cusp, but he had an ace in the hole even there. He had a friend.

Well, sort of a friend, anyway.

Brandon didn't know the siren's call, but he did know how he had attracted her attention before. Brandon walked toward the water, it rose up to keep him out. He stepped back, then did it again. Stepped back once more and once more the water fell back into the sea. Then he waited. The minutes seemed like hours.

Finally Rhodes was there, as was her rock perch, one that hadn't been there before he tried to enter.

Her musical voice tripped along the water, somehow adding the sound of the sea to her smile. "Son of Assiah, willing friend. Hast thou another promise thou wish to spend?" As before, she posed, thrusting out her breasts, giving him a sly smile. Her tail swayed side to side, trying to lure him in.

Nothing is free, Brandon reminded himself. "What would it cost me to find out if your 'sister' has returned to Yetzirah?" he asked.

Rhodes instantly dropped her seductive expression and posture. "I have not seen Bethany, son of Assiah, but your voice tells me that you fear for her." She looked concerned.

Brandon stilled. No rhymes, no thee's and thou's. No seductive pose, no attempt to seduce. "I do fear for her. She is not where I left her in Briah. If she crossed over into my world, she could be in danger. There is a taint there, a predator I can't identify. I'm afraid she might be hurt or frightened. I thought perhaps she might come to Yetzirah to find help or safety," he admitted.

"If Bethany was injured or frightened, she would come to me." Rhodes told him seriously. "If she were able," she added on a more solemn note.

"You called her Bethany," Brandon looked at her with confusion.

"She prefers nicknames," Rhodes smiled. "Roberta Griffin becomes 'Bobby' in Assiah, Bethesicyme becomes 'Bethany' in Yetzirah. Formality has never been her style. She will use her true Yetzirah name with our Mother, sister and near- brother, but with me she is a little sassy."

"She is that," Brandon agreed, stunned by Rhodes knowledge of Roberta's full name. Names had power, only given to another with complete and total trust. Roberta must really believe Rhodes was part of her family in Yetzirah.

Rhode's smile faded to a look of genuine concern. "I do not like that you are worried for Bethesicyme, or that she has entered a world not of her making. She was created for me to protect."

Brandon frowned. "Created for you?"

Rhodes laughed, but it wasn't even vaguely humorous. "Those of you from Assiah know so little of our elemental worlds. Bethesicyme swam within our mother's womb of Yetzirah long before she breathed the air of Briah or entered the body of her Assiah mother to finish becoming. I willingly shared my heart with my true sister from the day of her awakening. I had never thought to see her as a woman grown in form true, but she came back to me and I love her still. Whether adult or child, I do not wish to lose her again."

"Nor do I."

Rhodes nodded. "You love her." It was not a question.

Brandon didn't hesitate. "Yes, I do. She is my mate."

"Then she is yours to protect, where I cannot."

"Always and forever."

There was a long pause. "That is as it should be. I will search for my sister, as will our mother. If Bethesicyme is here, she will be found," she told him.

"Thank you."

"I will also ask from you a boon."

Nothing is free, Brandon again reminded himself. "What would you have me give, Rhodes?"

"When you create my near-sister or brother, I ask you to tell them of me, even if Yetzirah is closed to them. If they are able to come into Yetzirah, tell them I will protect them and love them, as I always have their mother. They may come and go between Assiah and Yetzirah as they please, but they will always be safe in my near-father's realm." Her smile turned a little bit sly. "And teach my near-sister or brother to be just a little bit sassy."

"On that, my sister to be," Brandon answered with a return smile and lightening heart, "you have my word. Willingly."

Rhodes gave him a formal bow of her head. "Search thy tainted world within Briah, brother to be, search my sister's Briah world as well. I and all the creatures of Yetzirah will search for her in this realm. If we find her, I will send her to you safe. If you find her, you will do the same so that I might see her safe."

"I will," Brandon promised.

With that, Rhodes nodded again and dove into the sea, leaving no ripple in the water to show she had ever been there. This time, however, her posing rock did not disappear with her.

Brandon quickly returned to the Briah side of Roberta's cusp world, turned back into an eagle and searched with his eagle eyes for more than an hour, but found nothing. She wasn't there.

Once again he followed the stream into his own world of Faucon d'épée. Again, no Roberta, but his world still felt contaminated. It nearly overpowered him with its stench of wrongness.

Suddenly, he remembered the white stag. It had been beautiful, yes, but it didn't fit. He had never created animals in his world that large.

The Seth. *(To be blind to danger is imprudent).*

Damn! He had seen the danger, had known Faucon d'épée was contaminated, but he'd ignored it because the stag had looked harmless. He'd been blind to the fact that it didn't belong.

He returned to where he had first seen the stag and changed back into his natural form as he landed. Within the shade of a tree close to where he landed, he found their makeshift backpack, the apples and bananas were scattered around it as though dropped in a hurry. Or in panic.

She had reached his world. She'd found the taint, the danger.

Or, he realized with mounting horror and rising assurance, the danger had found her.

He sat down and waited for the stag to find him. He had a definite knowing that it would, just as it had found Roberta.

***

Roberta opened her eyes, above her she saw only white. She was flat on her back on a soft surface. A bed, she realized.

"Milady, awakens," said a sultry feminine voice.

Roberta looked in that direction. An exquisitely beautiful woman with long light brown hair flowing down to the back of her knees stood there. She was wearing a sheer iridescent rainbow hued gown that shifted colors continuously, hiding very little of her perfect form. A ribbon of the same ever-changing rainbow was threaded through her hair. Her eyes were a satiny silver, shifting to pale blue.

"Hasten, Flit, tell thy Lord, Milady awakens!" another voice said from the other side of the bed.

Roberta turned her head and looked over. Another woman stood there, wearing the exact same clothing as the first. There was a hint of wings on both their backs, not quite visible, but she knew they were there. Not wayside fairies like little Tansy had been, but full grown Fae, taller than she, close to six feet, she determined. They were identical twins. Delicately beautiful in both face and form.

"Who... art thou?" Roberta asked carefully. God only knew what kind of new trouble she was in now, but using formality was always the way to speak to Fae. (Thanks, Mom, for making me read those stupid girly novels).

"This one is oft called Delisa," the one on the left side told her, with a graceful bobbing curtsy

"This one is oft called Asiled," the other said at almost the same time, with an identical bob.

Roberta sat up cautiously. She was now wearing a shimmering blue gown threaded in silver thread. It was more substantial then theirs, but equally beautiful. "I..." She touched the sleeve of her gown curiously. The material was exquisite, but far more fragile than anything she would ever considering wearing in real life. It would tear with a sneeze.

"Thy clothing was most sadly abused, Milady, forgive ourselves if thou believe an intrusion was made upon thy person," said the Fae on her left.

Was that twin Delisa, or Asiled? Roberta wondered, then repeated the names to herself. Ah. Mirror twins, mirror names. Clever and more than a little weird.

Roberta touched her hair. It was no longer in a braid, but down. She pulled it over her shoulder. It curled down in long graceful waves. It had been washed in something that made it shine like it had been re-touched for a television commercial. More red than auburn, she thought.

"Thy tresses were so tightly wound, ourselves feared thee might suffer pain whilst thee rested," said the fairy on her right.

"Our Lord said to assure thee that thy modest person hast only been tended by maidens such as ourselves," said the fairy on her left.

Roberta decided to give up on figuring out who was who, she had a feeling they would answer to either name, depending on which side they were standing.

"Our Lord desired us to see that thou were unharmed by the vicious creatures that attacked thee," the fairy on her right continued.

Great. She'd been strip searched, bathed and coiffed by virgin fairies. Roberta looked at her hands. Yup, manicured as well, her nails had been buffed to a mirror shine.

She tried to remember how the hell she got here. She had been fighting with something... well, swinging a large stick at it in any event, so that she could...

... a white stag. That's right, she had been trying to give the stag time enough to get away. "hyena." That was it. There had been a pack of hyena trying to kill the stag.

"As thee say," said the fairy on her left. "Though ourselves know not the names of such foul creatures," she added in a frightened voice.

"'Twas most distressing for our Lord." The fairy on her right told her.

"Thy abuse within his world was a most terrible happening." The fairy on her left agreed.

"My Lord's guards heard thy cries for help and were unable to assist quickly enough to save thee from all thy injuries," said the fairy on her right.

"My Lord is most regretful for thy hurt," added the fairy on her left.

Roberta was having a difficult time turning her head back and forth trying to keep up with the conversation. Her mind was spinning. Think. She was in some kind of bedchamber wearing new clothes and had been apparently groomed and polished by a couple of extremely talkative and annoying virgin fairies of some kind.

"Milady? Dost thy brow offend thee?" The fairy on her right asked with concern.

"My lord will be most distressed if ourselves hath not tended thee well," the fairy on her left sounded more than a little worried about that possibility.

Brow offend thee? What did... Ah. She was rubbing her temples, obviously indicating she had a headache. She dropped her hands from her head. Formality, she reminded herself. "This one's brow is merely alight with curiosity," Roberta explained. "How long hast, hath," damn which was the correct pronoun, hast or hath? Screw it. "How long have I been asleep?" (And where in the four hells am I?), she asked herself.

"A full moon-even and Sun-Day. 'tis moon-eve once again."

Roberta wasn't exactly sure which voice had answered, so she spoke to the fairy on the left. "Who is thy Lord?"

"King Orchis is our Lord, Milady," yup, it figured, the fairy on her right answered.

Damn, couldn't they decide on one as the designated speaker and the other one keep mute? "Thy King hath... has been most gracious to offer me aid," Roberta said to the fairy on the right, since she figured it was now her turn to speak.

"My Lord is always most gracious," the expected fairy answered. Then, surprisingly, she spoke again without her twin taking over the conversation. Obviously, Roberta decided, a trick of some kind to drive her nuts. "His concern for thee was most anxious."

"Our Lord hast asked if thee might join him within the court, if thou hath been tended to thy satisfaction," the left fairy told her.

Great. Hopefully, Brandon would also be in the 'court' and she could find out what the hell was going on and where the hell she was. More importantly, she felt she had a moral imperative to get away from the Bobbsy twins before she did them an injury she might not regret. They were driving her insane with this back and forth conversation. "I would be most honored to attend thy lord," Roberta started to stand up, then looked down. The floor was made of grass.

"Milady! Thy feet are not yet shod!" both fairies said at the same time and hastily kneeled down and put some shimmering blue silk shoes on her feet. She wasn't sure if the left twin fairy had flown over the bed, or was just an Olympic sprinter, she never saw her move. Naturally, the fairy on her left put on the left shoe, the fairy on the right, the other.

"I thank thee for thy tending," Roberta gave a slight incline of her head to each of the fairies as she stood, the fairies rising with her.

Both fairies bowed deeply, their foreheads nearly touching the ground. "Oh, My Lady," both said in unison, "thou art most gracious. 'twas our great favor to be of such service to thee!" They stood, gave two identical curtsies, then they rushed over to an archway, pulling polished white silk curtains to each side of the opening tying them back with a golden cord.

Music, laughter and conversation that should not have been silenced by the sheer curtains, filled Roberta's ears. A male Fae, walked to her side and bowed deeply. "Milady," he said in a deferential voice, holding out his arm, "might this one be so honored as to take thee to our King?"

Roberta looked around the room. Well, not quite a room. They were under an open-air tent, with soft warm breezes flowing in. It was near dusk outside. There was springy and well manicured grass under her feet. Everything was set up like some kind of formal reception. It looked a bit like the wine tasting reception where she had first met Brandon, but a lot fancier and a whole lot bigger, about the size of a square city block. Silk scalloped tapestries of rainbow colors hung partially down the sides.

Inside the tent there was a huge party going on with several hundred guests. Some were sitting at wood carved tables, most were dancing. Trays of wine and food were being carried by more rainbow dressed servants, everyone else was wearing single iridescent shades. Men and women wearing the identical colors to each other talked or danced together. Pale blues with blues, pale pinks with pinks, yellows with yellows. Combined, it all blended together like the inside of a polished abalone shell, shiny but muted. Music played from somewhere, but she couldn't see the musicians from her viewpoint.

She looked more closely at the women. Regardless of what they were wearing, they were all twins to Delisa and Asiled.

"Milady?" The man/fae still held out his arm. "May this one lead thee to My Lord's table?"

Roberta looked at him more closely, straining her neck to see him. He was close to six foot six maybe six eight. He was wearing the same rainbow colored cloth as the two twins who had 'tended' her but in male design. The top of his outfit was cut as a type of formal tunic, his leggings were also rainbow colored and fit like tights. She looked back at the dancers. All the men in the room were identical to this guy. They were Pod people that could only be distinguished by whatever color they were wearing. Hundreds of identical men, hundreds of identical women. She pulled a strand of her red hair over her shoulder to make sure she wasn't changing into an identical replica, then sighed with relief. She might not be as beautiful as these folks, but she was still herself.

Her male escort still had his arm extended as though he would wait forever if necessary. She placed her arm on top of his. Right, she remembered his previous question, he wanted to take her to his 'lord'. "Of course."

Her courtier thread their way through the dancers and groups of diners, finally ending up at an ornately designed wooden throne that looked like polished amber with tiger's eye detailing.

The man who had been sitting on the throne stood. This one was not a pod person, he was completely different from the others. His hair was a glimmering gold white, not soft brown. His skin actually glowed as though he had turned on a spotlight from within. He wore a deep purple half tunic and pants, a brilliant platinum white blouse with wide sleeves. Nothing about him was muted or subtle. He was so incredibly handsome it almost hurt the eyes to look at him. No crown, but there was no doubt he was the King of these people.

Again, silently thanking her mother for forcing her into all those etiquette lessons and fairy tales, Roberta managed a deep curtsey. Her escort silently faded into the background.

"Rise, Lovely Lady," an overly sensuous voice said gently. "Our meeting needs no formality, we are most pleased to see thee well." He took her hand to help her to her feet. He smiled when he looked at her face. "We welcome thee into our world of Briah into this one's garden of Faucon d'épée. I am Orchis."

His world? His garden of Faucon d'épée? Roberta's stunned mind raced, she tried not to let her expression show the shock his words gave her. "This one is called... Bethany, King Orchis." First rule in the True Science doctrine. Names have power. She'd almost forgotten and given her real name. But he was so incredible handsome, she had wanted to for a moment. Even now, she had to force her feet to stay still, she had an almost overwhelming urge to sway forward toward his glorious, shimmering light.

"Beautiful Bethany," his smile was enchanting, mesmerizing. "Our servant, Tansy, hath not done thy beauty full justice by her description." He smiled more fully, his teeth were a dream of any orthodontist or dentist. "Hair of sunset newly gone, says she, yet we think more of sunset newly risen. Eyes of sun-leaves turning from the early frost, says she, yet we detect no frost in thine eyes. Golden dust upon thy skin." He nodded with approval. "Of this she spoke truly. So enchantingly a mortal of Assiah, yet so lovely."

Okay, that was a bit over the top, but Roberta couldn't help but be flattered. Compared to the incredibly beautiful pod people, she had been feeling a bit like a junkyard dog. "Thy fulsome compliments art very kind, King Orchis."

"Yet sincerely spoken," Orchis gestured to an elegant table that suddenly appeared near them. "Thou must be fatigued from thy distressing ordeal," he said with concern, "We beg thee sit, replenish thy sustenance with us and tell us how our court might serve." He pulled a chair for her to sit, then took a seat next to her. They faced the dance floor so they could view the show, but Roberta still had trouble taking her eyes away from his incredibly beautiful face.

As soon as they were both seated, rainbow dressed servants placed a beautifully arranged crystal plate, purple in color, containing small pieces of bread and cheese, a glass of the same crystal was filled with a white wine and placed precisely where it would be easiest for her to reach.

Orchis raised his clear crystal glass, she picked up her own purple one, looking at the contents with concern. She was extremely thirsty, but... Fairy wine? What exactly did it do? Was it safe to drink?

"Our solemn pledge, Milady, our wine and food is both pleasurable to thy palate and will do no harm to thy person," Orchis told her. "Sip, tell us of thy needs so that we might assist thee within our realm."

Roberta took a careful sip of the wine. It was very mild, with a comfortable flavor. Not overpowering, but crisp, light, refreshing. She'd expected a type of ambrosia, an overwhelming taste. It was a nice surprise. "It's lovely," she told him honestly, taking another careful but longer sip. She put down the glass and gave her attention to Orchis. A rainbow hued servant immediately refilled her glass. "I apologize if I was trespassing in thy world, King Orchis," she started, "I was searching for my companion when accosted by the hyena. I fear my companion shall be worried that I am not waiting where he expects to find me."

"Ah. Thy companion who goes by the name of Sir Brandon," Orchis nodded. "Our guards seek him as we speak," He looked at her surprised expression and smiled. "Milady, We could not be King of Briah should we not know all that transpires within our kingdom."

Not to mention that little eavesdropping Tansy had a big damned mouth. He probably had spies everywhere in his world. What else had they said when the little sneak had been lurking? "Thank you, King Orchis."

"Such beauty as thine should not be left untended, Milady. We shall remind thy companion of our displeasure for treating thee thusly."

He looked toward the opening of the tent. "Ah. We see that thy companion approaches us now." He shook his head with distaste. "He doth wear the garments of a hunter. Not fit for our court, but we shall overlook his rough attire for your benefit, dear Lady."

Chapter 25 - Amethyst

Roberta turned and watched with relief as two guards escorted Brandon to the table. Their uniforms were white, but, again, with the exception of their military style clothing and the swords they wore at their sides, they looked exactly like the other men in the tent.

"My King," both guards bowed. "As thou requested, the companion of Milady hath been found and brought to thee in safety."

"Thou art welcome to our court, son of Assiah," Orchis inclined his head. "Join us, please."

"Thank you," Brandon sat in the chair offered and in a deceptively calm voice, turned to Roberta. "I thought you were going to wait for me," he said. "I've been searching for almost two days. Are you alright?" He studied her, she looked incredible in the glittering clothing she wore, but not like his Roberta.

Roberta subtly flicked her eyes toward Orchis. "I was unavoidably detained."

Brandon didn't miss the hint and frowned. "What happened?"

Orchis put his hand over Roberta's and answered the question for her. "We fear thy Lady Bethany was sorely abused within our world, Son of Assiah. This garden of ours was neglected for far too many years and hath attracted base elements that art not gentle."

Lady Bethany? Then it flashed in his tired mind. (Be not known by elements unknown to thee.) She had given this Fae King only her middle name and even that, according to Rhodes, was only a nickname in the elemental worlds. It was another warning. ("Don't trust this guy.") Rhodes knew her real name, she was known and trusted, but not Orchis, he was the unknown.

Orchis was still smiling gently at Roberta. "With sweet valor did Milady attempt to protect a white stag from the unsavory intentions of evil predators. Alas, the foul creatures perceived her as prey in the Stag's stead."

"A white stag and 'evil' predators." Brandon repeated skeptically.

"Indeed," Orchis shook his head with mild distain. "Thou hast put Lady Bethany in sore peril whilst in our world." He told Brandon. "Gentle ladies should not be so easily dismissed nor should they be dressed in such coarse attire with which she was clothed when she was brought to our court."

Brandon looked at him sharply. "Excuse me?"

"We excuse thee," Orchis raised a languid hand and nodded toward the plate of cheese and fruit, accepting Brandon's sarcasm as a true apology. "Please join us in our repast. Thou art most welcome within our garden, Sir Brandon."

Brandon looked at Roberta with surprise, then back to Orchis. She had hidden her name from Orchis but had given him his?

"Apparently," Roberta broke in, answering the question he hadn't asked, "the lovely wayside fairy we met a few days ago has been keeping King Orchis well informed," she told him dryly.

Orchis gave a musical laugh. "Thou art wise to our secrets, Milady."

"Is Tansy now within thy court?" Roberta asked him, sipping her wine. If so, she had severe and painful plans for that sneaky little eavesdropping fairy bug.

"Nay," Orchis answered, smiling, as though he could read her mind. "We have sent her on a most important errand."

Between frantically searching for Roberta and now being in this court located in his own Faucon d'épée, Brandon was feeling a little less than friendly. Two agonizing days worrying about her, not knowing if she was living or dead, now finding her in the hands of this creature was hitting him on the raw.

This 'King' was the taint he'd been feeling since before their arrival. The moment he had walked into this pseudo court, everything within it bore down on him like black rot. He'd found the problem, now what was the solution?

A crystal goblet of wine was placed in front of him by an extremely beautiful female attendant wearing a rainbow gown. He picked it up, looking at the crystal suspiciously.

"Our pledge, Sir Brandon," Orchis smiled, "our wine will do no harm to thy person."

Brandon frowned, hearing the truth, but still feeling a trap. "Amethyst," he nodded thoughtfully. "Crystal quartz colored by the tears of wine Dionysus wept in despair for her," he nodded. He put down the glass without taking a sip. The wine was clear and harmless, yes, but not the vessel that held it. He took Roberta's hand under the table and squeezed her fingers. With his other hand, he pushed her glass further away, knowing the wine surrounded by the amethyst would give her a feeling of lethargy, then hopelessness, sadness, despair. She returned the pressure, but wasn't sure if his touch would help. How many times had her lips touched the crystal?

"Thou knowes't of the legend," Orchis looked impressed.

"I 'knowes't of many legends and myths," Brandon answered looking him straight in the eyes. "There is a particularly interesting

Celtic one about a white stag that is used by the Fae of the Otherworld to send mortals astray," he told him.

"And dost thou believe we come from this 'otherworld'?" Orchis asked, showing interest.

"I have no idea what world you come from," Brandon answered. "But I do know that this world is not the otherworld, nor is it yours, King Orchis, it is mine."

Orchis laughed, the musical sound was now less than lovely. "Thou speak of thy world," he smiled as though talking to a child. "The shadow children of Assiah have no 'worlds'. Such imaginative gardens they create are vast to the young, perceived to be unending, but 'tis only a world whole to them," he assured him. "They are not true worlds, merely small gardens, a playground for children within my realm." He looked wistful. "We have oft watched shadow children design their pretty little gardens within our world of Briah. 'tis both amusing and touching, filling our heart with joy at their simple pleasures."

"How patronizing of you," Brandon answered.

Orchis again ignored the sarcasm. "Aye, we do feel as parents to the children of Assiah, 'tis true. Such innocent gardens they create shall remain in Briah, by our will, with no dangers, no fears to frighten those who hath no uncertainties." He looked at Roberta with curiosity. "Is this not how thee created thy perfect garden, Milady? No fears, no dangers?"

"Yes," Roberta answered, looking slightly dazed, "that is how I created my garden."

"'tis always so," Orchis smiled at her then sighed, his eyes showing sorrow. "We have never meddled in gentle fantasies when the children of Assiah come into our realm." He sighed. "Perchance this was an error we should not allow to continue."

"I don't understand," Roberta looked confused, "what error?"

"Children grow, Milady Bethany, they forget what they have created. That is a danger. Gardens, neglected, attract weeds, doth they not? Such lovely gardens revert to what they once were when left untended by forgetful children. Thy gardens no longer have perfect weather. Thy gentle animals become prey, not pets. A tender fawn will walk up to a hungry wolf and be devoured because of its own innocent curiosity. You have seen this with thine own eyes within thy companion's garden."

Roberta thought about the mother and fawn she had almost touched near the stream, then remembered the rabid hyena chasing the white stag. "Yes." Even now she didn't know if the beautiful stag had escaped and felt a wave of melancholy knowing that it probably hadn't. There had been ten of those villains, she couldn't have scared them all away. That beautiful stag was either dead or bleeding painfully waiting for death. She blinked back tears at the thought.

"Children grown are not vigilant, they care little for innocence and preservation." It was though Orchis read her mind. "'tis it not the same within thy unprotected gardens of Assiah, sweet Lady Bethany? A cruel circle of both life and death when thy lovely gardens are left untended?"

The mellow wine Roberta had sipped made her stomach twist. "'tis the same in Assiah," she admitted with a sinking heart. As children of True Science, they had created naïve gardens of Eden, with serpents and other predators waiting at the borders for their chance to venture in. In her own world... no, not world, in her garden of Adelie she had touched and petted bunnies and swans, had let tiny hummingbirds and butterflies land on her fingers. They were pets. They knew she wouldn't, couldn't, hurt them. They were easy prey. A once unpolluted, perfect world was being destroyed because adults didn't care about its preservation. Tears she couldn't contain started slowly flowing down her cheeks.

"Nay. Sorrow not, gentle lady," Orchis gently wiped her tears away with his hand. "There are not yet weeds within thy garden."

"But there will be," she said in a sad soft voice. "Weeds always prevail."

"No, no. Not always," he looked at her with concern. "Sometimes weeds merely need pulling. If thou wish it, I will be most honored to visit thy garden periodically. If thou wish it, the King of Fae will even tend it for thee when thee must return to Assiah."

"So kind. That's a very kind offer," Roberta answered, feeling a little prickle on the back of her neck as something tried to force it's way into her increasingly foggy and melancholy mind.

"'tis as nothing. Give its name to me willingly, so I might find thy tiny little 'garden world' and see it not neglected in thy absence. I shall promise to remove such unwholesome weeds with my own hands."

Willingly.

And there it was. Even in her overwhelming depression, Roberta recognized the trap. He wanted the name of Adelie, because he didn't know it. If she wished it, he would visit. That would be an invitation.

And there was still another clue piercing her foggy mind. For the first time since she'd met Orchis, he was using the words 'I' and 'my', not the royal 'we' and 'our'. He wanted this information for himself, not his 'court'. Brandon squeezed her hand again, but she didn't need the warning. Roberta looked at Orchis, keeping her expression bland. Orchis was good at this game. He wanted both the name and an invitation to Adelie. One she would never willingly give.

She had stupidly almost fallen for it. His logic had been impeccable and directed cunningly.

But the elemental worlds of children were not designed the same as Earth, the 'circle of life' criteria wasn't necessary here. There were no weeds in Adelie, not even now, there never would be. This wasn't a polluted world. It was her fantasy world to visit, a playground of imagination that was safe when the realities of the real world made her frightened or unhappy. It may have seemed too simple, too perfect for her adult self, but not for the child she had been.

The child she still was in many ways. She could still summon the undine and sylph, with the innocence of a child.

(Realize thy knowledge and convention of innocence.)

Fantasies needed to be an escape from harsh reality, not create more anxiety. The worlds they created didn't need the circle of life and death, they only needed to be dreamed of and loved.

(A world without despair or fear is subject to jealousy and avarice.)

Adelie and the two worlds on the sides of it were definitely worlds without fear or despair. "Dost thou not already know where my 'garden' is within thy realm?" she asked Orchis carefully.

Orchis gave a small sigh. "There are so many childhood gardens within my world," he explained, "and all are so fair with innocent beauty, 'twould be difficult to see one flower amongst the others."

Roberta worded her denial even more carefully. "In Assiah, I study the needs of nature. I have learned that a healthy world requires both predator and prey." She smiled with feigned admiration and adoration. Well, mostly feigned. Orchis was a stone fox. "Thou art most wise, King Orchis, thy words have touched my heart. The 'circle of life and death' as you say, should be allowed to follow its own path. I see now that I was remiss creating a 'garden' without remembering this most insightful truth." She sighed regretfully. "Thy wisdom has given me much to consider, King Orchis, and I thank thee for thy council. I now know, by thy gentle rebuke, that I should leave my world to find its own way, without any interference," she gave him a grateful bow of her head. "I thank thee for reminding me of that insightful obligation."

"Ah." Orchis leaned across the table and kissed Roberta gently on the lips. He pulled back, studying her eyes, then nodded in satisfaction as a handsome man wearing a polished blue tunic the same color as Roberta's gown walked up to her side. "Our gentle cousin doth seek thy attention, sweet Lady Bethany. Thou must honor him with a dance." He smiled. "I bid thee dance, Milady, whilst we speak of manly concerns with thy companion."

The 'cousin' held Roberta's chair as she stood. She gave him her arm and started for the dance floor.

"Rob... Bethany," Brandon said sharply, standing. Instantly, the two guards who had led him into the pavilion were at his side, holding him in place with a hand on each shoulder so he couldn't follow.

Roberta turned toward him at the sound of her name, but her eyes were glazed over.

She didn't see him.

Chapter 26 - Binding

"What have you done to her?" Brandon glared at Orchis, ready to do battle. She had been overcoming the wine infused by the amethyst, he had seen it, but this was different. This new geas she was under had been caused by something else.

Orchis took a calm sip of his wine, then also stood, towering over Brandon by several inches, giving him a superior smile. With an invisible gesture by their king, the guards let Brandon go, standing back a few paces, but continuing to guard, waiting for him to make another move. Orchis moved to the side of Brandon, turning and watching the dancers.

"Lovely, aren't they?" he asked as if they were simply two men at a singles nightclub checking out available prospects.

"What have you done to her?" Brandon repeated.

Orchis gave him an amused smile of arrogance. "Shadow taint of Assiah. Dost thou not know the power of a kiss by the King of Fae?"

"No," Brandon answered in an equally cold voice, deciding not to allow this creature to have any feeling of superiority. "I know nothing of you, or the power of your 'kiss'. In my world, you don't even exist as a shadow of a shadow. In Assiah, you are not a King using the royal 'we' as a signature of his own importance. You are nothing there, not even a glimmer of thought."

"Thou seek to insult us," Orchis looked amused. "Perchance thy words are even true," he shrugged without concern. "But we are in my world, shadow taint of Assiah, not thine, so it matters little."

Brandon cut to the chase. "What do you want, Orchis?"

"Thy companion confessed to a garden within my realm," he answered. "With great courtesy, we asked it to willingly give an invitation into that garden. It thought us a fool, that it could create a clever diversion, knowing we could not take the name or invitation from it with only coercion."

"She is not an 'it', she also not a fool," Brandon answered scathingly.

Orchis paused. "*She*, yes, of a certainty," he gave a graceful nod of his head. "We shall accept your censure, that was most unkind. She is not a fool, but she is a mere mortal woman of Assiah. The more gentle gender of thy kind understands little of what they truly want. They must be cared for and cherished, protected from that which they are unable to

189

understand."

"And what doesn't she understand?" Brandon asked.

Orchis ignored the question, looked over at Roberta and frowned. "That modest gown her ladies in waiting have chosen doth not frame her beauty to its full," he decided, and waved a hand. The blue dress Roberta was wearing turned into a formal pastel gown of green, her shoulders bare. The gown matched perfectly the color of the male she was now dancing with. "Ah. Much better. Such loveliness should not be hidden." He shook his head. "Gentle Ladies need to be clothed in gowns of the finest silk, not dressed as thy lady came to us, as though she were but a squire of no courtly station."

Brandon took a deep breath, staring at Roberta. Dressed like that, she took his breath away. But damned if he didn't prefer her in the dark green pants and blue shirt she had worn when they were traipsing around through Adelie. "What do you want, Orchis?" he repeated.

"The name of her garden in our realm. She will not willingly invite us, yet she invited thee." Orchis answered simply. "We would ask of thee to give us the name of her garden willingly and offer us the same invitation so we might protect its innocent nature."

"It is not my invitation to give," Brandon answered. Nor had he invited Orchis into his world, he knew. How was it that had he managed to trespass here, but couldn't get into Roberta's world?

Orchis sighed heavily. "We do not understand thy refusal. 'tis merely a mortal garden imagined by a child." He told him. "It resides in our world, not thine. 'tis merely a garden that will surely revert to chaos such as thy own garden has done. Its... forgive us, *her* childhood garden needs love, it needs the attention she cannot provide as a woman grown. She belongs in Assiah, as dost thee. Wouldst thou have her stay forever in our court dancing endlessly with our courtiers, only as 'shadow of shadow, less than a glimmer of thought', as thee say we appear to thee in thy world of Assiah?"

Brandon stilled.

Orchis smiled. "As thee see, Shadow of Assiah, as thee diminish us, so dost thou diminish thy sweet Lady Bethany."

Brandon finally found his voice. "You're saying you'll keep her a prisoner if I don't give you a name and invitation to her world? Is that your threat?"

"Prisoner. Threat. Such disagreeable words," Orchis sighed.

"And yet accurate," Brandon answered.

"Nay," Orchis smiled. "We ask for a simple invitation, so our lovely 'guest' might be released into thy tender care, into a world than is not just mere shadow to thee."

"It is not my invitation to give," Brandon repeated, his heart sinking.

"She gave it to you," Orchis answered. "Is it not thine to give as thee choose?"

"It's a matter of honor," Brandon told him.

"Honor has so many faces," Orchis shook his head. "Doth one not include an act of kindness and protection to thy lady? Her cherished world is being slowly tainted as we speak. It shall die without the care it seeks. Doth she truly know what is best for her world, her gentle dreams of childhood?"

Brandon started wracking his brain for something else he could offer to obtain Roberta's freedom. He used to be brilliant at negotiation, now he felt like an idiot. Think! The pearl of Yetzirah was in his pocket, but he doubted it would be to Orchis' liking. He also knew the name of the world in Briah that his Grandfather had created as well as his own. That name might have value to Orchis, but he knew it would never be enough. As long as Brandon knew the name and could give an invitation to Roberta's world, Orchis would want it.

(A world without despair or fear is subject to jealousy and avarice.)

The damned prophetic words of the Seth were burning a hole in his gut.

He looked at the dancers, searching for Roberta. There were all statuesque and beautiful. The women had same light brown hair, the same pearl white faces. Same nose, same chin, same eyes. They were the same height and weight as each other. When they changed partners, their gowns would magically transform to whatever pastel color the man was wearing. The men were also identical to each other, he noted. Light brown hair, pale golden skin. Same features, same physical size. They twirled their ladies in unison, leading with the same steps, the same movements.

Only one dancer was different and easily seen. Her footwork was slightly quicker because she was not as tall and needed more steps to keep up. The color of her gown changed like the others whenever she changed partners, but her auburn hair and freckled skin was like a beacon, a living burgundy rose surrounded by manufactured silk flowers. ('twould be difficult to see one flower amongst the others).

And he knew. He had a vivid *knowing*. The other dancers were droplets of water, rainbow mist, shadow vapor, nothing more. Orchis might be able to change Roberta's clothing, but he couldn't change the essential her. It was not difficult for him to see the one true flower amongst the others.

Roberta was real, the others were not.

Orchis was waiting patiently for the reward he believed would be his.

Again, in his memory, Brandon saw a shy little girl with vivid red hair, hiding behind a tree. ("It was my fantasy to fit in, just as I was.") She never wanted to be anything but herself in Assiah, she didn't try to blend in with the others, she simply wanted to be herself. She wasn't a fish, dolphin or mermaid in Yetzirah, she stayed herself, she wanted to fit in as she was. She changed into a more practical swimsuit when she entered the water, but the change was only on the outside, she didn't change herself. She didn't fly as a bird, butterfly or even a bee in Briah, she wanted to fit in, as she was.

She always stayed true to herself. Orchis couldn't change that absolute truth.

No one, King or Fae or anyone else, could transform Roberta into what she wasn't, no matter what world she happened to be in.

"She will never be only a shadow to me." Brandon stated firmly. Roberta was perfect to him, just as she was.

Orchis still waited, not knowing that Brandon had already voiced his decision.

Worlds within Worlds

"She comes! She comes!" shouted a tiny voice whizzing around the room. "Celandine has been told that Orchis, King of all Fae has captured the shadow taints of Assiah!" she exclaimed. "Was it not well done of Tansy? She comes! She comes!" Tansy danced in the air. "Tansy asked her to come and she comes!"

Orchis looked sharply at Brandon. "Thy heart and mind I cannot claim," he seemed more than a little ticked off by that fact. "Thy form shall be bound, but thy lips remain." He gave a cruel smile. "Know this, Shadow taint of Assiah, if thou doth speak without my leave," his violet eyes darkened, "thy companion's life will be to do with as I please. Thou knowest the legend of the cup of tears, the next cup she sips will heighten her fears. Should that not be enough, she will be given the wine of Sucellus."

Brandon felt the physical bounds gathering around him, similar to the binding the Magus had put on him when he was bound to the Seth-A-Tristan et Yetzirah. But this was far worse. He hadn't willingly submitted. He was frozen in place, trapped like the sylph he had released from the brooch. His body was so cold, he thought he might break like an ice sculpture if he tried to move or if someone tipped him over.

(Imagine for a moment being bound against your will, knowing there was no escape, no words to free you...)

Brandon didn't need to imagine it. He knew. Perhaps this was even worse than the trapping of the undine and sylph. He could move his eyes and see what he couldn't touch, his lips could move, he could talk if he wished, but he couldn't speak without endangering Roberta. First she'd feel renewed fear and despair from another cup of tears, then, if she were also given a cup of the aphrodisiac wine of Sucellus, she would give sexual favors unwillingly to any man or Fae who wanted them.

There were definitely times when his extensive study and knowledge of the mythology of wine was not such a wonderful gift. According to legend, Sucellus wine was a powerful form of a rape drug allowing both movement and full memory, but no conscious or willing self-control.

A bound and unwilling prostitute with Orchis as her cruel and heartless pimp.

"Aye, thee also knowest that legend as well," Orchis smiled with satisfaction. "She will spread her legs for all my brethren. Perhaps without her true desire, but her woman's womb will be for hire." He looked more even more pleased by the look of horror on Brandon's face. "A mortal child of a Fae might be assumed who shall willingly dance to her lord's every tune," he added just to twist the knife in Brandon's heart.

Orchis turned to his court and clapped his hands for attention, ignoring Brandon as less than the unwilling silent statue he had made him. "Sweet music for my Celandine! Have thy words entrancing. Graceful be thy dancing! Fill thy cups with wine of bliss, let there be naught in our court remiss."

The dancers moved more slowly. Words were softly spoken, gentle laugher was muted to a whisper of sound. They looked like music-box dancers, twirling in harmony, an animated backdrop designed with perfection. As before, Roberta was the only one who stood out among the others.

Tansy was still air dancing, singing with glee. "She comes! She comes!" The little fairy twirled with excitement. "Tansy asked her to come and she comes!"

"Silence, Fairy bug," Orchis batted the little fairy away, giving her a glare that offered worse violence. He walked over to his throne and sat with a negligent yet elegant pose. Chastised, Tansy took a subdued position near him, her wings drooping downward.

Brandon was frozen in place far to the left of Orchis, close to the opening of the Fairy Pavilion and waited for the next disaster. Who was coming that could cause such a stir?

The music started playing a softer, more lilting tune as a beautiful woman walked in. She wasn't wearing a ball gown like the rest of the court, but a soft green, very casual dress. One side of it was longer than the other, that side reaching only a little past her knees. Her eyes were a luminous blue, Brandon could see them from several feet away. Her dark brown hair fell almost to her waist in soft curls, pulled up and back on both sides by sparkling sylph lights creating an almost crown effect. When her bare feet touched the grass, they didn't leave a mark.

If Orchis was the Fae King, 'the shining one' that could mesmerize a woman with a casual kiss, this would be the Fae queen who could do the same to a man, Brandon decided. She didn't glow like Orchis but compared to him, hers was a more quiet beauty, more potent for its very subtly.

And like Roberta, himself, and Orchis, she was not a robotic clone, nothing like the others. She was not a mere shadow of life. She was not mist. She was very, very real.

And she terrified him. Was he going to be in thrall to her, the way Roberta was now in thrall to Orchis? Were they both going to be trapped in this damned fairy court forever, dancing like puppets to someone else's tune?

The woman walked directly to him and paused. Surprisingly, she was almost a foot shorter than he was and had no wings, visible or otherwise. He tried to avoid her gaze, to keep from being caught in her probable spell, but found he couldn't. Her eyes were too impossibly blue, too compelling. She looked nothing like the other Fae. But if she wasn't Fae, what in the four hells was she?

"Once more I greet thee, twelfth son of Tristan," her voice was sensual with a quiet grace. She gave him a slight incline of her head then added, only for his ears, "Thy chivalry defines thy outcome, Sir Knight of Swords."

Brandon's instincts were screaming at him. She greets him once more? She knew of Phineas Tristan? She knew a line from the Seth? What fresh deception was this? There was something else about her that raised the hair on the back of his neck and not in a particularly good way. With her this close to him, he could see a small golden star that hung almost invisibly around her neck, a very tiny sylph adorned its center.

Orchis' next words chilled Brandon to the bone. "Celandine, our chosen consort! I greet thee." His voice literally dripped with seduction.

She turned toward his voice. "As I greet thee, Orchis. Tansy tells me thou hast requested an audience."

"Tansy," Orchis looked with unfeigned annoyance at the little Pixie. "Did we not bade thee give our lady a golden invitation written in our own hand? Did thee not present it in a courtly fashion?"

Tansy looked abashed. "Twas so heavy my Lord, Tansy must look far and wide to bring Celandine to thy side. Her garden is far, never placed the same, but Tansy bade and still she came."

"Thou lost the golden invitation given thee by thy Lord?" Orchis spoke in a quiet voice that offered instant punishment.

"Twas only a mishap of my friend for sure," Celandine put in quickly, "One needs not a golden card for thee to lure," she added in a soft voice. "Thy message alone caused curiosity," she explained. "What is it thou wouldst have of me?"

Oh, Lady, Brandon thought to himself. What wouldst he have of you? Every man in the room knew the answer to that question. He looked at Roberta and actually caught her eyes as she was being twirled slowly around. She saw him, but only looked at him in confusion, as though she were trying to remember something just past her memory. The drugged gaze she had before was partially gone. She also looked at the mystery woman each time she was swirled in that direction.

"From me thee hide, when I would have thee by my constant side. Wouldst thou sit with me awhile? I have greatly longed for thy

195

enchanting... smile." Orchis moistened his lips. "Or perhaps thou would prefer more privacy? I have prepared a restful chamber just for thee."

Subtle this guy wasn't. Brandon looked at Roberta and rolled his eyes. He saw a flicker of amusement in response. His heart lifted. Apparently the 'kiss of a Fae King' wasn't permanent to a 'mere shadow of Assiah'. If he could somehow break this damned binding, maybe they could escape while the King and his 'lady fair' courted each other center stage. (And definitely before Roberta was coaxed or coerced into drinking any more wine.)

"An offer that is most difficult to decline, yet with thee I have no time to recline." Celandine gave Orchis a gentle smile, then waved a graceful sweep of her hand toward Brandon. "I have come to thee as Tansy spoke of a shadow-taint. Were her words spoken true, or merely a feint?"

Brandon was already frozen stiff, but it felt like he had stiffened more. She came because of him? Damn! Now he was part of center stage, escaping with Roberta was not possible when all eyes were on him.

Not good.

Orchis opened his hands with a negligent shrug. He smiled, glowing in his own unique beauty. "There truly is a shadow taint that trespasses within my world as you can see. Yet I must confess, 'twas mostly a ploy for thee to come to me," he admitted with a winning smile. "The taint is of little import and not worthy of thy notice. Think only of me, lovely Celandine," he added in a coaxing voice.

Brandon suddenly noted with interest that Orchis had dropped the royal third person when he spoke to this woman. Did that mean something? He looked toward where Roberta was still dancing to see if she had also noticed the inconsistency. Unfortunately, her dance partner had twirled her in another direction, she wasn't turned his way and didn't see him.

Celandine smiled. "A truly effortless request. Thy shining beauty could easily stray one from a *noble quest*."

Noble quest? Oh, damn, Brandon had been trying to get Roberta's attention again, what had he missed? The strange woman didn't turn toward him, nor were the words spoken with a different tone, but he had literally felt the words he knew were aimed specifically at him. He started paying closer attention to what she was saying.

"Let thy noble quest be thy willing choice to lie with me," Orchis suggested. "Doth my garden not tempt thee with its luxury?"

"This truly is a garden rare," Celandine looked around the landscape with marked consideration, "this new realm you claim has no compare," she told him. "'Tis very far from thy formal court, thus hard to see, what value is this land to thee?"

"Its grass is warm and softly spread," Orchis told her, almost purring, "an idyllic place for us to bed. We would love thee in our royal company," he gestured towards the dancers, "a gentle mating that all could see."

Whoa. He was back to 'we' instead of 'I'. Either Brandon was translating that wrong, or the gloves were off. Orchis didn't want to gently 'lie' with Celandine with probable lovemaking to follow, Orchis wanted that bedding held publicly in the full view of the entire court so they could appreciate his performance. He looked around feeling more than a little uncomfortable.

"Thy fulsome compliment doth flatter me much," Celandine answered, her voice still surprisingly calm. "Hath this world a name that one might... touch?" she asked.

The hesitant word 'touch', had its effect. Orchis paused a moment as though he was having difficulty remembering the question, maybe even his own name. Brandon realized his own libido was starting to rise in anticipation. The entire group had stopped dancing. They were now just swaying with the music, watching the interplay as though they were settling in for a promised porn flick. Maybe expecting a full-blown orgy in which they could all participate. Roberta's face was also turned toward the woman, waiting and swaying like the rest of the dancers for her response.

Apparently, when Orchis was sexually turned on, it infected everyone around him.

Yet, Brandon realized, with every rhyme she had volleyed, the woman had been rejecting Orchis' advances. She was skillfully saying her words with a clever double entendre, so they could be taken in several different ways depending on who was listening. She clearly wanted something, but it was also obvious to Brandon that it wasn't a public roll on the grass with Orchis.

"This garden's name is Faucon d'épée," Orchis finally answered, "but it needs no formal name for thee," he was breathing heavily. "All gardens that touch Briah are ruled by my invitation and bear your beauty with fruitful anticipation." He carefully brushed a golden lock of his hair over his shoulder and glowed more brilliantly, watching her with obvious lust.

Faucon d'épée. Brandon felt sick to his stomach. Orchis knew the name of his world. Names have power. Tansy again. He'd barbeque that little fairy bug first chance he got. Well, he finally knew how Orchis had found his world, but how in the hell had he gotten inside without an

197

invitation?

"All gardens that touch Briah are ruled by thy invitation?" Celandine looked astonished. "Truly a momentous claim of riches, Lord of Fae. My garden as well?"

Brandon knew that the last wasn't an idle question. She had quit talking in rhyme. Something was shifting, he watched the woman with increased interest. A memory tried to emerge, but it continued to slip past him.

Orchis, however, didn't seem to notice the change or the rhythm of her words, only waved a negligent hand. "Fear not, Celandine. For thy... bounty fair, I release thy garden into thy care."

"Dost thou? Such gracious generosity." She looked up for a moment then shook her head. "I can see have been most remiss in my duties. I was unaware my garden in Nebulae needed release or 'twas being held captive by a Briah lord of Fae." The seven pointed star around her neck sparkled, making itself fully noticeable, the elemental within it glowed a hot bright spark of brilliant white and blue fire.

Whatever that spark was, it no longer looked like an innocent sylph, Brandon thought with concern. Possibly not a sylph at all.

Evidently, her last words had some meaning of importance. The music stopped abruptly. Every leaf, every breath, everything alive stilled at her words. The dancers were no longer swaying.

Brandon also felt himself holding his breath for the next move in this verbal chess game. This was not good. He could taste fear in the air, the tension was like a nuclear weapon that was about to implode. There was obvious danger lurking and it was going to take out everyone in the room.

What the hell had she just said or done that caused everyone to so suddenly go on guard?

Orchis looked stunned, his eyes widened as though he had never truly seen the woman before. "Nay! Thou mistake my words!" he said quickly, his earlier seduction pose was no longer in evidence. It was as though she had given him an ice cold shower with her statement, then jabbed him with a sword of fire. His golden glow had muted appreciably. "None rule Nebulae. I make no claim to thy garden within it! No offence was intended!"

There was a long pause, as though everything, everyone, was still holding its collective breath. "Then none shall be taken," Celandine finally answered in a calm voice. The star at her neck settled back into its former near invisibility. The tension eased, but didn't completely dissipate. That feeling of doom was still hanging out there, somewhere very close. Something very deadly hovered without mercy, aimed at

198

everyone.

Then Celandine looked at Roberta. "I see Bethesicyme doth grace thy court. 'Tis good to see her safe, one thought her lost. Rhodes hath sorely missed her sister's company." She turned back to Orchis. "Dost thou claim thy riches also include the daughter of Amphitrite, near-sister of Triton?"

Orchis turned toward Roberta, who was still frozen on the dance floor. "Nay!" he waved toward her. Roberta staggered slightly and her partner took her arm to steady her, then gently let her go, giving her a courtly bow. Orchis turned back to Celandine. "I release the daughter of Amphitrite, into thy care. I beg thee tell Triton no offense was intended toward his near-sister."

"You may believe that I shall. His understanding will no doubt be... remarkable," Celandine told him.

Rhodes had come through, Brandon realized with surprise and a silent sigh of relief. Had she used her siren's call to get this woman to help her sister?

No matter how she had summoned this woman for help, Rhodes was rapidly becoming one of his new favorite relatives.

Orchis still seemed rattled. "Wouldst thou also ask that the companion of Bethesicyme be released into thy care as well?"

Celandine glanced toward Brandon and shrugged with no apparent interest. "Nay," she answered, with a negligent flick of her wrist. "'Tis his riddle to solve."

Brandon felt oddly complimented by her dismissal, but confused. His riddle to solve? What riddle?

"Dost thou wish more of me?" Orchis asked.

"Nay. I must decline remaining longer in thy court, Lord of Fae." She looked around her surroundings again. "Unlike thee, I need tend my garden."

There was a collective sigh of relief.

"Thy presence will always be honored within our garden world of Faucon d'épée," Orchis told her with a deep bow.

Celandine returned the bow. "I thank thee for thy invitation and would visit this world again. But... Faucon d'épée," she shook her head. "Nay. Its name doth not please me. An arrogant name that doth not ring true," she frowned again shook her head, looked toward Brandon, than back to Orchis. "Art thou sure this world within Briah was claimed by thee without offense, Orchis of Fae?"

The relief of the court was gone again, replaced by renewed tension. Brandon's more so than the others.

"'Twas no offense," Orchis assured her. "'Twas mine to claim without trespass."

"Why wouldst thou wish to claim such a world so far removed from thy formal court?" Celandine asked curiously.

"So we could give it our protection from the shadow taint as it was not tended well. If thou will it, there is witness to our claim."

"Not a necessity, surely, but I confess a curiosity of any world *dreamed by a child of innocence pure,* yet not well tended and so easily claimed," Celandine looked intrigued.

Once again, Brandon felt that her words were directed at him, but, again, he had no clue what she meant. Damnit, what was he missing?

Orchis gestured to Tansy, hovering nearby, she was biting her lip with worry. "Tansy, attend us."

Her small voice entered the discussion. "Tansy's sorry Celandine was worried, 'twas not kind of Tansy."

Celandine gave her a gentle smile. "'Twas but a very small worry, sweet Tansy, innocently intended, quickly mended," she answered. "Thy chosen King has claimed a world within Briah, because it was not well tended and that Tansy bears witness to his claim. Doth this be true?"

"Tansy does bear witness!" Tansy nodded eagerly. "'tis true, Celandine! The shadow-taint from Assiah willingly spoke the world name thrice! Tansy heard the name thrice! Tansy told her Lord true! Tansy told her Lord thrice! Faucon d'épée, Faucon d'épée, Faucon d'épée!" Tansy said in Brandon's voice. "My King heard the name true, My King heard the name thrice!"

"Aye," Celandine nodded gently at Tansy flitting near the arm of Orchis' throne. "Thou hath been truly faithful to thy King, Tansy, fear the wrath of none."

Brandon's stomach felt like lead. *(Realize thy knowledge and convention of innocence.)* Damn! Could he have been more stupid? A three year old child knew to keep the name of their world a secret, but he'd used it without thought the entire time they had been here. (Your free will, thrice given, acceptance thrice received). He thought back. Roberta had never said the name of his world or her own since leaving his office so many days ago.

No, he had not protected his garden well. He'd literally given it away with sheer stupidity.

The woman spoke again, her attention back to Orchis. "Thy servant hears truly, Orchis, but listens to but one voice and can not see the heart within a child of Assiah." She looked at Brandon and gave him a soft smile. "A wise Knight of the Sword knows to keep his council within the interested ears of Briah." She looked at him expectantly.

Brandon's mind was racing, as time itself seemed to stop. What was she talking about? ('tis his riddle to solve.) What was the riddle he needed to solve? Riddles. Roberta complained she hated riddles, they only seemed obvious after they were solved.

(*Reject that which has no purpose to thy quest.*)

The answer was there, in the line of the Seth. Brandon concentrated, his mind racing. Faucon d'épée was tainted, being destroyed with black rot. Sometimes a vineyard had to be permanently abandoned, plowed under, because it could not be saved. Was that what he had to reject? Did Faucon d'épée have any purpose any longer? Had its soil, its essence, played out? Should he destroy his world by rejecting it, denying its existence, quit believing it was real so that Orchis couldn't claim it? Was the fantasy world of a child even meant for an adult?

(Its name doth not please me. Nay, an arrogant name that does not ring true.)

Faucon d'épée did not ring true. But why? Because it was tainted, unreal, a mere fantasy, or for some other reason?

("A wise Knight of the Sword knows to keep his council within the interested ears of Briah.")

Hints. She'd been giving him hints. There was another answer. It was his riddle to solve. He'd kept his council within the interested ears of Briah. How? By blurting out the name of his world so Tansy could hear it and repeat it to Orchis, thrice given, thrice received? A hell of a lousy way to 'keep his council'.

(listens to but one voice and cannot see the heart within a child of Assiah)

Reject thy certainty.

Realize thy knowledge and convention of innocence.

(Dreamed by a child of innocence pure.... the heart within a child of Assiah)

Brandon stiffened. Oh, four hells. Oh, Damn. (An arrogant name that does not ring true)

Of course it didn't ring true! The answer was always there. Dreamed by a child of innocence pure. Sword-Point. That was the true name of his world when he'd created it. Not Faucon d'épée, Sword-point. He'd forgotten he'd changed the name to French when he was ten, because at the time he thought it sounded more grownup, classier, it fit in with his new French surroundings, his new language. But, as a child of six, he had named his world Sword-Point.

Reject that which has no purpose to thy quest.

Orchis. Orchis had no purpose to his quest.

He wanted to laugh and cry at the same time. Brandon suddenly felt so enriched with power it made his mind reel. Eyes burning with unshed tears, he turned his eyes to his captor, trying to keep his voice steady. "Orchis, Lord of Fae. My world within Briah is closed to all who have not received invitation. *Ki Akal Briah*, Orchis," he made certain to speak loudly so that everyone, everything, in the white silk tent would hear. "You may be King of Briah," he said with a voice strong and sure, "but there are worlds within worlds and my world is not yours. *Ki Akal Briah*, Orchis, my world is not yours, it can not be claimed, you have not its name, you have not been invited."

Sword-point, he thought to himself. His world. Dreamed by a child with innocence pure. It was *his* world, *his* childhood dream and he had never lost it, he had never given it away, it had simply been protected by a growing child's arrogance and pride, his need to fit in. He let out a choked laugh, his unshed tears finally fell. "*Ki Akal Briah*, Orchis, my world is not yours, it can not be claimed, you have not its name, you have not been invited," he said loudly for the third and final time.

With a shimmer of blinding light, the clearing instantly held only Roberta, Brandon and the mysterious Celandine. Even the tables, chairs and all the luxurious hangings were gone. Roberta ran to Brandon, wrapping her arms around his waist, holding on tightly. She was no longer wearing the ever-changing pastel gown Orchis had magically dressed her in, but the green pants and blue shirt she had worn before. Even the sea grass was still braided in her hair.

"Well done, Sir Knight," Celandine gave Brandon a sweet smile and a formal bow. "Forgive my trespass into thy world without invitation. I shall intrude no longer."

With that, the small golden star on her chest flashed white and she was gone.

Brandon and Roberta stood in the now clear meadow as the full moon bathed them in its light and just held each other.

"You look tired. How did the rehearsal go?" Pricilla greeted Aaron at the door.

"No real surprises, just the normal minor issues," he put his arm around her, pulled her close and kissed her. Since Aaron had made the decision to give her the star, she was always there when he came home. She had complete control, no more surprises, no popping in or out unexpectedly wherever he happened to be.

She was definitely her own anchor, finally given her own independent path. He could still call her like any other elemental, but he was only tempted to do so to prove that he could. Celandine or Ce-Cill, she was always his, just as Magus of Power, or simply A-Ron, he would always be hers.

He kissed her again with satisfaction before he answered. "The charity wants two shows instead of one because they sold out and have more pledges than seats. One of my assistants advised me she's pregnant and her husband wants her to quit by the end of the month so she doesn't jeopardize the baby. Then three stage lights overheated and blew up, starting a small fire that triggered the sprinklers and destroyed about a quarter of the props we'd already set up."

Pricilla grinned. "Which assistant is pregnant?"

"Allison," he told her.

"When's she due?"

"I didn't ask." Aaron admitted.

Cassie bounced into the room. "Cool! Can I take Allison's place?" she was wearing her usual cut off jeans and a new 'save the world' t-shirt exclaiming, 'What? You think water and Virgins grow on cherry trees?'

Aaron grimaced as he read the slogan. "We'll talk about it," he decided.

Cassie's face lit up. "I'll finish making the Cobb salad and set it up on the patio," she told him, anxious to please. She bounced off into the kitchen.

Pricilla laughed and started leading the way to the patio. "You just made her day. You do happen to remember that part of Allison's act was to light a circle of fire with a wave of Salamander heat, right?"

Aaron looked resigned. "Better Cassie practice and learn control surrounded by fire extinguishers and sprinklers at the theatre than here where she might accidently burn the house down," he kept his arm around her waist as they walked toward the patio. "I need a drink. So! What did you do at work today?"

"Watered my garden, pruned a few intrusive weeds," she told him. "Nothing to write home about."

Chapter 27 - Sword Point

"Are you sure this is the right tree?" Roberta asked, grabbing the branch above her.

"This is the right tree," Brandon told her for the tenth time. "We are not sleeping on the ground where just any Fae king can pull us into some fantasy trap. Just a few more feet and we'll get to the cote."

"You said that thirty feet ago," Roberta complained.

"Well, thirty feet for an eagle, is just a few flap of the wings," he told her.

Roberta said quietly, "I know. I'm sorry I can't fly with you, Brandon. It would be so much faster if I could change shape."

"Never be sorry," Brandon said almost harshly. "That's what saved you from Orchis. You never changed in Briah as a child, it wasn't part of your fantasy. By being true to yourself, he couldn't completely enthrall you. Never change for me or anyone else. You are perfect, just as you are."

Just as you are. Roberta held those words close to her heart, smiling down at him. "I think we're here."

"Just stay there and hang on tight," Brandon advised, "Let me get past and I'll pull you up." He stopped for a moment when he got to her side and gave her a quick kiss. He kept climbing, reached the flat branch above, laid down on his stomach and grabbed her hands, pulling her up.

As Roberta stood in the middle of what was essentially a large aerie nest, she whistled in appreciation. "Wow! This is huge."

"Not exactly a Swiss Family Robinson tree house," Brandon apologized.

"Better," Roberta assured him, checking out the details of the nest. The cote contained a pseudo bed of feathers and large leaves to cover them. The branches created a natural window opening that looked out over the meadow below. A water catch basin graced another section of the nest. Beside the basin was a small selection of Licorice root ready to be used as natural toothbrushes. "You've thought of everything."

"If you're hungry, there's food in the hollow," Brandon showed her the spot. "Nuts and carrots mostly. I steal them from prey for when I take on something other than bird form."

"I think I'll pass. We're going to be vegetarians before this quest is over," Roberta answered, "I am more than ready for a real old fashioned pot roast or cheeseburger. Eating like a rabbit is not my idea of a healthy diet."

Brandon decided not to mention the two rabbits and the tasty squirrel he had devoured before going to Rhodes for help. "This has been a very strange day," he said instead.

Roberta took off her shoes and sat on the bed, putting her back against a large branch. "No argument there," she answered. "I'm guessing that Tansy wasn't the deceptive 'elemental of air' the Seth mentioned. Orchis was the true villain." She shuddered in remembered revulsion.

Brandon also took off his shoes, sat next to her, putting his arm around her shoulders. "That's a given," he agreed. The thoughts of what Orchis had planned for Roberta would haunt him for years. He'd almost lost her. "By the way, I love you. You're the third to know."

"'By the way'?" Roberta turned her head to stare at him. "You let me in on that little bombshell when I'm helplessly trapped a hundred feet above the ground leaning against you in a very convenient feather bed?"

"Just thought I should mention it," he answered.

"Right. Just a 'by the way' that I'm supposed to take in stride?" Roberta sighed, then glared. "Wait a minute! What do you mean I'm the third to know?"

"First me, then Rhodes, now you. Have you noticed that three seems to be the magical number around here?"

"Rhodes? When did you tell Rhodes?"

"When I went back to the edge of Yetzirah looking for you. She was more than a little concerned and offered to help. And, I might add, came through. She's the one who sent Celandine to us."

"Rhodes sent Celandine?" Roberta asked astonished, then concerned. "At what cost to you?"

"Nothing I can't pay," Brandon assured her. "Mostly just that I come back to Yetzirah after I find you so she can see that you're safe. Celandine has probably already told her that you're alright, but we need to go back to your cusp world just to be certain."

Roberta was silent for a long moment. "Who exactly was Celandine, do you think?

"I don't know," Brandon answered seriously.

"Alright-y, then. Try another. What *was* Celandine?" Roberta asked. "She was too tall to be a pixie and too short to be fae. Definitely no wings."

"Something from Briah," Brandon decided. "She was walking around with sylphs in her hair, did you notice?"

"Yes, but it was more like they were willingly tagging along," Roberta answered. "Strange. I liked her, especially when she formally apologized for trespassing into your world without invitation."

He frowned. "It's odd. I have a feeling I should know who she is, but my memory seems a little hazy. Something the Magus said, I think."

"Back to the Seth," Roberta mused, then turned to look at him. "Wait. *'An Elemental of Earth and Nebulae* will contest for thee'. She said her garden was in Nebulae."

"And so started the life of Kether-et-Nebulae," Brandon mused. "The first story we read out of crystalis."

Roberta nodded. "Nebulae. She must have named her world after she read the story. Is Nebulae in Briah do you think?"

"Maybe," Brandon agreed, "but since she could talk to Rhodes, she could be on the cusp of air and water like you."

"Good bet," Roberta agreed. "She certainly has connections in Yetzirah. She definitely knew how to scare the shit out of Orchis by mentioning Triton, and I don't think she was bluffing," she grinned. "If Orchis is the bogeyman in Briah, Triton is definitely his counterpart in Yetzirah. Uncle Treat can be a real bad-ass and there is water in every world. Orchis wouldn't have stood a chance against him."

"Uncle Treat?"

"In Yetzirah, he's called my 'near-brother'," Roberta shrugged. "Intense, but he can also be a sweetheart. As I recall, he can make super fun storms if you hassle him enough," she grinned. "Kinda ticked him off royally when he finally figured out I was only bugging him just to get lively weather, when he was only trying to get me to back off and leave him alone."

"You ticked off Triton? God of the sea, son of Poseidon?"

She grinned. "It seemed a good idea at the time. Nixie and I used to love to surf the big waves."

Brandon shook his head, deciding not to ask who Nixie was, he was still reeling from the knowledge of Triton and the statement that she had intentionally pissed off a god so she could body surf big waves. He looked at her seriously. "Now, back to the original topic before you get me more sidetracked with trivia," he decided. "I told you I love you. That's a pretty major declaration. Care to respond?"

"Well," Roberta seemed to think about it, "I'd really like to reciprocate the statement, but you'd be only the second to know and, if we're playing by the magical number of three, I can't. Sorry."

Brandon looked stern. "Tell the damned tree, then," he suggested.

"Isn't that cheating?" Roberta looked at him innocently.

"No, " Brandon said firmly. "It's a living entity, therefore it counts."

"On your head be it," Roberta looked up at the branches covering high above the cote like a natural canopy. "I love him, tree," she said clearly, then turned to Brandon. "I love you. I have for as long as I can remember. I know it, now you know it, the tree knows it. That's three."

Brandon smiled at her. "You were the little red-headed girl behind the tree in Loire, weren't you?"

Roberta looked surprised. "You saw me?"

"Sweetheart, I will always see you," Brandon assured her and gave her a quick kiss. "By the way," he whispered. "Are you still nekkid under all those clothes?"

"I believe I am," Roberta speculated with a grin.

"What a coincidence. I happen to be nekkid under all my clothing, too."

"Well... no need to waste a perfectly good coincidence," Roberta suggested, putting her hand on his cheek and raising her lips for another kiss.

"None at all," he gently laid her down on the feather leaf bed, kissing her very slowly, then settled in next to her, working on the string ties holding her shirt together.

Sylphs were lighting up the branches above them, creating a very romantic atmosphere. Roberta looked up at them in surprise and wonder. "Okay, that's strange. Beautiful, but strange."

Brandon stopped unstringing her shirt. "Two people who have admitted they love each other and are about to make love, assuming you don't keep changing the subject, is strange?" He frowned at her.

"No," she told him, "How all this works. How everything in our fantasy worlds just seem to fit. A feather bed, romantic lighting... I almost expect a champagne breakfast in the morning. It's perfect."

Brandon looked up into the leaf canopy above them. The sylph lights sparkled, but what Roberta thought of as romantic, he didn't. He thought about how Orchis had planned on bedding Celandine in front of his entire court. The sylph lights weren't the same, but still gave him an uncomfortable feeling. The thought of an audience, even an elemental one, didn't feel right. He almost said as much to Roberta when the sylphs seemed to just flicker out, the aerie now only lit by the light of the moon glowing through the leaves. He breathed a sigh of relief.

"Well, that was rude." Roberta looked at the now empty leaves.

"My world," Brandon told her, "my fantasy," he answered, "Now everything is perfect," he told her.

"Yes, it is," Roberta told him as he finished untying her shirt and pulled it over her head. She started pulling off his shirt. "Or, it will be as soon as we make sure we're both nekkid under these clothes. How do you get this damned thing off?"

Brandon smiled. "As I was saying, 'my world, my fantasy'," he answered.

"Meaning?"

"If we both get naked too quickly, I might forget all my romantic intentions," he explained. "My fantasy is to make love to you very slowly, for a very long time." He carefully unbraided her braid, draping the sea grass over her shoulder while he fanned her hair out over her breasts. "God, you're beautiful," he told her against her lips before he drugged her with a long kiss.

"I love you," Roberta whispered. "Now take off your damned shirt," she continued to whisper.

"I thought you wanted to be wooed," Brandon smiled, leaning down and stroked one breast while he loved the other with his mouth.

"Consider me wooed," Roberta suggested huskily.

"Then comes the courting," Brandon kissed her neck, then paid attention to her other breast with his mouth.

"Consider me courted," Roberta's breathing became more erratic.

"Then comes the dancing," Brandon continued.

"No dancing," Roberta answered firmly, remembering circling around unwillingly in Orchis' court.

"Not that kind of dancing," Brandon told her, knowing her thoughts. "I don't intend to let your feet touch the floor or dance to any tune but ours," he moved down the length of her body, pulling her pants down as he went. "No fancy ball gowns," he kissed her stomach, "no phony courtly manners," he stroked her thighs, as he continued to pull down her pants, kissing each thigh in turn, "no artificial music," he pulled her pants completely off, then tickled the bottom of one foot.

Roberta giggled.

"Now that's real music," he told her, working his way back up her body as slowly as he went down, kissing every spot along the way. He listened to her every gasp, every sound she made, mapping out the spots she responded to the most favorably. She giggled again when he licked her navel. She was so incredibly responsive to every movement he made, every spot he loved with his hands and mouth.

When he was facing her again, Roberta thought she might lose her mind. She was more than just in love, her feelings when he touched her were more profound than she thought possible. He touched something deeper than just her body, he touched her heart in very way possible. "Brandon, I seriously love you." She wished she could think of something more important to say, something huge to let him know this was bigger than simple love. It was so very much more than simple love.

Brandon looked into the green eyes he wanted to see every day of his life. "I seriously love you, too. This is *real*, Bobby. We are real. What I feel for you is so much more than fantasy."

Real. That was the word she needed. Roberta reached down,

stroking him intimately through the pants he was still wearing. She bit the lobe of his ear. "It seems to me these pants are getting a little tight, right about here," she told him. unfastening the top of his pants and reaching within. "I'm pretty sure I've waited for you all my life," she continued to hold him intimately. "I am your Page and I was born to hold your sword."

"Sweetheart, that is not my sword you're holding," he assured her.

"Semantics."

Brandon laughed, quickly removed his pants and moved on top of her, taking her face in his hands and kissing her thoroughly. "Assiah, Briah, Yetzirah, your world or mine, it doesn't matter. We will always be together. I need you to know that." He entered her with one smooth movement and started moving within her slowly. "You are my Destiny Given."

He had entered her body as easily as if they had been designed for each other. "I do know that," Roberta moved with him, "because you're mine as well," she told him as her body rose to greet the physical joining. They continued with slow loving movements, gentle touches, then fun loving, tickles and kisses, play bites and serious nips, climaxing almost at the same time, but not exactly. That in itself was real, perfect.

She was not a screamer, Brandon noted, but not very quiet either. Then again, neither was he. No choreography could ever match the music they danced to, because it could never be duplicated within any simple fantasy.

As she snuggled into sleep, Roberta noted that Brandon snored a little and grinned at the comfort of the very human sound. She wanted to hear that soft snore for the rest of her life. She tucked the hand circling her waist between her breasts, her own hand holding his as they slept.

A half an hour later, Roberta woke and realized there was one very important element Brandon had neglected to put in his aerie. "Um, Brandon?"

"Hmm," he pulled her closer. "We're safe, love. Nothing can reach us here. It's been a long day. Go back to sleep."

"Brandon, we need to climb back down."

"Why?" Brandon awakened fully. "What's wrong?" he asked, worried.

Embarrassed, Roberta answered. "I, uh. I need to pee," she told him, "and the nearest bush is a hundred feet down."

Brandon relaxed. "Just pee over the side," he suggested.

"Reasonable for a guy," Roberta said with annoyance, "but us female types are equipped a little differently. We can't just point and shoot, you know."

Brandon sat up and sighed heavily. "Fine. Get dressed, I'll lead the way," he told her, dragging on his pants, "but we're coming back up afterwards."

"I love you, Brandon," she assured him, biting her lower lip, trying not to laugh as she put her clothes back on.

"I love you, too," he answered. "But, sometimes reality really does cause a few problems." As they finished dressing, the tree was once again filled with sylph lights, twining down the tree, showing them the safest way down.

He smiled with appreciation at the sylphs timing.

Adding a little helpful fantasy was sometimes a nice bonus.

Chapter 28 - The Griffin

After they climbed down the tree the next morning, Roberta asked the question. "Which way do we go to get to your Grandfather's world?"

"That's the way to Crow's nest," Brandon pointed toward the far end of his world toward the mountains that marked the border of Faucon d'épée, but didn't start walking in that direction.

"Crow's nest?" she whispered, looking concerned that once again he had spoken the name of a world out loud.

Brandon read her mind. "Not its real name. Grandpère was French. Very old world, never spoke English unless he absolutely had to. Even then his accent was so horrific you almost had to use a translator to figure out what he was saying. Translate Crow's nest silently back to yourself in his language," he smiled. "For that matter, Faucon d'épée is a bastardized translation of the name of my world in English," he told her. "That's why Orchis couldn't truly claim it."

"Because it wasn't the true name," Roberta's eyes widened. "Clever."

"No," Brandon confessed. "Arrogant and lucky. I'd forgotten I changed the name when we moved to France," he told her.

"Hmm," Roberta moved closer to him, resting against his chest. "Unconsciously clever, then," she decided. "Still, how was it that I could get into Faucon d'épée without knowing its real name?"

Brandon thought about it. "I don't think you really need to know the name at all," he speculated. "Maybe all you really need is to know where it is and be given an invitation into someone's world. The Magus mentioned that there are texts within texts. He said even he needed to be reminded of his own ignorance now and again."

Roberta considered it. "Maybe all that's needed are good intentions."

"Orchis didn't have any good intentions."

"That's for sure. Maybe just believing he was given the name three times and received it three times was enough. Celandine didn't know the real name of your world, either, but she got in, even apologized that she had entered without invitation."

"More puzzles," Brandon looked toward his grandfather's world, stopped and shook his head, frowning. "I don't think we should continue on to Crow's nest, Bobby. I don't want to put you into any more danger. I only flew over it quickly and I have no idea who or what we'll find there.

If Orchis and Celandine could get into Faucon d'épée through some unknown loopholes, it might not be safe. You're more important to me than any damned Seth."

"Very chivalrous and very sexist." She kissed him. "I vote we go on," she told him. "We've gone this far, we can't chicken out now. Do you want to fly ahead, do a little reconnaissance?"

"Absolutely not," Brandon answered, taking her hand and lacing his fingers through hers. "You are now on a leash, little girl, until we get back to Assiah. The last time I left you alone, you managed to get involved with a white stag who was probably Orchis or one of his cloned people."

"Noticed that too, did you?" Roberta smiled, squeezing his hand.

"Hard to miss. They were graceful robots all, but still carbon copied robots," Brandon answered.

"They were all a little too perfect." Roberta nodded. "When I was in my world in Briah, I kept thinking how boringly perfect everything was, like Sleeping Beauty in her cute little meadow dancing with a make believe prince animated by squirrels and owls and singing 'Some day my Prince will come'. I like your world better. Without the Fairy Court camping in the middle of it, of course."

"I saw Sleeping Beauty once, not my cup of tea." He shook his head. "I had to watch those damned girly movies whenever my little cousins came to the house. I was almost glad when Sleeping Beauty bit the apple, was put in her glass coffin and shut up for a while. She sang in that high pitched voice that hurt my ears."

Roberta laughed. "It was Snow White who bit the apple and had a voice that could shatter glass. Sleeping beauty pricked her finger on a spinning wheel."

Brandon shrugged. "Same thing, they both sang to little creatures in the forest. I just remember my eyes started glazing over when one of them sang 'whistle while you work'," he answered. "Or was that Mary Poppins?"

"No, Mary Poppins danced and sang on rooftops with chimney sweeps, not dwarves, or animated clothing. Still," Roberta admitted, "she did sing to birds like the others. Cartoon penguins too, as I recall." She tripped over a rock, letting go of Brandon's hand to get her balance. She sat down to rub her right toe. "Ow." She shook her head.

"Are you okay?" Brandon kneeled in concern.

"Fine," Roberta assured him, "just stubbed my toe. These boots are definitely not made for walking."

"Let's take a break," Brandon decided, sitting next to her.

"This was so much easier when I was ten," Roberta took off her shoe and rubbed her toe. "Being an adult sucks."

"Not always. There are a lot of adult benefits you seem to have overlooked since last night," he reminded her, pulling her down to the grass then rolling her on top of him.

"Good point," Roberta said softly as she kissed him. She crossed her arms on his chest and looked at him hopefully. "Care to remind me of those adult benefits?"

"Ow," Brandon said.

Roberta lifted up. "Ow?" she frowned. "That's your response when I'm throwing myself at you?"

"Stone in the back," Brandon explained, "Feels like a boulder."

"Oh. Well, if you're going to be picky," Roberta laughed as she got off him and started putting her shoes back on. "Definite mood breaker."

"Nothing will kill this mood," Brandon stood and pulled her back up. "Let's find a softer meadow," he suggested, putting his arms around her, kissing her and pressing her body next to his to show his obvious interest in furthering their discussion.

Roberta wriggled free and started running in the direction of Crow's Nest and a much grassier area. "Catch me if you can," she grinned back at him over her shoulder, then was blasted back several feet by a wall of air. Naturally, when she fell it was on yet another wayward stone. "Ow and Ow?"

Brandon hurried up to her. "What happened? Are you alright?"

Roberta looked ahead, there was nothing there. She gave him her hand to help her up then rubbed her backside. "Yup, definitely out of the mood." She looked up a Brandon. "Did you see that?"

"See what?" he looked confused, pulling her up.

"Go ahead a few feet," she suggested.

"Why?"

"I want to see what happens," she told him. "Just be careful."

"Okay," Brandon walked forward slowly, watching his feet, stopped then to looked back at her. "What's supposed to happen?"

"Keep walking," Roberta instructed, then got up, brushing the back of her pants, gingerly massaging her bruised butt. Maybe she should re-think her preference to his world rather than Adelie.

Brandon walked a few more feet, then turned and looked at her. "Well?"

"Watch," Roberta walked toward him, got hit again by the blast of air, this time she kept her balance by wind-milling her arms. It still pushed her back several feet. "Its like one of those fun houses," she grinned and walked forward again, once more being blown back. "That is so cool!"

Brandon considered it. "I'm guessing we left the boundary of Faucon d'épée," he decided. "I'm in Crow's Nest. I didn't realize we'd walked that far."

"Since we don't know whatever loophole Orchis and Celandine used to trespass into other worlds, I guess we have to play by the rules we know. Should I keep playing with the wind, or would you like to invite me in?" she held up a hand. "Nope. Wait. One more time," she smiled, then let the wind push her back a third time as she moved forward. "That is so fun! I want to do it again," she told him, then proceeded to do so.

Brandon stood there with his hands on his hips. "Done playing yet?" he asked.

Roberta gave a deep sigh. "I suppose," she answered in the, disappointed voice of a sulky child, dragging her right foot over the grass.

"I invite you into Crow's nest," Brandon said firmly, shaking his head.

Roberta frowned at him as she walked forward and no blast of air stopped her. "Grown-ups have absolutely no sense of humor," she told him, "you just wanted to ruin my fun because you can't do it."

"Sadly true," Brandon answered. "You get air blasts, all I get are tidal waves that try to drown me when I pass from one elemental world into another."

"Poor baby," Roberta stood up on tiptoe and kissed him. "I'll take you La Ronde when we get back to Assiah. Best roller coasters ever. Or Sea World in San Diego. They have water slides."

"Deal." He kissed her back, taking a little more time than necessary, then nodded toward some high mountains about a mile away. "That's where we're going." He took her hand and started walking.

Roberta looked at the mountains dubiously. The lush grass in front of them swayed in the breeze like a green sea. Glorious and vaguely familiar. "There's a trail leading up that land bound replication of the Cliffs of Moher right?" she asked him hopefully.

"Huh," Brandon studied the cliffs objectively. They did look a bit like the same famous cliffs. "You've been to Ireland?"

"Hmm. Let me think," Roberta frowned. "Ireland is surrounded by water, I'm a Doctor of Marine biology... Blue fin tuna, salmon, monkfish, bass, albacore, undulate rays... yup, I'm pretty sure I've been there once or a hundred times."

"Smart ass," Brandon determined, then looked curious. "What the hell is an undulate ray?"

"A ray that undulates," Roberta smiled. "Not as pretty as mantas in

215

my opinion, or especially endangered as yet, but interesting." She looked up at the cliffs in front of them. "Back to our current problem. Is there a trail leading up?"

"I don't know. We can only hope," Brandon answered, less than certain of that possibility. "If not, we'll figure something out," he promised.

"Right," Roberta frowned.

When they found a truly soft carpet of grass, they once again made the most of their newly found 'adult' benefits. After, they both lay naked on the soft grass for a long time, just looking up at the incredibly blue sky.

"I really like it here," Brandon decided. He'd never made love to woman in the open before. The freedom was incredible.

"You just like to see me nekkid," Roberta decided, rolling on her side, balancing on her elbow and stroking his bare chest. The warm sun caressed her skin, she was fully exposed to the elements, and felt wonderful. A little wicked.

He closed his eyes at her touch, and yawned. "Oh, yeah. If I was younger, we could do it again."

Roberta laughed. "Have you ever noticed that men get worn out after sex and women get more energized?"

"Nope, but I'll put it on my list of unfair perks that you get and I don't."

"Poor baby. You need a nap?"

"No," Brandon answered. "If I stay down here, I might never get up."

"Ah, well," Roberta kissed him quickly and stood, stretching a little to get the kinks out. "Back to our quest, old man. Sorry, I mean 'old Sir Knight'," she corrected. She started putting her pants back on.

"You could keep your top off," Brandon suggested, watching her with appreciation. "I'm sure my youth will come back more quickly with a little extra stimulation," he wiggled his eyebrows.

Roberta looked down at his nude form, studying him from head to toe, her eyes twinkling. "Let's make a deal. I'll keep my top off if you keep your bottoms off so I can see how that's working out for you." She stared without embarrassment a little lower than his waist. She'd never felt so comfortable with anyone before. (Not such a prude anymore, huh, mom?)

Brandon cleared his throat. "Deal breaker," he decided, sat up then stood, picking up his clothes.

"Thought so," Roberta laughed as she pulled her blue shirt over her head and started retying the laces while Brandon put on his pants.

When they finally got to the base of the mountain, holding hands, Roberta grimaced as she looked up. This close the steep mountain seemed to go on forever, she couldn't see the top. "This doesn't look too promising. Not that I even know how to use them, but I don't suppose you brought along ropes and grappling hooks?"

"Not even in the backpack that was left behind," Brandon studied the near vertical rock in front of them. "This is not going to be simple."

Roberta looked at him seriously. "For you it would be. Simply fly up as an eagle or hawk."

Brandon glared at her. "Not happening. We stick together."

Roberta decided not to argue. She wasn't too fond of the idea of being alone again either. "Well, let's explore," she suggested. "Maybe there are some decent handholds and foot bearing crevices somewhere."

They started walking again.

Brandon stopped at a likely climbing area. "This looks good. A lot of handholds anyway, like it was made for climbing."

Roberta studied the rocks and nodded. "Maybe it was. Did your Grandfather enjoy scaling mountains as a kid?" she asked. "It looks like they go all the way to the top in a zig-zag route with resting ledges. A little steep, but definitely doable," she told him. "What do you think?"

Brandon studied it. "Its terraced," he frowned, then nodded. "I'm sure Grandpère designed this. Reminds me of Tain l'Heritage in Ardéche, even if it is a lot rockier and steeper."

"Silvering the heritage?" Roberta translated his French. "I don't know what that means," she admitted.

"It's the name of a vineyard in Ardéche," Brandon explained. "Left bank, near the Rhône."

"O-kay," Roberta smiled. "That's a good thing, right?" she asked hopefully.

"I don't know," Brandon answered, looking up the steep incline, thinking about it.

"Only one way to find out," she started climbing.

Brandon was still thinking about the path when she stepped on the first ledge. He grabbed her around the waist to keep her from exploring further. "Nope. Bad idea."

Roberta looked at him curiously. "Why?"

"Snakes."

"What?" Roberta looked horrified. "Snakes?"

Brandon nodded. "Grandpère was afraid of snakes, he was bit by a viper when he was a kid in Ardéche, almost died before they could him get medical help. It happened when he was climbing some rocks just like these, probably because he put his hand in the wrong crevice."

Roberta looked at him curiously. "Then, since he created this path, wouldn't it follow that it would be safe and he'd make sure there weren't any snakes in the crevices?"

"Unfortunately no," Brandon shook his head. "Grandpère didn't like being afraid of anything, even as a kid, thought it was unmanly. His fantasy was to be a 'manly man'. If I were him, I would be a roadrunner, hawk or something else that liked to hunt, kill and snack on whatever it was that scared me. It would be both a stimulating challenge and adventure. Besides," he added with a smile, "snake is very tasty when you're a hawk."

"See," Roberta held up an index finger and waggled it at him, "that's what's wrong with boys," she advised him. "They are creatures of circular illogic. If you're scared of something, wouldn't it simply be easier to avoid it rather than eat it?"

"Not for manly men," Brandon argued, puffing out his chest.

Roberta rolled her eyes. "Macho rules, got it. The caveman hunts the wooly mammoth, the sissy little woman stays home and cooks it."

"After she picks then stomps the grapes for a nice Châteauneuf-du-pape," Brandon added with a hefty sigh. "Ah, those were the good old days."

"Talk about fantasy," Roberta answered.

"Then, of course, she massages his feet, his back, his front, his..."

"Time out," Roberta suggested, "or we go back and find that soft meadow."

Brandon pulled her to him. "Works for me," he told her, bending her back and kissing her ruthlessly.

Roberta grinned. "Later. Quest first, you need to rest up, I don't want to waste any massages that get me nothing in return," she told him, then looked back at the rocks. "As to the possible snakes, any suggestions?"

Brandon straightened her up and frowned at the mountain with resignation. "Despite the possible snakes, I think we'll have to chance climbing. The good news is, I doubt Grandpère would have created any actual poisonous snakes, even if he could. Kid proof, remember?"

Roberta looked skeptical. "Moray eels aren't all that poisonous either, but I'm not going to cheerfully put my hand into one of their nesting areas. They can still deliver an extremely painful bite. Do you think he took out their fangs, too?"

Doubt it." Bandon shook his head. "Wouldn't be sporting. Fangs are a snake's only defense. You don't fight another fencer when he doesn't have a foil to fight back with."

218

"Your grandfather was a fencer, too?" Roberta asked.

"I have no idea, but he *was* French," Brandon shrugged, as though that were an answer.

"Ah. So. What now? Do we climb or don't we?"

Brandon glared at the cliff. "Well, I'd fly you up, but, and don't take this the wrong way, I don't think I'm strong enough to carry a full grown person as either an eagle or a hawk."

Roberta stilled, her memory flashing back onto something else. "I used to watch you in Faucon d'épée the same as I did in Loire." She looked at little apologetic. "Our worlds were so close to each other and I..."

Brandon stared at her. "You were behind the tree you said was a nice memory," he smiled

"Yes," Roberta rested her head against his chest. "I called you my griffin," she whispered. "My very own griffin."

"Griffin?"

"Sometimes you flew as a griffin. Head of an eagle, body of a lion. Wings wide enough to block out the sun. You became my secret fantasy."

"Griffin," Brandon become thoughtful. "I barely remember being one, I only did it a few times. But I do remember," he answered, then he made the decision. "I'll change, then you get on my back. We are going to fly."

Roberta looked thrilled. "Really?"

"Really." Then, remembering his childhood fantasy in every detail, he changed. One moment he was a man, next a Griffin. Head and wings of a huge eagle, body of a strong lion from the shoulders down. He folded his wings to his side and looked at her expectantly with his eagle eyes, holding out a leg for her to climb up.

"Wow," Roberta studied him with awe. He was more beautiful than she remembered. His wings were golden brown, the feathers around his neck were silver white, as were the ruffs on his front legs. She used the step she was given and scrambled up on his back, lying down, stretching her legs down the length of his strong back so as not to get in the way of his wings. She tucked her hands under the ruff of his neck feathers, holding tightly.

Then, Brandon the Griffin spread his wings and took off.

For the very first time in her life, Roberta knew the feeling of real flight. It was glorious, his feathers were soft, his body was strong, her heart soared.

She was on her very own, her previously secret, fantasy griffin.

Chapter 29 - The Other Brandon

As they reached the top of the cliffs of Emboîtement de corneilles (Crow's Nest), Brandon flew to another meadow, let her climb off and changed back.

"That was fun!" she told him.

"No, that was scary," Brandon argued. "We should have backed up a couple hundred feet so I could have gotten a running start or at least a decent updraft. Instead I flew straight up without the wind and flapped like a barely hatched fledgling." His expression was slightly embarrassed.

"It was still fun," Roberta disagreed. "So. Where to from here?" she looked around. The meadow was fairly small with tall grass. In front of them were trees with several dirt paths leading through it.

"I did a flyover while you were flirting with Orchis. If I remember correctly, it's the path straight ahead, a little to the left."

"Okay," Roberta took his hand, they started walking, then she stopped, pulling on his hand. "Wait. Stop. Did you see that?"

"What?"

"That huge boulder over by that small tree," she pointed.

"What about it?"

"I may be going crazy, but I think it moved."

Brandon studied where she pointed. "Oh, damn. That's a Rowan tree."

"And I'm guessing that because you said 'oh, damn', that's not a good thing?" Roberta guessed.

"It means if you think that boulder moved, it very likely did and we need to get down," he told her, pulling her to the ground. "Try to look small," he commanded.

"Why?" Roberta said quietly. "Are you saying I look fat in this outfit?" she grinned.

"Don't be a smart ass," Brandon said sternly. "Roberta, this is a fantasy world, remember? Unless Grandpère was making wine from Rowan berries, which our family has never done, he put more than snakes in Crow's Nest."

"You can make wine from Rowan berries?" She asked with interest.

"Yes, but not the point."

"Okay, what is the point?"

"Just that, in mythology, Rowan trees are generally guarded by

220

dragons."

"You have got to be kidding!" Roberta stared at him, then back at the suspicious boulder. "Really?"

"Not so loud," Brandon whispered.

"Why on Earth would your grandfather put a dragon in a world called 'Crows Nest'?" asked in a similar whisper.

"No clue," Brandon answered, looking over the grass they were lying on. "But, apparently he did, or it found its own way in through yet another loophole we don't know about." He raised his head cautiously. "I see it now too. That boulder is moving, or rather, breathing and it has a tail."

"Swell," Roberta looked over the grass. "Yup, I don't see the tail, but its definitely breathing," she agreed, then heard another sound from that direction. "And snoring like a lumberjack," she laughed softly. "I think it's asleep."

"For now maybe," Brandon didn't sound hopeful that the situation wouldn't change. "Why do I get the feeling that its no coincidence that I've been promoted to a Knight of swords and knights are supposed to fight dragons?"

"According to True Science, there are no coincidences," she reminded him.

"Sadly true. Which means I'll have to play 'Sir Brandon the dragon slayer' and fight it."

"Fight it with what?" Roberta asked. "You have no sword."

"My page is supposed to lead my warhorse and carry my sword." He told her. "That was your job."

"So fire me," Roberta suggested.

Brandon gave her a quick kiss. "Not happening any time soon," he assured her, "but you are now on probation as my sword carrier."

"Can I still play with your sword on occasion?" Roberta questioned.

Brandon scowled at her. "Get your mind out of the gutter, woman, we have a bit of a situation here. Focus."

"Okay, I'll focus, but for some reason this just seems too silly to be real. What do you suggest we do?"

Brandon thought about it. "Stealth. We quietly sneak around it," he decided. "Ever do a military belly crawl?"

"No, but I've seen it done on television. Does that help?" Roberta asked. She peeked out over the high grass again. "Maybe it's a friendly dragon?" she suggested hopefully.

Brandon pulled her head down. "You want to bet on that?"

"No, nor do I really want to stealthily do a belly crawl through high grass," she told him. "Ever hear the expression 'snake in the grass'? The reason we flew up was to avoid snakes, remember?" She peeked over the grass again. "Uh, Brandon? It moved again, this time I can see its tail. It's wrapped around the tree."

"There goes stealth as an option."

Roberta nodded, "and I think it can hear us. It just opened one eye. It's looking this way."

Brandon put his hand over her mouth. "Then quit talking," he suggested reasonably in a quiet voice.

Roberta pulled his hand away. "Wait a second. I just thought of something," she said just as quietly.

"So have I," Brandon told her. "I'll distract it. When I do, you run as quickly as you can into the trees."

"But I just remembered..."

"Now, while its still groggy from its nap. Run!" he ordered her, slapped her on the butt to get her moving, then changed into a golden eagle and flew high, near the dragon. The dragon was as gray as the boulder it had pretended to be and much larger than it looked from a distance. Brandon let out a loud cry near its massive head to get its attention. As anticipated, the dragon turned its head toward it.

Roberta sighed, stood, brushed off the back of her pants and started walking toward the Rowan tree. "Manly men," she muttered to herself. "They have to make everything so difficult," she said in a normal voice. "They never *listen*." The dragon swerved its massive head toward her. She gave it a sociable wave. "Hello!"

In eagle form, Brandon looked with horror at his mate and dove closer to the dragon trying to get its attention away from her. Once again, the dragon turned toward him as Brandon let out a low Kee-ye! He made more certain he could keep its attention by pecking at its back. The dragon lazily unfurled a wing and batted at him. The breezed it created caused the eagle to tumble for a moment before he could compensate and dive toward it again.

Roberta walked up to within a few yards of the dragon and stood completely still. "Hi, there," she said in a friendly voice. "How's it going?"

The dragon looked at her curiously. "Qui êtes-vous, et comment est-il que vous pouvez juger la forme vraie?" Its tone was polite, but delivered in a near roar.

Its accent was thick and it spoke very quickly, Roberta frowned, understanding only a very few words. "Excusez-moi, ce qui?"

Once more, Bandon the eagle dove toward the dragon, trying to distract its attention away from Roberta. Once again, the dragon flapped a wing, spinning him off with a blast of air, never taking his eyes off

Roberta.

The golden eagle Kee-yed again, trying harder to get the dragon's attention. What in four hells was his mate doing? Why wasn't she running into the trees?

Roberta looked up at the eagle and yelled, "Brandon, would you please quit playing around and come down here to talk to Monsieur Dragon? I can't understand what he's saying." She turned back to the dragon. "Je fais des excuses pour mon ami. Je l'aime davantage que ma vie, mais il est un idiot," she said very slowly, hoping it would understand.

"Ce qui?" The dragon looked confused.

Well damn, Roberta grimaced. Evidently her Canadian accent was as unintelligible to him as his formal French accent was to her.

Suddenly, Brandon was next to her, pushing her immediately behind his back. "What in the four hells are you doing?" he asked her, not turning around to look at her, but keeping a wary eye on the dragon who was now looking at him curiously. "Are you trying to get yourself killed!?"

"No," Roberta stood on tiptoe and said quietly in his ear. "I'm trying to talk to your dragon," she told him.

"What?"

"According to the Seth, *an elemental of fire will not consume thee*," she quoted from the line of the Seth. "I tried to mention that before you took off on your brave kamikaze bombing mission, but you wouldn't listen. There's also the caveat that *to see danger where none exists is cowardice*. Your dragon seems mostly friendly, but it doesn't understand me."

"Probably because you don't speak dragon," Brandon answered, trying to sound reasonable, when all he really wanted to do was take her over his knee for again putting herself in danger.

"Neither does he," Roberta told him. "Not unless dragons normally speak French."

"What?"

The dragon was still studying Brandon, then in a soft roar asked him, "Que faites-vous ici, et comment est-vous lui que vous pouvez juger la forme vraie?"

"Good lord, he does speak French!" Brandon said in astonishment.

"I figured that out already. What's he saying?" Roberta whispered in his ear again. "He talks so fast and his accent is worse than yours."

"He wants to know what we're doing here," Bandon answered. "Nous sommes ici sur une recherché," he said to the dragon.

"You said we're here for research?" Roberta guessed.

"On a quest," Brandon corrected her. "This is really strange."

"Well, talking to a dragon is hardly normal," Roberta answered reasonably.

"That too," Brandon said, "But stranger still, his voice sounds exactly like Grandpère's."

"C'est le monde de Pierre's, vous enfreignent," the dragon said, sounding a little less friendly.

"We're infringing on what?" Roberta asked, still understanding only a few words.

"My grandfather's world," Brandon translated, still watching the dragon. "Pierre était mon grandpère, il nous a invités à visiter son monde. Vous avez mon mot," he told it. "And before you ask," he said to Roberta, "I told him Grandpère Rose invited us."

"Qui est votre compagnon? A-t-elle été invitée aussi bien?" (Who is your companion? Has she been invited as well?)

"Oui. Elle est mon épouse, également invitée." (Yes, she is my wife, also invited.)

"Où est Pierre? Je lui demanderais si vous parlez vraiment."

"Mon grandpère est mort," Brandon told it gently. (My grandfather is dead.)

The dragon looked utterly heartbroken. "Je m'afflige son dépassement. Il était mon ami."

Roberta couldn't follow the entire conversation, but her heart lurched when she saw the expression on the dragon's face.

"Il n'y a aucun besoin de peine, votre ami est mort sans tristesse. Il a vécu une longue et heureuse vie." (There is no need for grief, your friend died without sadness. He lived a long and happy life), Brandon assured him.

The dragon paused for a very long time. "Comment mon je vous aide, près du fils de mon ami?" (How may I help you, near son of my friend?)

"Nous devons passer et trouver une négligence dans les mers de Yetzirah," (We must pass and find an overlook into the seas of Yetzirah.) Brandon answered.

The dragon stayed silent again for several moments, then answered. "Si vous dites volontairement votre fils ou fille de moi, alors vous pouvez passer." (If you willingly tell your son or daughter of me, then you may pass).

It was the same thing Rhodes had asked him to willingly promise. Why was that so important to these creatures of fantasy that they be remembered? Brandon paused, then spoke very quickly so Roberta wouldn't have time to translate or understand. "Je promettrai volontairement, si vous accepterez volontairement de protéger mon fils ou la fille ils viennent chez vous dans ce monde ou tout autre." (I will willingly give such a promise, if you will willingly agree to protect my son or daughter should they come to you in this world or any other.)

"What did you say?" Roberta asked, "Did you make some kind of promise?"

"Later," Brandon answered brusquely.

The dragon gave a formal bow of his head. "Fait. Mon nom est Brandon."

Roberta gasped. That sentence she fully understood. She laughed with delight.

Brandon grinned. "Mon nom est également Brandon," he told the dragon with a duplicate bow, trying unsuccessfully to hide his surprise. He wondered if his mother knew why his grandfather had suggested that name to her.

If a dragon could smile, it did so, with two rows of extremely large and lethal looking teeth. "Bon."

Then the dragon stood, almost twenty feet tall, unfurled its wings and flew away. The Rowan tree disappeared as he left.

Roberta turned to watch the dragon, it was now merely a speck in the sky. "Wow," she exclaimed, then looked back at Brandon. "You were named after a dragon?"

"Apparently," Brandon answered.

"How cool is that? Doesn't that make him your Godfather or something?"

Brandon nodded, smiling. "I'm pretty sure that's what Grandpère Rose intended. He was a little eccentric."

"But how did your grandfather create an elemental of fire in Briah? Shouldn't 'Brandon the dragon' be in Atziluth playing with the rest of the fire folk? Was your grandfather on a cusp as well?"

Brandon shook his head. "No. Middle of May, more than a week away from the cusp," he answered. "The Magus did remind me that True science doctrine is not infallible and there is a lot we don't yet know or understand." He listened to his own words, that strange memory from his visit to the Magus still trying to surface. Was it the Magus who had said that? Or someone else? With the exception of his unforgettable binding to the mantle of Knight, it all seemed a bit hazy.

"Well," Roberta decided, unaware of Brandon's internal thoughts, "since your new Godfather has apparently left the scene, shall we walk the path to the viewpoint of Yetzirah?"

"Yes," Brandon took her hand as they started walking the path to the far side of Crow's Nest. "Oh, also remind me that I need to put you

225

over my knee for scaring the hell out of me."

"Scaring you how?"

"For walking straight up to an unknown dragon, who could easily breathe fire and turn you into a crispy dragon snack."

"I knew he wouldn't hurt me. I tried to tell you, you wouldn't listen."

"Try harder next time," he told her sternly. "He bruised me the last time when he hit me with his wing." He looked at his right hand, shaking his head in mock dismay. "I might have easily broken a claw."

Roberta started laughing.

Chapter 30 - Crow's Nest

It took less than an hour to walk the path to the edge of Crow's nest and the cliff overlooking Yetzirah. Predictably, a huge wave of seawater rose to greet Brandon, cutting off his view. He walked back several paces, the water returned to the sea. "Well that's just great," Brandon said with annoyance. "You get funhouse air blasts, I still get tidal waves. Does any of this seem fair to you?"

"No, but 'manly men' don't get the fun stuff, they're too grown up," Roberta answered, letting go of his hand. "Well, you can at least see the ocean," she pointed out, walking closer to the edge that was obviously closed to him, rolling her eyes when he warned her not to get too close. "I can see about twenty islands or more from this viewpoint. Any idea what we're looking for?"

"Well, it has to be an island that Grandpère could see without getting drowned," Brandon got as close to the edge as the ocean would let him.

"Any idea what it looks like?"

"According to my family apocrypha, it's a symbol of life," he told her.

Roberta looked at him curiously. "You mean like an ankh, or," she looked concerned, "oh damn, the yin yang symbol on the brooch that we've already used and pretty much destroyed?"

Brandon thought about it. "I doubt it. Old Phineas Tristan was a farmer from the nineteenth century, probably not terribly interested in other cultures and their mythological symbols," he told her.

"Then what do you think we're looking for?"

"I have no idea. Grandpère Rose only said that old Phineas was a prude and the symbol would be obvious if I ever got to Crow's nest. Then Grandpére laughed like a loon and wouldn't give me any more details. Said it was a symbol Phineas believed only the men in our family would fully understand. Unfortunately," he added, "Grandpére may not have been completely lucid toward the end, he was on 'happy' drugs."

"Were you and your grandfather close?" Roberta asked gently.

"Yes. I'm mostly sorry he couldn't have met you before he passed. He would have loved you," Brandon assured her, taking her hand and kissing her palm. He looked toward the part of the ocean he could see, then pointed off to the east. "There it is," he laughed. "Wow. That's got to be the island."

Roberta looked where he was pointing, her eyes widened. "That?

Oh, my. That looks like..."

"An erect penis and complimentary testicles," Brandon finished her thought with a grin. "Heh. Grandpa Rose always did have a warped sense of humor. He told off color jokes just to see my grandmother blush."

"I'll bet." Roberta stared at the huge phallic stone jutting out of the sea, the added flourish of two huge boulders on either side strengthened the illusion of very happy male genitalia. "Well, in a practical sense, that is definitely a symbol of life," she grinned. "That is really incredible."

Brandon nodded. "His last off-color joke. It also explains why only the male descendants of old Phineas were allowed to follow the family tradition of looking for the island and caves. I don't think an eighteenth century man would feel comfortable putting in a more specific description in the family apocrypha, knowing that his daughter or female descendants might read it before they passed it on to their sons."

"I love it!" Roberta bit her lower lip, trying not to laugh. "So. Now we know what we're looking for, how do we get to it since you can't get into Yetzirah?"

"Not a clue." He sat on the ground as close as he could get to the boundary, she sat next to him, Indian fashion.

"Any ideas?"

Brandon grimaced. "There's got to be something more of a clue in the Seth. Unfortunately, between Rhodes, Tansy, Orchis and my honorary Godfather Brandon, I've forgotten half of it."

Roberta thought about it. "Back to business," she took another glance at the huge phallic island, and stifled another giggle. "What was the last stanza of the Seth? Do you remember it? My brain is on overload, I'm drawing a blank."

Brandon nodded then quoted:

"Diomedeidae may aid thee, if thou will it.
Diomedeidae will be lofty, denying thee thy purpose
One quest begets the other
Thy chivalry defines thy outcome."

"Clear as mud," Roberta groaned. "Okay," she sighed heavily. "Diomedeidae is an albatross. A seabird. Presumably a creature of Yetzirah rather than Briah."

"That much I know. I googled the word as soon as I got the Seth," Brandon told her.

"'The Diomedeidae will aid thee if thou will it'," she quoted, confused.

"So. We just wait and hail the first Albatross we happen to see flying by and ask it to help us?"

"Not practical," Roberta shook her head. "An albatross can fly for years without landing."

"There's good news," Brandon decided with a frown. "Even if we get lucky, I don't speak albatross, you?"

"Nope. Then again, it never occurred to me that a dragon could speak French, either," she answered.

"Good point."

"Hmm. Maybe Rhodes can communicate with one," she speculated. "If so, maybe you could change into a smaller bird and get her to ask the albatross if it can carry you to the island on its back?"

"'While being lofty and denying thee thy purpose'?" Brandon gave a humorless laugh. "I doubt it. Even if it could, a wall of seawater would probably rise up and kill both me and the albatross."

"Which would definitely 'deny thee thy purpose'."

"Exactly. Not a good plan," Brandon agreed.

"Damn. I really hate riddles," Roberta sighed with frustration. "Maybe we're taking this too literally. What else do we know about the albatross?"

"Well, according to Google and the Rime of the Ancient Mariner, it's hung around your neck when you screw up," Brandon answered, then quoted,

"'Ah! well a-day!

what evil looks

Had I from old and young!

Instead of the cross, the Albatross

About my neck was hung'."

"Then everyone on the ship dies, as I recall from English lit," Roberta reminded him.

"Yup, happy ending all around," Brandon had a feeling of hopelessness.

Roberta thought about it for several long minutes. "Okay, after the Diomedeidae, the next line in the final part of the Seth is 'One quest begets the other'."

"It was also the first line of the Seth, the one that brought us to your cusp world," Brandon reminded her, his thoughts raced ahead, his posture stiffened.

"Round and round she goes, Beginning to end, end to beginning." Roberta groaned with annoyance.

"Back to your cusp world," Brandon decided and helped her up. "Somehow, the answer is there."

"That can't be right," Roberta shook her head. "It would be as though all we've been through was worth nothing."

"We released an imprisoned sylph and undine," Brandon reminded her, "that was worth something."

"And found each other," Roberta smiled. "That's the best part."

Brandon kissed her, holding on as tightly as he could. "Yes. That's definitely the best part. Now we go back to the beginning."

Roberta looked at him suspiciously. "You have another knowing, don't you?"

"Yes."

Roberta shrugged and looked at him hopefully. "Wither thou goest, Sir Knight," she smiled. "But it's a long way back to my cusp world. Maybe we should rest a bit." She wiggled her eyebrows.

"Not necessary," Brandon told her, facing away from the cliff, back toward the trees. "Let's fly. There's a good updraft here.

"We can we fly again?"

"Absolutely," Brandon smiled, as he changed back into a griffin and she climbed aboard. The knowing he had was not a return trip back to Adelie. It was back to Assiah, where they had first started. His mind repeated to himself the final words of the Rime of the Ancient Mariner, a finish Roberta obviously had forgotten.

(The Mariner, whose eye is bright,
Whose beard with age is hoar,
Is gone: and now the Wedding-Guest
Turned from the bridegroom's door.

He went like one that hath been stunned,
And is of sense forlorn :
A sadder and a wiser man,
He rose the morrow morn.)

Unlike his shipmates, the Ancient Mariner survived, living a long and lonely life.

Just like he would be living a long and lonely life.

Without Roberta.

She had to go back to Assiah, but he never could.

A sadder and a wiser man, he rose the morrow morn...

Chapter 31 - One Quest begets another

Brandon flew slowly, taking the long way around, passing all their previous adventures along the way, determined to hold everything in his memory. Emboîement de corneilles (Crow's nest), the place they had to go to find the island of Phineas Tristan so they could continue their quest. There, directly below them, they had met Brandon the dragon and promised he would never be forgotten.

'An elemental of fire will not consume thee'. Roberta had figured that one out, he probably would have fought his own Godfather and died in the process if she hadn't.

He flew from Crow's Nest into Sword-point, moving slowly over the tree that cradled his cote. The sanctuary where Roberta had first told him (and the tree, he smiled inwardly) that she loved him, where they had first made love, where they first physically consummated what they truly were to each other.

As though Roberta also remembered that moment in the cote, she ruffled her fingers into the feathers of his griffin's neck and whispered over the wind, "I love you, Brandon," with such genuine truth, his heart soared. He could carry her with his strong body and wings as if she weighed nothing, yet still he could feel the warmth and weight of her body because she meant everything to him.

He flew from their cote further into Sword-point, which was now clear of Orchis' taint.

'An elemental of air will seduce and deceive thee'. Where he realized for certain that Roberta would never be only a shadow to him, where he finally understood that Orchis couldn't hold her with the passionless kiss of a Fae king, because she could never be anything but what she was, what she would always be. His.

'One may be coaxed yet not coerced. One may be touched yet not imprisoned'.

Faucon d'épée, the arrogant pseudo name he had called his world, where the mysterious Celandine had argued for them and given him the hints he needed to banish Orchis and his court from his true world of Sword-point, dreamed by a child of innocence pure.

'An Elemental of Earth and Nebulae will contest for thee'. Celandine had definitely fought, contested, for them, but didn't tell him the answers. It had been his riddle to solve, his job to make his world safe once again as he had first imagined it as a child.

His riddle to solve. A gift and a curse.

He knew the answer to the riddle now. Nothing was ever free.

On from there, he flew past the 'special' tree where Roberta admitted she had peeked around as little red-headed girl, watching him fly, adoring him secretly from afar. He wished he had known her then, it would have changed everything in his life. They would have grown up together, bonded from that point on.

Along the stream they flew, leading to Roberta's garden within Briah, where she had grown apples on a cypress tree. That memory made him smile, even in his griffin form. It was where she had accused him of trying to get her 'nekkid', but where they were both oddly satisfied when he only held her in his arms as they slept and snuggled under the glittering sylph lights. Not just falling in love with her in her garden, but when he had the knowing that he already was. He seemed to remember that he had told her that he loved her then, but perhaps that had only been in his dreams. Dream or real, it was when he first knew that they were made for each other, heart, mind, soul. Little Tansy had been there as well, the little wayside 'fairy bug' who spied on them, learned the name of his world, and gave Orchis the power to temporarily take residence there.

They finally reached the edge of Briah near her 'landing site' world of Adelie and he changed form with her still riding on his back. She clung tightly for a few moments as though she would never let go, then slid down his back, taking his hand and naturally lacing her fingers with his. "That was fun!" she grinned, her hair was windblown framing her face, she was displaying her deep dimples with pure joy.

Brandon had been remembering the moments that now broke his heart and answered, "I'm glad," he returned the smile, then looked grave. "Because it might just be the last time you get to fly on a Griffin," he told her. "When you go back to Assiah, you won't be flying again unless you get on a plane." He held her face in both hands. "Roberta, I love you. I want to marry you. I want you to have my child."

"I love you too," Roberta answered. "I'd like that as well. So will both our mothers," she added with a grin, "they've been scheming, you know."

Brandon shook his head. "Sweetheart, you don't understand. When I took on Phineas' sephiroth to try and bring back the pearl he'd taken, it was only a promise to try, not necessarily to succeed. Well, that," he gave her a weak smile, "and to put the name Tristan somewhere in his male descendants name, first name or middle name."

Roberta smiled. "Not exactly a deal breaker," she told him, "its not like Phineas' last name was Beelzebub."

Brandon continued to look grave, unable to return the smile. "When I took on a formal Seth from the Magus, became a Knight, it became an obligation, not merely a promise."

"I understand that."

Brandon shook his head. "I don't think you do. I agreed for the entire family of Phineas Tristan, past present and future. That includes every male child born through me."

"I understand that too," Roberta assured him. "We get a *family* Seth, Brandon. We're a team. A formal Seth can go on for generations. If we don't succeed, our son, or our daughter's son, continues the obligation."

"You want that for our children?" Brandon asked incredulously.

"Oddly, enough," Roberta answered, "yes, I do. Its not uncommon for True Science families to have a formal Seth hanging around their necks like an albatross." She smiled. "'It's a riddle, wrapped in a mystery, inside an enigma; but perhaps there is a key', remember? Any child we have, or their children, will deal with it, I refuse to have any cowardly descendants. We've made mistakes on this quest, but we survived, Brandon. Our kids will probably make mistakes, but they will also survive. Eventually it will be resolved. We can go back to Assiah, write it all down, hand the pearl over to our kids in our wills if we can't figure it out before then. We warn our descendants of the hazards we faced, they tell their children of the hazards they faced, everyone keeps a diary. One of our descendants will figure it out." She told him.

Brandon touched her face with tenderness. "I'm sure they would. There are only a couple of problems they can't resolve."

"'Every step in a sephiroth lengthens the path, every answer you find gives you more questions, more responsibilities'," Roberta shrugged. "One of the first lessons to be learned in True Science."

Brandon tried to keep his new understanding of the problems gentle. "First question. How will they get into Yetzirah?"

"Well..." Roberta considered it, "someday, someone in the family will be born a Page of Cups. Or, not as likely, but possible, born on the cusp, like me."

"Okay. We get a male Page of cups in the family. Which begs the next question. How did we get here?"

Roberta grimaced. "The brooch and our kids won't have that option. They might be able to get here in their dreams, but they'll have to figure out another way to physically get here."

Brandon nodded. "Even if we get a page of cups in the future, they could, possibly, figure that out, but, here comes the next question. What happened when we first arrived? What was missing?"

"Our clothes, our backpacks, pretty much everything that belonged in Assiah." She considered the possibilities. Since she hadn't used any of the very expensive gear she bought for this adventure, she might be able to return it. Then again, everything had been on "sale", she probably wouldn't get that lucky.

"Which brings the next question," Brandon continued, breaking into her thoughts of financial practically. "If we send ourselves back, what will be missing?"

"Everything that doesn't belong in Assiah." She looked down at the outfit she was wearing. "Including our clothes."

"Exactly. They will stay here. And what happens to the Pearl of Yetzirah?"

Roberta paused and thought about it. "Oh, four hells," she looked annoyed, but not especially worried. "It stays here, too. Good catch. I didn't think of that." She shook her head. "So. We're stuck, because you can't leave the pearl and we can't take it back to give to our eventual kids so they can bring it back and take it to the island."

"Exactly."

Roberta thought about it. "Bummer," she didn't sound very concerned. "Okay then. We stay here to have our kids. Like you said before, we build a Swiss Family Tree house. Where do you want to set up housekeeping? Should we build in my world in Briah, or yours? We haven't really explored Crow's nest, maybe that would be even better. Or, we could put vacation homes in all three worlds." She smiled. "You make Rowan wine, I sell licorice toothbrushes to the fairy bugs."

"You'd really do that?" Brandon asked, astonished. "Leave your family, your job, everything?"

"Of course I would! I knew this quest would be dangerous, I put all my affairs in order before we left. What, you think I'd leave you here alone so you can live like Robinson Crusoe without your man Friday? The ancient mariner 'a sadder but a wiser man', forlornly rising each morning alone? Is that what you've been thinking?"

She looked at his expression. "Oh, my God, you were! Forget that," she said firmly, standing on tiptoe to kiss him. "I love you. That is not going to change. I've said it before, I'll say it again. 'Wither thou goest, Sir Knight, I'm your Page, I goest too'. You're stuck with me. Get used to it. As for missing our families," her eyes clouded a bit at the thought, but she continued with a gentle smile, "we'll make a new one."

"A new one," Brandon looked at her in astonishment.

Roberta nodded. "Think of the possibilities! Your godfather, Brandon the dragon, can teach us how to make fire so we don't have to always eat cold food. Maybe Celandine will come for a visit occasionally. She seems to know her way around. Maybe she even knows a few useful tricks we don't. We could make her an honorary aunt to our kids or something, assuming we can figure out how to get hold of her. We may have to deal with Tansy the traitorous fairy bug on that issue." She grimaced at the thought. "Or not."

"Celandine would be honorary Aunt to our kids," Brandon repeated slowly.

"Well, I know she's a little cryptic," Roberta responded, "and she does speak in annoying rhyme with a lot of thee's and thou's, but she might become a little less esoteric... eventually."

"Our kids will already have a real Aunt," Brandon said.

Roberta looked surprised. "You have a sister I don't know about?"

"No, but you do."

Roberta grinned. "Trust me. If my mother or father had ever conceived a child outside of their marriage, I'd have heard about it."

"No," Brandon shook his head. "Rhodes. She's your sister. She would be our children's aunt."

Roberta thought about it. "Oh! Well, if we're going that route, in Yetzirah our kids would have several aunts. Rhodes, Charybdis, Kymopoleia, then a couple of Uncles, or great Uncles, Albion, Triton. Then of course the Grandparents, Amphitrite, Doris, Nereus... I'm not sure of the whole family genealogy of Yetzirah, it gets confusing past those."

Once, again, Brandon had a knowing and kissed her again. "I love them all and you're brilliant."

"Yes, I know, I made straight 'A's' at University." Roberta answered, bating her eyelashes modestly. "As for loving all my Yetzirah relatives, you haven't met Amphitrite yet. She may very well be the Mother-in-law from hell. I love her, but she's very stuffy and, don't take this wrong, you're from the wrong side of the tracks." She waved a supercilious hand, "Briah people, you know," she said pompously, "so flighty, dear."

Brandon laughed, his heart suddenly light. "Lets go see Rhodes. I promised her I'd bring you back so she could see you were okay." He started leading her toward the water.

Chapter 32 – Return to Assiah

"Let me get her," Roberta suggested to Brandon when they reached the edge of Yetzirah. "I know where she usually hangs out."

Brandon frowned at her, getting as close to the water as he could without being drowned by the wave that would rise up. "You're not going to forget me again, are you?"

Roberta gave him a quick kiss. "Never." She ran into the water, her clothes automatically changing into the silver blue swimsuit. Immediately the three dolphins who had been her childhood playmates were there in the waves, leaping with enthusiastic flips, urging her further in. She turned to wave at him. "I'll be back in a bit." She swam out to greet them.

Brandon sat on the sand, hoping he was going to do the right thing. He wasn't quite sure about this particular knowing. It was, in fact, only a hopeful instinct. He watched Roberta and her dolphins, swimming in a world he would never be able to enter.

Moments later, Rhodes was sitting on her rock near the shore. "You have kept your promise, Son of Assiah," Rhodes nodded her head at Brandon. She looked out at the ocean and Roberta swimming. "She has always been so lovely and graceful in the water."

"She's lovely and graceful everywhere," Brandon told her.

"You see clearly now?"

"Yes, I believe I do."

"All is well then," she turned back toward the water. Suddenly, Roberta turned, gave them a cheerful "woo hoo!", then headed back, the adult dolphins swimming on both sides, the baby trailing behind.

Roberta reached the rock quickly, leaving her friends in the deeper water.

"Are you well tended, sister?" Rhodes leaned down and hugged her, acting as though she would never let her go.

"Yes," Roberta answered, hugging her back, "I am very well tended."

Rhodes pulled a fresh strand of sea grass from the water, turning Roberta to once again braid her hair, taking out the snarls with gentle fingers as she tossed away the tangled grass and weaved the new grass into a complex style. "So pretty you look, Bethesicyme. Our mother will be pleased with your grownup form true."

"Thank you for sending Celandine to assist us, Sister," Roberta turned when Rhodes tied off her hair.

Rhodes look surprised. "Celandine helped you?"

"You didn't send her to us?" Roberta asked in confusion.

"I did not," Rhodes answered, "I have never spoken to Celandine."

"You don't know Celandine?" Brandon asked from the shore.

"I know *of* Celandine," Rhodes answered Brandon. "Few have met her. I have not. She is not of Yetzirah and would not trespass, although she would be most welcome.

"Then where is she from?" Roberta asked.

"Nowhere, everywhere. Her garden is... within."

"Within what?"

"More I can not say."

"Can not, or will not?" Roberta asked, pouting a bit and beetling her eyes.

Rhodes smiled. "Always so curious, sister." She shook her head. "More I can not say," she repeated firmly.

"I don't understand," Roberta looked at Rhodes suspiciously. "She knew of you, our mother, our brothers and sisters," she told her.

Rhodes shrugged. "Perhaps the undine you released from its Assiah prison told her of us. It told all of Yetzirah that it was most grateful for your compassion and your Knight's chivalry."

Roberta looked confused. "She talks to undines but won't trespass in Yetzirah? How is that possible?"

"More I can not say," Rhodes repeated a third and final time.

"You're starting to bug me, Rhodes," Roberta gave her a good glare.

Rhodes dunked her under the water, holding her down with her tail. "Always so sassy," she smiled at Brandon as Roberta came blubbering up.

"You are so going to pay for that," Roberta splashed her.

Rhodes splashed her back, laughed and winked at Brandon. "She will teach your children well. Remember your promise to me, Son of Assiah."

Roberta looked at Brandon with worry. "You made another promise to Rhodes? Are you crazy?"

"Yes, I am," Brandon told her, then looked back at Rhodes. "Your promise to me is that you will help and protect your near-sister or brother as you have Bethany."

"Yes. I will keep my word. Your promise to me is that you will tell them of me, whether or not they are allowed to enter Yetzirah."

"I will keep my word as well," Brandon assured Rhodes. "All our children and their children will learn of you. You will never be forgotten for as long as our descendants live." He took a short breath. "I should also advise you that those of our children who can enter Yetzirah might be on a quest, searching for an island."

Rhodes looked interested. "A quest for an island? There are many islands in my fathers' realm," she told him, "which one is best when upon this quest?"

"This one looks... It looks like..." he looked at Roberta for help. Not only was it embarrassing to describe it, he wasn't quite sure if a mermaid who was a fish from the waist down would know the nude anatomy of a human male.

Roberta rolled her eyes at him and looked at Rhodes with a shake of her head. "It looks like a penis and balls, Sister. A very happy penis and balls. Evidently Brandon is too shy to describe it."

Rhodes laughed. "You'll have to work on that flaw, Bethany, if he stays shy I never will be able to meet my near-sister or brother."

"Do you know of such an island?" Brandon asked.

"We all know it well," Rhodes told her. "Many of the children born of Assiah and Yetzirah have commented on it. They laugh, they point. They find it very amusing."

Roberta grinned. "Intimidating to the girls, I would think. I mean, really, if they thought that something that size would be in their future, they'd probably enter into permanent celibacy. That is one huge..."

Brandon coughed, deciding to intervene before the two became more graphic. "Yes, well. Can you direct our male descendants to this island?" he asked Rhodes.

"I may. Or perhaps I will lead them astray," Rhodes eyes twinkled while she thought about it. "Will they be under the shadow of a Seth whilst upon this quest?"

"Yes," Brandon answered, noting with suspicion she was now speaking in formal rhyme. "They will be under the Seth-A-Tristan et Yetzirah."

Rhodes nodded, looking pleased. "Thou art then the twelfth son of Tristan?"

Brandon looked at her curiously. Where had he heard that description before? "Yes."

Rhodes nodded. "He was much enjoyed by my brethren, still spoken of often." She leaned down and whispered to Roberta so low that Brandon couldn't hear. "Favored by our sister Kym, yet still too young to hold form true." She tugged Roberta's braid playfully.

Roberta's eyes widened. "Oh."

"Can you tell us how the first Tristan got a pearl out of Yetzirah and into Assiah?" Brandon asked.

"Twas a gift, perhaps," Rhodes told him, looking innocent. "More I can not say." She winked at Roberta.

Brandon took a deep breath, then pulled the pearl out of his pocket, saying formally, "then I willingly give thee this bobble rare, as an adornment for thy pretty hair. 'tis for to thee to keep safe 'til the next son of Tristan doth take my place." He tossed it to her. It traveled between the gates of Adelie and Yetzirah without resistance. Rhodes caught it easily.

"Uh, Brandon," Roberta looked at him in horror, "not your best plan. What are you doing?"

"I may give it to him," Rhodes looked at Brandon a little slyly, "if thy descendant treads lightly and asks for thy bobble, *very* politely." She smiled at him then posed coquettishly as she first did when he met her. "Dost thou find my form lovely, Son of Assiah?"

Brandon gave her a courtly bow. "You are so very beautiful, sister to be, that you take my breath away," he told her truthfully.

"Thy words are pleasing to me. I shall accept thy token willingly." Rhodes smiled, then put the pearl in her hair. It became a ribbon of sliver blue light, threading down the length of her hair, sparkling with life. She looked at Roberta wistfully, and stroked her face. "Come to me again, Bethesicyme, only in thy dreams if you cannot hold form true. Thou art sorely missed and always loved." With that, she again splashed Roberta playfully, then both she and the rock she had been sitting on, were gone.

"Okay," Roberta looked at Brandon with confusion, "What willing promise did you make to Rhodes when I was out of earshot?"

"Only that I would tell our children of her, never let her be forgotten. I made the same promise to Brandon the Dragon."

"That seems harmless enough," Roberta didn't sound completely convinced.

"I don't know if it is or not," Brandon answered, "But it seemed to be vitally important to both of them that they never be forgotten."

Roberta considered it. "True immortality," she answered slowly with a knowing of her own. "You always exist somewhere if you're never forgotten."

"Children forget their dreams of youth," Brandon agreed. "I'd forgotten about being a griffon until you reminded me."

Roberta turned toward the water and looked thoughtfully back at the open sea. "I'd almost forgotten Rhodes and Nixie and Jennifer until I came back." She felt a wave of sadness. "But they never forgot about me."

"And I never even knew about Brandon the dragon until I came here. My grandfather never told me about him, but Grandpère was remembered by him, he grieved when he learned of his passing," he answered. "Now Brandon the dragon will never be forgotten either, as long as our family survives."

Roberta nodded. "But I still don't understand. Why did you give Rhodes the pearl?" She walked back up to dry land, her clothes changed automatically when she reached the Adelie side. "Did you make that promise, too?"

"Nope."

"You do realize that she might just keep the pearl for herself, right? That she has now become part of the problem and the solution?"

Brandon pulled her to him and kissed her. "Every quest needs a challenge, Bobby. Our male heir only needs to come here in his dreams, not physically. Still, I'm sure Rhodes will make sure whatever Tristan shows up will get an interesting adventure. What fun would our family Seth be if it's too easy to solve?"

"So we're going back to Assiah?" Roberta determined, feeling a little sad at the thought.

"It's where we belong. This is a world for children, a place to create memories and adventures that will shape who they become as adults. We've done our part. We brought back the pearl to Yetzirah." He smiled.

"But not to the island," Roberta pointed out.

Brandon shrugged. "It doesn't matter. Returning the pearl to the island will be the problem for the next son of Tristan. Rhodes will keep the pearl safe until he tries to fulfill the Seth-A-Tristan et Yetzirah," he told her. "I trust her. She's family. We give him a few cryptic hints, tell him about Rhodes and Brandon, our family dragon, write our story, tell him of our travels through Yetzirah and Briah, tell him to write his story. If he can't resolve it, it continues to be the Seth of the next son of Tristan. As you said, some Seths last for generations. Perhaps it will be solved in our lifetimes, perhaps not. It doesn't matter. The only promise that can never be changed and will be added to our family Seth and apocrypha is that the memory of Rhodes and our family dragon must always continue. We will never let them be forgotten."

"I like that promise," she smiled.

"So do I." He put his arms around her waist. "Let's go home, get married and start that family so we can keep our promises."

"Just like that?" Roberta looked at him.

"Exactly like that," Brandon answered without a trace of doubt. "Take my hands, love. This time, we think like adults." He quoted, "'One quest begets the other, two of earth, two of air, one of water'."

Roberta's back was to his front, she held tightly on to his hands.

"Don't let go," he warned her.

Roberta smiled. "I'll never let go," she promised, turning her head to give him a quick kiss.

"On three we take each other home," Brandon started counting. One, two... Now."

"*Ki Akal, Assiah, Page of Swords et cups et Assiah,*" he said clearly, sending Roberta back to Assiah.

"*Ki Akal, Assiah, Knight of Swords et Assiah,*" Page said at the exact same time, holding his hands securely, intent on keeping Brandon with her, keeping herself with him.

In less than a thought, they were back in Brandon's office, wearing the clothes they had on when they first started their quest. The unused backpacks, supplies and the now empty brooch of Assiah were at their feet.

There was only one true difference that Roberta noted. The sea grass of Yetzirah that Rhodes had lovingly braided through her hair was still there.

How she had brought something to Assiah from Yetzirah would remain a secret between herself, Rhodes and the daughter of cups she would one day carry.

The same secret Phineas Tristan had taken to his grave. He had not taken the pearl, it had been given to him.

Everything from an elementary world was a gift from the heart; for one and from one who would always be loved and never forgotten.

Heart, mind, soul.

Epilog

Aaron read the letter from Brandon Grayson, fingered the now sylph and undine free brooch and smiled. "Well," he looked across the breakfast table at Pricilla, handing her the now lifeless gold, "the elementals are taken care of and our new Knight of Swords and his Page have invited us to their wedding."

"Ooh, shopping!" Pricilla brightened. "New clothes for me and a gift for the bride and groom," she answered.

"Right," Aaron shook his head. "Focus on the important things."

Pricilla smiled. "And the Seth-A-Tristan-et-Yetzirah? How's that progressing?"

"Not my problem any more," Aaron told her, shaking his head.

"It's still formally in The Major Apocrypha," Pricilla reminded him.

"True, but it's also formally resolved, even if the descendants of Tristan don't know it," he shook his head. "No one ever reads the fine print of a formal Seth."

"Like you not reading the fine print of the Seth-A-Ron and giving the key to Amme and leaving me in limbo, oh mighty Magus of Power of Eternal Lemniscate?"

"Thanks for the reminder, brat," Aaron glared at her.

"Do I get spanked?" Pricilla looked at him hopefully.

"Later," Aaron promised. "Anyway, the key issue outlined in the Seth-A-Tristan-et Yetzirah, was that the Page on the cusp of Yetzirah and Briah finally gets a formal sephiroth, which she did, the undine and sylph were to be released into their own worlds, which they were, and the pearl taken back to Yetzirah, which it was," Aaron shrugged. "If our new knight wants to complicate things and have it returned to the specific island it was taken from as per his familial apocrypha, that's his problem, not mine."

"All's well that ends well," Pricilla saluted him with her orange juice.

Aaron frowned. "Well, for the moment, but I did also get a letter from Hamish."

Pricilla looked at him with concern. "Is he alright? Is Aunt Vanessa okay?"

"Physically, yes."

"But..." Pricilla put down her glass and looked at him expectantly.

"The knife Curt used to kill Amme. Apparently, it was stolen from

242

Vanessa's family about six decades ago."

"Five hells," Pricilla sagged in her chair. "And I'm guessing it's an artifact of power of some kind?"

"I have no idea. But Hamish stated very firmly that it has to be recovered. And, according to Paul, since its now evidence of a crime, it will be sitting in the property room of the police department forever unless someone can prove its value and providence to claim it."

"In other words, Paul gets another fool's errand to follow, we sit around and wait for the fallout," Pricilla translated.

"Pretty much," Aaron answered with resignation.

"Okay then," Pricilla shrugged. "Back to the important things. What do you think we should buy Brandon and Roberta for a wedding present? Crystal or China?"

Aaron thought about it. "Mother of pearl napkin rings with gold trim," he answered.

"Open air of Briah, abalone circle denoting Yetzirah, gold of Assiah," Pricilla nodded. "Brilliant," she agreed. She immediately started imagining the design she would send to Tiffany's. Expensive, but it was Aaron's idea, he could hardly complain.

"Of course it's brilliant," Aaron said pompously, "I am the Magus of Power by Eternal Lemniscate."

"Ah, huh," Pricilla nodded absently. Maybe she should add a delicate necklace with the same open air design for Bethesicyme to wear on her wedding day, with a tiny dolphin or mermaid adorning its center. Oh! And a small silver/gray tie-tack in the form of a dragon for Brandon.

She'd send those items anonymously, of course, Celandine no longer existed in Brandon's or Roberta's memories since returning to Assiah. Besides. Why ruin the mystery?

Aaron looked at her suspiciously. "What are you plotting, Cilla?"

"Me? Nothing at all," Pricilla answered, then smiled at him with pure innocence.

End

Next up: The Hermit

Made in the USA
Lexington, KY
14 May 2016